IN THE CORNER

Part Three of the Operation Jigsaw Trilogy

MARK HAYDEN

Paw Press
www.pawpress.co.uk

Copyright © Paw Press 2014
All Rights Reserved

Cover Design - Hilary Pitt, 2QT Publishing.
Design Copyright © 2014
Cover Images Copyright © Shutterstock

This edition published 2015 by Paw Press:
www.pawpress.co.uk
Independent Publishing in Westmorland.

ISBN-13: 978-1514643198
ISBN-10: 1514643197

For Caitlin & Charlie

I hope I'm still around when you get to read it!

Acknowledgments

This book would not have been written without love, support, encouragement and sacrifices from my wife, Anne. She agreed to carry on full time work and let me step down so I could write. I also do the cooking and ironing, so it's not a one-way deal.

Thanks also to the tribe of readers who gave the thumbs-up to the books (with the occasional thumbs-down to certain sections): Jen Driver, Jane McQuillin, Martin Marriott, Mark Nicholson, Gail Sheldrick, Bob Smith, Martin Trent and Chris Tyler. Speaking of Chris, thanks also to the fellow members of Kendal Writers' Café.

A special mention has to go to former DC Nick Almond of Cumbria Constabulary for sharing his experiences with me (and to his daughter, Amy, for introducing us).

Finally, I am grateful for the professional services of the team at 2QT Publishing. Thanks are owed to Hilary Pitt for designing the cover and to Joanne Harrington for proofreading. It should be emphasised that any remaining errors are entirely my own and not Joanne's.

If you are thinking of publishing your own work, I can strongly recommend the services from 2QT.

IN THE RED CORNER

PROLOGUE

ANGLESEY

NOVEMBER 2001

The match flared, and flame slowly took hold of the wick. He held his palm around the candle to shield it from the draughts invading the cottage until it was steady enough to be left alone. Conrad Clarke tossed the spent match into the fire and stood back to admire his handiwork.

Romantic candles – check. Romantic smells coming from the kitchen – check. Blazing log fire – check. Dramatic surprise – check. But where should he hide the ring? He didn't want to risk putting it under the sofa in case it disappeared, and the dresser was too far from the hearth. I know, he thought, I'll move her picture on to the mantelpiece and hide it behind that.

He was just straightening the picture when he heard a car engine and the crunch of gravel. He rubbed his hands on his trousers to dry the nervous sweat, grabbed the umbrella and went out to meet her.

The sports car slid to a halt, the rear end drifting by a foot as she over braked. Her father had promised her a car for her twenty-first birthday, with the style and quality dependent on her degree results. Amelia had collected a first class Honours degree and a brand new sports car, and then gone travelling.

The rain was squally rather than torrential, but he didn't want her to get her hair wet. He stood over the car with the umbrella as she put things in her bag, then climbed out. Her long legs unfolded from the front seat, and she shook out her hair. Conrad's heart leapt as she threw her arms round him and planted a big kiss on his lips.

'Missed you,' she said.

'Missed you, too. Let's get inside before you freeze.'

He ushered her into the cottage ahead of him, and she paused inside the door to take in the scene.

'Conrad, wow! That's so romantic.'

She flung her arms round him again, and he ran his hands down her back as their tongues reacquainted themselves with each other; her body felt even better than he remembered, She slid her thigh up between his legs and nudged his groin. When they broke for air, Conrad could feel sweat forming on his back.

'I don't know which I want more – food or your body,' she said. 'They both smell delicious.'

'The food will wait. I don't think I can.'

They made love on cushions in front of the fire because he knew how cold it was in the bedroom. Before they got dressed, he poured them some wine. Amelia sniffed the glass and then sniffed the room.

'I've just realised,' she said. 'It doesn't smell of cigarettes in here.'

'No. I said I'd give up while you were away, and I have. Five months now.'

'Well done.'

Conrad caught a whiff of something starting to burn in the kitchen and kissed the top of her head. 'I think I'd better get that food out.'

During the meal, he told her about his promotion to flight lieutenant and the commendation he'd received for a particularly difficult helicopter rescue he'd carried out in the Lake District. She described the horror and madness of being in America when the Twin Towers came down (although she hadn't been in New York, she was a little vague about exactly where she was on 9/11).

Conrad picked up on that and said he would be going to war, almost inevitably. He was being taken off air-sea rescue and fast-tracked on to the Chinook transport helicopters.

When he mentioned war, she put her hand to her mouth and said, 'Oh no. For God's sake, take care, Conrad.'

After the meal, Amelia collapsed on to the cushions, and Conrad thought there would never be a better moment. He took the box from behind her picture and got down on one knee.

'I've missed you so much. I don't want to do that again. I know you've only just got back, and you haven't decided what to do yet, but I want us to do it together.'

Amelia had sat up halfway through his speech. The look in her eyes wasn't promising, but Conrad pressed on, opening the box.

'Amelia, will you marry me?'

'Oh, Conrad.' She closed the box on the ring and wrapped his hand round it. 'You don't understand. It's been great, but it's time for both of us to move on – I'm not the one for you.'

A horrible realisation dawned on him. 'You only came for a goodbye shag, didn't you?'

She looked away at the fire; tears glistened in the light. 'I'm sorry.'

He stood up and shoved the ring into his pocket. 'I'll get the spare quilt. You'll be warmer if you sleep on the couch; that bedroom is freezing.'

She turned her face up to him with a puzzled look. Clearly she was anticipating a longer scene, and more emotion. Well, she would have to manage without the drama, for once.

While he was upstairs, she went out into the rain and brought in her bag from the car. He left the quilt to one side and put the cushions back on the couch. She rummaged inside her bag and held out a small package with a ribbon round it.

'Here. I bought this in the States.'

'No. You keep it.'

She walked deliberately over to the dresser in the corner and placed it on top. 'When you open it, I want you to know that I meant it. I really did.'

He ignored the package and made some coffee. She told him that she was going back to America because she had been offered a job there. Going up the short staircase, he felt the cold strike his chest. He wondered how she had managed to make him feel guilty for proposing. He shook his head and climbed into the damp bed.

After she'd gone the next morning, he looked at the gift on the dresser. He tore off the bow and the wrapping paper to find a brass Zippo lighter inside. Engraved on the side were the words *To Conrad, with Love from Amelia*.

He tossed it in the drawer with the ring. If he ever started smoking again, he'd use that lighter to remind himself what a fool he'd been.

Chapter 1

Nine Years Later

Blackpool – Hong Kong

Wednesday – Thursday

3-4 November 2010

Tom felt two things at the same time: the noise slapped against his head like someone boxing both his ears, and a huge weight landed on his back, bouncing him into the air before tossing him across the pavement and into the road. He tried to sit up.

A car had stopped in front of him, and the passenger door was opening. How ironic would that be? Survive the bomb and then get run over.

The man who got out of the car was holding a gun, and when he started shouting at him, Tom realised that it had all gone quiet. The man was wearing a baseball cap which said *Police*. Tom couldn't hear a word he was saying, so he just put his hands in the air and shouted, 'I'm a police officer. I've gone deaf.'

The armed policeman raised his gun, then lowered it and took a step towards him. Tom couldn't decide whether it was more interesting to look at the man with the gun or the blazing wreck of his car, when something else caught his eye. There were flames climbing up his sleeve.

He flopped back on to the ground and started to roll around. Someone grabbed his arms, and he saw the nozzle of a fire extinguisher being pointed at him before it all went black.

Conrad Clarke stretched out his legs in the luxury of business class (at Kate's expense) and started to think about what to do next. The first leg of his journey, from Kabul to Delhi, hadn't offered any such opportunity for reflection: the cramped seat, his height and the wound in his leg had made it an ordeal to be endured. Now they were on the way to Hong Kong, he could think about what to do.

What had Rick said in *Casablanca*? "Of all the bars and all the gin joints in the world, you had to walk into mine." Something like that. Of all the ex-military she knew, Kate Lonsdale had chosen him to be her knight in shining armour. Him, the man who had recruited her boyfriend for a smuggling operation, the man who had arranged a helicopter crash to cover up Vinnie's murder.

That would have played on his conscience all right, would have given him difficult choices – but it was the nature of the hole she had dug for herself that made it a prize-winning moral dilemma. Either by accident or by design, Kate had been drawn into the shadowy world of private intelligence contracting. Why hadn't she just gone to GCHQ when she left the Army?

Clarke knew, had always known, that Operation Red Flag was connected with the private military sector, but he didn't know how. He knew that the vast profits Red Flag was making would come to an end one day, and he knew that his masters would probably co-opt him into something else that was equally nefarious, but he had never guessed that they might recruit Lonsdale.

The flight attendant passed by with the trolley, and he took another small Scotch. It would dull the pain, and if he stuck to just two glasses he wouldn't be too drunk to think when they arrived in Hong Kong. What the attendant couldn't offer him was a chance to smoke.

Kate was in trouble. She was hiding out somewhere among the skyscrapers and chaos of Hong Kong after three canisters of pure heroin had been planted in her luggage.

He rolled the ice round in his glass. He had seen a couple of those containers himself. They held two kilos of powder, and the street value in London was about £130,000 per kilo. The TV headline would say something like this: *A former Intelligence officer has been arrested in Shanghai with drugs worth over half a million pounds. The sentence for drug smuggling in China is usually the death penalty.*

Whoever had planted the drugs would have got them very cheaply. In fact, the fake battery cases in which they were packed they were packed cost more than the drugs, but that was beside the point. That person had wanted Kate to disappear into a Chinese jail for so long that she might as well be dead but, clever girl, she'd seen the ambush, dodged the bullet and asked Conrad to help her out.

Unfortunately for Kate Lonsdale, Clarke had been ordered to deal with her. Somewhere in the shadowy background his smuggling operation and her private intelligence work were joined together. When the Commanding Officer called him and said *We've got a problem in Hong Kong,* he sounded furious. The sort of fury that comes from having to clear up someone else's mess. It was the only clue he had to what might be going on.

He finished the Scotch. He was going to have to choose: did he follow orders and ensure that Kate Lonsdale disappeared, or did he try to make up for what he had done to her in the past? He remembered Mina's words on that freezing cold day in Essex – *For what you have done in the past, the slate is wiped clean. It's up to you what happens in the future.* Kate Lonsdale had done nothing to deserve a Chinese noose. In fact, there was only one thing in the world he wanted less than Kate Lonsdale's death, and that was his own.

He chewed on the ice cubes from his Scotch and reclined his seat. There were three hours to go. He closed his eyes and slept.

The blue flashing lights showed dimly through the ambulance windows as they sped towards the Royal Preston Hospital. In his newly silent world, Tom wondered if they were using the sirens, too. He also wondered why they were going to Preston instead of Blackpool. The paramedic was strapped into her seat for the journey, but kept a close eye on him. Tom was strapped in, too – face down because his back was in agony from the burns. The only conscious act he had performed since the ARV officers had put out the flames was to extract his warrant card and shout the basic facts about who was in the car and that an unknown IC1 male was the bomber. There was another seat in the ambulance, and it was occupied by a uniformed policewoman.

The A&E department seemed quiet. Tom tried to smile because everything seemed quiet at the moment. He was alive. He hadn't lost any limbs. He wasn't blind. If hearing loss was the price he had to pay for survival, right now he was happy to pay it.

He was wheeled into a cubicle, and tried to sit up on the trolley. The paramedics grabbed his hands to steady him, and one of them shouted something in his ear. Tom shook his head. 'Sorry. No good. Completely deaf.'

The paramedic held up her hand in a *Stop* gesture. A doctor had arrived, and Tom could see them talking but had no idea what they were saying, so he looked around and realised that three of the four people crowding his cubicle were women. Having registered this, his brain couldn't take the thought any further and he giggled. The police officer gave him a worried look and said something to the doctor. His back was starting to throb in time to some unheard beat. He tried to lift his left arm and pain shot through him. The male paramedic took his wrists in a gentle hold and placed them on his lap before repeating his colleague's *Stop* gesture. Tom closed his eyes and listened to the throbbing in his back. How bad could it be?

Someone tapped his hand, and he looked up. The paramedics waved goodbye and were replaced by a nurse. The doctor was scribbling something on to an A4 notepad. After a minute, she showed it to him. Tom peered at the pad and said, in what he hoped was a normal voice, 'Your handwriting is terrible. Did you know that?'

The doctor took the pad back and jotted in the corner: *Point to words you can't read.*

After some pointing and rewriting, he was able to decipher this message:

We need to cut the clothes off your back. You need anaesthetic. Can't give you a general. Going to put you on morphine drip for 20 mins then start. Police say they need *all* your clothes and belongings for evidence. Your left arm is burned. We'll help you to undress.

Tom looked around him. 'Are there no men in this hospital?' The doctor, nurse, and police officer looked at each other as if he'd spoken in a foreign tongue. He shrugged, and lifted his feet for them to undo his shoelaces.

Kate was waiting in the smoking section outside the arrivals area of Hong Kong airport. A driver was waiting inside with a board that had Clarke's name on it. Kate would slip into the car behind him, as if they'd met on the plane.

She was wearing a baseball cap but she was under no illusions. Since this morning, she hadn't seen a single western female who looked anything like her – a few backpackers had the same height, but they were years younger and mostly slimmer. The armed security men had taken a good look at her when she passed.

If she pressed her nose to the smoked glass, she could just make out the arrivals boards above the gates. Conrad's flight had landed now, and he would be making his way through passport control. He had sounded very confident on the phone – he had a plan and he would help her out. But Conrad always sounded confident. According to the Movements Officer, he had sounded just as confident when he booked out the helicopter flight that killed her boyfriend and the pilot, as well as leading directly to Gareth Wade's suicide and his own shattered leg.

'Are you not smoking?' asked a Chinese businessman, who had learned his English with an American accent.

'I gave up,' she lied. 'It's only by standing here that I remember why.'

The man was about to take the conversation further when Kate saw the tall figure of Conrad limping towards their driver.

'Nice to meet you,' she said, bowing to the man before scuttling towards the car park. She glanced through the main doors and saw that Conrad had stopped to power on his phone.

There was now a full-scale concert playing inside Tom's head. The rhythm section in his back had been joined by a brass band. Something was happening to his ears, but he couldn't say whether or not this was a good thing. Was his hearing coming back, or was this the beginning of tinnitus? There was so much morphine still in his system that he didn't care.

According to the doctor's second scribbled message, the procedure to dress his burns had gone well. She had spent a long time writing him a note which said that his sartorial vanity had saved him from more serious injury: the woollen cloth of his suit and the thick cotton shirt had acted as a barrier when the man-made raincoat was ignited by flying petrol. There would be scarring, but not too much. They might have to think about a graft on his upper left arm, but that was for later.

The nurse had helped him climb into bed after the procedure, and he was lying in the only position he could – curled up on his right side with his back and his left arm well away from the sheets. That gave him a very limited field of view, and he couldn't see the man coming in until he shoved a warrant card under Tom's nose. He focused on the name: Detective Chief Superintendent Hulme, Lancashire & Westmorland Constabulary.

Twisting his neck, he could see that Hulme was saying something.

'Still deaf. Can't hear a word,' said Tom.

Hulme started to fish around his pockets for something. There was already a pad and pen on the nightstand, but Hulme was looking for something specific. When he flicked through the pages of his notebook, Tom guessed that the man was going to show him the official Caution and arrest him.

'Going to sleep now. Too much morphine,' mumbled Tom, and closed his eyes.

No one shook his shoulder or disturbed him, and in a few seconds he succumbed to everything that had happened and drifted off to a deep sleep.

Lights were burning all over St Andrew's Hall. Sir Stephen Jennings' older daughter was visiting with the grandchildren, and there had been tears, tantrums and much running about the building before they settled down to sleep. He wished they would arrive earlier – children need routine not excitement in the evenings. Still, it was always good to see them.

He went around switching off lights and shutting doors to keep the heat in. At this time of year the cold soon crept in through the casement windows, and even though he could afford to heat the whole building, he refused to pay good money to the foreign bloodsuckers who owned the energy companies. Another bloody shambles – the infrastructure that his ancestors had slaved to build had been handed on a silver platter to feather-bedded eurovampires.

Before retiring to the drawing room for a nightcap in front of the fire, he stuck his head into the kitchen. Susan and Olivia were seated at the kitchen table next to the Aga, a bottle of Chardonnay and two glasses between them. Susan sipped her wine while Olivia was doing something with her new phone. The way she flicked and tapped at the screen was a revelation to him – it seemed like only yesterday that these smartphones had been launched, and now they were everywhere – except in his pocket. A friend in security had told him that they were so easy to track that you might as well walk around wearing a sandwich board with all your personal information on it.

Olivia put down the phone and gave him a kiss. 'Thanks for getting the boys off to sleep, Dad. They love your stories.'

'Flatterer.' He pointed to the phone. 'Does that thing tell stories yet? I'm sure it will, sooner or later.'

'They won't be as good as yours. Unless you record them and make money. It's the future, you know.'

'Part of it. What's so important that you can't wait until morning?'

'I was just texting Julian to say we're going to bed. Then I checked the weather for tomorrow.'

'I could tell you that. It's going to rain.'

'And the news. There's been an explosion in Blackpool, apparently.'

Susan sucked in a sharp breath. Any bad news from the Fylde peninsula set her on edge – it was where Olivia and Julian lived. The fact that her daughter was three feet away from her in their Oxfordshire kitchen meant nothing. Sir Stephen kept his poker face: this could be bad news.

'Gas leak?'

'No. Looks like a bomb.'

Jennings checked his watch. It was five minutes to eleven. 'I think I'll catch the news on an old-fashioned television. With a drink,' he said. 'Don't stay up too late, girls.'

'There's a full bottle here,' said Susan, topping up their glasses. 'We'll be as long as it takes for Olivia to tell me about what Amelia's been up to.'

That could take a very long time. Their younger daughter's exploits sometimes made his bed time stories seem quite prosaic – even if they weren't suitable for small children. Jennings grunted and went into the drawing room.

He switched on the television, poked the fire into life and poured himself an Islay malt.

The end of the weather forecast was showing. He was right – it would rain in the morning. The news began with the presenter putting on her sombre face.

There has been a bomb explosion in Blackpool with at least two fatalities. Police are not linking it to Islamist terrorism at this stage, but they say that it is too early for a definite conclusion. We are going straight to our reporter at the scene for the latest developments.

This had to be Offlea's doing. He wasn't surprised that his lieutenant had been so extravagant in exacting vengeance, but he hadn't expected it so quickly. The reporter was standing next to a police cordon. Lights could be seen behind him where the forensic teams would be gathering evidence. He summarised the news about a car being blown up and then said something which made Jennings sit bolt upright in his chair.

Unconfirmed reports say that a police officer from London was near the car when it exploded and that he has been taken to hospital for treatment.

Damn! Damn and blast.

Offlea had overreached himself this time. Not only was Kate Lonsdale on the run in Hong Kong, but now it looked as if he'd struck at Tom Morton and failed.

Jennings clicked off the television and downed his whisky. He went through to the study and opened the safe from where he took a bag full of mobile phones, each one labelled for different contacts.

He was putting on his coat as he passed through the kitchen. 'Something's come up,' he told his wife and daughter.

Susan was becoming increasingly impatient with his sudden absences. She was of the belief that he should be fully retired and not dashing out in the middle of the night any more, and she made her feelings known.

He shrugged. 'Don't wait up.'

Olivia opened her mouth to protest on her mother's behalf, but Susan put her hand on her daughter's wrist and shook her head. Jennings grabbed his keys and left.

He drove to Cherwell Valley service station and then past it to a lay-by up the road. If he was going to make these calls from a popular location, he didn't want his car's number plate showing up on their CCTV. Pulling up his collar and pulling down his cap, he walked back up the road and cut through a hedge to get into the service station. He found a wall away from the cameras and turned on the first phone. He didn't wait to see if there were any messages: he just dialled its only number. Offlea answered straight away, and Jennings could hear the sound of driving.

'What in God's name has happened, Will?'

'Do you want the good news or the bad news?'

'Stop pissing about and tell me.'

He heard the tick-tick of an indicator as Offlea made a turning, and then the noise of his vehicle accelerating.

'Adaire and his sidekick are blown to pieces. That's a good many of the brothers avenged, I can tell you.'

'Was the survivor Tom Morton?'

'Aye, the lucky sod. He rolled out of the car and missed the blast. I didn't stick around to find out how badly hurt he was.'

'He's alive and in hospital, apparently.'

'I think it would be best if I went to ground for a bit.'

Jennings grunted to himself: Offlea wasn't a huntsman. When a fox goes to ground, the hounds pursue it until they have the beast cornered, then the huntsmen dig it out, and the hounds finish the job. A bombing in England and the near death of a police officer would unleash more hounds on Offlea's tail than he could ever shake off. And when the first fox was killed, they would go looking for the next one.

'I stopped at the farm to collect my gear and I'm heading south,' said Offlea into the silence.

'Well, you can keep going until you get to France. You're going to have to lie low for a long time after this. And Lonsdale is on the loose in Hong Kong. Your friend messed that up too.'

'Shit.'

'Precisely. I've sent someone to deal with her, but now that Morton's safe, it's too risky to act against her. I'll call him off.'

'That'll be for the best. I've got plenty of cash, but I need more if I'm going to keep a truly low profile abroad.'

'Call in at the printing works and clear out anything they've got. You've got keys, haven't you?'

'Sure I have. Are you going to close them down?'

'Probably. Counterfeiting is not my top priority any more. And throw away that phone. We'll have to communicate by secure email from now on.'

'Gotcha. I'm sorry about missing Morton, but I couldn't allow Adaire to carry on breathing God's air.'

Jennings sighed. 'I know, Will, I know. I'd have done the same myself, and I'm glad he's finally got his just deserts. Remember what I said – go abroad and keep a low profile. Very low. Good luck.'

'Thanks, sir. Goodbye.'

Jennings took a deep breath and considered his options. There was only one person he could think of who could fill Will Offlea's shoes. It was a risk but if everything he'd worked for wasn't going to come crashing down around him, he needed someone to get up to Fylde and keep the show on the road.

He fished in the bag and took out another phone. This time he sent a text – *Call me on receipt of this message. Take no further action until then.* He checked his watch. With luck, it shouldn't be long. He took out his hip flask and took a swig – it was a risk, driving after the Scotch and now brandy, but being seen on the CCTV buying a coffee would be a bigger risk. He walked around the service station to keep warm, and ten minutes later the phone rang.

'Is that you, Clarke?'

'Sir?'

'There's been a serious development. You're needed over here.'

'What about my current mission?'

'Abandon it. Leave her to her own devices. I need you back in England asap.'

'Roger that, sir. I'll need to come back via Kabul, but I'll be as quick as I can. I left too much stuff over there.'

'Fine. Destroy the phone you're using and just come to my house. Discreetly.'

'I know this is not a secure line, sir, but can you give me a clue as to where I might find you?'

Jennings laughed. 'Use your initiative, man. I'll give you a clue – nine years ago, you proposed to my daughter.'

There was a long silence from the other end. 'Sir,' was Clarke's only response.

In Hong Kong, there was a man holding up a board saying *Clarke*, but he didn't want to run into Kate Lonsdale just yet. He needed time to think and he needed a cigarette. He squared his shoulders, went up to the driver and asked if he spoke English.

'Yes. I drive many Americans.'

'Good. I need a smoke.' Clarke mimed the action in case the man's English wasn't as good as he claimed. 'Ten minutes. Okay?' He held up ten fingers and pointed to his watch.

'Yes, Mr Clarke: I understand. Shall I take your bag? We'll be in the holding area to the right.'

Clarke smiled. It was better to be safe than sorry. He gave the man his carry-on case and offered an apology.

'No need, sir. I'll see you when you're ready. The smoking area is to the left.'

The driver walked off, and Clarke left the building, lighting a cigarette as he walked.

He didn't know what had shocked him most – the sudden resolution of his moral dilemma about Kate, or the fact that his Commanding Officer was Amelia's father. Bloody hell. The emotional kick was too strong. Instead of thinking about whether he wanted to be dragged deeper into Operation Red Flag by the father, he could only think of the daughter. Gorgeous, vibrant Amelia, who throbbed with life and who'd made him feel like a prince every time he wrapped his arms around her. The bitch. He had no idea of where Amelia Jennings was or what she was doing. He hoped she hadn't gone home to mother.

He lit a second cigarette and swigged some water. He was putting the lighter back in his pocket and running his finger over the relief portrait of Ganesha when he felt himself being watched from the corner of the building.

He looked left, and saw a tall man in fancy dress – that was the only explanation for the felt hat pulled low over his face and the cloak that must feel sweltering in the subtropical heat. Clarke looked around for a film crew or other obvious justification for his appearance, but when he looked back, the man had gone. He walked up to the corner, and there was no sign of the apparition nor any obvious sign of where it might have gone: no alleys, no doors, no bushes. Just a featureless concrete wall and a road where no cars had been. It had been a long day. He shouldn't have had the second Scotch.

He turned his thoughts back to the question of Kate Lonsdale. To stop her suspecting he was involved in her plight, he would have to continue with the deception. Not only that, he wanted to help her get out of Hong Kong with her reputation intact. Captain Lonsdale was not an easy person to help: unlike Amelia, she made a virtue of self-reliance.

He crushed out the cigarette and sought the holding area. By the time he arrived, his limp had almost disappeared. The driver was standing outside the car. There was no sign of Kate.

'Very sorry, sir. The lady has had to go somewhere urgently.'

'Did she say why?'

The driver gave a very European shrug. 'I left her watching the BBC World News channel on the car's TV, and she said something had come up. She seemed very worried. She told me to take you to the hotel. She also gave me this.' He offered Clarke a mobile phone and charger. 'She said that she would be in touch.'

Instead of a taxi, the man was offering him the back seat of a Mercedes saloon. Clarke shivered at the memory of Moorgate Motorhire's fleet of vehicles, but he climbed in and made himself comfortable. The driver had thoughtfully left the TV on, but it was giving him news of the Tokyo stock market. 'I think the next UK news is at half past four. It'll take me longer than that to drive into the city.'

'Thanks.'

This was his first trip to Hong Kong, and he asked lots of questions about the city, trying to steer the conversation around to Kate whenever possible, but it became clear that she had employed their chauffeur partly because of his discretion. He gave nothing away about where Kate had been or where she was staying. Eventually the British news came on, and Clarke raised the volume.

Bloody hell, he thought. *Is that her cousin in hospital? Has Barbarossa lost the plot completely?* No wonder Amelia's father had his knickers in a twist. Things could be very interesting when he got back to Britain.

Chapter 2

Blackpool – Hong Kong – Earlsbury

Thursday –Friday

4-5 November

The next morning brought four things to Tom – breakfast, great pain in his back, the return of his hearing, and the return of DCS Hulme. The nurse who looked at his dressings did at least give him the option of waiting for a doctor before allowing the detective inside.

'Mind you,' she said, 'I think Mr Hulme has been up all night. He looks worse than you in some ways.'

'Not if you look at his back, I think.'

'No. You're right there. Shall I send him in?'

'Is he on his own?'

'I think so.'

'Then yes.'

When she left, a rushing noise filled his head, like a windy day on a shingle beach. He could hear again – if that blessing came with added sound effects, he was cool about it.

The Lancashire & Westmorland officer stood in the doorway. The nurse was right: Hulme did look terrible. He was three ranks above Tom – three difficult levels of progression. There weren't many detective chief superintendents about. The senior detective on the Earlsbury case (DCS Winters) was at the end of his career, and had obviously put in a long shift at each rank. Hulme was different. Tom reckoned the man wasn't that much older than he was – and if Hulme continued at his current rate, he'd be a chief constable before he was fifty. He stared at Hulme's suit. No, that cloth wouldn't prevent serious burns. You can't beat good Yorkshire wool.

'Can you hear me, DI Morton?'

'Yes.' When the man spoke, the noise receded a little. Good.

Hulme shut the door behind him and came towards the bed. Tom couldn't prop his back against the pillows, so he was sitting up with his legs crossed. He felt like his sister when she was going through her yoga phase.

'Mind if I take the weight off my feet?' said Hulme, pointing to the padded hospital chair.

'Only if you're not going to arrest me.'

'No. Well, not yet. Probably.'

'What's changed since the early hours?'

'We found a reliable witness. A taxi driver dropped someone off just across the road as it all kicked off. Both he and his passenger saw a male get out of the car and run off before you did your Houdini act.'

'That witness. He wasn't one of Adaire's minicab drivers, was he?'

Hulme raised an eyebrow. 'Nothing wrong with your memory, then. No, he isn't. His passenger was a bit worse for wear, and I wouldn't trust her testimony in court, but he was solid. Now then, this is the $64,000 question: what made you jump out – assuming you didn't know the bomb was there beforehand?'

'Instinct. I was already deeply suspicious of my … passenger. He had said that he wanted Adaire arrested by your lot, and then – all of a sudden – they're climbing into the car. When Adaire and his hatchet man got in, and my passenger got out, I knew that whatever he'd put in the boot wasn't an early Christmas present. Even if it hadn't been a bomb, Adaire's man would have shot me first and asked questions later.'

Hulme thought for a moment. 'That makes sense. As far as it goes. What it doesn't tell me is what the man was doing in the back of your car in the first place.'

'Can you pour me some water? Got to keep the fluids up.'

Hulme passed Tom a full glass and settled back with his notebook. Tom took a drink, a deep breath and started his story.

It took two glasses of water before he'd finished, and Hulme had taken very few notes. Tom wondered whether the man was going to nod off. Typical – you nearly get blown up and then your audience falls asleep.

Hulme closed his notebook. 'I spoke to DCS Winters before I got here. He said that there's a hidden infra-red camera at the BCSS car park, which might show your passenger arriving. They're checking the footage as we speak. For what it's worth, Winters also said that you were devious but not dangerous. I'm not sure if that's a compliment or not.'

'At the moment, I'll take what I can get.'

'Someone will be in to take a full statement after lunch. I've got enough for the briefing.' Hulme yawned. 'And I'd better get changed before the press conference. Thanks for your time.'

'Good luck trying to catch him. You'll need it.'

Hulme laughed. 'Yeah. I'd be very surprised if he's still in the country.'

Tom lay down on his right side. His back was aching from sitting up, and throbbing like mad from the burns. DCS Winters was a good judge of character – *devious but not dangerous*. Well, it depends on how you define dangerous, doesn't it? Tom had kept back one piece of information: the tattoo on the bomber's wrist. If he'd told Hulme about it, the detail would soon emerge, and the man would have it removed PDQ. Tom was keeping that to himself.

'Is everything okay?' asked Clarke when Kate finally showed up at the hotel. He was sitting at the bar – showered, shaved and refreshed from a couple of hours' sleep.

'Yes and no. Do you remember me telling you about my cousin, the one I went to school with who joined the police?'

Clarke nodded and tried to look encouraging without showing undue interest.

'It was such a shock. I saw on the news that there'd been a bombing in Blackpool, and that a policeman had been injured. Something made me check on him. He's okay. According to Aunt Valerie, he's burned but not too seriously.'

Clarke frowned. 'Blackpool? I thought he worked for the Fraud Squad in London.'

'He was on a case in the Midlands. Last time we spoke, he said there was a link to Blackpool, and I've seen at first hand just how vicious those people can be.'

'How awful. Do you want a drink?'

'I'd prefer some food. Have you eaten?'

'No. I was hoping you'd be able to recommend somewhere.'

'Drink up and follow me.'

She led him a short walk down the hill, almost to the harbour. When they arrived at the restaurant, the waiter put his arm around her in a most disconcerting way. Given her reputation, the fact that she didn't deck him could mean only one thing: they knew each other quite well. He mentally tipped his hat to her.

Over a very extensive and tasty meal, she outlined her position. Clarke encouraged her to tell him as much as she could. She hesitated a little when it came to specifics, but he had the advantage of knowing that she was no longer in real danger. He pushed her to tell him everything about the mission, how she'd been recruited and what Leach was like.

'How quickly could you get hold of the battery, or whatever it is?'

'It's here. In the kitchen.'

'That was quick work. Do they know what they've got back there?'

'Sort-of.'

'And do you want to carry on working for Anthony Skinner?'

'Perhaps. When I've got some answers about what's happened here.'

'Then let me handle it.'

She frowned and pointed a chopstick at him. 'Look, Conrad, I'm sorry I dragged you here. I've probably over-reacted. I don't need you to solve my problems – just help me figure out what to do.'

He held up his hands. 'I know, I know. You're a big girl and you can look after yourself.'

She jabbed him with the chopstick. 'Less of the "big", all right?' She jabbed him again. 'And less of the "girl", too. I'm a woman.'

'I know that, Kate. It seems the waiter does, too.'

She went a gratifying shade of red. He followed the colour down her neck towards the cleavage emerging from her cotton blouse. He caught sight of a gold chain.

'Sorry, Kate. That was just too tempting. Tell me: is that my old ring on the end of that chain?'

Her eyes glistened with moisture and she took a sniff. 'Yes,' she said, and drew out the chain. The ring he had offered to Amelia Jennings in Anglesey glittered as it swung about. 'Look, Conrad, I feel really guilty about this. I know Vinnie never paid you, and if it were me, I couldn't afford to lose an asset like that. On your salary back then you couldn't have afforded this without a bank loan.'

He couldn't take his eyes off the ring. Could he really be about to meet up with Amelia again after nine years? It was time to finish things off. 'I wonder how much it would cost today,' he said.

'Avi Leaming offered me six thousand pounds for it – if you signed a note to say it wasn't stolen.'

The only thing stolen had been his heart. And Vinnie Jensen's life, he supposed. 'I'll give you a choice,' he said. 'Let me take the canister off you and sort things out with Leach and Skinner. No questions asked. In return, you can either give me the ring or pay me in instalments.'

She didn't hesitate. With practised fingers, she undid the catch and slipped the chain from her neck. Clarke held out his hand, and she dropped the ring into it. 'Are you sure?' he asked. 'Do you have anything else to remind you of him?'

She shook her head. 'I don't know why I'm telling you this … Perhaps because I lost touch with so many friends when I left the Army, or because you were there when he died. Anyway, I don't know whether I would have accepted him.' She tried a smile. 'Just like the woman who turned you down. Whoever she was.'

'Amelia.'

Kate moved some of the spilt food around the paper tablecloth with her chopstick. 'I have pictures … memories, a pair of earrings from Tenerife. That's enough for what we had.' She looked up at him and the tears that had started to form were gone. 'What now? About my other little problem?'

He breathed an inward sigh of relief. 'Do you know if Leach is still around? Have you got a number for him? … And for Skinner in the UK. Give me the canister and give me twenty-four hours. In fact, you can go online when we've finished here and book yourself a flight home for tomorrow evening.'

She mumbled into the coffee. 'I left my credit cards in the hotel. Just in case they tried to track me. I've nearly run out of cash.'

Clarke sighed. 'That wasn't your brightest move, was it? And how are you going to pay my expenses? It's not cheap flying here from Kabul.'

'You're not short of a bob or two. I'll transfer the money when I get back to England.'

'Your bank will still be open in Britain. Get on to them and arrange some emergency credit for your flight. Now, let's have some more coffee, and you can give me the numbers.'

Twenty minutes later, they parted outside the restaurant. Clarke had the canister of heroin in a takeaway carrier.

The forecast had been right. It was starting to pour with rain, and there was no chance of golf today. Patrick Lynch was trying to think of an alternative activity when the phone rang.

'Hello?'

'Hello, Paddy. How's things?'

'What the feck are you doing ringing this number? Don't you know the police have been all over me?'

It was him. Red Hand, the man from the Principal Investors. Patrick had never expected to hear from or see that man again. This could not be good.

'We need to meet.'

'I'm not sure that's a good idea.'

'Did you see the news this morning? That bomb in Blackpool settled a few scores, I can tell you. Benedict Adaire won't be causing any more trouble, and his wee fella – the one who shot your nephew – he's paid for his sins, as well. We need a short meeting, Paddy. Do you remember the place we first met? Under the bridge?'

'Of course. When?'

'Now. This weather's terrible. Don't bother about lunch; just get in your Jag and come over. Before I come to see you.'

That was the clincher. There was no way he was having that psychopath in his house. If Fran found out, she'd kill them both – starting with Patrick.

They had given Tom more painkillers after lunch – along with a warning that because they were so addictive, he could only take them for three days. That was not something to look forward to, because the pain beforehand was horrendous. They were just kicking in now, and unlike the morphine, they didn't make him fall immediately asleep. At least the silver nitrate cream they'd put on his back had a pleasant smell. Whenever he dropped off, the tang of melting plastic seemed to creep back into his nostrils.

The nurse checked his dressings, and he lay down to rest. In her absence, the shingle beach noise came back: he couldn't work out whether it was receding or not, and he started to doze. A loud knock on the doorframe awoke him.

One of the few male nurses stood there. 'Hi Tom, I've got some people to see you.'

He struggled up to a sitting position, and the nurse continued. 'That detective who left this morning said that they weren't going to leave a guard on your door, but that all visitors had to give their ID.'

'Who are they?'

'One of them says she's your sister and the other one says she's your partner, but there was nothing on your form to say you were in a relationship.'

'I'm not. What's her name?'

He looked at a Post-it note. 'She says her name is Kris Hayes.'

'Oh. She's my work partner, or she was. She can come in afterwards. Send Diana in first.'

He looked at the note again. 'She says her name's Fiona.'

Damn. How could he forget his other sister? The one who lived just down the road in Southport? Perhaps because they hadn't spoken for nearly three months, that's why. 'Sorry. I was expecting the other sister. Send her in.'

Fiona marched into the room. Her hair was shorter than he remembered, but just as well cut, and the tailored blouse / black trouser suit & heels combination was what you'd expect from someone on nearly three times his salary. Fiona was a GP.

'How do you think that makes me feel?' she said. 'I live twenty minutes away by car and Diana is in London, yet you expect to see her first.'

It looked like the haircut was the only thing that had changed. Fiona was living proof that you could love someone dearly without liking them very much. As if to prove him right, she went straight to the foot of the bed and picked up his case folder.

'They have doctors here, you know. Some of them quite good.'

She looked up, and he could see the strain on her face. He held out his right arm tentatively, and she dropped the folder and came to him for a hug. She was crying – and so was Tom when she wrapped herself around his burnt arm. He tried to grit his teeth but couldn't stop a hiss of pain escaping. She jumped back as if it were she herself who had been burned.

'What's the matter?'

'Nothing. Just my left arm. It's a bit raw.'

'Sorry. I hadn't got that far in the notes.'

'You could have just looked.'

'Read the notes before doing the examination. That's the rule.'

He was going to say *Try being a sister first and a doctor second*, but he bit that back, too. He'd done a lot of that when they were little.

'Mum rang me in the middle of the night. She was going to drive down this morning, but I said I'd get some time off and see how you were. What were you doing, Tom? How did you get into this mess?'

'I can't say. It's classified at the moment.' It wasn't, of course, but if his mother was coming sooner or later, he'd rather tell just the one relative. She could pass it on. 'All I can tell you is that it wasn't supposed to end like that.'

'You mean with the bomb?'

'No. With me alive: I was supposed to be incinerated along with the other two.'

She picked up the folder again and spoke without looking up. 'We even had a mysterious call from Cousin Kate. I'm surprised she didn't beat me to it now she's not at the Army's beck and call.'

And there it was. Fiona's jealousy of her cousin even after all these years. Yes, their grandparents had taken pity on Kate and given her hospitality, but they had never pretended that she was a Morton. Tom tried to be diplomatic. 'She's in Hong Kong. I think. I've barely seen her since the spring.'

'Even though you're neighbours?'

'She's got a new job. Takes her away a lot.'

'Let me guess: it's classified.'

Fiona put the folder down, evidently satisfied with its contents. She took a seat across from him and tried to ask non-medical questions about his health.

'Just come out with it,' said Tom, 'and ask me how bad the pain is on a scale from one to ten.'

'Sorry. I can't remember the last time I visited someone in hospital who wasn't a patient.'

Tom asked about his nephews, and while she was telling him, he caught her looking at her watch. If he had been one of the patients whose appointments had been cancelled so she could dash off, he'd be pretty upset. 'Thanks for coming, Fi. It really means a lot.'

She stood up, evidently relieved.

'Tell me one thing before you go – why am I in Preston Hospital, not Blackpool?'

'Regional Burns Unit. I wouldn't want you anywhere else. Tell me something – who's the black woman with the funny accent outside?'

'A copper from Earlsbury.'

Fiona raised a quizzical eyebrow.

'Near Birmingham. We were working together before this case blew up.'

'I see the bomb hasn't damaged your sense of humour. Shame.'

She leaned over and kissed him.

'Take care, Tom,' she said, before straightening her jacket and marching out.

Hayes slipped nervously into the room a few seconds later. He hadn't expected to hear from her ever again after the stunt she had pulled in Earlsbury. He could have forgiven the insults (with a suitable apology), but he would struggle to forgive her for ducking out and going on the sick.

She stood inside the door, wringing her hands and looking down. It was guilt, he realised. In Hayes' mind, she had left him in the lurch, and he'd been nearly killed. Cause and effect. He let her squirm for a few seconds until she opened her mouth. He cut in ahead of her.

'It wasn't your fault. Not the bomb. That would have happened anyway, as soon as he got me on my own.'

She stared at him. 'What can I say?'

'What do you want to say?'

'Sorry.'

'Did you want to say that to me before you found out about the bomb?'

Her look said it all. It was still guilt speaking to him, not repentance. He thought about her mother and the church.

'Look at it this way, Hayes. You've had a Road to Damascus moment, but you don't know what it means yet.

You've seen the light but you don't know how it changes your perspective on being a copper.'

She took a deep breath and looked him in the eye. Properly. She was wearing jeans and a vibrant yellow top under her padded jacket. The golden cross on her neck, which must always have been there when they worked together, was clearly visible today. He expected her to touch it after he mentioned St Paul's conversion, but she didn't. Instead, she put her hands together in front of her and balanced her weight on both feet.

'I was wrong. I still want to be a copper – but only if I can find a way of doing the job properly. I don't know if your way is the right way, but you got the job done without breaking the law. That's better than not doing the job at all.'

It was a start. If she was willing to walk into his room and admit she was wrong, it was worth trying again. Besides, he might need an ally, because Tom was not going to give up until the man with the tattoo was behind bars – and if Hayes had to arrest him for Tom's murder, then so be it. So long as *someone* arrested him.

'Good. Now sit down and hand over the chocolates.'

'Sir, I'm sorry…'

'What? You've driven all the way up here to see a man who was blown halfway across Blackpool, and you haven't brought me any chocolates?'

'I…'

'Sit down. You can bring them next time.'

'Will there be a next time?'

'Yes. We've got unfinished business.'

She sat down and put her bag on the floor. 'I guess you're okay, from what your sister said. If you don't mind me saying, she's got a loud voice.'

Of course. Fiona hadn't shut the door behind her, and Hayes would have heard his sister's side of the conversation.

'Yes, I am. I'll tell you all about it in a minute. If there's no chocolates, tell me this: have you signed yourself off the sick yet?'

'No. I was going to go in tomorrow.'

'Don't. See your doctor and get a sick note until the end of next week. If you go back before my status is resolved, they'll send you to Coventry. Literally and metaphorically. I need you doing things.'

'What do you mean ... your status?'

'I can't investigate the bombing. That only happens on TV, as you know. I'm a material witness. I need to make sure that I'm reassigned to the MCPS investigation.'

'Is there one?'

'Yes, thanks to you. That printout you got for me from the hotel – it's conclusive proof that a police employee sent DS Griffin and DC Hooper to be shot at. We're going to find them, and that's the first job you can do for me. Everything in the car was destroyed except me and my clothes – laptop, documents, the lot. Even the proof that Adaire's sidekick was at Wrekin Road has gone up in flames. Doesn't matter, though. They're both dead.'

'So how can I help?'

'I can rebuild most of my computer files from backups, but Griffin's phone records and the hotel printout were in my suit pocket – along with my phone, warrant card and wallet. And the keys to my flat. It's all been taken for analysis, but they should be finished with it by Friday afternoon. Your first mission is to get it all back.'

'Right. Will do.'

'And what else?'

She looked nonplussed.

'Bring some chocolates, Kris. Bring some chocolates. Now, do you want to hear what happened?'

'Yes. Of course – but I'm surprised you haven't asked me to get you a cup of tea. That's what you normally do.'

'I was just about to.'

Hayes smiled for the first time that afternoon and headed off to look for a vending machine. Or something better, hopefully.

The receptionist answered the phone in two languages, giving the hotel's name in Mandarin and then English. Clarke asked if he could be put through to Mr Leach's room.

'One moment.'

The phone rang but went to voicemail. No surprise there – according to Kate, the man would be out on the pull somewhere. Clarke didn't leave a message.

That narrowed things down. If the man was using the same city centre hotel as before, there was a good chance that he had the same mobile number. Clarke sent him a text: *I'm a friend of your missing associate. I'll pick you up from reception tomorrow morning at 10:00 so that we can get this mess resolved. Look out for a white Mercedes with a white man in the back.*

Less than five minutes later he had a reply:

No chance. I'll meet you in the coffee lounge at the same time.

Good. At least he wasn't dealing with a complete idiot – if the man had agreed to get into the car, Clarke would have been worried that he was armed.

Clarke's final message read: *OK. Look out for tall man with limp.*

Business concluded for the night, he stretched out his legs and waved the waiter over for another beer. It was nice to be in a civilised country where you could still have a drink with your fag. He tucked the carrier bag full of heroin further under the chair.

The rain had formed a little stream down from the old football ground towards the canal. It was dark, too, and Patrick had to put his lights on when he passed under the M5 flyover. The little turning circle by the canal was just big enough for him to swing the Jaguar around and point it towards the way he'd come, and at first he didn't notice the van. It had reversed into some weeds and was invisible from the approach road. It was fully visible from the canal, of course, but this wasn't one of the tourist waterways.

He sat and waited, like he had last time. There was no way he was going to walk over there now. He was no one's servant any longer except his own. If Red Hand wanted to see him, fine – but it was the other man's turn to get his coat wet. He had barely formed this thought when the van door opened, and a heavily muffled figure sprinted over. Patrick unlocked the doors, and the man climbed into the front.

'I've got something for you,' said his visitor, and started to unzip his waxed jacket.

'I'm having nothing to do with you or your friends any more.'

'Not after today, no, but there's one more piece of business.'

The man reached inside his coat and pulled out the evil-looking gun that Patrick had seen in his glove compartment. Pat knew nothing about guns, but this one was square, professional and looked like something he saw the American cops use on the telly.

'Take your phone out and pass it over.'

Patrick hesitated for a second. He was deeply in trouble, he knew that, but if he was going to get out of it he only had one weapon – his charm. It was a shame the other person wasn't a woman. He handed over the phone.

'Keys.'

They followed the phone into the man's pocket.

'Now your pills.'

'What in God's name do you want them for?'

'For your sake, Paddy. If I have to tie you up, and you have one of your funny turns, I want them handy. And if I have to leave you, I want you to have them out next to you. So you can pick one up with your Pope-licking tongue.'

With a grimace, Patrick handed over the pills, and Red Hand opened the door. In all this time, the gun hadn't wavered, and even if Patrick were trained in unarmed combat, it was so far away that he'd never have reached it. The man backed out of the Jaguar, keeping the gun level. When he was standing up he said, 'Now you. Get out, shut the door, get into the passenger side of the van and fasten the seat belt.'

As he crossed the gap between the vehicles, Patrick could feel his heart starting to constrict. He took a deep breath and climbed into the van. The smell of fish was almost overwhelming this time, and he gagged. 'Can I wind the window down?'

'Sure. And when you've done, put your hands on the dashboard.'

Patrick did as he asked and waited. Red Hand walked round to the same side of the van and slid back the side door. Before Patrick could move, he was behind him. There was no barrier between the two compartments.

'Okay, Paddy. Keep looking ahead.' There was a rustle and a bleep from behind him. Patrick tried to concentrate on his breathing. 'Now then, you've got a choice. You can die of a heart attack, or you can have a bullet through your head. If you choose the latter, I'll have to make another visit afterwards.'

The surge of pain hit his chest like a hammer. If he had his pills on him, he would have taken one straight away. His hand lifted off the dashboard, and he tried to massage his heart. With shallow breaths he struggled out the words, 'What other visit?'

'Hand back on the dash.'

He straightened out his arm with difficulty, and from over his left shoulder, Red Hand showed him a picture on his phone. It showed three girls in St Modwenna's uniform, one of them his daughter. The bastard.

'If you make me shoot you, I'll have to take a little insurance with me to France, won't I?'

Patrick saw it clearly. If he died in the van, no pills in his pocket, the waters would be very muddy, and his death would be pronounced as natural causes. If he were shot, the murder squad detectives would have a forensic field day. He made a decision, and the pain receded a little. 'How are you going to make me have a heart attack?'

'Easy. Just close your eyes.'

Patrick did as he said, and there was a noise from behind. He snapped his eyes open as something came over his face. It was cling film, wrapping around his mouth and nose and then around the headrest. His hands came up in a reflex attempt to drag it away.

'Quit struggling. Now!'

Putting his hands back down was the hardest thing Patrick had ever done in his life, but he managed to get them away from his face. The film was pulled tighter, and another layer was added. When the pain swelled up again, he lifted his hands off his lap but they never made it to his face.

Instead of going black, everything went white, and Patrick knew he had made the right decision. Fran would be okay. His daughters would live their lives free from the dirty mess he had made of his own.

The white light resolved itself into a tunnel with a shining star ahead of him. Free of his body, he rushed towards it. At the end of the tunnel, he could see Dermot waiting for him. That was all right, then. Heaven or Hell, he'd have some company when he got there.

It was fully dark by the time Francesca Lynch got home. She had finished work in the middle of the afternoon and tried to get hold of Patrick, but there was no reply. She wanted his help with the weekly shop – not that he could do much heavy lifting, but she enjoyed his company, and having someone to push the trolley made things much faster. She didn't think he'd be playing golf, but he was obviously up to something – the Jaguar was missing from the drive.

She unlocked the kitchen door and lifted the hatchback on her car. Grabbing the first two bags of shopping, she went into the house and flicked on the lights. She carried the shopping over to the worktop and was about to plonk it down when she saw something very worrying. Neatly arranged on the end of the counter were Pat's phone and, even worse, his pills. She dropped the bags with a thump that sounded like breaking eggs, and dashed around the house calling his name.

It was dark everywhere, and in each room when she flicked on the lights, there was nothing. Fumbling out her phone, she rang her daughter.

Chapter 3

Hong Kong – Earlsbury – York
Saturday
6 November

The chauffeur-driven Mercedes dropped Clarke off at the hotel, and he made his way into reception. To the right was a bustling coffee lounge. He headed over to an empty table, exaggerating the pain in his leg so that everyone in the room could see that he was the Tall Man with Limp. A young waitress took his order for a pot of coffee, cream, and two cups. Before Leach could appear, he took out his cigarettes and placed them on the table next to the newspaper he'd bought on the way over.

'I think I'd prefer the non-smoking area,' said Leach.

The other man was in his forties and wearing a crumpled linen suit which sorted well with his five o'clock shadow. With his eyes on Clarke's cigarettes, he hovered by the table.

'If we're quick, you can escape before the smoke gets on your clothes. On the other hand, it might help mask the smell.'

Leach sat down as the coffee arrived, and Clarke picked up his lighter. He rubbed Ganesha's tummy for luck and rubbed the little fish on the other side for love. Then he lit up a cigarette and poured the coffee. Leach was waiting for him to make the first move. The man might be odious but he very clearly wasn't stupid – so why was he mixed up in this?

'Just so you know,' said Clarke, 'We know some of the same people. In fact, I suspect our closest mutual acquaintance is a certain Ulsterman with red hair. Or a red beard. Or possibly a shaven head. He usually wears long-sleeved shirts to hide the Red Hand tattoo on the inside of his left wrist, which must have been painful when it was done. I don't know his name, but I'll call him Barbarossa.'

Leach sipped his coffee, but said nothing.

'I'll assume that Barbarossa was responsible for the heroin planted in Captain Lonsdale's luggage – or rather that he got *you* to do it.'

Still Leach said nothing.

'Okay, I'll go a step further. I don't think this operation, job or whatever you call it was on the straight and narrow from the word go. I have great respect for Captain Lonsdale's work, but she's a novice at undercover. The stakes don't get any higher than this. The two of you shouldn't be taking on the People's Republic of China on your own.'

Leach put down his cup. 'It was a test. Lonsdale thought we were collecting disassembled surveillance kit. No chance. Those circuit boards and components in her case were bits of old computer. There's no way we would have tried to smuggle the real thing in our luggage. It was all a test to see how she reacted when she was stopped by security … what she did, whether she's ready to go on to the next level.'

Clarke gave a reasonable nod, as if to say that subjecting your colleagues to a dose of the Chinese security police might be all in a day's work. Maybe in Leach's world it was. 'Something tells me that the heroin wasn't part of the plan. That was a death sentence waiting to happen.'

The skin around Leach's eyes crinkled just a little. Whatever leverage Barbarossa had over the man must have been quite powerful to get him to try having Kate killed.

'Have a look at this,' said Clarke, unfolding the newspaper and tapping one of the stories. Leach took it from him and scanned the article.

'What's this all about?'

Clarke had pointed out a report into the bombing in Blackpool. 'That was our mutual friend's handiwork too, except he botched it, and he's gone on the run. He won't be active for a long time. The operation against Captain Lonsdale is over. You can ask higher up the chain if you want, but I wouldn't recommend it.'

Leach topped up his coffee and slowly added a little cream. 'So what do you suggest?'

'You've been very lucky, old man. Very lucky indeed. I am your new best friend, because Kate has no idea what's in those canisters. She still thinks they might be a bomb. If you have a word with Skinner in London, this can all be fixed.'

'How?'

'Tell him that you added three real batteries as an additional test. Tell him that Kate sussed it out and went to ground. Get him to debrief her as soon as she arrives in London – she's already left the Territory. The heroin can be our little secret.'

Leach sat back. 'What's in it for you?'

Clarke picked up his lighter and stroked Ganesha. 'Good karma. It never hurts to make a deposit in the karma account. I might need to make a withdrawal soon.'

'Okay. That should work.' Leach nodded and pushed away his coffee, half drunk. 'What about the missing canister?'

'One phone call and my driver will deliver it wherever you want.'

'Give it to me now. Out front.'

Clarke sent a text message and stood up. He held out his hand, forcing Leach to shake it. By the time they reached the drop-off zone, the Mercedes was waiting, and the driver passed the package over to Leach. Clarke dropped into the back of the car and let out a long breath.

'Where to, sir?'

'Do you know a jeweller who will buy gold and diamonds for cash?'

The driver hesitated for a second. 'I know someone who might know that person. Let me make a call.'

Clarke felt the ring in his pocket. He wasn't after the money, though he would take it gratefully: he wanted that cursed thing destroyed before it ruined any more lives. He was going to make the jeweller melt down the gold in front of him. That way he could be sure he'd never see it again.

The detective flicked through Pat's passport and put it back on the coffee table.

'I understand your concern, Mrs Lynch, but at the moment there's nothing we can do except put out an alert for his car. Are you *sure* that there wasn't a tracking system fitted? It's a very expensive vehicle.'

'Of course I'm sure,' snapped Fran. 'He had it taken out so that you lot couldn't follow him.'

'Yes. We can't avoid the fact that your husband has a track record of evading the law.'

Fran slapped her hand on the table. 'I've told you. He's *not* evading the law, he's missing. Something's happened to him, and you're only bothered about him failing to answer his bail.'

'Of course we're concerned. Does your husband have any bank accounts or credit cards that you don't have access to? I assume you're monitoring all the joint accounts.'

'Yes.'

'And you've spoken to all his friends – and associates.'

'He didn't have any associates left. They've all been murdered or arrested. You should know about that.'

The detective was like a Teflon-coated robot. He responded to no human emotion, and nothing seemed to stick to him. Helen put a calming hand on her arm and spoke in a level voice to the detective. 'We spent all last night on it. As soon as Mom discovered that Dad had gone and left his medication behind, we started ringing everyone from the golf club to my half-sister. Not a single person had heard a word from him in seventy two hours. All of them are on the lookout for him.'

The detective made a note in his book and answered Helen instead of Fran. 'So, you see, there's nothing else that we could do. There's no one else we could turn to for information that you haven't already spoken to.'

'What about the other officers?' said Fran. 'That DI Morton from London and his woman?'

'That's difficult.' For the first time, the detective seemed on the defensive.

He wasn't going to add to his comment, so Fran said, 'Why is it? Tell me.'

'I thought you might have realised. DI Morton was badly injured in the Blackpool bombing, and DC Hayes has been off ill since last week.'

Fran put two and two together. Blackpool. Adaire. Morton. The counterfeit money. And now Patrick. It couldn't be a coincidence. She lay back on the settee and caught a whiff of Pat's aftershave clinging to the leather. Across the decades, she heard an echo of his youthful bravado: *When I go to meet me Maker, it'll be with a bang not a whimper. Sure it will.*

And it was.

'You alright, Mom?' said Helen.

'Can you show the detective out, love? I think we're finished here.'

With a worried glance at her mother, Helen jumped up and held open the door to the hall. The detective put his things together methodically and said his goodbyes.

Helen came back, and Fran started to tell her about what had been going on and why she wasn't expecting to see Patrick again in this life.

'How's the patient?'

'He's fine, he's fine. Come in, both of you.'

Kate had been hanging back from the door when they arrived at Tom's parents' house in York. She had let Diana go first – it was her mother who was answering the door, after all. They had travelled up from London together by train – a mostly silent journey because Diana was worried about her brother, and Kate was still scared by what had happened in Hong Kong.

Mrs Morton, Kate's Auntie Val, gave her as big a hug as she had given her daughter, and told them that Tom was asleep. 'He made me promise something,' she announced, while they were still standing in the immaculate Georgian hallway. 'When I told him you were both coming, he said I had to tell you the story first. His throat is still sore from smoke inhalation. Come through to the sitting room, and I'll make you some tea.'

A likely story, thought Kate. Tom has an official version of events which he wants his mother to give out. Then he doesn't have to remember what he's told people. She chose the least-comfortable looking chair as Diana flopped on the couch.

The tea was accompanied by cakes (of course), and she didn't realise, until her aunt had finished the story, that they had eaten every one of them. Kate had been shot at many times, and a vehicle she had been driving in Iraq had been hit by an RPG, but she had never come as close to death in the Army as Tom had in Blackpool.

She sat back and looked across at Tom's sister: Diana had gone white. Auntie Val's phone rang, and before answering it she said, 'That's him. Easier than shouting down the stairs.' She took the call, and after a few seconds, she said, 'Yes, they're here. Shall I send them up with some tea? ... Good.' She disconnected. 'Right. Up you go. He's in the main guest room.'

'I'll make the tea and bring it up,' said Diana. She brushed some hair out of her eyes. 'You go ahead, Kate.'

'Are you sure?'

Diana nodded and started clearing the tea things. Kate went upstairs and knocked. Tom's voice (remarkably free of smoke effects) invited her in.

He was struggling into a sitting position and held up a hand to keep her away. 'I can manage, thanks. If you try to help, you might touch my left arm – that's the bit that hurts most.'

There was a fan heater in the room, despite the house being warm, because Tom obviously couldn't have anything touching his upper body. There were dressings across his back and all over his upper arm.

'It's not as bad as it looks,' he said. 'Except for the arm. That's worse.'

Two chairs were drawn up by the bed, and Kate took the further one. 'Was it the same gang? The same one as in Essex?'

He nodded. 'Effectively, yes. I told you there was someone behind the scenes, pulling the strings, didn't I? Well, I think he was in the back of my car two nights ago. Now I'm going to get the bastard if it kills me.'

He delivered his declaration in a matter-of-fact voice as if it wasn't news any more, and as if his near-death experience was unrelated. Kate swallowed a lump in her throat and felt the cake weighing heavily on her stomach.

Tom continued. 'What about you? I wasn't expecting you back from the Far East for ages.'

She looked down. 'I had problems too. Nothing like yours, but it didn't go according to plan.'

They heard the creak of two hundred year old floorboards as Diana approached, and Tom said, 'Tell me later. When Di goes off to see her mates – which she will do now she's here.'

Curiously, Diana didn't ask any questions about the bombing. They talked as if they were in London, sharing a meal at Di's Hackney loft.

'One thing,' said Diana. 'Who's this young, Afro-Caribbean woman who visited yesterday? That's Mum's description, by the way, not mine. She was asking if I knew her. Apparently she landed on the doorstep and just said, "I'm Kris, with a K." And after her visit, you told Mum she was, "Just someone I know who brought me some things." What's going on, Tom?'

He put on a serious face. 'It's the pain, you see. I can't manage with the drugs they gave me at the hospital. That was Kristal Hayes and she's my dealer. She brought me some of the good stuff.'

'No, she isn't,' said Diana, a little too quickly, as if she might have believed it.

'Yes, she is. Her name really is Kristal Hayes and she really brought me some stuff.' He left them hanging for a second. 'But she's a copper from Midland Counties. She brought my phone and wallet from the evidence room in Blackpool. And some chocolates.'

He pointed to the largest box of Thornton's chocolates that Kate had ever seen. Diana jumped over and grabbed the gift tag that was still attached to it. '*To Tom from Kris. I'm Sorry. X X.* What's going on, eh?'

'Nothing,' said Tom. 'She forgot the chocolates the first time she visited and overcompensated yesterday.'

From his expression, Kate thought that there was both more, and less, to his statement than he would admit. There was something going on with Tom and this woman, but Kate doubted that it was romantic on either side. No woman would ever buy a giant size box of Thornton's as a romantic gesture – whatever it was that Kris-with-a-K was apologising for, it was connected to the bomb in Tom's car.

He joined them for an early dinner, and everyone tried not to look at his chest and his wounds. His father was almost silent and spared both Kate and Diana his usual digs at their expense – Kate for her single status and Diana for lack of a proper job. After the meal, the patient said to Kate that she could help him get back to bed.

'Are you alright? Can you manage the stairs?'

'Of course I can. I need someone to carry the bottle of wine and two glasses.'

'One glass,' said his mother.

'Two. I asked the district nurse: she said that if I lay off the blue pills tonight, I can have a drink. So there.'

Kate followed him as he gripped the banister, taking one step at a time, and then he collapsed on to the bed, almost out of breath.

'Give me a minute before you pour,' he said as he adjusted his position. Kate had pulled her chair up close to the right-hand side of the bed so they could talk. He slowly reached out his hand towards her and poked her in the stomach. 'Chinese food agrees with you. You've put on a few pounds.'

He was right. When she had put on her cold weather clothes after the heat of Hong Kong, the waistband of her jeans had protested loudly. 'My gain has been your loss,' she responded. Tom looked beyond gaunt. His face looked hollow in places, and he must have banged his head because there was a bruise around his eye. She looked again. The bruise was quite yellow – it must have been a while ago.

'Go on then,' said Tom. 'Tell me all about it.'

So she did. The panic when she found the batteries in her luggage, calling in Conrad to help her, and the shock when she got back to find it was a test – and that she'd passed. He told her the truth about Hayes and what had gone on in Earlsbury, including where he got his black eye. She flinched when he told her about fellow officers calling him an *oberleutnant* to his face and referring to him as a *gauleiter* in messages.

'Are you done with the spying game?' he asked.

'No. It's all I'm good at, and I don't want to retrain as a teacher or anything. But I'm going to take a break. There's unfinished business.'

'What do you mean?'

'I gave up too easily on what happened to Vinnie and Gareth Wade in Afghanistan. Now I'm out of the Army, I can pursue it. In fact, when I got home there was a message from Army Welfare – Vinnie's parents would like to talk to me. I'm going to see them on Tuesday evening. What about you? Have they given you a prognosis?'

'They're going to do a skin graft on Monday morning. They only let me come to York because I said I'd go privately. It's not a big deal. I should be feeling much better by Wednesday, but I won't go back to London until the end of the week. The Director of CIPPS is coming to see me on Thursday.'

'What's CIPPS again?'

'Keep up, Kate, it's who I work for: the Central Inspectorate of Professional Policing Standards.'

'And the boss is coming all the way up here just to see you?'

'As if. No, he's launching an investigation up here and he can fit me in. Now then, Cousin. What aren't you telling me about Hong Kong? I noticed you were very vague about where you spent the night on a couple of occasions. Remember, I do interviews for a living.'

Kate flushed. She'd left out Li Wei from her narrative. Not because she was embarrassed about having a fling with a Chinese waiter, but because Tom had been around attractive women for weeks, apparently, but hadn't made a move on a single one of them.

Chapter 4

London – Oxford – York

Tuesday – Friday

16-19 November

Over the weekend the weather had turned crisper and drier. The fading November sun was making an effort when Clarke arrived at the temple in Putney. Instead of showing it up as being in decline, the light picked out the newly painted doors. The more persistent weeds had been cleared from the forecourt too. On the way over from the car, the sun caught his eyes, and he saw the man again – the one with the cloak and the felt hat.

He whirled around and there was no one there. This time, he had seen the figure against a brick wall – there was nowhere a real person could have gone. It *must* have been an illusion, but was it a trick of the light or was it something inside his head? As soon as he was finished in Oxfordshire, he would see a doctor.

The door was answered by a new priest. Both men stared at each other, neither expecting what they saw. Clarke broke the silence.

'Sorry to bother you. I'm a friend of Mr Joshi. Is he about?'

'Yes. Please come with me.'

The man's response was delivered with a heavy Indian accent (of some description – he certainly wasn't a native speaker of English). Clarke followed inside and slipped off his shoes. He was shown into the small office, and on the way he noticed that the lobby had a new carpet.

He shook hands with the older priest and was offered a chair. Joshi put the kettle on and peered into the corridor. Satisfied that his colleague was out of earshot, he closed the door firmly behind him.

'Changes all around,' said Clarke. 'My donations wouldn't have played a part in the makeover, would they?'

Joshi smiled and poured the boiling water into a teapot. 'Up to a point, Mr Clarke. Up to a point. I wasn't willing to spend money on a building with no future, but when one of our sister temples offered to send me a junior priest, I thought it would be a good investment. He's very devout, you know.'

'You make that sound like a bad thing.'

'The older I get, the more I realise that fundamentalism is the enemy of religion – Islam we hear about all the time, but in the USA there are Christian fundamentalists – and in India too we have our brothers who would like to turn back the clock. I am hoping to show him that our faith aims to change the soul, not the world.'

'Good luck with that. Here's something for the next phase.'

Clarke handed over an envelope stuffed with cash and put the carrier bag containing it on the floor for later. Joshi accepted the offering with a bow and made the tea.

'I'm glad you have come in person, Conrad, though I wasn't expecting to see you for a long time.'

'My contract finished early – they even paid me a bonus. I'm going to be based in the UK for a while. Probably.'

The priest nodded and stirred his tea. 'I went to see Mina only last week, and I was wondering how to tell you the news.'

Clarke sat up in alarm. 'What's happened to her? Is she okay?'

'Yes, yes, she has come to no harm. The problem is with the future. She saw the prison dentist last week, and they have told her she must have a denture. They will not allow her any further private treatment, and certainly won't do the work themselves.'

Damn. That was bad news. The surgery on Mina's jaw had been so successful that the surgeon had said she could have a combination of bridge and implants to give her something to chew with on that side of her face. She would be devastated with the news.

'I see. Let me think about that.'

Joshi nodded, and they talked of cricket and other interests. Clarke even asked a couple of questions about the chapter of the Mahabharata that he'd been reading. Tea finished, Joshi led the way into the devotional area, and Clarke took out the small offering of Chinese sweets he'd brought back from Hong Kong. He laid them on Ganesha's altar and knelt in front. Joshi said a familiar prayer, and at its end, he continued with another prayer that Clarke hadn't heard before. He thought he heard the name *Mina* a couple of times.

They shook hands again, and Clarke went back into the sunshine. There was no one waiting for him, either real or imaginary.

Kate took a taxi to the Jensen family home in North London. There were regular curving streets of small semi-detached houses, and she was glad she hadn't been forced to use an A-Z. Just before they arrived, she spotted a short cut to the High Street and a tube station. She'd go back that way.

Margaret Jensen welcomed her with tears and questions about her health. The woman was probably around seventy, but she had aged a lot since the funeral. Kate was ushered into the sitting room she'd viewed from Camp Bastion over the video link. It was unchanged except for a large photograph of Vinnie in his dress uniform which now adorned the wall. Kate took a seat where she couldn't see it.

'Is Mr Jensen not here?'

'No. He's gone to the Emirates for the football. I told him it was all right – he didn't need to be here. Let me get you some tea.'

The gas fire was on, and Kate used the waiting time to take off as many layers as decently possible.

'I see you've still got his ring round your neck,' said Margaret when she returned with the tray.

Kate tried to lie, but the words stuck in her throat. She coughed and lifted out the chain; on its end was her mother's wedding ring. Margaret's face fell with disappointment.

'I didn't want to tell you, but I found out that Vinnie had only borrowed the ring from another soldier. It was meant to be symbolic – he knew it wouldn't have fitted my big hands. I had to give it back when I found out. This is my late mother's ring.'

'I'm sorry, Katy. I didn't know. Vinnie didn't talk much about your family, really.' Margaret shifted in her seat. 'Who carries around a ring like that in a war, I wonder? He could easily have lost it.'

'If you'd met the man who had it, you'd know why. Conrad's full of surprises.'

'Conrad? No ... Vinnie never mentioned no one by that name.'

Kate slipped the ring back down her top, and Mrs Jensen picked up a large brown envelope from the side of her chair. 'It's lovely to see you again, Katy, but I wouldn't have bothered you except for this.' She extracted some papers from the envelope and put them on her lap. 'Vinnie made a will years ago, just to keep things simple. I guess that comes from being in the Army.'

Most soldiers did make a will, it's true. Even Kate had dashed one off a few years ago. Mrs Jensen continued. 'He left everything to his sisters, divided equally, with me and his dad named as executors. We got a firm of lawyers to do it, but they've said that there's going to be death duties because of all his property. Did you know anything about this?'

'What do you mean?'

'He owned this house in Devon. Worth a fortune it is. I knew nothing about it. And then the solicitor says he had all these houses in London – *Buy to Let* he called 'em. There's far more here than a soldier should have. I know you was close and I know you feel guilty about what happened to him, so I started thinking. Is any of these houses yours? Were you, like … partners in any of this?'

She held up the papers, and Kate was itching to ask *Could I take a quick look?* But that would imply she knew something about it. 'Sorry, Margaret. We weren't partners. He took me to the Devon house once, but I thought it was owned by your family as a holiday home, you know.'

Margaret's expression said that hers was not the sort of family to have property on England's expensive seaside. A time-share in Spain, perhaps, but not this. 'Oh. That's a shame. I was hoping that you might have been entitled to a share, but never mind.'

Kate saw Mrs Jensen's eyes flick to a wall clock, and it was approaching the hour. She guessed that her hostess would be about to watch a soap on TV, and she took the chance to make her excuses. Margaret didn't try to detain her.

On the way to the tube, Kate considered what she'd learned. Vinnie had been up to something. He clearly had a source of income beyond his Army pay, but what could it be? Was it connected to his death or just a result of some long-ago piece of good fortune, coupled with canny investments? Without the details, she couldn't go digging, but she knew someone who could: Tom. This sort of financial web was bread and butter to him.

But of course, he wouldn't act on this alone (even if he were fully recovered). Kate had never forgotten the way that Gareth Wade's widow approached her outside the inquest. She had more-or-less said that Wade had had a second income, which had stopped with his death. Coincidence? Possibly.

It was time for a trip to Wales.

Come to my house. Discreetly.

That had been the order. Conrad Clarke had a theory about orders: When your commanding officer tells you to do something sensible, it's an instruction; when he tells you to do something daft, it's an order.

He was riding a gentle old gelding – the first time he'd ridden a horse in a dozen years. Well, what could be more discreet? He certainly wouldn't be on any CCTV cameras as he worked his way along the bridle paths from the stables to St Andrew's Hall. Then again, he was so deep in the countryside that there weren't any cameras anyway.

Although he had hated his physiotherapist at Valley Edge Rehab clinic (the feeling was mutual), she did know what she was doing. She had asked him about his sporting interests, and he had said *cricket*.

'That's a good game, but what exercise do you do to prepare for it?'

'Cricket is the exercise.'

'No, no, no. It will make your leg worse. You need to rebuild your strength all over the body before you play cricket again.'

He hated exercise. It was so boring. Cricket is fun. It's a battle of wit, skill and psychology that can only be played in the summer. What could be better?

She had given him a list of suitable activities, and most of them were non-starters as far as he was concerned – swimming, weights, running, and cycling were just *so* tedious. He had enjoyed the yoga classes and half promised himself to enrol when he was discharged, but life got in the way. Kabul is not renowned for its tolerance of yoga.

There was one last exercise at the bottom of the list, which had an asterisk next to it: horse riding. The asterisk led to a footnote which explained that he would have to provide his own horse. Ha! The Army owns more horses than tanks, and they couldn't spare one for a decorated war hero?

He had first got into the saddle when barely a teenager, to get closer to a spectacular girl at school, and discovered that he loved it far more than he loved her. The co-ordination, judgement and sense of direction that made him a good helicopter pilot were first developed on horseback. His parents indulged him, and on his eighteenth birthday they had bought him a hunter – with the proviso that the livery costs and the hunt subscription were coming out of his salary when he left school. That was one reason why he had joined the RAF instead of going to university.

He had kept the horse for seven years, and when it died, so did his enthusiasm for the sport. By then he was being picked for his RAF team as a spin bowler, and he had long realised that girls who hunted were out of his league financially. He went to the hunt ball one last time, and someone introduced him to Amelia.

He had discovered a lot about his new master before coming here: it would have been dangerous not to. Sir Stephen Jennings had inherited St Andrew's Hall (and the baronetcy) at the age of eight, when his father had been killed in the Korean War. The old man had won a VC during the Normandy landings, too. That must have been a hard act for the young Sir Stephen to follow, but follow it he did, winning medals of his own with the King's Oxford Lancers.

If Clarke had inherited a house like that and had three children to follow in his footsteps, his attitude to life might have been very different.

He nudged the horse down the hill and lost sight of the house. The animal's rocking motion was having an effect;

he was already sore but he was loving it. Another reason for arriving on horseback had also turned up during his research: Sir Stephen had been Master of Foxhounds in his day, and had a bizarre listing on the Companies House website – he was Chairman of Fylde Gentleman's Sporting Club Ltd.

A little digging showed that this was the holding company for a racecourse and hotel in Lancashire. What on earth was an Oxfordshire squire doing with a racecourse near Blackpool? His son-in-law was listed as chief executive, and for a paralysing second he thought that this must be Amelia's husband … but no, Julian Bentley had married the older daughter, Olivia. On the other hand, Amelia was listed as a director.

He crossed the road at the bottom of the hill and dismounted at the open gates to the Hall. Before him stood an Elizabethan manor house: all brick and chimneys, with original leading in the windows. The small front garden featured a gravel circle around a fountain. Small ruts in the gravel pointed to the side of the house and led to a utility area with two cars and a stable block. By the time he'd tied up the horse and found a blanket, Lady Jennings was standing by the back door with her arms folded and wearing an amused expression.

'I never forget a face,' she said. 'Even one I've only seen in a holiday snap.'

He walked towards her, and she held out her hand. 'Conrad Clarke,' he said.

'I know. Founder member of the Jilted by Amelia club. Don't worry, she's not here.' Lady Jennings turned to go inside. 'Leave your boots in the scullery and come through. Would you like something to eat?'

'I'm not sure if I'm invited for lunch.'

'Ignore Stephen. If you've been in the saddle, you'll need something inside you, and so will the horse. Give him some feed and have a cigarette. You can't smoke in here, I'm afraid.

Clearly, she had been doing as much research into him as he had into her husband. In the flesh, it was difficult to believe that Lady Jennings was sixty. She was dressed in a flattering pair of jeans and had buttoned a blue cardigan over a white blouse. The blue picked up her eyes and complemented the honey highlights in her hair.

He dug out some food for the horse and considered his position. The lady of the house may have come to welcome him herself, but he was still going through the tradesman's entrance. Clarke had been to a private school, yes, but few outside Gloucestershire had ever heard of it. He had ridden to hounds and never been short of money, but he wasn't rich. Although his mother had enjoyed her work at GCHQ enormously, his parents had needed her salary to keep themselves afloat. There was a bigger distance between his world and Amelia's than between his world and the semi in North London where Vinnie Jensen had said he'd grown up.

He and Vinnie were both tradesmen. Thanks to Operation Red Flag they had both become richer tradesmen, and he wasn't about to lose that if he could help it. He went into house and took off his boots.

The kitchen was straight from the pages of an interiors magazine. He knew this because they had framed a copy of the article and hung it in the scullery. In one of the photographs, Lady Jennings was flanked by her daughters. He flinched and went through to the hall, pausing to warm his hands at the Aga and sniff with anticipation at the smells of home cooking. How would Mina feel coming to a place like this? Was the dream of country living a purely English phenomenon, to which she would be immune? Can you cook curry on an Aga?

He paused on the threshold of the oak-panelled hall where modern lighting had been used to supplement the stained glass windows in the gallery. The space was large, immaculate and utterly useless for modern living, unless you were hosting a party.

Most of the walls were bare, to show off the centuries-old panelling, but occasionally there was a picture of an ancestor. In pride of place was a grouping of living family portraits. In the centre was a joint portrait of Sir Stephen and Lady Jennings in evening dress, standing in this very hall. A banner had been draped over the gallery, and he could just make out the number 25 – presumably their wedding anniversary. Underneath this picture were a couple of wedding pictures and a large studio portrait of Amelia. He didn't think he could take much more of this.

He looked around again, and the only military reference anywhere was in their son's uniform at his wedding (he had followed his father into the King's Oxfords). There were no medals, certificates, old swords or suits of armour. You wouldn't guess that Sir Stephen was chairman and formerly chief executive of CIS – Consolidated International Security, the largest private military contractor based in the UK.

'In here, Conrad,' said Lady Jennings from a doorway. 'And you must call me Susan.'

He smiled, and was ushered into a more modest room than the hall, though still unmistakably old. A Labrador slept on a rug in front of the log fire, and Sir Stephen was putting down the *Daily Telegraph*. At least the man stood up to greet him.

'A beautiful house, if I may say so, sir.'

'Yes, it is. Thanks to Susan. She rescued it from my neglect and my father's penury.'

'Has it been in the family long?'

Jennings stared at him. 'Don't bullshit me, Clarke. You know exactly how long it's been in my family, and everything else there is to know about me and my family that can be found on the internet.'

Of course he did. 'Sorry, sir.'

'Now sit down and tell me what you've put together with that devious brain of yours.'

He did as he was bid and let the dog lick his hand in welcome. Jennings had gone to the sideboard and returned with two small glasses of a richly coloured malt whisky. Instead of handing one over, he stopped a few feet away and waited for Clarke to tell his story. That's how the rich stayed rich – they didn't give tradesmen a drink until they'd proved their worth.

'Well, sir…'

'Drop the "sir". We're neither of us in uniform any more, and I don't believe you mean it when you say it.'

Sir Stephen Jennings was obviously older than his wife, and his active life was written in the lines across his face. He was wearing an old pair of twill trousers and a check shirt; a heavy pullover had been discarded over the arm of the chair. He stood before the fire like an old tree – securely rooted and going nowhere.

Clarke moistened his lips and tried not to stare at the Scotch with too much eagerness.

'I know that I've spent the last five years smuggling vast amounts of hard currency out of Iraq and Afghanistan, and now that I know your involvement with CIS, I can see how it worked – and I've a good idea that the currency came from reconstruction money – but apart from that, I'm none the wiser.'

'Good. If you can't find out with your inside knowledge, then things must still be pretty secure.' Jennings handed over the Scotch and raised his glass. 'To the future.' They both drank, and Jennings relaxed into the couch. Clarke echoed his body language and tried to look as if he belonged.

'Did you ever speculate what happened to it after you loaded it on to the transporters?'

'Of course. I know that it must have been going somewhere for laundering first, but the ultimate destination? I assumed that it would work its way back to the people who skimmed it off in the first place. Together with someone like you, who was pulling the strings.'

This assessment was met with a grimace. 'A little reductive, but there's some truth in what you say.' Jennings took a deep breath. 'From the moment the cash was separated out of the fund it came from, to the moment it reached its final destination, I reckon that eighty per cent was paid in bonuses like yours, in taxes and other expenses, commissions and dividends to our investors. It's the final twenty per cent that got me involved.' He leaned forward and stared at Clarke with the gaze of a much younger man: a man about to inspire his troops for a dangerous mission. 'That twenty per cent supplements a key part of the national security budget. And that's all you need to know.'

Clarke drained the last of his malt whisky. So that was their game. The intensity of Jennings' stare said that he believed what he was saying, but Clarke didn't care whether the money ended up paying for assassinations in Pakistan or buying a new roof for St Andrew's Hall. So long as he got his share, Jennings could play whatever games he wanted.

He put on a need-to-know face and said, 'I understand that, but you've brought me here and told me that for a reason. Presumably there's something you need me to do.'

'Yes. Will Offlea did a variety of jobs for me, but I only want you to cover some of them.'

'Sorry. Who?'

Jennings laughed. 'The man you called Barbarossa is really Will Offlea – or at least, that's the name he's used since he left Northern Ireland. He acted as liaison officer for a number of jobs in Afghanistan and elsewhere, but his main role was to co-ordinate the absorption of the cash into the banking system. That's the part I need you for.'

Aah. Money laundering – he'd never heard it called *absorption of cash into the banking system* before, but it was as good a euphemism as any. 'How many schemes are we talking about?'

Jennings frowned at his use of the word *schemes* but said nothing. 'As you know, we've been having problems. A year ago, we were running three Operations – Red Flag, Green Light and Blue Sky. You know all about the income side of Red Flag, and that's continuing – or it will do as long as we have boots on the ground in Afghanistan.'

'You think that's about to change?'

'Yes. I've had word from a friend that our beloved prime minister is going to make an announcement this week that we're pulling out during the lifetime of this parliament. By the next election, there won't be any British troops – or airmen – in the country. We've got a couple of years to find an alternative source of income.'

Clarke nodded. 'And that work I did for you in Essex was to wind up Operation Blue Sky.'

'Yes. It was doing quite well until those criminals got greedy and messed it up. In fact, it was doing so well that we grafted the counterfeiting on to our operation in the Midlands – Green Light. That idea blew up spectacularly last week.'

'What happened?'

Jennings took his empty glass and poured another nip of malt whisky for them both. 'Bad luck and bad judgement. Somehow, Sergeant Morton from the Fraud Squad followed the money up the M40 from London and started sniffing around. We managed to divert the flow of cash to a new contact in Blackpool, and that's where the bad luck came in. Unbeknownst to me or Offlea, the purchaser in Blackpool was an ex-IRA man. He let his face be seen in Earlsbury, and one of his past sins came back to haunt him. Before the bombing with Morton, did you read about the shooting of a policeman? … two in fact.'

'And two other men as well, wasn't it?'

'Yes. The dead officer was our man in CID. That made life very difficult. What made it worse was that bloody Morton – Inspector Morton now – wangled himself into the investigation and discovered the identity of the IRA man – Benedict Adaire. Will Offlea had a personal score to settle with Adaire. He decided to take out Adaire, Morton and Lonsdale in one go. He succeeded with Adaire but failed with the other two. That's why he's gone abroad.'

'If I might ask, what was the element of bad judgement? Was it giving Offlea the Kill order?'

'I didn't give him the order; that was his decision. I couldn't stop him, though. If you knew what Adaire did to his family, you wouldn't have tried to stop him, either. No, Conrad, the element of bad judgement was in trying to keep the counterfeiting operation going. We should have stopped it dead.'

Susan Jennings' footsteps echoed across the hall she approached them. 'Time for lunch, Stephen, before you offer any more hospitality of the liquid kind.'

Tom had never seen his mother so happy. Not for years, anyway. Mrs Valerie Morton had received official confirmation. She was going to become Lady Morton in the New Year Honours List.

Strictly speaking, it was his father who had received a call telling him that he would become Sir Thomas. That was a minor detail. She was so radiant with anticipation that she almost forgot to provide lunch for Tom and his bosses. She rang her favourite deli and wheedled the manager into sending someone round with a few platters just before Paul Ogden, the Director of CIPPS, and Leonie Spence, his deputy, arrived. Never one to miss out on good food if she could help it, his mother joined them for lunch.

Tom knew about Leonie from talking to Samuel Cohen, but he'd never met her before, and he wasn't expecting her today. As well as being a woman in the police service, Leonie had risen despite not being a police officer – she had been a barrister before joining CIPPS. His mother and Leonie assessed each other in that covert way women do. She was tall, but not as tall as Kate, and much slighter. Her hair was dyed blond and parted at the side in a bob. This meant that a large fringe was prone to sliding down over her face. On their way to the dining room, her heels echoed on the tiled floor. That had been the part of her outfit that his mother had focused on most. That, and the fact that she wasn't much older than Tom and wasn't wearing any rings.

The hostess arranged the guests so that she could focus on the boss rather than his deputy, and after pleasantries about the journey from London, she opened the bidding.

'Tell me,' she said to Ogden, 'and I'm asking this because Tom is a bit vague on the subject, what does CIPPS do that the Independent Police Complaints Commission doesn't do?'

Ogden, a fellow Yorkshireman although not a graduate, looked at Tom as if he were responsible for his mother's question. He had never been responsible for what she did, although occasionally he had been held accountable. Tom shrugged.

'It's a long story, Mrs Morton.'

'Take as long as you've got,' she replied with an expansive wave.

'For starters,' said Ogden, 'the IPCC has a much bigger budget and a lot of staff. They handle the big cases – deaths in police custody, for example, or if a member of the public is shot by armed officers. They are in the public eye a great deal, and quite rightly too. We are much smaller and can respond much more quickly, and we restrict ourselves to cases of corruption or criminal activity by serving officers. It isn't always practical to bring in serving officers from the other end of the country so that's our job — if Inspector John Smith or Jane Jones is accused of taking bribes, and the chief constable wants a quick result, they give me a call. When they do call in an outside force to investigate, we're the ones who make sure they do a good job.'

His mother nodded throughout Ogden's explanation, and Tom wondered why on earth she was asking this. He was opposite Leonie Spence during the meal and he noticed that she used her wayward fringe as part of her communication strategy. When she needed time to think or needed someone's attention, she would brush it out of the way.

His mother made coffee and left them to it. Leonie asked the way to the bathroom.

Ogden began by asking about Tom's health and recovery.

'I'm getting there. The only issue is the skin graft — they're going to look at it again on Monday, and I should get the all-clear to return to work then. I may need to wear something other than a suit for a while.'

He had tried to cover the last remark with a smile, but Ogden seemed concerned. He delayed responding until Spence returned. The wayward fringe had now been pinned back with a gold slide.

'And that's the issue,' said Ogden when his deputy was seated. 'What are you going to return to?'

Tom tried to keep his voice level. 'Midland Counties, sir. There's a major problem there.'

Spence frowned, as if this was not the answer she wanted to hear.

'Go on,' said Ogden.

Tom took a folder from the sideboard and laid it in front of them. It contained the printouts which proved that Detective Sergeant Griffin had been sent to his death by a senior officer in MCPS. As he outlined the facts, Ogden's face lengthened and he sucked in a breath through his teeth.

'That's a right mess and no mistake,' he said when Tom had finished. He looked at his deputy. 'Leonie?'

Her speaking voice was deeper than Tom expected; her accent was London Lite. 'I agree,' she said. 'There are clear grounds for a criminal investigation here – of a most delicate nature.'

Tom said nothing. Ogden picked up the papers and studied them. 'Are you up to it?' he asked. 'Not just physically, but in terms of dealing with half a dozen senior officers from England's third-largest police force?'

'I've been nearly blown to pieces so far, sir, and I'm not going to let that stop me.'

'I was afraid you'd say that.'

'The thing is,' said Leonie, 'we can't really have a lowly DI, no matter how good you are, investigating a chief constable. It might look as if we aren't taking this seriously.'

'It's not the Chief,' said Tom. 'I have evidence that the corruption goes back well before he was appointed. My strategy was to work with him as far as possible.'

'Are you sure?'

'As sure as I can be.'

Ogden nodded.

'There is something else you could do,' continued Tom. 'You could promote me to DCI.'

Ogden laughed. 'Nice try, lad. Nice try.'

'Actually,' said Leonie, 'that might not be a bad idea.' Ogden spluttered something about his budget but she held up her hand. 'Hear me out.' She looked at Tom. 'From what I've heard, this case is a bit of a crusade for you, isn't it?'

'Up to a point. I haven't acted unprofessionally in any way but, yes, I want to get to the bottom of it.'

She nodded. 'Would I be right in saying that CIPPS wouldn't have been your first choice of career path?' She didn't wait for him to answer. 'How about this for a solution? I'll be nominally in charge of the investigation, but you can run it in whatever way you see fit. I'll join you when you meet the Chief then go back to London. We'll promote you to DCI on the understanding – the clear understanding – that you'll do at least another year in CIPPS after this is finished before you even *think* about looking for a job elsewhere. Would that work, Tom? Sir?'

Ogden rubbed his jaw. 'Works for me.'

Tom was a great believer in the Art of the Possible. He wasn't going to get a better offer anywhere else. He stood up and extended his hand to Leonie. 'I look forward to working with you, Ma'am.'

She shook his hand firmly in response. 'It's Leonie, not "Ma'am". I'm not your commanding officer, I'm your manager.'

Ogden shook his hand too and then asked about support.

'I want to use DC Hayes from MCPS. She's good and she knows the case.'

'Fine. Please thank Mrs Morton again for the lunch. She's a right good cook. Come on, Leonie, shall we head off to Harrogate?'

Ogden went to get his coat. Leonie leaned towards Tom and gave him a conspiratorial wink. 'Your mother knows a good deli, doesn't she?'

Tom whispered back, 'I learned everything I know about cooking from our housekeeper.'

She patted him on the shoulder, and he tried not to grimace with pain. At least it was his right shoulder.

They left the house, and he made a quick phone call to Hayes with the news.

'That's great, sir.' she said. 'I don't want to put a dampener on things, but I've heard on the grapevine that Patrick Lynch has done a runner. Well ... he's been reported missing by his wife, and his Jaguar's disappeared.'

'That's not good. Look, Kris, I can't start until Wednesday at the earliest. When you get back on Monday, can you dig around a bit?'

'No problem.'

Tom thanked her and rang off. His next call was to the insurance company to continue arguing about the value of his burnt out car, currently sitting in the forensic lab.

Clarke and his hosts adjourned to the kitchen where the smells of cooking turned out to be from a rich, heart-warming French onion soup. After they'd taken the edge of their hunger, Lady Jennings put down her spoon and looked at Clarke.

'You're going to have to meet her again, you know.'

He tried to grin in response. 'I'm good at keeping a low profile, you know.'

'Not easy with your height, I imagine.'

Clarke bowed his head towards her and brushed his hand over it. 'I'm losing my hair as well as having a limp. Soon I'll be just as anonymous as the next man.'

Susan kept a straight face. He couldn't figure out whether this topic was being raised for his benefit or their daughter's. Was he going to be warned to stay away from her clutches or to keep his hands off her?

'According to Stephen, you're going to be moving in one of her circles,' said Susan.

He turned to Jennings. 'That's news to me.'

Jennings looked down at his soup. 'We haven't got round to specifics yet. Still sorting out the context.'

'I don't want to steal your thunder,' she responded to her husband. To Clarke, she said, 'Amelia's had a chequered career since you split up.'

Clarke wanted to put his cards on the table. He was guessing from their attitude that a number of men had been smitten by Amelia over the years. It was a good job they didn't know that he'd hung on to the ring for nine years.

Well, it was gone now. 'I think "since she dumped me" rather than "split up" would be a more accurate description, Susan. It was a long time ago and I've travelled a long way since then.'

'I'm sure you have,' said Susan. 'It's just that Amelia has a tendency to look on her exes as a resource to be exploited. Just to warn you, that's all.'

'Noted. What's she been up to career-wise? She told me she'd been offered a job in America when we last met.'

Sir Stephen interjected, 'It's a bit more complicated than that.'

Susan glanced at her husband then put her hand on Clarke's. 'He's trying to spare your blushes, Conrad. What he means is that when Amelia was touring the States, she hooked up with a US congressman and had an affair. He was married, of course, but Amelia convinced him to take her on as part of the team in advance of his bid for the Senate in 2002.'

'Oh,' said Conrad. He had never given a thought to whether Amelia had been faithful to him during their time apart. The important thing was whether she came back and stuck to him. He shouldn't be surprised to learn that she had slept her way to a job. Susan patted his hand now that she'd broken the news and started to eat her soup again.

'How did he get on?' asked Clarke. 'In the election, I mean?'

'He won. Before the polling day, however, his wife found out about Amelia and gave him an ultimatum: get rid of the Limey or I'll dump you during the election. The congressman got Amelia's Green Card revoked.'

Sounds like they were well suited, he thought. He kept the thought to himself, however, and nodded his understanding to Susan.

She finished her soup and pushed the bowl aside. 'Once he'd done that, he made it up to her. He used one of his contacts to get her a job in London and, professionally speaking, she's never looked back.'

'Is she still in politics?'

'She never was in politics,' said Sir Stephen. 'She was in PR and happened to work for a politician. She's taken a sideways move and works as an event planner for celebrities now. Not a world you're familiar with, I'm sure.'

Clarke deflected that assertion by asking Susan if Amelia had arranged the article about the kitchen.

'It was her idea of a bloody birthday present.' said Jennings.

Clarke looked at the couple – Sir Stephen was still harbouring some resentment about having his home invaded by photographers and plastered all over a magazine: the little smile on his wife's face as she got up to fetch some cake said that it might have been the best birthday present she'd ever been given. Her friends and neighbours would have been green with envy.

She asked him about his health over tea and cakes, and then Sir Stephen stood up. 'You'll be wanting a smoke,' he said. 'I'll show you round the garden.'

His host collected his dog and his pullover from the drawing room, sneaked a portion of cake for the dog and waited whilst Clarke put his boots back on.

Jennings led him through a dormant kitchen garden to the formal gardens at the rear, then to a lower, less formal lawned area with an old tennis court, tucked away from sight of the house. He made no effort to talk about the gardens and passed through them as if they were like the house – just *there*. What he did do was throw a tennis ball for his dog while Clarke lit a cigarette.

'You'll be working with my son-in-law,' began Jennings.

'At the racecourse?'

Jennings threw the ball and gave him a grin. 'Absolutely. Best place I've ever come across for laundering money. All those on-course bookmakers.'

Clarke had been to many race meetings and enjoyed a flutter, but he had never been a gambler away from the track. 'I think I might be a bit out of my comfort zone there.'

'You'll get the hang of it. Julian knows roughly what's going on and he can point you in the right direction. He also has a key to Offlea's cottage and knows where the books are kept. You'll need them.'

Clarke smoked for a moment and contemplated his fate. He had passed within a mile or so of Fylde Racecourse when he went on an RAF visit to the jet fighter factory at Warton, but otherwise the area was terra incognita to him.

'That's not all,' continued Sir Stephen. 'There's an interchange arrangement that Julian knows nothing about.'

'I'm sorry. You've lost me there.'

'Do you remember how those bundles of notes looked when you shipped them out?'

Clarke was hardly going to forget what a half a million pounds looked like. Or dollars. Or Euros. The mere thought made him feel faint. He nodded.

'The Foreign Office and the MOD kept track of the serial numbers of those banknotes. We couldn't have them just turning up by the truckload in Lancashire. Nor could we invent planeloads of Eurozone and dollar gamblers for the racecourse. All the currency needs to be turned into used, non-sequential Bank of England notes.'

'Did Offlea do all that himself? Sounds like a full time job for a small team, not a part-time job for one man.'

'He just did transport. Other people arranged the exchange, and some of them are quite dangerous to know. You'll need to protect yourself.'

'I'm sure. I'll be very careful.'

'I know. That's one of the reasons I chose you, Clarke. For such a risk taker, you have an extraordinarily well-developed sense of self-preservation.'

The dog was sitting in front of them, patiently wagging its tail. Jennings rubbed the ball in his hands to get his scent on it then hurled it as far as he could into a group of shrubs before starting to walk back towards the house.

'You'll have to find somewhere up there to live, but you can stay at the Sporting Hotel until then.'

An idea was forming in the back of Clarke's mind. 'Excuse me asking, but what's going to happen to the counterfeiting operation? I can't imagine the printers will want to just stop.'

'I told Offlea to help himself to whatever they had already printed and take it with him abroad. You're right, though, the printers will keep going – as will the Principal Investor who brought them on board.'

'That could be dangerous.' He was about to say *for you*, but changed his mind. 'For us, I mean.'

'How so?'

'Our dogged little Detective Inspector Morton won't let a bomb blast stop him. He'll be back on the case when the notes start showing up. If he's more successful this time, you can guarantee that the printers will point the finger in our direction if they're caught.'

'A good point. Perhaps we should try to find an outlet abroad for them.'

'I might have a safer idea. Give me a couple of days to think about it.'

Jennings nodded. They stopped between the stables and the back door: clearly he wasn't being invited back inside. 'One more thing,' said Jennings. 'Now that Susan's satisfied her curiosity, you'll make all future visits by arrangement with me. Understood?'

Clarke nodded.

Jennings took his hands out of his pockets. He gave Clarke a firm handshake with his right, and with his left he passed over a mobile phone.

'Good luck.'

'Thank you, sir.'

Now that the chain of command had been firmly established, it seemed right to slip back into calling his boss *sir*. Clarke resisted the urge to salute and turned to untie his horse. As he did so, the figure of a cloaked man slipped around the corner of the Hall. He couldn't put it off any longer. He had to book himself that appointment with the neurologist before he did anything else.

Kate stood in the tube station with her bags packed at her feet. She studied the map and tapped her Oyster card against her hand. Paddington or Waterloo? Should she see her father first or go straight to see Gareth Wade's widow?

She put her Oyster card away and sent her father a text. *Hi dad. W'd like to visit tonight. OK? X.*

He could be giving a lecture and might not reply for a while, so she left the ticket hall and went in search of a coffee. Before she could locate one, she got a reply. *Want to see you soon but not this weekend. Busy. X.*

That was strange. If she didn't know him better, she might almost think he were up to something. She turned around and headed back to the tube: *Paddington it is.*

'Thank you for fitting me in,' said Clarke.

'Not a problem,' said the neurologist. 'Let me just look at the EEG printout for a minute.'

He had been there for an hour already, and spent twenty minutes lying down while a medical technician taped electrodes to his head for an electro-encephalograph. The neurologist had breezed in carrying a coffee, and had started looking at the results before she had even taken her coat off. She was of Indian extraction, but obviously second- or third-generation judging by her Midlands accent. As a private patient, Clarke had been well looked after, and was dunking a biscuit into his second cup of tea.

She looked up at him and switched on her smile. 'I don't have all the notes here from your extensive trauma event.'

'You mean the crash and the explosion.'

'Yes. I'm sorry about your leg, but it's the crash I'm more concerned about. Did you bang your head at all? Were you treated for any head trauma?'

'I blacked out, I know that much, but it can't have been for more than a second or two. I didn't have any visual problems and all my reactions functioned as they should. Good job they did or I wouldn't be here.'

'That's a good sign. Did they do any scans when you were repatriated?'

'No.'

She went on to ask about headaches, seizures, blurred vision and so on. She looked in his eyes and made careful notes when he described seeing the man in the cloak. After all that, she went back to the EEG.

'The good news is that I don't think you have an advanced case of anything,' she said with some enthusiasm. Clarke was inclined to agree about the *good news* part and waited for her to go on with the inevitable *bad news*. 'On the other hand, Conrad, there are many things that don't show up on an EEG, and there's one thing that has. Have a look at this.'

She passed over the printout and pointed to one of the lines. 'See here. There's a small flat section, then a big spike before it returns to normal. Only in one place, though. I'd like to have a proper look with an MRI scan.'

'How soon can you do it?'

'About a month on the NHS. Or tomorrow if you can afford £375. I can go through the results with you on Monday.'

'Where do I sign?'

She laughed. 'Good. You should be alright to drive for a while. There's no indication of any generalised irregularity. As I say, you don't have an advanced case of anything.'

'That's a relief. I'll try not to fly any helicopters until we've seen each other again.'

She took him seriously. 'I think that's a good idea. Oh ... before we go any further, is there any shrapnel in your neck or head?'

'I don't think so. Why?'

'We need to be sure. The magnets in the scanner can pull a hairgrip right off someone's head. Imagine what that would do to a piece of metal in your brain.'

Ouch. He tried not to think about that.

'Thanks, Doctor, I'll see you on Monday.'

The receptionist sorted out the scan for tomorrow, and Clarke left the building. Lighting a cigarette, he looked around. No men in cloaks. Good. He walked to the end of the street and hailed a taxi to take him to a solicitor's office in the City.

Stopping for a drink on the way home, he saw the muted television in the bar tuned to a rolling news channel. Pictures of the prime minister in the desert, talking to soldiers, were supplemented by captions: *PM's pledge to troops: total withdrawal by 2015 ... "We are not abandoning Afghanistan and our soldiers can be proud of what they have achieved." ... Arsenal keeper signs long-term deal ...*

'Proud? Tell that to the ones who came home in a body bag,' he muttered to himself.

Chapter 5

Wales – York

Saturday

20 November

The house had been easy enough to find. Gareth Wade's widow had several public listings, and Kate located it on the map then planned a circular walk from the village that would take her past the Wade residence and on to the coast before returning to her hire car.

It was bitterly cold and snow had begun to appear in the forecast for Wales: she needed every layer she had brought with her, and it wouldn't be out of place to wear a scarf over her face. She set a brisk pace to try and get some warmth into her legs and enjoyed battling up the hill.

Almost at the top, the house appeared on her right, slightly raised up and commanding uninterrupted views of the sea. It must be beautiful in summer.

It was a modern dormer bungalow in a style that someone once called *Southfork on Sea*. The original property had been added to at the side, and the whole front was glass. Triple-pane sliding doors would open to a terrace for barbecues. Perched on the sloping drive was a people carrier: Mrs Wade and her tribe were at home.

She continued her walk and soon reached the exposed headland. There were no more layers to put on, and she could feel the wind seeking out the smallest gap in her waterproofs. Kate had nearly been arrested for impersonating a police officer not so long ago, and wasn't going to try that again. So, Mrs Wade, is it going to be *good non-cop* or *bad non-cop*? Picking up her rucksack, she walked back down to the house. Right up until she pressed the bell, she had no idea what she was going to say.

A boy of about ten or eleven answered the door, and Kate asked if she could speak to his mother. He trailed off into the house. 'Mam, there's someone at the door for you.'

A distant voice shouted, 'Ask him in and close the ruddy door. It's freezing in here.'

The boy returned and stood aside. Kate noticed the pile of shoes on a mat and started untying her laces as best she could with numb fingers. After closing the door, the boy disappeared upstairs.

A shout – *Evan!* – came from the back of the house. If that were the boy's name, he'd never hear because sounds of a computer game were already drifting down from his room. A few seconds later, Mrs Wade appeared through the door into the kitchen.

'Oh,' she said. 'I thought you were a man.'

Kate decided on good non-cop. 'You aren't the first to make that mistake.'

'No, no, I mean Evan didn't say that you was a woman. I just thought it was a man at the door. I didn't mean that I thought *you* was a man.'

She had her hair pulled back and was wearing a long top over leggings and fluffy slippers. On top of all this was an apron. Flour and make-up were smudged on her face.

'Please … it's okay,' said Kate. 'I'm sorry to interrupt – I can come back later if you're baking.'

'I'm not baking: my daughter is. Officially, that is. For the Christmas Fayre at school, would you believe … except if we don't practise now we've got no chance next month – and the rugby's off 'cos of the weather, so Evan and his friend are upstairs.'

She wiped her hands on her apron and looked at Kate properly. Recognition slowly dawned on her face. Kate realised that she was never going to be good at this – so few women had her build that once noticed, she was rarely forgotten.

'Aren't you…?'

'Yes. I'm sorry we argued last time we met. The inquest must have been terrible for you.'

Mrs Wade looked back into the kitchen. 'Cerys, can you put some of those things in the dishwasher and start to wipe down the surfaces? That's a love. I won't be long.' She took off her apron and hung it from the kitchen door. 'Come with me.'

Kate followed her into the front room with its floor to ceiling windows overlooking the bay. It was spectacular, but even with double glazing, she could feel the heat leaching out. Mrs Wade pointed to one of the chairs arranged to face out, and Kate sat down, unzipping her jacket to make herself look more like a welcome visitor and less like an intruder. It didn't work.

'It's Captain Lonsdale, isn't it?'

'Not any more. I resigned my commission in the summer. It's Miss Lonsdale, or preferably Kate.'

The other woman nodded, but didn't offer her own first name in exchange.

'The reason I called,' said Kate, 'is that I went to see Vinnie's parents the other day. His mother was going through his affairs and found that he had more money than she thought he would have been able to save. I just wanted to make sure that you had a good lawyer who was on top of things. In case, you know, that Gareth had been ultra-careful with his assets.'

'You've come a long way to say that, haven't you?'

'I do contract work now. I had a job in South Wales and I thought I'd make a long weekend of it in Pembroke. That's the thing about the Army – like everything else, your spare time comes in rations, so you have to make the most of it. I'm not used to being a civilian yet.' She was getting nowhere. Mrs Wade hadn't made eye contact, nodded or shown any sign of engaging in a conversation. Kate was starting to waffle, so she just shut up and left a silence. Mrs Wade broke first.

'We're doing all right, thank you. I'll have to go back to work after Christmas, but we'll be okay.' There was a pause before she continued. 'I don't know how the kids are going to cope without him on Christmas Day, mind. Even when he was on a tour of duty, he always Skyped them. I think Cerys is still expecting his face to appear on the computer any day now. I had to stop her from replaying all the old sessions that she'd recorded. Pretended to her that the computer had broken.'

She was laying it on with a trowel. Kate didn't doubt a word of what the woman had said, and she imagined that the children would be wandering around for years expecting to see their father, just like she had done when her mother died, but the Grieving Widow act was even less convincing than Kate's Concerned Colleague. She'd seen enough.

'I'd better let you get back to your baking. I'm sorry to have bothered you.'

Mrs Wade smiled with relief and stood up. She stood for a long time with her hand on the front door catch, waiting for Kate to retie her shoelaces.

She drove to the nearest pub and ordered some lunch, picking the first thing on the menu that came with chips.

She knew a brush-off when she got one. She had also checked various estate agents' websites, and there was no sign that the Wade home had been put on the market. Therefore, Mrs Wade must have found enough money to carry on in the short term. What would Tom do now?

Well, there had been three men in that helicopter. Two of them had been receiving money from an unknown source: what about the third? Could Conrad have been in on something with them?

It had taken all her determination to speak to Mrs Wade: she hadn't a clue where to start with Conrad Clarke. The man was just so *plausible*. He was the sort of bloke that a husband might find in bed with his wife – and then end up going down the pub with him, because Conrad had convinced the husband that there was a perfectly innocent explanation. If she didn't get anywhere else, she'd think about tracking him down.

Her food arrived, and she devoured it in minutes. Around the bar, couples were eating lunch, and groups of men were chatting over a pint. She had never felt so alone in her life. Tom was with his family, her friends were in the Army, Vinnie was dead and she had no colleagues.

She dug out her phone and sent Anthony Skinner a text:

Ready for the next job so long as it's not in Hong Kong. He might respond on Monday … it might be weeks – or never.

She thought back to Tom's injuries. Whatever he was into, it was very serious, and he had told her last night that he was back on the case in Earlsbury. Could she do anything to help him? Something behind the scenes?

It was nearly nine months since the Valentine's Day shootout at Four Ashes Farm in Essex. There was one other loose end – Mina Finch. On the day that Mina's husband had been stabbed – and Mina had shot his killer – Kate had found herself staring down the barrel of a gun being held by a very small woman, who seemed to have been expecting her. Perhaps she could visit Mrs Finch in prison and put her on the spot. No. Bad idea.

She had got an out of season bargain at the hotel – a five star room for a three star price. Included in the deal was access to the gym and pool. Kate picked up her keys and left the pub. She was going to have a nap and then hit the gym. Tom's throwaway comment from his sick bed had reminded here that there was one part of her life she could control – and that was her waistline.

After her nap, she checked her phone and found a message from Skinner suggesting a meeting at a completely new location – the London HQ of Consolidated

International Security. Had he got a new job for her? She replied and told him *Any time after 15:00 Monday.*

It wasn't a day for looking at new cars. A coating of snow had given way to sleet, and Tom's father had very quickly suggested – after visiting the BMW garage – that the internet would be a lot warmer. Tom agreed. When they got home, his father had to manoeuvre around a small hatchback partly blocking the drive. His mother was waiting for them at the back door.

'There's a journalist in the hall,' she hissed. 'She says there's going to be a story tomorrow that you should comment on.'

Tom had no intention of commenting on anything.

'Why did you let her in?' asked his father.

'Would you leave someone outside in that weather?'

Tom and his father shared a glance. *Yes, they both would. Without hesitation.* 'Don't put the kettle on until she's gone,' he said to his mother, then went through to the hall. Too late. The journalist was already enjoying a cup of tea.

'DI Morton. How can I help you?' he said in a voice which implied he had no such intention whatsoever.

She introduced herself as Juliet Porterhouse, and Tom insisted on checking her credentials. Most journalists know better than to doorstep police officers, and Tom had learned early on that the ones who did so were invariably freelancers or (worse still) bloggers. He never talked to either type. This one, however, was a staff reporter for one of the Sunday broadsheets. When he saw the name of her paper, he vaguely remembered her.

'You've come a long way, haven't you?'

'I was in Blackpool last night. I'll file my copy from here then head back down the A1.'

She looked at the door to the sitting room, hoping to be invited in. Tom said nothing, and she began by asking about his convalescence. He gave polite but truthful answers about his health and played a straight bat when her questions shifted to how he had come by his wounds.

'I've come here for a reason,' she said. 'We're going to be running a story tomorrow which identifies Benedict Adaire as the leader of a Republican hit squad in Northern Ireland. The Lancashire and Westmorland Constabulary have already identified the bomber as coming from Belfast, and he would be the right age to have been a terrorist himself during the Troubles. We want to give you a chance to explain what you were doing in that car. The Lancashire & Westmorland press office has given us nothing at all.'

Porterhouse opened her notebook. 'Are you really working for Professional Standards, or is that a cover for something else?'

Tom looked around him. His instinct was to send her packing, but the very last thing he wanted was his picture next to the article and veiled hints that he worked for MI5. 'I'll give you two quotes,' he said. 'One for free and one with a condition.'

'Let's start with the free one,' said the journalist. 'Do you mind if I record it? My fingers are too cold for shorthand.'

'Go ahead.'

She took out a recording device and held it up.

'I'm a very lucky copper. Or a very unlucky one,' he began. 'Most of my work for the police has been in fraud and money laundering. I'm very handy with a spreadsheet and normally I don't even carry handcuffs. On that night, I was in the wrong place at the wrong time. That was the unlucky part. The lucky part is that I'm still alive and I'll make a full recovery.'

'And the second quote?'

'The condition is that you do not begin your piece by saying: speaking from his parents' luxurious Georgian house in York where his father is a judge... '

The look on her face said that she hadn't been thinking of saying that but wished she had. She nodded, and Tom pointed to her recorder. 'Say it for the tape, if you wouldn't mind.'

'Fair enough. Minimal personal context. You are married, though?'

He pressed his lips together. 'Very nearly divorced. Just waiting for the judge to pronounce that life in the marriage is extinct.'

'Sorry about that. Go on.'

'Benedict Adaire was a common criminal, and so was the man who murdered him. They were both involved in a wide variety of crimes in England that had nothing to do with their past in Northern Ireland. Crime, not paramilitary violence, is what brought them together and crime is what made them fall out.'

Porterhouse switched off the recorder and considered what he had said. 'Okay. Not what I hoped for, but more than I expected. Thanks, Inspector.'

He showed her to the door, and she buttoned up her coat. Patches of icy sleet were beginning to accumulate at the edge of the lawn. 'Drive carefully,' said Tom. 'It's a long way.'

'You're not joking. I'm going to head off now and phone my copy in from the services.' She dug her hands in her coat pocket to retrieve her gloves and pulled out a business card with them. 'Here,' she said. 'If you like what you read tomorrow, bear me in mind for the future.'

He made a point of putting it in his wallet, and she smiled at him before making a dash for her car. It never hurt to have a contact in the press.

On the way back to the kitchen he received a text from Kris Hayes.

Body found in Earlsbury. Inside info says Patrick Lynch. Do you want me to start digging now?

He responded: *Wait until Monday. Dig gently.*

IN THE RED CORNER

Chapter 6

London– On the Train – York – London

Monday

22 November

Clarke's second appointment with the neurologist was at the ludicrous time of eight o'clock on Monday morning. It was the doctor herself who admitted him to the building, and this time she didn't bother to take off her coat. Neither did he: it was too cold.

'Sorry to drag you into town so early, Conrad. I'm pleased to say that this won't take long.'

'Oh good. I like the sound of that.'

'I accessed your MRI results yesterday – it beats trying to cook Sunday dinner. You have no tumour and no stroke damage. They were my main concerns.'

'There's a "but", isn't there?'

'Isn't there always? I think you might have had some very minor trauma damage, possibly in the crash. Can I show you this?'

She pushed her computer monitor around, and several multi-coloured scans of his brain were revealed. 'Can you imagine standing on top of a very tall building?' He nodded. 'These images are like looking down at floor plans. Each one shows a different level through your brain. It's not quite the same because they're rotated through 90 degrees, and the first one is close to your left ear, the last one is close to your right ear. Got that?'

'I think so.'

'Normally, this section talks to that section.' She pointed to two different parts of his brain. 'But in your case, there might have been some damage – even a temporary break in the circuit. There's no way of knowing this, but when you crashed, I think that this section stopped talking to that section for a few seconds, and because the brain is very adaptable, it found a way round via here.'

It was all a bit much. She was pointing to different parts of his head as if meant something to him, and it meant nothing.

She pressed on regardless. 'When you woke up, normal service was resumed, but it now seems that there is a scenic route in your brain. Very, very occasionally, some of the signals don't go down the motorway. They go for a drive round the coast and pick up a passenger – a man in a cloak.'

He rubbed his chin. 'That's a very nice metaphor, Doctor, but what does it mean for me?'

'It means that I want – I insist – that you have another scan in six months' time, to see if there is any change. In the meantime, carry on as before unless the symptoms get worse. Or you could try psychoanalysis – perhaps the man in the cloak isn't a neurological phantom but something surfacing from your past.'

That was a relief. Probably. His doctor was smiling like a TV advert on *pause*. She was waiting to see if he had any questions. 'Thank you,' he said, and she started to close down her computer. On one of the bookshelves was a tiny statuette of Kali.

He stood up to go. 'Tell me Doctor, do you think the man in the cloak might be Ganesha?'

She sat there with her mouth open as if she'd suffered her own short-circuit.

'I don't like therapists,' he said. 'I wondered if a priest might not be more use.'

She closed her jaw and stood up. 'Whatever floats your boat, Conrad. Whatever floats your boat.'

His new laptop was working, his new(ish) BMW was sitting on the drive, and his new skin was healing nicely. *That's the glass half full view of the world*, thought Tom. He had never been a glass half empty person.

Snow had been forecast for tomorrow, but he wasn't in a position to leave now. The hospital had insisted he get dressings from the district nurse, who couldn't come until tonight.

Kate had pointed him in the direction of an encryption system for videoconferencing, and he told Hayes to check it out. Before long, he was looking at a low resolution image of her in a conference room at BCSS.

'How was your first day back at work? Any problems?'

She shrugged. The encryption system added a slight delay, and her shoulders seemed to spasm. 'It was okay. I went to Human Resources and told them the Griffin investigation was still active, and that they should ring CIPPS in Lambeth. They couldn't be bothered. It'll take a few days before ACC Khan even realises I'm back.'

'Good. What news on Patrick Lynch? Is it definitely him?'

'Yes. Because we had arrested him, it wasn't too difficult for me to find out what was going on.'

'Even better. Take me through it from the beginning.'

There was a flash and a flicker as the connection nearly disappeared, then Hayes looked down at her notebook to give him the story.

'On Saturday morning, a delivery driver followed his satnav down a dead end. He couldn't turn his waggon round in the lane and went through into an old loading dock by the canal. This is about two miles from Earlsbury centre, under the M5 flyover. The driver had to do a careful ten-point turn and came face to face with an old van in the bushes. He could clearly see a body in the front and dialled 999 straight away.'

She paused to see if he had any questions. He waved for her to continue – and four seconds later – she did. 'The body was in the front passenger seat and slumped over the dash. There was no obvious sign of foul play, but the officer attending recognised Patrick Lynch, and the full Major Incident Protocol was observed.

'However, there was nothing to find. There were no prints on the van at all except Patrick Lynch's. The keys were missing, but the door was unlocked. The only forensic note of any significance was that the van has been used regularly for the transportation of fish.'

'Fish?'

'Yes, sir. The van had false plates but the VIN proved that its last legal owner was a fresh fish business based in Fleetwood, Lancs. They sold it to a man who gave a false name and paid cash.'

'Interesting. Fleetwood is very close to Blackpool, unless I'm much mistaken. Have they got cause of death yet?'

'The post-mortem results came in today: a heart attack. Apparently he left his pills and his phone at home when he went out. He had a massive angina attack and just died. Time of death is consistent with shortly before the time that Mrs Lynch reported him missing several days ago.'

'Presumably he wasn't driving the van. How did he get there? Was he picked up at home?'

'No. He took his Jaguar, and that's missing. There's been too much rain since he disappeared to check for tyre tracks at the scene. There's an alert on every traffic camera in the country for it.' She flicked through the notes. 'Wallet still in his pocket. No bruising or other signs of a struggle. The consensus view is that he went to a rendezvous, had a heart attack, and whoever he was meeting just left him there. And stole his car.'

Hayes looked into the camera, her report concluded. Tom rubbed his chin. 'What do you think?' he asked her.

She echoed his gesture of stroking her chin, though presumably she hadn't felt any stubble when she did so. 'Well, Tom, if you'd asked me that question six months ago, I would have said, "If it quacks, it's a duck." By that, I mean the official story is overwhelmingly the right one.'

'But you don't think so. Why?'

'The phone and the pills. They were on the kitchen worktop, near the back door. You couldn't miss them if you left the house. You and I both saw him having an attack. That man knew he was just a few seconds from death without those pills. I can't see that anything would make Patrick Lynch leave the house without them.'

'Neither can I, Kris … but I don't know what it all means. Thanks. That's good work. I'll see you at the Earlsbury Park Country Club on Wednesday night, if they'll still allow me to stay there after getting the place turned over.'

'Use a false name, I would.'

Tom thought about it. That wasn't a bad idea. 'Thanks. I'll book us in under Leonie's name. She'll be there overnight and seeing the chief constable with me on Thursday. She wants to meet you.'

Hayes frowned. 'Are you sure she'll let us get on without any interference?'

'I've got to trust her. No alternative. But she did make a good first impression.'

Hayes's mouth twitched upwards in a smile. 'I'm sure she did. Sir.'

He tried to give her a baleful look, but he doubted that it came over on the screen. They disconnected, and he went back to the fireside. He lay face down on the rug and dropped off to sleep. It was the most comfortable place in the house.

Of course Kate had heard of Consolidated International Security, but she had never expected to be walking through its doors. Their London office was close to her flat, but the look was very different: CIS occupied the whole of a three storey building where the top two storeys thrust out over the pavement, like a fighter sticking out his chin before a bout.

She could see a large and comfortable reception area beyond, but all visitors and staff first had to pass through the security lobby first. This area was unusual in having two guards who enjoyed their work, and who spent quite some time verifying her identity and checking with Skinner's office before admitting her to the warmer zone within.

She had to report to a second desk inside, and was issued with a photo-ID just for this short visit. 'Please wear that on top of your jacket so that it's visible at all times. You will be stopped if it isn't.'

The lanyard on Kate's pass was red. Members of staff had attractive purple ones, and more favoured visitors were given blue, they told her when she asked. All of them had CIS running through the fabric.

Skinner's assistant appeared very soon afterwards, and surprised Kate by being a man. She said nothing about that, and neither did he. They went through a secure door, and into a small meeting room. 'Red badge visitors can't be left on their own,' he explained, while they waited for Skinner.

'Good job I don't want to go to the ladies room.'

'Yes, it is. For some reason, women find it difficult to pee when I'm standing at the cubicle door.'

Kate flushed bright red and her bladder gave a spasm of sympathy. She couldn't stop herself crossing her legs.

'That's why we're meeting down here,' said the assistant. 'Saves me having to give you the body search.'

Skinner appeared, and his assistant left with a parting grin that Kate did not reciprocate.

Her host placed two cups of coffee on the table and said, 'Let me guess. You've just had the cubicle door conversation. Don't worry: if you really need to go, one of the girls will accompany you. It's safe to drink the coffee.' He took a sip of his own and continued. 'Now you know why I prefer to meet people off the premises. Much simpler, and the added benefit is that you won't appear on any surveillance tapes. Either our own or our competitors'.'

'It also means you can keep jobs off the books.'

He shook his head. 'If you do a little digging you'll see that Andrew A. Sinker is listed as chief executive of CIS. Anthony Skinner is just a small variation of that. I don't want the Yanks poaching my best people: they often have a camera on our front door.'

Tom would have found all that out before taking a job with Skinner because he hated loose ends. 'I don't think you can count me as one of your best. Not after Hong Kong.'

'On the contrary. You have great promise, Kate, but I'm wondering if I wasn't pushing you in the wrong direction.' He took a piece of paper and passed it over. 'Would you do a job like that? It's based on a real operation, by the way, but some details have been changed.'

The paper was headed:
URGENT FIELD MISSION. PESHAWAR. PAKISTAN.

She skimmed over it.

Client: *Landowner sympathetic to Pakistani government.*

Problem: *Son kidnapped by forces linked to Pakistani security services.*

NATO Response: *None.*

Mission: *Seek and rescue.*

It sounded like the scenario for a spy film, but she knew the reality of life in Pakistan. It was all too plausible. The fee mentioned was astronomical, if the son was returned unharmed. No alternative fee was mentioned.

'I can tell from your face that it's not your cup of tea,' he said.

'No.'

'But what if you had been ordered to support that mission by gathering intelligence on radio traffic in the area?'

'Remotely?'

'Yes.'

'An order is an order. We spy on Pakistan all the time.'

'And what if you had been asked to support our mission when it became clear that the lad was being held in Afghanistan?'

She hesitated. Her team had regularly supplied intelligence to the Afghan National Army. They also supplied it to the American PMCs at work in Kabul, but they did not lay intercept devices on other people's behalf. 'That's getting a bit too hypothetical. I couldn't say.'

Skinner retrieved the paper from the table. 'Vinnie said *Yes*, and so did Gareth Wade. They both provided support to CIS operations in Iraq and Afghanistan. Your visit to Pembroke was very enterprising, Kate, but Mrs Wade was in touch with me before you got back to your hotel.'

She sat back, stunned. The implications of this were enormous. Serving soldiers and airmen were using public resources to assist private companies – and being paid for it. This must have been approved at a high level. Was it corruption or deniability?

Her mind baulked at the implications of what she'd heard. Going to Wales had taught her just how much she was on her own. Skinner's show of strength today with his high security fortress made it clear what she was up against. She settled for something more important to her life and her peace of mind.

'What about Squadron Leader Clarke?' she asked.

'I know Conrad.' The smile on Skinner's mouth showed that he wasn't lying. 'However, as he's still very much alive, I can't comment on his involvement in any operation. You could always ask him yourself.'

'Not without a truth serum. That man tells tales for fun. I wonder if he even lies to himself about what he's up to.'

'A good point. I can tell you that no matter how hard you look, you won't find any payment from this company or any of our associates to Squadron Leader Clarke, and that's not because we've hidden them. They simply weren't any – until this summer.'

'Kabul? The helicopter pilot training?'

'Yes.'

'I can ask him when he gets back. That'll be an interesting conversation.'

'He's already back. Contract's over – and again, I can be honest: I have no idea of where he is or what he's doing right now.'

Kate finished her coffee and turned the mug round with her finger until the handle was pointing at Skinner. 'What about me?'

'Have you any objections to Dublin?'

'No. I've always wanted to go there. What's up?'

'There are a lot of companies headquartered there for tax reasons, especially digital ones. Our client had a data leak a few months ago, and their product turned up on the internet for sale to the highest bidder. They asked us to investigate, and our hacker found that the crooks had accessed the system using authentic credentials.'

'In other words, it was an inside job.'

'Yes.' He pushed the file across to her. 'You've got a flair for investigation. They want to know which of their employees let the bad guys into the vault.'

'On my own?'

'Yes. This is an official CIS operation, so you can draw on all our resources here if you need them. Take as long as you like when you get there, but you need to start on Monday.'

She looked at the file. Pinned to the top were her fee and expense limits. 'Book me into somewhere nice, and I want four days at home every fortnight.'

'Deal.'

They shook hands, and Skinner escorted her to reception. One of the women on duty upgraded her lanyard from red to blue and put all her details on the system.

Chapter 7

London – Fylde – Earlsbury – In Prison
Wednesday–Saturday
24-27 November

It had been a long time since Conrad Clarke had owned a vehicle of any kind (he wasn't counting the poor little Micra he had driven into Croxton's Mercedes). He spent some time in the guest room of his Notting Hill flat (there being a tenant in residence) and decided that the only option for life on the Fylde peninsula was a Land Rover Defender – the old fashioned kind that farmers use. He tracked down a relatively new model at a dealer close to his new home and started packing.

On the way to Euston, he called at a self-storage unit and arranged for a wooden crate to be shipped overnight. Then he caught the train to Cairndale.

Between the city of Lancaster and the county town of Kendal lies the river Cowan. Its waters form the border between Lancashire and Westmorland, and straddling its banks is the town of Cairndale. Clarke had never been there before, and it was well into the evening when he arrived. The Midland Hotel was opposite the station; he was soon asleep in one of its beds.

He made one stop in the morning before completing the purchase of his new vehicle, then drove down the A6 towards Preston, turning right before the city and making his way to Fylde racecourse. The racecourse entrance was wide, and had pillars more suited to a country estate than a racing venue. As his Land Rover climbed up the slope, he realised why, and stopped to take in his new base of operations.

Fylde racecourse is built on a plateau above the Ribble estuary, and on the north side runs the railway. Horses were unloaded there, and on race days the excursions from Blackpool and all over the North West would disgorge the punters who filled the stands. None of this was visible from the south, where Clarke was staring up at the Fylde Gentlemen's Sporting Club.

Where the plateau sloped down to the river, a monumental five-storey classical building had been constructed. At its rear was the grandstand for the finishing line: from the front it was supposed to be a haven for local gentry and professional men with rooms and restaurants open all year. Clarke had read that Jennings and his son-in-law had rescued it from ruin and turned it into an upmarket spa – now known as the Sporting Hotel.

Impressed and bemused in equal measure by Victorian excess, he continued towards the front and was directed to a modern extension on the left, concealed from the road by trees. He was expected.

Two hours later, he was ensconced in Will Offlea's cottage, surrounded by ledgers and notebooks. He was going to have to put his plan into action a bit quicker than he had intended.

'I'm very sorry,' said the waitress at Earlsbury Park, 'but the Christmas menu doesn't start until next week.'

'That's a relief,' said Tom. 'I'm sure we'll be fine with the normal menu.'

The waitress looked amazed that guests wouldn't want roast turkey in November, but she said nothing and poured their water. Tom was finding it hard enough to cope with the enormous artificial tree that had appeared in reception since his last visit.

'I see from your expense forms that you've been here a lot recently,' said Leonie. 'What would you recommend?'

'Anything but the steak. Unless you have the rib-eye, and you need a big appetite for that.'

Kris had barely spoken since she had joined them at the table, and she made eye contact with Tom rather than the deputy director. She kept sneaking glances at the senior officer, mostly when the older woman was brushing the hair out of her eyes. Here was an example for her – a woman who had risen through the ranks and achieved a senior position without being openly aggressive or loud. Except, of course, that Leonie was a white graduate from London, not a black football player from Earlsbury.

When the manager brought the wine list, Leonie looked brightly at the other two and suggested a bottle of Australian Chardonnay. 'Not for me, thanks,' said Hayes, in something close to a mutter.

'Me neither,' said Tom. 'I'm on enough drugs as it is.' He wasn't, but didn't want Hayes to feel even more left out than she already was.

'Okay,' said Leonie. 'Run it by me again. Who's on your list of suspects, and why?'

'It comes down to John Lake,' said Tom. 'He's the security liaison officer who came to BCSS – it's the big police station where we were based. Lake told us about Benedict Adaire and his Republican connections. The man in my car – the bomber – quoted verbatim from what Lake said. Therefore, the person we want must have been at both meetings. The phone call to Griffin was made from Victoria Hotel, and they must have heard Lake speak as well.'

Leonie nodded, ate some of her food and then put the knife and fork aside. That was how she stayed so thin. Hayes looked nervously from her plate to the other woman's. Tom carried on eating as heartily as he could manage.

'There are other possibilities,' said Leonie. 'For example, one of the people at Lake's briefing could have talked to someone else.'

'That's true. Given the serious nature of the information, I think there would have to be a very close working relationship between them, though.'

'Or there could be two people. One who did for Griffin and one who tried to do for you.'

'I hope not: it's too implausible. One bad apple, yes – but two completely rotten ones? Don't forget, the bomber is intimately connected with the counterfeiting. I agree with you about the possibility that someone talked, but I still think we should start with people who were in both meetings.'

She nodded her agreement and turned to Hayes. 'You've worked here longer than Tom. What's your view of these people?'

'I'm sorry, ma'am, I'm only a DC. We don't have much contact with the senior officers.'

Ouch. She shouldn't have said that, and Leonie's expression made it very clear. She shifted her chair very slightly to focus even more on Tom.

They finished their meal with speculation about how much the government was going to cut from police budgets, and Leonie stood up to go to the bar. 'Join me for an orange juice, Tom?'

'Yes. No ... I mean can you order a pot of tea?'

Leonie's expression said that it would be a very short drink in the bar if Tom was going to be drinking tea, but she nodded and left.

When she had gone, Hayes gave a small smile. 'Thanks for trying, sir. I appreciate that.'

'Trying what?'

'Trying not to make me feel even more left out of the evening than I already was.'

'I'll butter her up tomorrow. Don't worry. Look, Kris, will your mother be at home when I pick you up tomorrow?'

'Yeah. What on earth do you want to know for?'

'Can I come ten minutes early? I need someone to put a new dressing on, so that I can wear a shirt. It wouldn't do you any good to see me half naked.'

She didn't know what to make of that, but she nodded, and then – on an impulse – she reached up to peck him on the cheek. 'Welcome back, Tom, and congratulations on your promotion. I hope Leonie hasn't eaten you by the morning.'

In the bar, his tea was steeping nicely, and Leonie was checking her phone. When he sat down, she put the phone away and leaned on the back of the booth next to him. 'You shouldn't be here,' she said.

'In Earlsbury Park? It's quite good value, and there aren't many alternatives.'

'No. I meant that you shouldn't be in CIPPS. I was on holiday when Sam Cohen recruited you, and there should have been a proper interview. It was naughty of the boss to let him get away with it.'

The clip was back in her hair; the blue eyes were steady. Tom looked back at her. 'There aren't many good coppers wanting to join CIPPS, and you know that. Cohen is a mate, not a close friend, and I don't owe any loyalty to him, only to the job. I won't embarrass you, let you down or stab you in the back. That's a promise.'

She sipped her wine. 'Fine words, Tom, but … as they say round here, fine words butter no parsnips.'

'No, they don't. That's what they say where I come from. God only knows what they say round here.'

He had broken the spell. Leonie laughed and told him to pour his tea before it went cold. While he was doing so, she asked if Lancashire & Westmorland had made any progress on locating the bomber.

'No. There was no magic piece of evidence, and the trail is colder than the weather outside. Finding the rotten apple in MCPS is our best hope.'

When she relaxed, he quite liked her. She asked about his parents' house and he asked about where she lived. 'A small flat near the river. Not too far from you, if you cross the wobbly bridge. A relic of my divorce.'

'Sorry.'

'It was a long time ago now, or seems that way. Trouble is, it's so handy and it's worth a fortune … but if I sell it, I'll never get another place so central. Almost none of our old neighbours live there now. It's a mixture of foreign nationals and bankers using them as their city crash-pads. Anyway, time for bed. I hope your next case is in London. It must be lonely out on the road.'

'You can be lonely anywhere. I'll see you in the morning.'

The rain had turned to snow overnight, and Tom took great care in joining the slow moving traffic.

'Go on. You're dying to ask me,' he said to Kris.

'I won't give you the satisfaction,' she responded.

'You mean you don't want to know what your mother said to me in the kitchen when she was changing my dressings?'

'Of course I want to know. I'm just not going to give you the satisfaction of asking.'

The traffic came to a standstill, and he turned to her. 'Actually, she was very nice. She said almost nothing that wasn't related to my injuries or how I was going to get back to London in this weather.'

Hayes grinned in triumph. Tom hadn't been entirely truthful because Mrs Hayes had also said *So that's what a chief inspector looks like with no shirt on*. But there was no way he was going to repeat that.

Eventually they escaped the jam, and Tom parked as close to the entrance as possible. Every time he'd got into his new car, he'd checked the back seat carefully for unwanted guests. They slipped and shivered their way into the building, and Tom had to go through the process of renewing his accreditation. Hayes slipped away into the offices, and Tom found Leonie waiting for him outside the Boardroom (as the posh meeting room was known).

'Let's not hang about, Tom. I want to get back to London before the country grinds to a halt.'

'Is he here?'

'Yes. He said to just go in when we're ready.'

'Right. This is it.'

Leonie knocked and led the way into the Boardroom. Tom guessed that its nickname came from the real wooden tables, padded chairs with proper arms and a deep carpet with the force motto worked through it. Every time you looked down, you were reminded of your duty: *Protecting All*. The Chief was working his way through a pile of reports.

He had a reputation as a Copper's Copper. Yes, he was a graduate, but he had worked his way up the uniformed ranks, and all of his promotions had been to operational roles. He stood up and shook hands with both of them. He turned his attention to Tom first.

'If you're back on duty, you must be doing all right.'

'Yes, sir.'

'Good. Have a seat.' He turned to Leonie. 'I hope the first thing you're going to do, Ms Spence, is to tell me why I've had to come out here in the snow, and why you telephoned me at home to make the appointment.'

The look on the Chief's face said that he was giving her the benefit of the doubt, but only just.

Leonie put her hands flat on the table, one on the other, crossed her legs and turned her shoulders to face the Chief. Her voice was professional and steady.

'There's no easy way to put this, sir, but we have reason to suspect that one of your Command Officers or – just possibly – your PA was involved in the Griffin case.'

'Go on.'

Tom would have fidgeted at this point but Leonie kept her cool, not moving even a finger.

'When DCI Morton uncovered DS Griffin's mobile number, we established, with independent witnesses, that Griffin received a phone call directing him to the Great Western Goods Yard. We have tracked down the origin of that call to an extension in the Victoria Hotel, Edgbaston. It was just outside the Lickey Hills suite.'

In the silence that followed, Tom noticed that Leonie had retrospectively added herself to his investigation by saying that *we tracked down the origin of the call* instead of *Tom and Kris tracked down the call*. It's what Samuel Cohen called *chutzpah*, and his grandfather called *brass neck*. Having said that, she was the one talking to the Chief, not him. She was welcome to it.

Finally, the Chief spoke. 'We were all there. The whole senior team gathered to discuss budget strategy – or how to save twenty million pounds.' He rubbed his hand round his jaw and looked at Tom. 'Proof?'

Tom slid over the relevant printouts. Now the focus was off her, Leonie uncrossed her legs, and he could see a red mark on her thigh through the nylon where one leg had gripped the other.

'Why exclude me from your investigation?' was the Chief's next question. It was addressed to both of them, and Leonie gave Tom the slightest nod for him to answer.

'We have a statement from the late Patrick Lynch that shows Griffin had a boss – a handler, if you will. That statement also shows that the relationship pre-dates your appointment to this force. Although some of the team have been promoted since you arrived, they were all with MCPS at the relevant time.'

'The whole team? I can't trust any of them?'

'No, sir. You can't trust *one* of them. There's another factor.' Tom repeated the story of the bombing, and that the bomber had quoted John Lake's words to him.

The Chief didn't need to ask: he knew straight away who was present on both occasions. 'Niall, Malik, David and Evelyn,' he said, almost to himself. He turned back to Leonie. 'Let's be clear. You want to investigate my deputy, one of my assistants, my media relations guy and my own PA?'

Leonie answered what Tom thought was a rhetorical question, 'Yes, sir. And the reason it should be CIPPS is that we can move faster and more discreetly than any other professional standards team.'

The Chief shook his head. 'I've got no choice, have I? Not that I should be looking for one. I can't see an alternative explanation.' He sighed heavily. 'How low a profile can you keep this investigation?'

'I think it better if Tom takes the lead at first,' said Leonie. 'He and Kristal are known around here, and they can work the background case to see if anything comes to light. No formal interviews will take place without my authorisation.'

'What do you want from me?'

'A letter of authorisation to your HR manager so that Tom can review their personnel files.' The Chief nodded. 'And a description of the events of that evening, if you've got time.'

'As it happens, I don't.' He took a diary from his pocket and flicked through it. 'Can you meet me at the Victoria Hotel tonight, around six o'clock?'

'Of course,' said Tom.

'If you don't require me directly for the meeting, sir, I'll head back to London,' said Leonie.

The Chief stared at her for a second and then nodded. 'It's a big place,' he said to Tom. 'I'll be staying the night and they know that my details are not to be given out lightly. Text me when you get there. Here's my personal number.' He had to dig deep into his wallet to find a card with the relevant details, and passed it to Tom. 'You can type that letter of authorisation to HR yourself, as I can't use my PA to do it. Bring it tonight and I'll sign it.'

There was a knock at the door. 'Wait.' shouted the Chief. Tom and Leonie both flinched at the volume he used. He pointed to a smaller door across the room. 'You can leave through the kitchen. ACC Khan is waiting outside. He's going to tell me which police stations he thinks we can close without provoking a riot, and I don't want him seeing you two with me.'

They were halfway to the door when the Chief said, 'One more thing, Morton.'

'Sir?'

'If you're going to pick another fight with my staff, watch out for Evelyn. She has a nasty right hook.'

'What was that about?' said Leonie when the door was safely closed behind them. They were standing rather close to each other in a small kitchen. Tom could smell her perfume. It was the same one Caroline had used when she wasn't in court – *Expression of Woman*.

'I got into a fight with the DCI from Earlsbury division. He gave me a black eye.'

Leonie shook her head. 'For such a quiet man, you don't half attract trouble.'

'It must be my magnetic personality.'

'In your dreams, Tom. Anything else before I go?'

'Just the one. Unless you want to wind her up deliberately, don't call Hayes "Kristal". It's "Kris".'

Leonie bristled and took a breath. Then she let it out again and said, 'Don't go native on me, Tom.'

'That's what my grandfather said when I went to London. I've tried to follow his advice.'

Leonie shook her head and walked away.

Tom headed towards the canteen. Hayes would look for him there. With any luck she would already have bought the tea.

The priest had given special dispensation for the heating to be turned on. At other times, the volunteers were expected to wear gloves and coats in cold weather, but today, with so much work to do, the Church of Our Lady was warm and bright as its worshippers prepared for Advent.

Since Patrick's body had been found, Fran had discovered that work doesn't stop you thinking about things, it just stops you going mad. Not that she would have minded going mad: it might have been a relief from the pain. She was here in the church because she didn't want Elizabeth going mad and because she had to stay sane for her daughter's sake.

She wanted her to go back to school as soon as possible, but that wasn't going to happen this week. The poor child was beyond devastated. She was just numb. Fran let Elizabeth lead, and no matter how slowly her daughter worked, she fell into step. Helen, always more impatient, would drift off and come back.

The outside door opened, and a gust of icy air rippled along the wall and shivered its way down Fran's arms. She didn't hear it close, and turned around to see who was letting all the heat out.

In the doorway stood Theresa King and her surviving son, James. He put his hand into the small of her back and ushered his mother into the church. Fran dropped the florist's wire and nearly swore. Theresa put her hand to her mouth and looked as if she wanted to run away, but James held her gently and urged his mother towards the altar.

Fran, Helen and Elizabeth stood in silence and watched them genuflect, cross themselves and kneel down. The radiators clunked as they expanded, more sleet blew against the windows, and a lorry laboured up the hill outside. No one moved.

James broke the silence with an Amen and stood up. He walked over to the flickering rack of votive candles and cleared some of the burned-out lights away. From his pocket he took three red candles and placed them carefully on the ledge. Fran put down her fake garland and walked over, crossing herself on the way.

'The Father doesn't like people bringing their own candles,' she said. 'He says it's a fire hazard. We're supposed to use the safety ones.'

'If only we could buy *safety* guns and *safety* knives to go with them, the world would be a better place,' said James.

Fran stiffened, and James bowed his head. 'I'm sorry, Mrs Lynch. Your loss is terrible. Please forgive me.'

She pointed to his candles. 'Is one for Patrick?'

He took out a box of matches (another thing frowned on by the young English priest, but used all the time by his Irish and Polish colleagues in the team ministry). James struck a match and put it to the candles, naming each one in turn. 'One for my father, one for my brother, and one for my sister's father.' He blew out the match. 'It would not be right in my soul to pray for Dermot because I didn't know him and my prayers would not come from the right place.'

They both stared at the candles for a second. Fran glanced over at Theresa, who was still in prayer. 'Why red candles, James?'

'For the blood that was shed. Their own and others.'

She stepped forward and whispered hotly in his ear. 'My Patrick died of a heart attack, and he never, *never* shed anyone else's blood.'

She grabbed the third candle, blew it out and thrust it towards James. He took it from her and rolled it in his hands. 'He let my father's killer walk away, and he let that man come back to kill my brother,' said James.

Fran was aware of movement in the church. Theresa had climbed up from her knees and was moving unsteadily towards them. Helen was coming out of the shadows. Her oldest daughter was like that: she wouldn't let her mother get outnumbered.

If only it were so easy. James wasn't the enemy, nor was Theresa. Admitting it to herself was the hardest thing, but he was right: Patrick had been like one of those little fish on the wildlife programmes, swimming around the sharks. And now one of the sharks had turned and swallowed him.

James seemed to be reading her mind and said, 'That heart attack. I heard he didn't have his pills with him.'

'Leave it alone, James,' said Theresa. 'Let them have the place to themselves.'

Theresa was so bundled up against the cold outside that only her face was visible. She put her hand on James's arm, partly to restrain him and partly for support.

Fran took the candle out of James's hand and relit it from the other two. She jerked her head towards the back of the church and said to Helen, 'James and I are going to nip out for a smoke. Can you tell Theresa about the funeral arrangements? Or lack of them.'

Out of the corner of her eye, she saw Lizzie standing in the shadows, still clutching a plastic garland. She couldn't think what to say to her and pretended not to have noticed. She grabbed her coat on the way, and James followed her out of the little door at the east end of the nave.

The church of Our Lady almost fills its plot completely, but there is a small garden at the back, stepped down the hill. Ashes are scattered there, and brides have their picture taken there in the summer.

Fran was going to stop smoking after the funeral. That was her promise to herself. She didn't need it like some of them did, and she'd done without for years. Unfortunately there was no sign of the Coroner releasing Patrick for burial. She lit two cigarettes and passed one to James. He'd never be able to roll one of his own in this weather.

'What do you think happened?' she said.

'I'm only looking from the outside. What did the police tell you?'

'That there were no signs of a struggle, and that the only crime committed was the theft of his car.' She blew smoke away from them and shivered.

'It was Hope who told me about the pills and the phone being left in the house. I don't think he would ever have done that,' said James.

Fran was vehement. 'I know he would never have left them behind. Never.'

James nodded. 'Do you think it was a coincidence that Benedict Adaire was blown to Hell just before this? I don't.'

'Neither do I. It can't be a coincidence.'

'Have you spoken to the one that arrested him? Inspector Morton, wasn't it?'

'Haven't you heard? He was in the car that got bombed. He only just escaped with his life. Apparently, the other one – the woman – she's on the sick as well. There's no coppers interested in Patrick now he's dead.'

James dropped his cigarette in a puddle and then carefully placed the filter in a waste bin. Fran felt obliged to do the same.

'They'll be back,' said James. 'At least Morton, will be. When he is, if you need any help to convince him, let me know. In the meantime, try and think of anything that Patrick was holding back. Anything that might help them.'

Fran pulled her coat more tightly round the neck to keep the wind out and went back into the church. James was right, if ever there was a policeman who didn't give up, it was that Morton bloke. The last time she had met him, he had threatened to take Lizzie away. Did James realise that the man was close to being a shark himself?

'Are you sure you should be going back to London tonight?' said Hayes.

'Are you worried about the weather or about me deserting my post?'

'Both, I suppose. They say the snow's going to get worse in the South and, you know, we've only just started this investigation.'

He was giving her a lift home before heading against the traffic into Edgbaston for his meeting with the Chief. They had spent the day negotiating with the BCSS Facilities Manager to get a small room and a secure cabinet. Even telling the man that it had been authorised by the chief constable had no effect. The only way round it was for Tom to ask for the bill to be sent to CIPPS.

'I need to see Leonie tomorrow.'

'Missing her already?'

'Leave off, Hayes. She's not my type.'

'I don't know what your type is. Sir.'

'I'll tell you this much – she's too dangerous for me. What about your type? You've never said anything about your private life other than football and the church.'

'When I know what my type is, I'll let you know.'

He was nearly at her house and changed the mood. 'There is a good reason for seeing her. Not only do I have to explain the facilities bill that's going to land on her desk, I also want her to be the one asking for the personnel records.'

'She won't like that, will she?'

'Tough. You would have gone ballistic if you'd seen the way she blithely told the Chief that "we" found out about the Victoria Hotel. If she wants the credit for an arrest in the future, she'll have to work for it.'

He pulled up outside her house – her mother's house. 'Are you clear on what to do tomorrow?'

'Yes. Go through DS Griffin's entire arrest record and see if there are any patterns. I can't wait.'

'At least you'll be warm. Is there a match this weekend?'

'No chance. See you on Monday.'

She sprinted up the drive, and Tom set the satnav for Edgbaston. What should have been half an hour took him nearly ninety minutes, and instead of quietly texting the Chief, the man was waiting for him in the bar, already wearing evening dress.

'Don't apologise,' said the Chief. 'There's already been ten people cry off tonight's dinner. It's the Mayor's charity auction, and all those who do get here will blame me for not having more traffic patrols out. Or blame the Mayor for not gritting the roads. Drink?'

'No thanks. I'm driving to London afterwards, and this won't take long.'

Tom took out the letter to HR, and the Chief studied it carefully before signing. 'It's easy to tell you were a lawyer,' was his only comment.

Tom took out his notebook. 'Thanks for this, sir. I just want you tell me as much about that evening as you can.'

'Follow me.'

They set off down some corridors which led from the old building into a new extension. The largest space was called the Warwickshire Room and doubled as ballroom and wedding venue: it was where the Mayor's dinner was being held. Beyond that was a locked door into darkness. A wooden plaque named it the Lickey Hills Suite. From a pocket in his dinner jacket, the Chief produced a key and unlocked the door.

'They lent me this so I could show you the exact disposition.' He paused with his hand on the door. 'We'd rented the rooms for the whole day. Evelyn arrived first and opened them up.' He pushed the door open and switched on the lights. There was a lobby with four doors leading off it on one side and another at the end. He pointed to the two doors in the middle. 'Those lead to the main room. At either side are what Niall and Malik would call breakout rooms, where small groups can brainstorm before feeding back. We were in and out of those rooms all day, as well as going to the rest of the hotel.'

Tom looked around the lobby. On a window ledge was a telephone. He went over and checked the extension number. It wasn't the same as the one on the printout. 'This isn't it.'

'I'm not surprised. Far too public. Have a look through the end.'

Beyond the lobby were male and female toilets. Hanging from the wall, almost unnoticed in the corner, was a second telephone. This was the one. He also noticed a fire door that gave on to the car park.

'We were exhausted by the end,' said the Chief. 'Just after the general election, I had a telephone call from the junior minister saying that there would be major budget cuts next year. He said that wise police forces would get planning sooner rather than later. I asked him for a ballpark figure, and he said that twenty-five per cent over three years would be a good starting point.' The Chief shook his head. 'I'm surprised that your lot has been allowed to carry on as you are. I would have thought that some bean counter in the Home Office would have merged CIPPS with the IPCC.'

'I think I've got the answer to that,' said Tom. 'Leonie told me that Ogden has done a deal. We're going to charge you for our work from April.'

'What? Was that her idea or his?'

'If it works, it'll be her idea. If it doesn't, I suspect Ogden will carry the can.'

'Sounds about right.'

'If you don't mind, sir, can you remember anything about that evening – who was where, what was going on?'

'I've done nothing but rack my brains since this morning. As I said, we were exhausted. We had lunch in the restaurant, just to get a change of scene. I ordered sandwiches at about five o'clock and by half past seven I couldn't think straight. Neither could anyone else. I set a deadline – we were finishing at eight o'clock, regardless of anything else. If I remember rightly, it was a few minutes before that when I threw in the towel.'

'What happened next?'

'My finance director had set the agenda and brought all the papers. She started to pack everything away. Evelyn gave her a hand. Everyone else turned on their mobile phones. I'd given strict orders for them all to be turned off except for mine, and in seconds it sounded like an amusement arcade in here – there was pinging and ringing and all sorts of farmyard noises.'

'The call was made about ten minutes after that. Can you remember anyone disappearing?'

'In ten minutes, we'd all disappeared. No one wanted to be hanging around. I asked Evelyn if she wanted me to lock up, but she said that we had to leave it open for the kitchen staff to clear up, but she did give me the key. I handed it in to reception and signed the bill. She helped the finance director carry stuff to the car park.'

It was dark outside, and the windows showed only reflections of the lobby. Tom put his face to the glass and peered out. The car park was extensive and not well-lit at this end.

'Did you see anyone outside when you left – talking, perhaps.'

'I left via the front door. One of the perks of the job is having my own driver. He collected me at ten past eight. You reckon that whoever it was came back in through the fire door?'

'It's the only logical explanation. They must have received a call or message at eight o'clock from a third party and been afraid of contacting Griffin directly. Otherwise they could have just sat in their car. The person I'm looking for must have spotted the phone by the toilets and left the fire door ajar. It was still a huge risk, but they were playing for high stakes.'

'Are you done?'

'Thank you sir. That's a great start.'

The Chief said nothing as he turned out the lights and locked the door. Ahead of them, other guests were gathering for the Mayor's banquet. He handed the key to Tom and wished him a safe journey before going to study the seating plan.

Outside, it had stopped snowing, but the clearing sky threatened a serious frost. Tom paused briefly to look at the hotel from the rear. It would have been easy to get to that fire door without anyone noticing a thing.

Life in prison was a lot like school in many ways, Mina had discovered. There were gangs, and then there was everyone else. Mina didn't like gangs, but if you weren't in one you ran the risk of being picked on, and that was very bad news. Almost as bad as being picked on was befriending one of the existing victims: your turn would come next.

At least she had a single cell, and for twelve hours a day she was locked up with nothing but her books for company: she hadn't been inside long enough to qualify for a radio. Things had improved when she was transferred away from London because she was identified as having the potential to work in the call centre.

'A call centre? You mean selling insurance or something?'

The welfare officer gave a smile. 'Not quite. That would be wrong in so many ways. No, it gives advice. You train on welfare, benefits and things like that and women from other prisons ring you up for help. It's a good job.'

And so she had begun to work through the self-study manuals, and she was now in training. Some of the women envied her, especially the ones on outside duty in this weather, but most of them started to pick her brains during association time, and she realised that she would probably be safe for now.

She was just taking her seat for a couple of hours' work when a prison officer came up with a slip of paper. 'Lawyer's visit this afternoon,' he said.

'I think that must be a mistake.'

He showed her the slip. Dominic McEwan was coming out to see her. Unless his secretary had got out the wrong file, of course, in which case he would turn up somewhere else, and they would refuse him access. 'Thank you.'

She put on her headphones and took her first call. A woman wanted to know if her mother could get child benefit to look after her boyfriend's son by another woman, who had just been arrested. She got a lot of calls like that.

Only a little after the time on the slip, she was taken from the association area, searched her and shown into the consultation room where Dominic McEwan was waiting.

'Mrs Finch ... how are you?'

She gave a perfunctory response and got straight down to business. 'Why are you here? I have no appeal and I'm not going to sell my house until next year.'

He shuffled the papers and pushed them to one side. 'I've had a proposition.'

This was alarming. McEwan had a number of clients who sailed very close to the wind. She hoped desperately that one of them hadn't been in touch with him about her past. She nodded for him to continue.

'I know this sounds strange, but I've had a tip-off that we might be able to use in your favour.'

'Who from?'

'Anonymous, I'm afraid, but they know what they're talking about. This person has some information which the police might be interested in. They want to give the information to you so that *you* can give it to the police in return for a reduction in sentence and a transfer to a fully open prison. From there, you can get some dental treatment in the community.'

Mina held on to the table to stop herself swaying. This sounded very dangerous, and far too good to be true.

'Are you okay?'

'Yes. Please go on. What's this all about?'

He passed her a sealed white envelope with no name or address on it. Mina looked around the room. It was strictly against the law for the prison to eavesdrop, but she knew from talking to her fellow inmates that it happened quite often. It was usually audio only, though, so she carefully unsealed the letter and scanned the contents.

It was printed, blunt, factual, and contained only one clue as to the author: a tiny drawing of a little fish at the bottom with an X after it. Conrad? What on earth was he up to? How did he get hold of this information?

'I take it you don't want to know what's in here,' she said, pointing to the paper.

'Not until you're ready to give me a legal instruction.'

She looked at her solicitor. 'I might have some information that might interest the City of London Police about the location of the printing works. Who should I contact?'

'Destroy that,' he said, pointing to the message. 'Don't even think of leaving this room with it in your possession.'

She ripped off the top half of the paper with the printing on and put it in her mouth. She couldn't chew very hard, but she masticated gently for a few seconds and placed the wad in the envelope before folding it up and leaving it on the table. McEwan didn't notice that she slipped the bottom fragment into her sleeve.

'I'll give the CPS a call and start the ball rolling,' he said. 'Out of interest, why did you mention the City Police?'

'Oh, it has to be them. Trust me.'

Dominic McEwan was a man who trusted no one. She thought that if he took off his shirt, the words *Plausible*

Deniability would be tattooed over the place where his heart should be. In fact, taking off his shirt was quite an attractive idea. He was the first halfway decent man she had seen in months.

It had taken Clarke two days to figure out that Will Offlea was not keeping his secrets at home. All the ledgers appeared to relate to the legitimate business of Fylde On-Track Ltd. This was the company that rented out pitches to bookmakers on race days and which was part-owned by Offlea himself. From the ledgers, Clarke had no way of knowing which was legitimate business and which was the laundered money. In the end, it was the first thing he had seen in Offlea's cottage that gave the answer.

Offlea had put all the ledgers on the dining room table before doing a bunk to France and he had placed a Post-it note carefully on the top. The note had two cryptic numbers written on it which Clarke took for a bank account. He put it carefully to one side and looked in the books. The first night and the next morning, he looked at the yellow note again, and the longer number looked more familiar: finally, it had come to him last night. It was a ten digit grid reference. The real books were somewhere else. In the rather sparse bookcase, there was a selection of maps which pointed him to a small farm. He called the owner.

'I think someone I know might have left something with you for safekeeping,' he said.

'What makes you think that?' said a man with a strong local accent.

'He left me a note with your location written on it.'

'Bring the note with you tomorrow. And a month's rent.'

The phone was put down at the other end, and Clarke wondered whether it was a two-part test – find the note and figure out the amount. He went back to the books and found it buried in the outgoings as Ribblegate Farm – milk supplies. Quite what a bookmaker wanted with £1,500 worth of milk each month was a very good question.

The Fylde peninsula had escaped the worst of the weather so far. The snow was coming in from the North Sea, dumping on the Pennines and leaving the west coast cold but dry. Even so, Clarke was glad he'd bought the Defender as he bumped up the track towards a small farm about four miles north of the racecourse. He had been to many farms in his time, but when he arrived in the yard, he reckoned that this was one of the most precarious.

The farmhouse was designed for Victorian communal living. Three of the downstairs windows illuminated the kitchen, and the fourth would be the utility room. There was no extension to offer the residents a modern living room or any other breathing space, but at least the windows themselves were double-glazed. That could make a big difference in the winter.

The same could not be said of the agricultural buildings. They were mostly corrugated iron, except for the two stone sheds further up the track. Repairs had been made to the rusting ironwork with cladding, plastic and in one place, sheets of asbestos. He jumped out of the Land Rover and felt his leg twinge in the cold.

He knocked on the back door and went in. A woman of about thirty was seated at the kitchen table with a small baby which she was encouraging on to her breast. At least it was warm in here. He closed the door behind him, but stood on the mat, reluctant to tread mud any further into the house.

'Sorry to bother you. I rang last night, and a gentleman invited me over to have a look at something.'

She looked mystified. Her hair had been dyed blond and the brown roots were growing out noticeably. They were probably about as old as the baby. 'Are you the locum vet?' she asked.

'No. I'm in business. Could it have been your father I spoke to?'

'Father-in-law. He's in the cowshed.'

'Thanks.' He was about to make small talk and ask the baby's name, but its mother had already returned to feeding it. In a remarkable display of dexterity, she started to send a text message with her left hand whilst holding the baby with her right. Turning to go, he saw artwork from an older child pinned haphazardly to the cupboards.

He closed the door carefully behind him and crossed the yard. One of the doors was wide open, and he went in to find a small herd of Holstein cross dairy cows standing on wet straw and huddling together where possible against the wind. One of the beasts had been separated into a pen, and two men were looking at her udder.

He walked over and called a greeting before getting too close: he didn't want to startle the men or the cow. The two humans stood up and turned around. It looked as if the father's genes had been passed straight to his son without any interference from a woman: other than time, nothing separated their appearances.

Clarke held out his hand. 'How do you do? My name's Conrad Clarke.'

The farmer shook hands reluctantly and adjusted his cap before speaking. 'Have you brought the note and the money?'

'Yes. Sorry, I didn't catch your name.'

'That's 'cos I didn't give it to you. I don't really want to know yours either.'

'Come on, man. This is the twenty-first century, and you've got a dairy herd in here. I could find out everything about you in five minutes if I rang the Ministry. And if they hadn't misfiled your paperwork.'

That produced a small chuckle. The quickest way to a farmer's confidence is to slag off the Ministry. 'Reckon you would, at that. It's Kirkham. I'm Joseph, and this is my son, Joe.'

'That's not my real name,' said the younger version. 'I were christened David but everyone calls me Joe 'cos they reckon I look like me dad.'

Of course they did. Clarke was beginning to like it round here. 'What's wrong with the cow?'

'Are you a vet? You look like you might be one,' said Joseph. 'Otherwise, why bother asking?'

'I'm just trying to prove that I'm different to my predecessor. I bet he never asked about the herd.'

'No, he bloody well didn't. He once drove straight into a ewe and blamed me for it. She was carrying triplets, and he killed her straight out.'

'Tell him the rest,' said Joe.

'Some other time,' said his father. 'If you really want to know, the cow's in perfect health. We're even thinking of showing her next year. Now, let's get you sorted.'

Joseph led him up the yard towards the stone sheds. The building faced away from the farm, and when they got to the front, Clarke saw that one of the structures had a metal roller door fitted over it. The other one was open to the elements. Inside the open shed, miscellaneous farm equipment and parts surrounded an empty space in the middle.

Joseph pointed to the shutter. 'They're both yours, of course, but that's the one you'll want the note for. See? There's a combination lock on it.'

Clarke took out the Post-it note and bent down as best he could to enter the code.

'Are you alright? Your leg looks a bit stiff.'

'War wound. It aches terribly in the cold.'

'Really? You're a soldier?'

'No. Royal Air Force. I used to fly helicopters until one crashed and I got my leg half blown off.'

Joseph grunted in sympathy. Clarke's fingers found the combination and he slipped off the padlock.

'Have you got the cash?'

'Of course. Hang on a second, and I'll just get this open.'

'Not so fast, Mr Clarke. I don't know what's in there and I don't want to know. Just give me the money and you can do what you like.'

Clarke slipped the padlock into his jacket and dug out the envelope with the cash. Joseph Kirkham stood in the freezing cold wind and counted every note before stuffing it in his pocket and touching his cap. 'Thanks. The only reason we're still in dairy farming is getting the rent on this place. If you want a brew when you're done, pop inside.' He turned on his heel and disappeared around the corner.

Clarke heaved at the shutter, and it glided upwards on a counterweight. That must have cost a pretty penny. Inside he saw a light switch and flicked it on.

It was like looking at a room within a room. Builders had created a plasterboard frame inside the raw stone walls, and there was an assortment of Swedish flat-pack kitchen units with worktops. Resting on these were several currency-counting machines and half a dozen mobile phones next to their chargers. Underneath one of them was a note. He pulled on some latex gloves and picked it up.

Don't use the phones here. Too easy to trace. I've texted all contacts to expect someone different. Books in cupboard. 1st Shipment in crate.

There were more Post-it notes with code names next to the phones. The ledgers in the cupboard were headed with the same names: should be easy to work it all out. Clarke plugged all the phones into their chargers to give them a boost and opened the wooden crate in the corner. Still wrapped in blue plastic – and stamped with the US Treasury logo – was half a million dollars.

He also saw that there was a fan heater in the shed and switched it on. With the roller door pulled down to keep out the wind, it was almost cosy. He perched on a stool and started to read the books. There was no elaborate code system here, just cash in from Afghanistan and the amount of laundered currency received from Offlea's contacts. According to recent transactions, the five thousand $100 bills in the crate should fetch him £240,000. That was simple enough. All he had to do was arrange an exchange, and then find some way of putting the money into Fylde On-Track. That might be more of a challenge.

He poked around a bit more and found some other useful items. First was a sack barrow for moving the crates. He had wondered how Offlea managed that bit. The man was strong, yes, but he wasn't built like a piano shifter. Second was an adjustable ramp for getting them into vehicles. Also logical. The most interesting item was a stand-alone printer that churned out vehicle number plates along with a box of vinyl films and blank plates. He would enjoy playing with that.

He left everything where it was except for one of the phones and locked up behind himself. Knocking on the farmhouse door, he found the family sitting around the kitchen table. The baby was asleep in a basket, and a young girl wearing a tutu had joined them. She was clearly the cupboard door artist, judging from the felt tip pens scattered amongst the mugs and teapot. If old Joseph had a wife, she was nowhere to be seen today. They didn't stand up to greet him: he just took off his wellingtons and joined them at the table. Joe poured a cup of tea.

'You've met Kelly,' said old Joseph, nodding at his son's wife. 'This is her daughter, Natasha.'

Ouch. That made things very clear. Kelly had brought a child on to the farm who would be forever labelled as not belonging to Joe. The child carried on drawing, oblivious.

Young Joe passed the tea and said, 'There's something we should ask you. Do you mind if we keep the hurdles and stuff in the other shed? If you have a bigger van, they might get in the way.'

'I haven't got a van at the moment,' said Clarke.

'You're not into fish as well, are you?' said Kelly, wrinkling her nose in distaste.

Even Natasha joined in. '*Smelly* fish.'

'You've lost me there,' said Clarke.

'Your predecessor used to keep a van up there,' said Joseph. 'He'd leave his Range Rover and take the van for a couple of days at a time. Or more. When he came back, he liked to dump rotting fish out in the pasture. I wouldn't have minded, but there was a lot of scallops mixed in. They'd have fetched a packet if they was fresh.'

'I'll try not to do that.' Clarke finished his tea. 'One more thing before I go. I'm staying in a hotel at the moment. Do you know anyone who might have somewhere to rent for six months?'

The two men turned to look at Kelly. She shrugged and said, 'I don't mind. So long as we can spend the money on doing it up after.'

Old Joseph spoke for them. 'We have a little bungalow on the edge of the farm. It's where my parents retired to, and we've had it as a holiday let, but it's not been doing too well. We're not exactly on the tourist trail here. The youngsters were going to move in after Christmas but Kelly's right, it could do with a bit of sprucing up first.'

'Does it have heating? Furniture? A telephone?'

'It even has Wi-Fi,' said Joe. 'We put it in because the lettings agency said we could get more for it, but it's just been a waste standing empty. How much should we charge, Dad?'

Joseph stroked his chin. 'For a residential let, I think six hundred a month is the going rate.'

'Here's the deal,' said Clarke. 'I'll give you six months' rent in advance, in cash. You keep all the services in your name, and I'll pay for them at the end.'

'When do you want to move in?' said Joe.

'How about Monday? Give you a couple of days to get the place warmed up and aired.'

Joseph held out his hand, and they shook on the deal.

Ian Hooper was in a thoroughly bad mood. It made things worse that he knew he was in a bad mood, but could do nothing about it. The hospital had finally discharged him this morning, and he discovered that his first-floor flat was effectively a prison. Getting up the stairs had almost incapacitated him, and he wasn't going anywhere until Monday morning, when he was back at the hospital for a physiotherapy assessment.

Ceri had been marvellous. Again. She had walked one step behind him as he tackled the stairs and done her best to make him comfortable on the settee. And then she went out.

He had encouraged her to go out. He had told her that he wanted to watch the rugby, and that she should go and see her friend and that he would be alright. Well, he wasn't alright at all.

England had been trounced by the South Africans at Twickenham. The two beers he had allowed himself had gone straight to his bladder, and the effort of getting to the bathroom had felt like his stitches were bursting. And what were they going to do tonight? Unless he could think of a better idea, in a couple of hours he was going to be watching *Strictly Come Dancing*.

He reached into the sports bag next to him where Ceri had put all his things from the hospital. He had told her that he would finish a couple of puzzles or read Matt Dawson's autobiography, but it was neither of these things that he got out of the bag. It was last week's *Sunday Examiner*.

The man who had shot him was pictured on the front page. Benedict Adaire. Every time he looked at the picture, he was taken back to the Goods Yard and he could hear Adaire's voice saying *we know where you live, we know where your wee girlie teaches*. And on the second page was a small picture of DI Morton, taken a long time ago.

Morton had told him to decide whether he wanted to be a copper or not. He had talked about having to decide where his loyalties lay. Morton was happy being a copper and serving whatever Higher Power he thought was in charge of the universe. Ian wasn't. His loyalties began and ended with Ceri. He heard light footsteps outside and put the newspaper back in his bag.

Chapter 8

London – Earlsbury – Fylde

Monday – Tuesday – Wednesday

29 November-1 December

It was five o'clock in the morning. Tom and Kate were huddled around her laptop, drinking coffee. Both were checking the travel news: Tom for the M40, Kate for Heathrow. Although snow had been falling through the night, both motorway and airport seemed clear.

'Let's go,' he said. 'It'll take me ten minutes to get the car. There shouldn't be any traffic wardens at this time of day.'

He rinsed his mug and put it on her drainer, then crossed the small landing to his flat next door. His cases were packed, and he lugged them downstairs, leaving them at the front door. In ten minutes' time Kate would wheel all their luggage out of Horsefair Court, and he would meet her on Carter Lane.

He slipped twice on the way to the long-stay car park, and felt the dressing move on his arm. That would need attention later. Neither of them spoke as he drove through the whirls of snow towards the West End. The local radio told them that the motorway in Kent was closed due to a multiple accident, but fortune smiled on them, and Tom was soon on the road to Heathrow.

'For the last time,' he said. 'You're sure that this job is on the level? No one's going to slip poteen into your luggage? Or leprechauns?'

'Not this time. I've already been in touch with my new client, and the chief executive is fuming about the leak. I'll be alright, Tom, but I'm worried about you. This Jigsaw crew are a violent lot when you get close to them.'

He dropped her at Departures and stepped out of the car to remove some of the layers of clothing he'd put on for the walk from the flat. A quick kiss and she was gone to Dublin.

Two hours later, he pulled into a colder but less snowy Midland Counties Police headquarters and signed for two document boxes, which HR had left for him to collect. He completed the journey to Earlsbury, and at half past eight he was finishing his breakfast in the BCSS canteen where Hayes joined him.

'Blimey, sir, what time did you get up this morning? I thought you might be snowed in down there.'

'That's one reason I left so early. Another reason was that I wanted to pick up the files from HQ.'

'I am impressed. Want another tea? Of course you do.'

'Let's take them to the office.'

Steaming mugs on their desks, Tom pointed to the sealed cartons from HR. 'This is the point of no return, Kris.'

'That's a bit dramatic for a Monday morning.'

'But it's true. If you're with me when we open those boxes, you can't pull out. No matter how nasty it gets, you'll have to stay the distance.'

She hardened her expression and crossed her arms. 'I've already apologised for bailing out last time. It won't happen again. Besides, how nasty can it get? I can't see the Chief's PA planting a bomb on us.'

Tom winced and felt his shoulder.

'Sorry,' she said. 'I didn't mean that. Look, sir, one of the reasons I couldn't hack it last time was that I didn't want to believe that it had happened. I didn't want to find out that even more police officers were bent. I just wanted to work in a place where you could trust people. When I heard what happened to you, when I saw you in hospital, I realised that you can never trust *everyone*. We can make MCPS a better place doing this.'

'I hope so, Kris, I really do. Okay, let's begin. First of all, did your efforts with Griffin's arrest records throw up any interesting connections?'

She grinned and opened the secure cupboard. There was nothing inside it except three slim folders which she passed to Tom. He took the scissors out of the desktidy and offered the handles to her. 'You open the personnel records: I'll read these.'

Old Joseph climbed into the Land Rover and gave Clarke directions to Ribblegate Cottage. 'It's not a cottage at all,' he said. 'It's a bungalow.'

Clarke turned round in the yard and drove past some trees and down a dip. Typically for farmers, they had built the new house on an unproductive piece of land at the bottom of a sloping area of scrub grass and backed by trees. By using this land for building, there had been no loss of grazing. The plain brick walls almost oozed damp, but the Kirkhams had been true to their word. Inside the bungalow, the oil-fired heating was on, and Joseph took pride in showing him the power shower. It was fitted over the bath, but it would be a welcome boost during the cold weather.

'Where are you staying at the minute?' he asked.

'At the Fylde Sporting Hotel. Do you know it?'

'Just a bit. You'll have met my great grandfather then.'

'I don't see how, but tell me anyway.'

'If you've been up the grand entrance to the old building, you'll have seen some portraits in the gallery. My great grandfather was the younger son of the Earl of Morecambe Bay. He was a great sportsman and reckoned that if he built a racecourse near Blackpool he'd get all the trippers to come along.'

'Sounds like a good idea. In principle.'

'Aye, in principle. But he was too much of a gentleman to stick to racing. He thought that if he built a gentlemen's club, he could get all the quality folk to go there too – have shooting parties and such like. Fool.'

'It didn't go well, I take it.'

'Trouble is, there weren't enough rich folk around here to make it pay. He had to sell the racecourse after only a couple of years. Some theatrical entrepreneur from London bought it. Great grandfather took to drink and left his wife and child to fend for themselves. A hundred-and-odd years later, here we are, still fending for ourselves.'

'You're trying hard to make a future for Joe and Kelly. And the grandchildren.'

'Grandchild. I've only the one so far. Plenty of time yet.'

Double ouch. Clarke opened the fridge and found a pint of milk already in place. He offered to use it to make them tea.

'Another time. I'll let you settle in. I need to see how David's getting on with the sheep. We keep a few over winter.'

'David? Oh yes – young Joe. Of course.

The farmer left, and Clarke set about moving in. He had brought everything except the storage box, which had been couriered from London. He wasn't sure what to do with that yet. Half way through hanging up his shirts, he got a phone call from the Race Office.

'Mr Clarke? I've got Mr Bentley for you.'

It was his boss. Or nominally his boss. The Chief Exec of all things Fylde Racecourse (and son-in-law to Sir Stephen Jennings) had only spoken to him once, when he handed over the key to Offlea's cottage. Bentley had told him to make an appointment for next week. Maybe he couldn't wait. The assistant connected the call, and Bentley spoke. His tone was far more conciliatory today.

'How's things, Conrad?'

'I'm just moving into my new digs.'

'Glad to hear it. Listen, I've had Sir Stephen on the phone.'

'Oh yes.'

'It's Olivia's birthday this weekend and it's something of a Jennings tradition to celebrate it up here. We all gather for supper on Friday night at the Sporting Hotel, then next morning we head up to Hartsford Hall for a shoot. After that it's Livi's birthday dinner at their Michelin-starred restaurant.'

'Very nice, I'm sure.'

'Yes. The thing is that Stephen would like to see you for a chat and thought you might like to join us for Friday supper and the shoot – if you're into that sort of thing.'

Clarke tugged his forelock. He wished Bentley were there in person to see him do it. On the other hand, Clarke had never been a proud man. Although excluded from the fancy dinner, he wasn't going to turn down a day's shooting. He was less sure about the family supper, though.

'Sounds good. Where's Hartsford Hall?'

'It's the Earl of Morecambe Bay's country house. Or it used to be. He lives in part of it now, and the rest is a hotel. It's near Cairndale – we get a minibus there and back. It's good sport.'

Clarke had done some research on Bentley. He had gone to a school not dissimilar to his own, and then a minor university, and then a career in the City. He was doing well at it, apparently, until he married Olivia Jennings. A couple of years later, he became squire of the racecourse. To hear the man talk, you'd think his family went back to the Domesday Book.

'Thanks for the offer,' said Clarke. 'If you can lend me a gun, I'd be grateful. I haven't got round to applying for a UK shotgun licence since I left the RAF.'

'No problem.'

'About the supper, though … I really don't want to intrude on a family occasion.'

'Stephen was most insistent. Not only does he want to talk business, he said that you'll need to bite the bullet at some point.'

'That's what worried me. You mean that Amelia's going to be there, don't you?'

'"Fraid so, old chap.'

Sod it. Jennings was right – the sooner he met her and got it over with, the sooner he could disappear back into the woodwork. He tugged his forelock again and asked Bentley what time he should be there on Friday.

'Any time from eight o'clock. Supper's served at nine. See you there.'

Despite signing up to a horrendously expensive deal for their minuscule office and secure cupboard, Tom and Kris did not yet have a connection to the BCSS switchboard. If they did, they might have received warning of their first visitor on Tuesday morning.

'This is where you're skulking,' said a woman, who burst open the door and nearly knocked Hayes flying.

Tom spent half a second noting that she was dressed for the cold before recognising the Chief's Personal Assistant, Evelyn Andrews, from the photograph in her file. He stood up and moved between the woman and the two desks where confidential paperwork was strewn everywhere.

'Good morning, Mrs Andrews. I'm DCI Morton. How can I help?'

She stepped right into his personal space so that she could close the door. Tom couldn't help flinching. Then she stepped back and said, 'You can tell me what's going on. I had a phone call from a friend last night. She told me that my personal file had been copied out to Professional Standards. What's going on?'

'Have you talked to the Chief about this?'

'First thing this morning. I asked him what on earth was happening, and he wouldn't tell me. At least he had the decency to look embarrassed about it. I had to ring around every station in the West Midlands until I found you lurking here. Now tell me, what's going on?'

Tom pointed to his colleague. 'This is DC Hayes. Kris, could you pack the files away?' and to his visitor, 'Please, take a seat.'

'I'm not going to ask again. Tell me what's going on.'

Tom took a deep breath and signalled for Hayes to start work clearing away. Then he sat down as calmly as he could and gestured to the plastic chair he'd stolen from the canteen.

Mrs Andrews kept her fur-trimmed boots firmly planted on the floor. Tom started to count to ten in his head and had got to four before the heating came to his rescue. She had clearly marched straight to their den from the exposed car park and was now in a subtropical office. She either had to walk out or unfasten her coat. She chose the latter and sat down at the same time. Coat and bag were dumped on the floor.

'Can we get you a drink? I'm afraid I'll have to send Hayes to the canteen.'

'No.'

'Fair enough. I'm not going to ask you the name of your friend in HR.' He paused.

'So?'

'She should be dismissed for what she's done. I could have your phone records within half an hour, and she would be out of the door by three o'clock.'

Evelyn Andrews sat back and took a sharp breath. Hayes paused in her tidying up and gripped the file she was holding.

'Now, shall we start again?' said Tom.

'Just leave that bit out of your report,' said Evelyn.

Tom nodded and pointed to the tray of empty mugs. Hayes put the last folder away and slipped out to the canteen.

'Now that you're here,' said Tom, 'you've got a choice. You can answer some questions off the record or you can refuse. I'm afraid the rules are different for serving officers – if I talk to them, it has to be official. For you, it's not. If you're willing to co-operate informally, all that will ever need to appear on the record is a short witness statement. Unless I need to arrest you, of course.'

'Never, in thirty years' work, have I had a complaint against me. If you tell me what it's about, I'll answer your questions, but I won't collaborate with you. I'm not a Quisling.'

Tom had heard them all now – *Gauleiter, Quisling, Fifth Columnist, Collaborator*. There was an entire field of the English language which hadn't moved on from the Second World War.

'People have complained about *me*,' said Tom. 'My first sergeant told me that if you don't get at least a few complaints, you're not doing your job. Villains will complain about anything if they think they can get some mud to stick. I've never had a complaint from an innocent person, that's for sure. I don't know if it makes a difference, Mrs Andrews, but this is not about a complaint.'

Hayes returned with the drinks. She also brought biscuits in an attempt to keep the peace. Tom looked at their visitor properly. She was eight years younger than his mother, but looked older. He guessed that this is what happened when you worked full time for a living. On the other hand, she fizzed with an energy that Valerie only showed when she was plotting a coup on the York Minster Arts Committee. Mrs Andrews was wearing a tailored suit, and sticking out of the top of her bag was a court shoe.

'If it's not about a complaint, then what's going on?' said Mrs Andrews, after finishing a biscuit.

'This is an investigation into serious professional misconduct, almost certainly amounting to criminal activity. Serious criminal activity.'

Mrs Andrews had noticed the files when she came in and pointed to the boxes. 'I'm not the only person under investigation, am I?'

'No, you're not. I can tell you that the chief constable has authorised this enquiry, and I can tell you that we're only looking for one person. One rotten apple.'

'It's not me.'

'If it isn't you, then it would make my life – and the Chief's – a lot easier if you say nothing about this interview to anyone until the investigation is over.'

'I can keep my mouth shut if I have to. I do it all the time. For example, I haven't referred to the fact that Kristal Hayes is in here. I read all the case papers, you know. I think you were very badly done by, DC Hayes. I hope it doesn't make you bitter towards MCPS or the Chief.'

'I want to be a police officer, not a martyr,' said Hayes.

'And there's something not in those files,' added Tom. 'Her name is Kris.'

Andrews nodded.

Tom took one of the three Griffin folders from his drawer. 'Can you tell me how your husband's business is doing?'

She immediately bristled. 'He's got nothing to do with the police. His firm is squeaky-clean in all respects. They have to be.'

'But they *were* involved with the police. When the factory burned down. It was arson.'

'Yes, it was. And a bunch of kids were arrested for it. That fire was *not* an inside job.'

'At the time of the fire, your husband was chief engineer on the production line. When the new factory was opened, he became operations manager.'

'So? He's good at his job.'

'I see that one of the investigation team was Detective Sergeant Griffin. He even wrote the final report for the DCI to sign.'

Mrs Andrews said nothing. Either he was hitting a nerve or she was very good under pressure.

'The thing is,' said Tom, 'insurance companies don't always pay out, even when it's arson. They wait for the police report. An inconclusive report means that the victim of the fire has to sue for the money. In a civil court, the burden of proof is on the balance of probability, as I'm sure you're aware. In this case, the police report exonerated Earlsbury Plastics completely. They were up and running again in no time.'

'Are you accusing me – or my husband – of bribing a police officer?'

'It's a coincidence, that's all. It might be something, it might be nothing. It depends on what happened the at the budget strategy meeting in the Victoria Hotel.'

She rolled the idea round in her head. 'It was all strategic. Nothing specific. I can't see how there would be scope to be unprofessional, let alone criminal, in that meeting. Incompetent, yes. Unhelpful, certainly. But not unprofessional.'

Her answer put her in the clear. He had seen enough of Evelyn Andrews to realise that she was a sharp woman who could probably hold her own in a game of poker, but she wasn't an actress. If she had made that phone call to Griffin, it would have been the first thing she thought of when he mentioned the Victoria Hotel. She would have given herself away immediately by jumping to what happened after the meeting instead of during it.

Tom relaxed a fraction in his chair and caught his arm on the desk. 'Ow! Sorry. Would you mind if DC Hayes made a note of your answers from now on? They'll form the basis of your statement. You can read her notes at the end.'

'If it makes things quicker.'

Hayes' notebook was already open. She picked up a pen.

Tom tried not to rub the dressing over his skin graft. 'Could you think carefully, Mrs Andrews? I want you to take your time and describe everything you can remember, from the moment the Chief wrapped things up to the moment you left the premises.'

She opened her mouth to ask a question, but changed her mind and thought for a moment. 'It was about five to eight when we stopped. The exact time is in the minutes; I always look at my watch and jot it down.'

That was good to know. It might be crucial.

'I put my notepad away and stood up. Everyone did. We'd been sitting down so long that we were all numb. The finance director started packing things away, and when I'd cleared the plates off the table, I gave her a hand.'

'What was everyone else doing at that point?'

'Turning on their blessed mobile phones. I know they're all senior officers, but the world doesn't stop turning if they're in a meeting. If there had been an emergency, we'd have heard about it in seconds. The control room has the Chief's number, and he never turns his phone off. Even on holiday.'

'Can you remember any of their reactions?'

'No. I was too busy clearing up. I do remember that no one actually made a call from the meeting room. They just checked their messages and their voicemails.'

'And then what happened?'

'We – that's the finance director and me – left the room together. We could only just manage the crates and flip charts between us, but we didn't want to make two trips. Oh yes … the Chief asked if I wanted him to lock up. I told him that wasn't necessary, but could he drop the key off because my hands were full?'

That tallied exactly with the Chief's account. The next two questions would either solve the case or put them back to square one. 'Think carefully. Did you see anyone go to the toilets? Was there anyone left in the room when you walked out?'

She gave the questions serious consideration. 'We'd had a toilet break at half past seven. I think everyone went straight out at the end, but I couldn't swear to that. Someone *might* have still been in the loo. Because we weren't locking up, I didn't need to check them.'

It was disappointing, but only to be expected.

'What did you see outside?'

'Very little. It was quite busy in the car park, with people leaving and arriving for dinner. Oh yes. It had just started to rain, so we dashed to the car to stop the priceless budget strategy getting wet. I dumped stuff in the FD's boot and got in my car. It was next but one to hers. I never looked back.'

Ah well, it was too much to expect that she could solve the case for them. It would have been nice, though.

'Thank you, Mrs Andrews. I know you'll be discreet, but if you could keep the questions about the Victoria Hotel to yourself, it would much appreciated.'

She was on her feet and picking up her coat before Tom had finished speaking. 'I know when to keep my mouth shut, Chief Inspector.'

With no farewell, she was gone.

Hayes breathed a sigh of relief. 'She should be on the force,' she said. 'I'd confess to anything if she was asking the questions.'

'Me too. What do you reckon, Kris?'

'It's not her.'

'Why do you say that?'

'She was too vague about the meeting. If she was hiding something, she'd have added lots of details. Not only that, I can't imagine DS Griffin doing anything that a woman told him to do.'

It was a good point. He and Hayes had come to the same answer from different directions.

'Who's next?' asked Hayes.

'I think we'll look at Niall Brewer.'

'Why's that? I'm only asking so that I can learn.'

'He's not a copper. We can do things to him that we can't do to ACC Khan or DCC Nechells.'

'Fair enough. Pick off the weak ones first.'

'You could say that. I'd say that Mrs Andrews was anything but weak.'

The day after Evelyn Andrews came to see them, Tom decided that it was going to be a good day. The breakfast at Earlsbury Park seemed to have improved on this visit, and the Black Country had escaped the worst of the weather overnight. There had been significant snow falls in Yorkshire; his grandfather had been getting noticeably more frail recently, and Tom hoped that he wouldn't go out trying to rescue any sheep. Today, he was sure, they would find something to help them get leverage on Niall Brewer.

A couple of the waiting staff seemed to be looking at him as he finished his meal: perhaps word had spread among them that he had arrested the Golf Club steward. When he dropped off his key at reception, the girl behind the desk (who knew exactly who he was and didn't care) said, 'Good luck.'

Tom said nothing, but he was half looking over his shoulder as he went out of the front door and didn't notice the camera crew until the microphone was thrust under his nose and a woman journalist started to introduce herself as coming from the local BBC News.

'It's Detective Inspector Morton, isn't it?'

'Chief Inspector, but yes it is.'

'Chief Inspector Morton, I understand that you are from the Professional Standards Team in London. Is that right?'

'Yes. You'll appreciate that all police work is sensitive, and ours can be very sensitive. If you contact the press office in Lambeth, they may be of more help than me.'

During his comment, Tom had started to edge towards his car. The journalist and camera crew moved with him and obstructed his path. They didn't block it, exactly, but he couldn't walk past them without crossing the line of the camera in what would be a very unflattering shot. The journalist pressed on. 'I understand you were recently involved in the Blackpool bombing. Are you now conducting an investigation that's linked to the bombing?'

It wasn't good journalism that had brought them here: someone had been talking. Someone had leaked this story – someone who thought that publicity would be to their advantage. Tom would have to stonewall. He couldn't just walk away from this.

'I am conducting an investigation at Midland Counties Police Service. My Inspectorate conducts enquiries all the time. These have to be confidential, but they are always fully reported at the end. On our website and via the press office. I'm afraid that I can't comment further until then.'

'We understand that the subject of your enquiry may be linked to the bombing,' she persisted. 'In which case, isn't there a conflict of interest? You are not only a witness to the bombing, but aren't you also a victim?'

Shit. Not only had his mission been leaked to the BBC, the argument had been made for them. He would have to say something and hope that it didn't come back to bite him on the bum. 'I can categorically state that none of the subjects of my enquiry are suspected of the Blackpool bombing or of having arranged it. More than that, I cannot say.' He wanted to take a step towards the woman, but that would look very bad on TV, so he put down his briefcase and thrust his hands in his pockets. 'Most enquiries are ruled *no case to answer*. Those officers are innocent and deserve privacy. If I were the subject of an enquiry, I wouldn't want a trial by television. Would you?'

The journalist pulled a face and backed off. She formally thanked him for the camera, and he picked up his case. He left them outside the hotel filming reaction shots and got into his car. *Oh dear*, he thought. *This is going to be very tricky.*

Chapter 9

Earlsbury – Fylde – In Prison
Wednesday to Monday
1-6 December

Tom had a situation that needed careful handling. He had never been on TV before and didn't think he would relish watching his performance tonight. He told Hayes about it on the way to BCSS, and she was as appalled as him.

'Is it really a set-up?' she asked.

'Got to be. One of those three people has leaked this story and put a spin on it that could undermine everything we do. I've committed myself on TV that we're not looking for a link to Blackpool. If we get so much as a sniff of that now, I'll have to hand over the case straight away.'

'What are you going to do?'

They were getting out of the car. Tom said, 'Ring Lambeth and tell them to expect a call from the BBC, if they haven't already had one. Then ring Leonie. You know what to do.'

'Yeah, get two teas.'

The facilities manager had finally installed their extension yesterday, and he used it call the CIPPS press office and then Leonie's mobile. They had told him she was out on a case.

'Hello, Tom. You'll have to keep this quick. My phone's running out of charge.'

'Is there a landline number I can call you on?'

'Hah! That would be good. There's no landline, no power, no water. I'm in a nice little B&B in Sussex that's been completely cut off from the outside world. According to the radio, it could take days to dig us out. I've never seen snow like it in England. I hope you've got some good news for me. Things are pretty pear-shaped here.'

He took a deep breath and made her day worse. She swore a lot.

'We've got no option,' she said after venting her anger. 'You're going to have to proceed as lead officer until I can get out of here. Just don't talk to the media again. Under any circumstances. Can you hack it? Would you like Sam Cohen to take some of the flak?'

That was the trouble with Leonie. She was so political that you couldn't work her out. Was she offering Samuel's help out of concern for Tom, or because she might be able to dump responsibility for the case on to someone else, now that it was looking shaky?

'Thanks for the offer. It's much appreciated, but I'd rather press on than have to brief someone else.'

'Fine. Good luck. I wasn't joking about the phone, either. It may be a smartphone, but the battery's not very clever. I'll turn it off to save power. Text me if there are any serious developments, and I'll pick it up later. That's if the mast hasn't gone down.'

Outside their office, Tom had noticed that Hayes was standing guard. When he put the receiver down, she opened the door to admit Nicole Rodgers, the deputy media relations manager.

Rodgers was her usual impeccable self. A black shift dress was pinched in at the waist and her boots had polished steel spike heels. He offered her a seat, and she took out an iPad.

'I've just had a call from the chief constable,' she said. The expression on her face implied that this wasn't a daily occurrence. 'He knew I was in BCSS and asked me to handle any follow-up from your ambush by the BBC this morning.' She crossed her legs and smiled. 'In fact, he asked me to continue with this as long as necessary, for some reason.'

Either the Chief had stated it directly or she had worked it out for herself, but Rodgers definitely knew that her boss was implicated in the investigation.

'I'm sorry you got dragged into this,' said Tom.

'Don't worry: it's my job to help you get on with *your* job. That's what media relations are for. Among other things. Perhaps if you could give me a general outline of what you're looking into.'

'No.'

She smiled again, folding her hands in her lap, leaning forwards slightly and pointing her knee at him. 'Most of the work I do is off the record or anonymous,' she said. 'When you watch the news, and it says *A police spokesperson commented...* then that's me. We make sure that the media are supportive, not intrusive. A little co-operation can go a long way.'

'I agree completely. That's why I've already briefed the Lambeth press office. I suggest you point all the journalists in their direction. It'll save you a lot of bother'

She must be used to this, he thought, *judging by her reaction*. Nicole Rodgers kept smiling and stood up. 'That's good to know,' she said. 'Of course, if you get anywhere with your investigation then it will become our business as well. You'll need to keep me in the loop when that happens.'

It was Hayes who spoke next. Rodgers had positioned her chair so that her back was to the detective constable, who had been making mutinous faces over her shoulder. Hayes opened the office door and said, 'Don't worry, Nicole. We'll get there.'

When Rodgers had left, Tom said, 'From the look on your face, you've got previous with her.'

'Too right, I have. She was all over the enquiry when I complained. She offered herself up on a plate to every bloke she spoke to.'

'Not your type, then.'

'You're harassing me. I could complain.'

'I know. It's a growing sign of your maturity that you won't.'

Hayes sat down and tapped her hands on her knees. 'Now that we've got some breathing space, what are we gonna do?'

'There's only one thing we can do,' sighed Tom.

The Coroner's office had been in touch. They were finally releasing Patrick's body for burial. The Coroner himself called to explain that he was signing the death certificate as Natural Causes. He had said: *there may or may not have been aggravating factors on the day – an argument, perhaps, in the van, and it was entirely possible that his pills might have made a difference, but when it came down to it, Mrs Lynch, there was no evidence of anything but a heart attack.* She could nominate a funeral home to call at the hospital any time from tomorrow and could someone call into the Coroner's office for the paperwork?

'Yes. Of course. Thank you.'

Helen called in after work, and Fran broke the news. They started to talk about the funeral and what might happen, when Lizzie appeared at the living room door.

'Are you alright, love?' said Fran.

'Were you talking about Dad?'

'Yes, love. I'll explain it to you later. When Helen's gone.'

Lizzie accepted this in silence, as she seemed to have accepted everything since Pat disappeared. 'Can I watch the local news?' she said. 'We might want to go out at the weekend, and I want to see the weather forecast.'

'I'll go,' said Helen. 'Do you want me to come with you tomorrow?'

'No. I'll manage.'

Fran showed Helen to the door as Lizzie switched on the television. Fran went back and sat next to her daughter, putting her arm around her and pulling her in. Lizzie put her head on her mother's shoulder, and Fran nearly missed the next item on the news.

That detective, Morton, was on the screen. Fran grabbed the remote and pressed Live Pause. She backed up, raised the volume, and watched it again. So, he was back and he was still digging.

Leaving her daughter to watch the weather forecast, Fran went to call James King. He could break the news about the Coroner's decision to Hope and Theresa. She also wanted to pick his brains about how to approach Inspector – sorry, Chief Inspector Morton.

It was the morning after his appearance on the TV news, and Tom was not happy about anything. Leonie was still snowed into Sussex, and he was fighting the traffic as he headed into Birmingham without a proper breakfast.

For the second time this week, he pulled into the MCPS Headquarters and signed in to reception. Under *Destination* in the visitor's book, he wrote *Command Conference Room*. On the third floor of the building, Evelyn Andrews was waiting at the lift. Her expression was five degrees colder than the outside temperature.

'I now realise that you should have given me a warning before our little chat on Tuesday. They're all waiting for you.'

Tom leaned in to whisper in her ear. 'If we hadn't had our "little chat", Mrs Andrews, you'd be sitting next to Niall Brewer this morning. Be thankful for small mercies.'

She pursed her lips, but said nothing, and led him round the corner to the conference room. He paused in front of the door and took a deep breath. Then he walked in.

DCC David Nechells, ACC Malik Khan, and Niall Brewer were seated together behind one table. The Chief was at one side, and a chair had been put out for Tom in front of the table. He wasn't having that.

He said *Good morning* from the threshold and then took off his coat. He took a second table and placed it at an angle to the three suspects and put a chair behind it. Tom was now facing the Chief and the others were lined up at the side. They all got the message.

The Chief began the proceedings by standing up and going to the door. 'It's not my place to witness this,' he said. 'You all know the drill, and you all know that you cannot be compelled to attend an interview with DCI Morton or anyone else from CIPPS. Over to you, Chief Inspector.'

That was really not useful, thought Tom, but Nechells corrected his assumption after the Chief had gone.

'What he means,' said the DCC, 'is that we are all expected to see you if we don't want our careers to be blighted.'

Khan managed a wry smile, 'He put it to us like this: *How many times have you told a suspect that if they're innocent, they've got nothing to hide.* Now let's get this over with so that we can all get on with our work.'

Nechells and Khan were radiating hostility to him so strongly that it would probably register on a Geiger counter. He could live with that. They had both been the subject of complaints during their careers and both been completely exonerated. Brewer was sweating heavily.

Tom gave notice that an investigation had been convened and that they would be required to give witness statements. He concluded by repeating the Chief's assertion that they could not be compelled to attend an interview. He passed letters to them all and said that he would be in touch. As Nechells and Khan received their letters, they stuffed them into their pockets and left the room with great purpose to demonstrate that they had better things to do with their time.

Brewer sat in his place and opened his letter, quickly scanning the contents. Tom locked his briefcase and put on his coat. He adopted a conversational tone. 'It's Thursday today, Mr Brewer. There are a few more files to look through, and I'm going back to London for the weekend. Just in case the weather gets worse, and I'm late on Monday, shall we say Tuesday morning? Ten o'clock at BCSS.'

Brewer folded his letter back into the envelope.

'I'll confirm that in writing,' said Tom.

The radio in Clarke's Land Rover only worked up to about sixty miles an hour; after that, the vehicle's various knocks, rattles and roars made listening impossible. For that reason, he was bowling along in the slow lane of the motorway at fifty miles an hour listening to Classic FM. His passenger was not amused.

'Can't you put something else on? Or go faster?' said Joe Kirkham. 'This music's rubbish.'

'It helps me relax and bear the strain of the journey.'

'We're only going to Manchester. We'll be there in half an hour.'

'Don't you dare retune the radio on the way back,' said Clarke. 'It took me ages to find this station.'

'I'll turn it off, then.'

Clarke completed Joe's misery by singing along to the *Ride of the Valkyries*. At the end of the music, Joe said nothing about helicopters, despite Clarke having given him a potted history of his RAF career: *Apocalypse Now* wasn't as popular as it used to be.

They finished their journey at an anonymous industrial unit to the west of the city. Clarke left his Defender and passenger around the corner and walked carefully over the icy pavements. He had a large lump of titanium in his left leg. The laws of physics said that the blood vessels surrounding it should keep the metal exactly at body temperature. It didn't feel like that: it felt like his rod and pins were connected directly to a deep freeze.

He found the address and went into the tiny office of a small company supplying parts for commercial vehicles. He checked – there were no cameras. 'Are you the man for the van?' said the only person around – a woman with two coats on. He didn't blame her.

'That's me.'

'This way.'

She led him into the warehouse, where a small van was sitting. True to his word, the owner had removed his logos from the side and had taken the vehicle to be re-sprayed white.

'Take a look,' said the woman, handing him the keys. 'But if you want a test drive, you'll have to wait until my husband gets back.'

'Is it okay to start her up?'

'Sure.'

He knew enough about vehicles to check the obvious things, but no more. After a quick inspection, he started the engine and peered carefully under the bonnet. There were no unnerving noises. He switched it off and took out a wad of cash.

Back in her unheated office, the woman counted the money and handed over the spare keys and one part of the vehicle logbook.

'I need a name and address to send to Swansea,' she said. 'Otherwise, they'll think we still own it.'

'Of course. I've written it down for you to copy out.' Clarke offered her a piece of paper with a fake name and fake address on it. He took it back when she was finished. His fingerprints wouldn't be on the document now.

'Do you mind if I just check a couple of things over before I leave?'

'Sure. Let yourself out. I can close the warehouse door from in here.'

In perfect solitude, Clarke put false plates on the van, raised the shutter and drove back round the corner. Joe had turned the Land Rover's engine on to keep warm.

The young farmer got out to look at Clarke's new transport and made admiring noises.

'Where did you say you were going?' he asked Kirkham.

'The Trafford Centre. It's not far from here.'

'Oh yes. Shame we couldn't have brought Kelly.'

'She'll get her chance before Christmas. It was our first wedding anniversary not so long ago. I couldn't afford to get her much. This is a bonus.'

'I take your point.' Clarke handed over a hundred pounds. Joe was going to drive the Defender back to Ribblegate Farm – after some shopping.

'Thanks,' said Joe, pocketing the cash. 'Are you sure you haven't got any other jobs lined up? You pay much better than farming does.'

Clarke hesitated. He had an appointment on Tuesday with the men who would turn his US dollars into used Bank of England notes. It could be dangerous, and an extra pair of hands might be very useful.

'Not at the moment, thanks, but you'll be the first to know if I do.'

Was it the secrecy of his operation that stopped him press-ganging Joe? Or was it the sight of Kelly, Natasha and the baby at the breakfast table this morning? He didn't know. Having driven the whole way from the Fylde without smoking, he reached into his pocket and took out his cigarettes, and a thought struck him.

'Actually, Joe, there is one thing you can do for me.'

'What's that?'

'When you get your present for Kelly, can you get something for me?

'Yeah. Sure. What is it?'

'I'll write it down.'

He jotted some instructions on an envelope and passed it over with some more cash. Joe looked at the note and was clearly overcome with curiosity. Conrad lit a cigarette and winked at him.

Before being sent down, Mina had no idea that women prisoners were allowed to wear their own clothes. It was only a casual chat to the dock warder at the hearing which made her realise that she should make plans. Her face alone, both the colour of her skin and the damage to her jaw, would make her stand out, and she had no wish to do that. Her bin liner of personal possessions ran almost exclusively to black – leggings, tops, underwear and trainers.

When it came to today's interview, she had to borrow. To prevent bullying, there were regulations about 'borrowing' clothes, but most of the women found a way round them. Mina would have liked to borrow a sari and tunic – but of the two Asian women closest to her size, one of them was a devout Muslim, and the other was a lifer who had murdered her own child before attempting suicide. Mina was not keen to be associated with either of these women. In the end, she swapped her Clinique moisturiser for a powerfully-coloured print tunic belonging to a much taller woman. On Mina, it came down to her knees.

Dominic McEwan gave her a briefing. The interview would be conducted by DI Fulton from the City Police: also present would be Frazer Jarvis from the Bank of England and a man from the CPS.

'And you're sure of this deal? They won't go back on their word?' asked Mina.

'You just answer the questions; leave the rest to me.'

She asked to go to the bathroom before it started and gave her hair one final brush to make sure it covered the scars, and then she was ready.

The first shock was DI Fulton. He was black. Mina hadn't expected an inspector from the Fraud Squad to be from an Afro-Caribbean background, but why shouldn't he be? His hair was short, curled close to his head and mostly grey, unlike his suit: that was a rather flamboyant blue. Fraser Jarvis and the man from the CPS (she never learned his name properly) were much greyer altogether although Jarvis was wearing a brightly-coloured tie.

Fulton gave her the Caution, but pointed out that she wasn't under arrest. The interview was being taped, but not recorded on video. The prison was not equipped for that.

'The most obvious question,' began Fulton, 'is why you are volunteering this information now, and why you didn't do so at the time of your initial arrest. As my CPS colleague will tell you, that would have helped a lot, and might have reduced your sentence even further.'

This was a very good question and it had worried Mina since the subject had first come up. She could hardly say *My secret boyfriend sent me a message*. Because she was looking down at the table, the men didn't see her smile when she thought of Conrad. She had been thinking of him a lot lately.

She lifted her head and brushed some of the hair away from her face. 'That was because I didn't know, then. When I was arrested, you had two people who knew the location – George and Adam Thornton. They didn't tell you either.'

Fulton looked uncomfortable and didn't respond to her comment about the Thorntons. Instead, he said, 'So how come you know now?'

'A simple coincidence,' replied Mina. 'George and Croxton used to make jokes about the money. They said it was "French" and that it "stank to high heaven". I thought they just meant it was illegal.'

Fulton and Jarvis conferred for a second, and then Fulton asked her to continue.

'After I started paying my debt to society, I heard one of the girls say something, and I put two and two together.'

'Does this prisoner have a name?'

'Who said it was a prisoner? It might have been a guard or a teacher, or anyone. I'm sorry, that's for me to know.'

'What did she say?'

'It was a throwaway comment about some work she had done, and she mentioned the name of the printer who did it. Something made me think of the counterfeit money, and when I was given my current prison job, I was able to do some searching on the internet.'

The man from the CPS was appalled. 'You get the internet in here? I thought that was strictly off limits.'

'It is, but my prison work is at a computer with access to various benefit websites. It doesn't take much to get unrestricted access, although it's risky. Sooner or later they'll find out, and I'll be back in the laundry or the kitchen garden.'

Fulton spread his hands. 'Okay, we can check on that, but it's time to deliver, Mrs Finch. Who are they?'

Mina looked at Dominic, and he took his cue. 'Is the deal still on? No record that it's my client who provided the information. Release on licence from next June. Immediate transfer to an open prison of our choice and unlimited access to off-site dental treatment. At my client's expense, of course.'

The three men moved back and started talking. Fulton and the CPS went back and forth for a few seconds and Jarvis shrugged. It was Fulton who came back to the table first.

'This is completely conditional. If the information is useless, there's no deal.'

'Understood,' said McEwan.

Mina took a deep breath. 'Garlic. Garlic & Sons, Commercial Printers, North London.'

Fulton and Jarvis both wrote the name down. Mina waited until they'd finished. 'There are a lot of printing firms within driving distance of Moorgate Motorhire, but I had a suspicion that it was about half an hour away and to the north. This firm has exactly the right profile to have gone into counterfeiting.'

'Should we try this out with Thornton?' said Jarvis.

'Not if you want to catch them,' said Mina. 'I'm sure that Thornton would deny everything and then tip them off.'

'She's right,' said Fulton, 'and we've said enough in here.' He terminated the interview, took the tapes out of the recording machine and passed one of them to McEwan. He held up the other one and said, 'If your information is good, this goes in the bin. You have my word.'

'Thank you,' said Mina. 'I got the impression from Sergeant Morton that you dealt fairly with people. I'm surprised he didn't come today – he seemed to be very invested in this case.'

'He is, but he's moved on. Apparently it's Chief Inspector Morton now. If they let you look at the internet again, you should check out a bombing in Blackpool recently. Try the *Sunday Examiner* if they've got a decent website.'

'Why?'

Fulton gave her a cryptic smile, and the three men left the interview room.

'Do you want me to look it up on my phone?' asked McEwan.

'No, don't bother. There are back copies of a month's newspapers in the library. I'll read about it there.'

'How bad is it?'

'It's getting worse, I'm afraid.'

Damn. Clarke rubbed his hand over the top of his head and looked in the mirror. He knew that his bald patch had been spreading, and the barber confirmed the worst of his fears. If he didn't do something soon, he would be entering comb-over territory, and that was not a good look.

'You *are* quite tall,' said the barber. 'Most people won't notice.'

'Time for emergency action. Cut it all off.'

'Are you sure? A complete shave takes a long time to grow out. How about a one-eighth fuzz? Just enough to give a shadow.'

'Go on then.'

The barber did a good job, and Clarke was satisfied with the result. Of course, he couldn't trim it himself afterwards, unlike a complete shave, so he would have to keep coming back to the barber. He paid and walked out on to the main street. It was no hardship coming to Garstang. He had never heard of the little market town until the other day, and he quite liked its single street and the sense that everyone knew everyone else. It also had a Booths supermarket, another pleasant discovery. He was going to eat well if he shopped there.

He peered into the windows of two jewellers and chose the second one because there was a woman behind the counter. He went up to her and said, 'I've got fifty pounds to spend on a birthday present for a woman I've never met, whose birthday party I've been invited to. What would you recommend?'

'Earrings,' said the assistant, and showed him two trays. He chose a yellow gold pair and asked for them to be gift-wrapped.

He wore a suit but no tie for the supper. It was supposed to be informal, after all, and he arrived at twenty to nine. His one concession to vanity was parking the Land Rover well away from the grand entrance, so no one saw him arrive in what amounted to an agricultural vehicle.

On his way to the private dining room, he stopped to look at the pictures. Sure enough, there was Joseph's great grandfather in hunting pink. The caption said his name was Charles Kirkham Malbranche. They must have dropped the last bit.

He went to the top floor and down an unfamiliar corridor. Approaching him was Julian Bentley, leading two small boys in pyjamas. 'Hello Conrad, glad you could make it. It's bedtime for these two, so just go in and say hello.'

'Thanks, erm, Julian. Excuse me for asking, but which one's the birthday girl?'

Bentley laughed. 'Blonde hair, gold dress. Can't miss her.'

Clarke tried to walk into the room as if he belonged there when everything from his shaven head to his parade-ground shoes said he didn't.

The buffet was under wraps at the back of the room, and in front of it was a mixed crowd of friends and relatives. At least, he assumed they were friends, because the Jennings family couldn't have produced so many cousins in their thirties.

'She's not here yet,' said a voice from behind him. It was Lady Jennings.

'Susan. Did you get here all right? No snow?'

'Not so much. Amelia is bringing her latest conquest tonight. Apparently he's quite a big name in entertainment, but I had to look him up. He's some sort of music producer.'

'Good for her. Now you're here, would you mind terribly introducing me to Olivia – it is her party, after all.'

'Fair enough. You've made your point. Come with me.'

Clarke really was fed up with this. The whole family seemed to be assuming that Amelia had broken his heart, and that his single status, nine years later, was self-evident proof that no one could replace her. The real problem was that until he'd met Mina, they'd been right.

Susan Jennings led him to her older daughter. Olivia was indeed wearing a gold dress, but it was one that Clarke thought more appropriate for someone's twenty-fourth birthday, not their thirty-fourth. He could see plenty of her legs, but they would have looked better in jodhpurs. Her mother introduced him, and instead of referring to the *Jilted by Amelia Club*, she said that he was replacing Will Offlea. Then she left them alone.

Olivia gave him two air kisses and said, 'You're not an actor as well, are you?'

'As well as whom?'

'As well as William, of course. He was always going down to London for jobs and changing his appearance.'

God above, that man is a piece of work, he thought. *Only Will Offlea could land up on the Fylde peninsula and pretend to be an actor.* Clarke shook his head, both to deny that he was in the profession and also in wonder at Offlea's cheek.

But there was more. Olivia leaned closer and swayed ever so slightly on her heels. 'We looked him up, but there was no sign of him anywhere. I asked him what sort of films he made, and he winked at me and said *Adult entertainment, with the emphasis on adult.* Can you imagine? A porn star.'

Clarke could not imagine Offlea as a porn star. His head was bursting with the idea, and his brain was in danger of shutting down at the thought. He focused on bundles of US dollars to wipe the image out of his mind.

'Sorry to disappoint you,' he said. 'I was in the RAF until recently.'

Light dawned in her eyes. 'Oh, you're the one who proposed to…'

He cut her off in mid flow. 'You run the Fylde Equine Research Centre, don't you?'

She patted his arm. 'Yes. That's right. Well, I run the livery side. I'm not a scientist but I know my horses.'

'That's fascinating. I used to hunt, and it seems that riding is good for my wound. Do any of your horses need exercising?'

'Really? Gosh, that would be great. If you're sure you're up to it…'

'Only one way to find out. When's the big day? Your birthday, I mean.'

'Yesterday. Don't ask how old.'

'Many happy returns for yesterday, then,' he said, and handed over one of the gift-wrapped packages he had brought with him.

Olivia gave him her drink to hold and was just opening the box when her husband returned.

'Look who's here,' said Bentley.

She wasn't an actress or a politician. Even so, Amelia Jennings made all the heads turn when she walked into the room. Unlike her sister, she had dressed down for the occasion in trousers and a black blouse. Except that her trousers were leather, and the blouse was the finest silk, accessorised with a diamond necklace.

Her other accessory was a man in early middle age who was wearing a loosely cut jacket to hide his emerging paunch. He followed two steps behind and seemed as far out of his comfort zone with the country set as Clarke would have been at a London nightclub.

Amelia scanned the room and made a beeline for her sister. By the time she arrived, Clarke had disappeared into the background.

Supper was served five minutes later, and he managed to grab Sir Stephen on his own.

'I need to talk to you,' said Jennings, 'but not here. Can you really shoot, or will you embarrass me tomorrow?'

'I won't let you down.'

'Good. I've arranged for us to be paired together. Lunch is provided, and there's transport back here afterwards for those excused the dinner.'

'You make it sound like a chore. I hear the food is rather fine at Hartsford.'

'Food is food: It's getting dressed for dinner that bothers me. Olivia insists that it's a black tie occasion, and

I'm getting too old for the penguin suit. I'll see you tomorrow.'

Jennings joined the queue for the buffet, and Clarke looked around. In the middle of winter it was easy to forget that the Sporting Hotel was part of the racecourse. All down the left-hand side of the dining room were doors opening on to an exclusive area of the grandstand. He saw Amelia's escort taking out a packet of cigarettes and asking one of the hotel staff a question. The waiter pointed to a curtain, and the man nipped outside. Clarke followed him.

They made typical smokers' small talk, and Clarke discovered that the other nicotine addict was still married to his second wife, 'But things don't look good,' said the man.

'Do you want to get back with her?'

'I want to go home. I'm living in a rented flat, and she's in Islington.'

Clarke nodded. 'Let me guess. After your first date, Amelia made sure there were pictures of you in the papers.'

'Yeah. Funny, that.'

'Do you want my advice?'

'Not really. I'm getting a lot of that at the moment from everywhere. Especially Twitter.'

'Sorry. Never used Twitter, so I wouldn't know.'

'You don't know how lucky you are.'

'Oh, I do. I had half my leg blown off by the Taliban, so I know exactly how lucky I am.'

'Really? Straight up?'

Clarke stuck his cigarette in his mouth and rolled up his trouser leg. The scar was long and livid in the light from the dining room.

'Then what would you advise, Mr War Hero?'

Clarke stuck out his hand. 'It's Conrad, and I'm no hero.'

'Gerard. Pleased to meet you. Go on then.'

'Well, if I were you, I'd dump Amelia. Very publicly and humiliatingly, but not here: she has too many friends and there are no paparazzi. Do it soon. Then I'd go down on one knee to your wife and grovel. Also in public. At the same time, I'd find a rich Russian or Indian who wants to buy your house and get your lawyer to hint that your wife will have to move out before Christmas unless she takes you back.'

They both lit a second cigarette, and Gerard mused on his advice. Before he could comment, the door opened, and Amelia stood silhouetted against the light.

'There you are. Come inside: you haven't met anyone yet.'

Clarke didn't move. He looked at her, and she glanced at him. The light was shining from inside on his face, and she suddenly recognised him. 'Conrad? Is that you?'

'Hello, Amelia. How are you?'

Gerard was alarmed that they knew each other, and Amelia was put out to find him talking to her escort. She was torn between whisking Gerard away and stopping to assess Clarke's long-term health. He took another drag on his cigarette, and she wafted away the smoke with her hand. 'Are you going to the shoot tomorrow?'

'Your father invited me.'

Satisfied that she would get her chance later, she stepped aside for Gerard to go back. 'Nice to meet you,' he said to Clarke, and then took Amelia's arm.

Conrad fingered the other package in his pocket, the one Joe had brought back from the Trafford Centre, and he considered whether to cut and run. That would be a shame; the Sporting Hotel did excellent food and he was starving. He headed for the buffet and found Olivia stuffing an open sandwich into her mouth. She waved her fingers in front of her face, and he picked up a couple of tasty morsels himself.

When she had finished chewing, Olivia said, 'Just trying to soak up the wine with carbs. I saw you coming back from outside with Gerard. What's he like?'

'Prey.'

'Pray for him? Why?'

'No. Prey with an E. He said his name was Gerard. What's his last name?'

'That's it. Or he doesn't have one. Even his Twitter handle is @JustGerard. Thanks for the earrings, by the way. They're lovely.'

'You're welcome.' He finished stacking his plate. 'Excuse me, I need to rest my leg. I'll take you up on that offer of a ride, perhaps when the ground's not so frosty.'

He left her at the buffet table and started searching for a quiet corner.

Kate's flat was full of life. Unfortunately, all of it was concentrated in the fridge in the form of mould, bacteria and fungus. As he cleared it out, Tom wondered if the Army inoculated its personnel against these things. He had promised to keep an eye on her flat while she was in Dublin; she expected him to make sure the pipes didn't freeze, but he was up early and thought he'd clean both flats properly. They were only tiny, after all, and he was full of nervous energy. Tonight, he was going to do something different. Tonight, Tom Morton was going speed dating.

There had been a leaflet on the hall floor when he got back yesterday – *Speed Dating in the City – Square Mile Residents Only*. He read the small print and rang the number. There was still room for men under forty, so he was booked in. Only when he disconnected the call did he realise how madly stupid this was. He was going to die of embarrassment. He knew it.

That was why he was up early and cleaning the flats – too much nervous energy and too cold to go anywhere outside. He tied up the bin liner full of Kate's rubbish and put it on the landing. Then the door buzzed – for him.

'Hello?'

'Hi Tom, it's Pete. Pete Fulton. Are you busy?'

What on earth was his ex-boss doing in the City on a Saturday morning? He buzzed him in and shouted down the staircase for him to come up. He shoved the black bag in Kate's flat and closed the door. He had the kettle on before Fulton got to the top floor.

His visitor held up two bottle bags when he came in and then put them on the breakfast bar. 'When you left, I didn't get you a present,' he said. 'I was pretty hacked off about you leaving, but I got over it and bought you a nice bottle of wine. I know you're a bit of a foodie.'

'Not so much lately.'

'Well, I never got round to bringing it over. Then I heard about the bomb, so I upgraded it to a single malt, and still didn't bring it round. Been sitting on the floor of my office, tempting me, it has. And then I heard you'd got DCI, and I was going to keep them both.'

Tom handed over a mug of coffee. 'What changed your mind?'

They sat on stools, and Fulton looked around the studio flat. 'Bit like a monk's cell, this, innit?'

Tom shrugged. It was better than being compared to Mr Bleaney: at least monks had a vocation.

Fulton continued, 'It was yesterday that changed everything. I've been out to a women's prison. Not my normal hunting ground, but we had a call from Mina Finch's lawyer.'

Tom looked up sharply and spilt some of his tea. 'What did he want?'

'A deal. Early release for Mina Finch in exchange for the location of the printing works.'

'Did you bite?'

'Too right, we did. The deal's conditional on her delivering the goods. I'm on my way up to North London to see how the surveillance is going.'

'Why now? What made her give it up so long after being arrested?'

Fulton repeated Mina's story, and Tom said, 'Load of rubbish.'

'That's what I thought, but you don't look a gift horse in the mouth. Well, not too closely.'

'When are you going in?'

'Monday morning. We've had a bit of a problem tracking down the owners. It seems that the list of directors at Companies House is a bit out of date.'

'Will you let me know what happens?'

'Straight away. You bust that distribution ring on your own, Tom, and it's a shame you can't get the glory for taking down the printers. As soon as it's safe, I'll be on the phone.'

Tom kept his own counsel. He had a firm opinion about what they would find on Monday morning, but he wanted Fulton to discover it for himself.

'How's things in the Midlands? I saw your appearance on the TV.'

'Not my finest hour, was it? How come you saw it? I thought it was only on the local news.'

'It was on the internet. The whole office had a look.'

'Great.'

'I thought you did okay, considering you was ambushed. Anyway, how's your wounds? It looked bad from the papers.'

Fulton was suitably sympathetic. Unlike most of the money laundering team, he knew what it was like to be on the receiving end of criminal violence. Tom found it made a difference to talk about it with someone who'd been there and come back again. It made him think of Ian Hooper in Earlsbury. There was some unfinished business there as well.

When his ex-boss had gone, he was left with some cleaning materials, two expensive bottles of drink and the speed dating leaflet. He resolved not to touch the drink until afterwards and to arrive at the dating event sober. That way he could enjoy the full horror of his humiliation.

The minibus from the Sporting Hotel dropped its passengers at Hartsford Hall and drove away. Clarke wandered over to Julian Bentley and asked, 'No Gerard today?'

There were very few women on the shoot. Olivia, her mother and friends were having a day in the spa at the Sporting Hotel: Amelia was here, but without her escort.

'According to my sister-in-law, he's never fired a gun, and he needs to make a call to New York this afternoon,' said Bentley with a shrug. 'Here's the gun I promised.'

Clarke examined the firearm. It was an old and rather plain double-barrel, but it was in good condition. Probably Bentley's first gun, now replaced.

'Thanks. Much obliged.'

He stuffed his pockets with shells, and skirted the groups of guns waiting for the gamekeeper to call them to order. He found Sir Stephen talking to a man he vaguely recognised from Iraq and Afghanistan when he had ferried mixed parties of intelligence people around the combat zones. The memory came into focus when Jennings introduced the man as Anthony Skinner, Chief Exec of CIS.

'He's brought me some news,' said Jennings, 'but I'd rather he told you in person over lunch. We're off now.'

They were led around the Hall and over a field to where the pegs were laid. Both men got their guns ready, and Jennings said, 'Listen, Clarke, do you want any of these birds or not? They're costing me thirty-five pounds each. There's no need to slaughter them if you're not going to do anything with them.'

'I just want a brace for my landlord, if that's okay.'

'Good man. We'll do that, and then I'll get the hip flask out. You can even smoke if you want to.'

As the man paying the bills for the Jennings party (there was another group too), Sir Stephen had got the best peg, and they soon had two brace of pheasants. Between the first and second drives, they swapped pegs with Bentley and his friend to allow the others better sport.

'Julian's a good man,' said Jennings. 'A bit arrogant sometimes, but he's a real entrepreneur, a good father and a good shot. His friend couldn't hit a barn door.'

The promised hip flask was passed around, and they enjoyed watching the less competent guns blaze away on the second drive. Spurts of white smoke drifted and dissipated in the cold breeze. If you were wrapped up warm, it was a great day for blasting pheasants out of the sky. Clarke had enjoyed proving that he was a good shot, but that was all.

Sir Stephen got down to business.

'How are you finding things?'

'I think I'm on top of it. The currency exchanges will be interesting, and I've got my first handover on Tuesday. I see that one of the exchanges is in France. I hope they speak English.'

Jennings grunted. 'No idea. Will's fluent in the language, so it wasn't an issue for him. Don't use Eurotunnel and vary your embarkation ports.'

'Will do. There is one thing I'm concerned about, and that's the basic mechanism. I can't see how Offlea's little company launders the money – all I've got is accounts for bookmakers' payments.'

'That's all there is to it. When the next race meeting is on, you circulate around the bookmakers and they will give you the same cash sum and you make up the difference from the slush fund. Easy. The receipt you give them will show a much higher amount. That way, the bookie has a large payment to offset against his earnings, so he's happy, and the cash is taken away by security guards and banked. All legitimate.'

'That won't account for all the money coming in, surely?'

'There's Fylde Events, too, don't forget.'

'You've lost me there, sir.'

Jennings pulled a face. 'Don't tell me Offlea's taken it all with him.'

'He must have. There's no trace of Fylde Events in the cottage or in the lockup.'

'It was another cash business. He was the sole director. On paper, Fylde Events would book the conference room at the Sporting Hotel for things like race nights and charity auctions. He would sell "tickets" for cash and run a nominal cash bar. A couple of days after the phantom event, Offlea would bank a load of cash from Red Flag into the Fylde Events account, and then pay the Sporting Hotel's invoice from it. That was how he got part of his earnings – that and the profits from Fylde On Track.'

Jennings took another swig. 'Awkward blighter – he must have been skimming off more than I thought, if he's taken the books and the bank details with him. You'll need to set one up on your own. Julian will expect at least a hundred grand's worth of business from you that way.'

'I could run swingers' parties. They sound like fun, and I'm sure some of Olivia's friends would be up for it.'

'The worrying thing about you, Clarke, is that you might do exactly that. Well, don't.'

'Perhaps next year. In the meantime, I'll settle for a run out on one of Olivia's horses.'

They were soon reminiscing about the good old days before the hunting ban, and Sir Stephen was telling him the best ways to get round it, when lunch was called. Rather than head straight for the van dispensing food, Jennings waved over Anthony Skinner, and they had a conference in the middle of the field.

'Tell Clarke what you told me,' said Sir Stephen.

'I might have set you up for something,' said Skinner. 'We've had a bit of a problem with Kate Lonsdale.'

'*Another* problem?'

'Yes. No sooner does she get back from Hong Kong than she sets off for Wales and stalks Gareth Wade's widow.'

The more Clarke heard about what Kate was up to, the more he admired her and the more he pitied her. The woman was a complete bull in a china shop.

'Luckily, we'd primed Mrs Wade not to talk,' continued Skinner, 'so I called Kate into my office and told her a story. I said that Wade and Vinnie Jensen were both being paid to support private military ventures in war zones.'

That was clever. Very clever. Lonsdale's inherent loyalty and discretion would mean that she wouldn't go blabbing to anyone, but it didn't mean the end of things, because Clarke could see what was coming next.

'What did you tell her about me?' he said.

'I hedged my bets, but implied you were involved somehow. I said that CIS had never paid you – which is technically true – and I think she trusts you. If you can come up with a plausible account, she might just call it a day and leave things alone.'

'Thanks a bunch, old chap. That's the sort of favour I can do without.' He gave a theatrical sigh. 'Where is the good lady now? I'm surprised she hasn't already been in touch.'

'I've sent her off to Dublin on a wild goose chase. Well, it's a legitimate job, but she hasn't got a cat in hell's chance of accomplishing the mission. I'm sure she'll be up to see you when she's had enough Guinness and blarney.'

Clarke looked at Sir Stephen and then said to Skinner, 'As the North West's newest bookmaker, I'll give you three to one *against* her solving it. Our Kate does like a challenge, you know.'

Jennings' mouth twitched at the corner. 'You'd better put up or shut up, Anthony.'

Skinner burst out laughing. 'You're on. A hundred quid says she comes back with her tail between her legs.'

The men shook on the bet and headed off for lunch. As they approached the other guns, Clarke noticed that Amelia was on her own. He decided that it was now or never and walked over to her. She could have been a model on a photo shoot for country casuals. Her hair had remained unruffled, despite the ear defenders, and she sat on the folding chair with one leg elegantly crossed over the other.

'Hello Conrad.'

'Hello Amelia. Did you have any luck this morning?'

'I got a brace. I'm a bit out of practice these days. I'm sure I'll do better this afternoon.'

'I'm sure you will. You're looking very good. I hope Gerard realises what he's got and doesn't take you for granted.'

'I won't let him. I'm sorry to hear about your injuries, but what have you done to your hair? Father said you'd caught one in the leg, not the head.'

'It's age catching up with me. Besides, I've never relied on my looks.'

'And you mean I have?'

'No, Amelia, I would never say that about you, although you are very good looking.'

She rewarded him with a smile, and his heart reminded him exactly why he had fallen head over heels in love with her all those years ago. It was time to move on.

'I've got something for you,' he said, and dug the Trafford Centre package out of his pocket where it nestled amidst the unused shotgun cartridges. 'Here, I don't have a use for it any more.'

She frowned at him and put down her drink to open the package. When she unwrapped it, there was a brand new

Zippo lighter, freshly engraved with the words *To Conrad, with love from Amelia.*

She was puzzled and angry, but she couldn't work out why. She held the lighter aloft and said, 'But you've started smoking again.'

He took out his own lighter and showed her the image of Ganesha. With a grimace, Amelia looked around and realised that she couldn't just drop it on the ground. Not here in the manicured grounds of Hartsford Hall. With distaste, she shoved the lighter and packaging into her pocket.

'It's a shame you couldn't be a complete replacement for Will Offlea,' she said.

That was alarming. Was she trying to tell him that Offlea had been one of the many notches on her bedpost? What if she was? She could do what she liked – it was the twenty-first century, after all, and if she chose to sleep with Loyalist paramilitary psychopaths, that was her business – but she had piqued his curiosity.

'In what way?' he asked.

'That story he told Olivia,' she replied. 'The one about him being a porn star. Well, he certainly had the equipment for it.'

Conrad knew when to withdraw from the battle. He had achieved his strategic objective in handing over the lighter and could only suffer damage if he remained in the field. One of the few lessons his father had instilled in him was *Always let the woman have the last word.* It had worked – still worked – for his parents, so with no more than a smile, Clarke nodded to Amelia, and went off to eat his lunch.

Only the roads on the trading estate had been gritted, and not very well. The pavements and car parks – and what few pieces of open ground existed amidst the concrete – were all covered in snow.

Detective Inspector Peter Fulton had been to monitor the operation twice over the weekend. There had been no activity at the printing works since surveillance began on Friday night, and it seemed that one of the partners in the business was on holiday. The other one was at home, or at least his family had been seen coming and going.

Fulton had decided to raid the premises at eight thirty on Monday morning, and so he was sitting around the corner in his car with Frazer Jarvis from the Bank of England's anti-counterfeiting unit.

Fulton spoke into the radio. 'Still no sign of anyone at work?'

'Hold on, Boss. I think I see a van.'

Fulton waited, and the officer said, 'Yes. That's it. A van with the target's name and logo has just come on to the estate.'

'Wait until he unlocks the door then we go on your signal. All units.'

They acknowledged his order and two minutes later he was given the signal.

The raid happened in slow motion. Not because of the adrenalin but because of the snow. All the police vehicles drove carefully up to the target premises, then a dozen police officers and SOCOs, arms held out for balance, tiptoed their way to the front door and went in. Fulton, brandishing the search warrant, took the lead.

Inside, he found one man still turning on the lights. He announced himself, and the man, who clearly watched too much television, immediately raised his hands in the air and dropped to his knees.

'Get up,' said Fulton. 'We're the Fraud Squad, not the Flying Squad. Is there anyone else here?'

The man struggled to his feet. 'No. The bosses should be here by now.'

'Isn't one of them on holiday?'

'No way. We're flat out busy with the Christmas rush.'

Fulton's shoulders drooped, and Jarvis, standing just behind him, kicked a box of photocopy paper in frustration.

'We're going to conduct a full search of these premises,' said Fulton to the still-petrified employee.

'You'll want to start in the back room,' said the man.

'Oh? Why's that? Do you know what's in there?'

'No. I've never been in there,' came the reply, accompanied by a vehement shake of the head. 'And it's always locked.'

Fulton waved forward his team and made his way to the back of the factory.

Tom drove cautiously in the middle lane of the M40. The outside lane was covered in weekend snow and only foolhardy 4x4 drivers were risking it. The slow pace gave him plenty of time to consider Saturday night's trauma.

His first two partners in the speed dating had been very pleasant. A little earnest, perhaps – and if he was honest – a little old for him. The third partner sat down opposite and said, 'Hello Tom, I'm Elspeth. What's your idea of a good night out?'

It was Elspeth Brown, the City Police receptionist. When she saw the look on his face, she took great offence. 'Don't be like that. I'm just joking.'

He mumbled through the next four minutes and the rest of the evening passed in a blur. At the end, he marked *No Interest* in any of the women and fled the room.

Overcome with embarrassment, he had even described it to his father when they spoke on Sunday. Dad had found it very amusing at first, but then he'd got serious.

'You should try online dating, son, if you're genuinely ready to dip your toe in the water again.'

'Really?'

'Yes. I know of at least two silks and a judge who've done it. One of them is expecting her first child after Christmas.'

His reflections on his love life were interrupted by an incoming call over the BMW's hands-free system. It was Pete Fulton.

'Hi Tom. Can you talk?'

'Yes. How did it go?'

'You were right all along. I'm sorry.'

'Why? What happened?'

'There's been a leak. We raided the factory ten minutes ago, and we've found all the gear. High-end presses, hologramatic printing machine, cotton-based paper, polychromatic ink, the lot. Even the plates. A real coup.'

'But…'

'But the owners fled on Friday afternoon, before we got surveillance in place. Well, one of the owners left with his family and the other one left with his mistress. The Met raided the wife's house, and I could hear the screams of abuse down the phone.'

'Any idea where they've gone?'

'We found something else in their back room – a bundle of blank passports.'

It gave Tom absolutely no satisfaction to have been proved right. He knew something like this would happen, and he didn't even feel any schadenfreude at Fulton's expense. He was surprised that they had even got the presses, never mind the plates.

'You'll catch them eventually,' he said.

'You always were a glass-half-full sort of bloke, Tom. I'd better go, but I'll keep you posted.'

'Thanks.'

He was only a few miles closer to Earlsbury when Kris Hayes called him.

'Sir, I've had that journalist from the *Sunday Examiner*, Juliet Porterhouse, on the phone. Says she's got some important information – as in so important she can't print it. She asked if you could call. I've got her number.'

'So have I. Call her back and tell her I'll give her a ring from the next service station.'

'Will do. Any excuse for a cup of tea, eh sir?'

'Haven't you got work to do, Hayes?'

'I'm on it.'

He called Porterhouse as promised, and she came straight to the point.

'I've just had an anonymous email making allegations against someone in MCPS. Serious allegations.'

'Why you, I wonder? Why not the woman from the BBC News?'

'This is different. I saw that clip, and it was hostile. Whoever sent this stuff to me must have read my piece and decided I was sympathetic to you. This is stuff that you're expected to act on.'

'I see. You know I'm not going to offer you an interview, or an off-the-record briefing, don't you.'

'I thought that.'

'So are you going to tell me what it says or not?'

'I hate to admit this, but I'm conflicted. The allegation is definitely malicious, and I don't do malice. I don't want someone dragged into an investigation unnecessarily. We all know how they can ruin people's lives.'

'I don't want that, either.'

There was a pause. 'I've been straight with you,' said Juliet, 'and if you'll be straight with me we can sort this.'

'How do you mean?'

'If I give you a name, will you tell me if they're already under investigation – just a simple Yes or No. If it's No, I'll delete the email. If it's Yes, I'll send it to you. How about that?'

It was a delicate moment. The investigation might turn on whether he got this information, but if he refused her offer, she could find out who was on his hit list with a little digging, anyway. On the other hand, if he accepted her offer, would he be in hock to her?

He found himself wondering what Leonie Spence or Pete Fulton would say if they were in his shoes. Fulton would refuse to co-operate and see what the response was; Leonie would agree, but do so with her fingers crossed behind her back.

'Okay,' said Tom. 'What's the name?'

'Are you investigating Niall Brewer?'

'Yes.'

'Then that's that. Give me your email address, and I'll send it over.'

Tom did so and headed back to his car to continue the drive to Earlsbury. When he arrived at BCSS, the email from Juliet Porterhouse was waiting for him. He flicked through the contents of the attachments and couldn't help smiling.

'What?' said Hayes. 'Go on, tell me.'

'I've got a mission for you, and the good news is that you won't need to leave the office to carry it out.'

Kelly Kirkham stood with her hands on her hips. 'Get them out of here. I told you: no dead birds and no dead rabbits in the house, and no moles strung out on the fences where Natasha can see them.'

Clarke's gift of the brace of pheasants wasn't going down as well as he had hoped. He had taken them into the farmhouse when Kelly returned from taking her daughter to school. The three adults were sitting round the table, and Kelly had stood up to get the kettle from the Aga when she saw the birds and let rip.

At least her anger was directed at her husband rather than Clarke. Young Joe got up and ushered him into the yard.

'Don't mind her,' he said. 'She wasn't brought up on a farm, see, and she still likes to think that steaks come from the supermarket, not from beef cattle. I'll take the birds, if the offer's still open.'

'Of course.'

They walked across the yard, and Joe hung the birds in a shed that was colder than most refrigerators. Clarke noticed some electrical equipment in the corner.

'Is that welder yours?'

'Aye. I did a course on it a few year ago when we were trying to diversify. I still get bits of work from other farms, and with our buildings, it comes in very handy.'

'In that case, I've got another little job for you, but I need it doing today.'

'I'd rather be welding than fixing the fence in the top field. What do you want?'

'I'll bring the new van down and explain it to you.'

Mina was beginning to regret her choice of prison clothes again. She had been sent down during a mild spell, and she didn't realise how cold it could get. She was going to have to contact Mr Joshi and get him to send her something. The call centre was warm, but it had been built outside the walls, and it was a long walk back with a long wait to get inside again. She shivered and started to bounce up and down to keep warm while they waited for the gates to open.

When the officer waved them through, and they'd been searched, she was kept behind by the deputy governor.

'Is there a problem, ma'am?'

'That depends. From the look of things, I'd say you've got what you wanted.'

The deputy waved a piece of paper at her and said, 'Pack your bags, Mina, you're on the move tomorrow.'

She breathed a huge sigh of relief. It had all worked out – Conrad's information, the arrests and the deal had all come through. 'Where am I going?'

'HMP Cowan Valley. It's a fully open prison and you've been given access to dental treatment. I hope it goes well for you.'

The relief was still coursing through her when she realised she had no idea where she was going.

'Excuse me, ma'am, but is Cowan Valley near Oxford?'

'What? No, it's near Cairndale.'

'And where's *that*?'

'Up North. Between Lancaster and Kendal.'

Was this a joke? Had someone decided to take their revenge by sending her to the other end of the country? There was no way Mr Joshi could visit her up there: she would be even more isolated than she was now.

For the first time in years, she ran her fingers over her jawline. The bone was smooth and the scars were hidden under her chin. There was just a huge gap where her teeth – bottom and top – should be. In this new prison, she could come somewhere close to being normal again, and she was now due for release in six months. Mina realised that she loved life more than she had thought. She wanted to be normal, to walk the streets and buy new clothes, and not hide her face from other people because she looked like a freak-show attraction.

She held out her hand, and the deputy handed over the movement notice before opening the door into the main building. 'Wrap up warm,' she said. 'I hear Cowan Valley is quite exposed.'

Mina headed for the payphone. She was going to ring Mr Joshi straight away and get him to prepare an emergency parcel.

'It's not like you to play your cards so close to your chest, sir.'

Hayes was standing in front of Tom's desk with the outcome of the job he had given her. Tom was going through the rest of the email from Juliet Porterhouse and had said nothing to his DC.

'It's tricky, Kris, that's why. I don't think Porterhouse fully appreciated the incendiary nature of the material she sent me, or the implications for Niall Brewer. Admittedly, Porterhouse doesn't know him from Adam, and she hasn't got his personnel file in front of her, but even so.'

'Don't be a tease. What's in it?'

'Financial information, gossip, and those photographs I gave you. The problem is that the financial information could only have been gathered illegally, and some of it relates to third parties. The same with that photograph. I can't use this information directly in our interview with Brewer. It depends on how it goes with him, but I'll definitely tell you more afterwards, okay?'

Hayes nodded somewhat reluctantly, but she accepted his decision. Tom didn't like keeping her in the dark, but he wasn't sure himself what to do with his illicit knowledge. He asked how she had got on with tracking down the photograph.

'I think it will add nicely to your "financials", sir.'

He studied her brief report and said, 'Good work. You can lead on that in the interview tomorrow.'

Chapter 10

Earlsbury – Heathrow – Cairndale – London

Tuesday – Saturday

7-11 December

'Sit down, Mr Brewer,' said Tom. 'I saw you reading the letter I gave you last Thursday. I'm sure you've taken advice since then.'

'Yes, I have.' The media relations manager had recovered his composure since their last encounter. Instead of a sweating, rumpled disaster area, Tom was faced with a man wearing a much more expensive suit, shoes and shirt than he could afford. The armour was back in place.

'Then I'll be brief. This is a witness interview. It will not be recorded, and it is not admissible as evidence on its own. You are therefore not entitled to legal representation during the interview unless I arrest you. Is that clear?' Brewer nodded. 'However, DC Hayes will make notes during the interview, and a statement will be prepared for you to sign. That will be a sworn statement, which is admissible. Do you have any further questions?'

'No.'

'Then I'll begin. You were promoted to senior media relations manager two years ago. Am I correct?'

'Yes.'

'Thank you. And before that you worked as a senior editor in television news.'

Brewer had done enough interviews to know when to keep silent. Tom had stated a fact; Brewer didn't respond.

'That was rather a step down, wasn't it?'

'There wasn't much difference in salary.'

'But there's no more chance of promotion now, is there? You're at the top. Not only that, you're out of the loop. You're now the man who used to be a senior editor. You wouldn't find it easy to get back inside.'

'Who says I want to? I enjoy my job and I enjoy helping a vital public service to get the best out of the media. Good placement for a story can mean a huge difference to public reaction.'

'Indeed.' Tom looked up from Brewer's personnel records. 'I've got your reference here. Very good it is, too, but what would your former boss say if I arrested him? Would he tell the same story under a police caution?'

'Why shouldn't he?' said Brewer in all innocence, but his hands gave him away. They had been folded on his lap, but the left one moved up under his jacket to scratch his right collar bone. Tom had the scent in his nostrils. To his left, Hayes made a note in her book.

'What would he say, do you think, if I asked him about your inappropriate relationship with a victim of crime?'

Brewer flinched and put his fingers on the edge of the table. 'Who told you that?'

'We protect our sources, too, Mr Brewer. Is it true? What do you journalists say? *Do you want to tell me your side of the story?*'

'There is no story. My team were doing an exposé about a fraudster in Coventry. He'd swindled hundreds of people, and one of them came to us. Because she was the first, we had to do a lot of handholding, and I spent a lot of time with her. After the story was broadcast – I repeat, after the story was broadcast, we did start a relationship. I did nothing wrong.'

Tom gave Hayes a chance to write down what Brewer had said, and made a point of asking her if she had written it correctly. Brewer did not look happy about seeing the details go into Hayes's notebook.

Tom continued. 'Shortly after you began this relationship, you separated from your wife and applied for the job here. Is that correct?'

'Yes.'

'And you divorced eighteen months ago.'

'Yes. I'm not proud of that, but I do my best as a father.'

'Does that include paying maintenance on a regular basis?'

He had tipped Hayes off about this question. When he asked it, she pushed her notebook forwards and held up her pen in readiness for Brewer's answer. It had the desired effect. Brewer's face flushed and he scratched under his jacket again. Perhaps it was a new shirt that needed a good wash to get the starch out. Or perhaps the anonymous source had given Juliet Porterhouse some very good information.

'I don't see how on earth that's of relevance to the investigation into DS Griffin,' said Brewer.

'You're right,' said Tom. 'What we need is the bigger picture. As you know, I used to work for the Fraud Squad in the City. It's a cinch to get hold of financial records – both yours and your ex-wife's. If I did that, would I find regular maintenance payments by bank transfer or would I find the maintenance as cash payments into her account with no corresponding payments out of yours?'

'No comment.'

Hayes' pen dived on to her pad and she wrote it down. Brewer watched her trace out each letter of his reply.

'Try again,' said Tom. 'This is not an interview under caution, and if you're going to be like that, I can soon arrest you.' He patted his folder of information. 'I know, you see. I know that's the case, and I can easily get proof. And there's more. DC Hayes, could you show Mr Brewer the picture?'

Hayes took a printout from the internet and laid it in front of Brewer. In the picture, a smiling Brewer had his arm round a younger woman as they shared a cocktail on the beach. 'Could you confirm that this is you and your new partner in the photograph, and that this image was taken on holiday in St Lucia?'

Brewer studied the picture for far longer than was necessary to confirm his identity. 'This was on Facebook,' he said. 'How did you get access to my private pictures?'

'Please answer the question,' said Hayes.

'All right, yes it is.'

It was Tom's turn. 'I believe that this holiday was booked through the Edgbaston branch of a travel agent, and that it was paid for in cash.'

'I spoke to them yesterday,' added Hayes. 'They remember you.'

'Cash,' said Tom. 'It's almost radioactive these days: if you don't know what you're doing, you can get burned. Most of the villains in money laundering take precautions. You didn't.'

The police officers sat in silence. Tom looked steadily at Brewer and Hayes had a new page open in her notebook. On the other side of the desk, Brewer was not so much crumbling as melting. The silence continued, and Tom thought that he was nearly there, then Brewer seemed to rally. He shifted in his seat and took his jacket off. Then he folded his arms and said, 'So? I still don't see what this has to do with DS Griffin. You may have the chief constable's grudging co-operation, but you're not popular here. You can't find anything that will link me to Griffin, and without that, all of this is speculation. If you had more, you'd have shown it to me.'

Tom nodded, as if thinking over what Brewer had said. 'Have you been to see Ian Hooper since he was shot?'

'No. And that's not because I've got a guilty conscience: it just wouldn't be appropriate for me to visit an officer who's on sick leave.'

'Perhaps I should arrange a visit for you. Gunshot wounds are terrible things, Mr Brewer. If you saw how badly injured he is, you might realise just how committed I am to nailing the one who did it.'

'The one who did it is dead. He was killed in that bomb blast – in fact, I might say that your enquiry has more to do with your injuries than Hooper's. That's what the local news was saying last week.'

'Not so: it's about the brains behind the operation. You've got brains, haven't you? You can see what would happen if I decided to arrest you and start digging. It comes down to this: either you sent Griffin to his death or there's some other explanation for these irregularities.' Tom swept his hand over the paperwork and tried to make irregularities sound like minor misdemeanours.

Brewer's gaze lingered on the holiday photograph. Tom went in for the kill. 'In fact, I'm really only interested in you at all if you did for Griffin.'

'What are you saying?'

'DC Hayes, could you get Mr Brewer a glass of water?'

Kris closed her notebook and slipped out of the interview room.

Tom leaned forwards. 'What I'm saying, Mr Brewer, is that I've got limited resources. I know enough about you to start digging, but I don't care about the rest. If you convince me there's another explanation, and if you answer a few other questions, then this folder here goes in the shredder.'

Tom let his fingers rest on the folder. Brewer hesitated until they both heard Hayes' footsteps returning along the corridor.

'I was selling information,' said Brewer. 'If you've got the contacts, you can get a lot of money for certain hot items. A tabloid journalist who can find out the name of a victim or the identity of a suspect ahead of the pack will pay a fortune for an exclusive.'

The door opened and Hayes came in with three plastic cups of chilled water. Tom said, 'Just one more thing. Whoever tipped off the BBC about my investigation wanted me to fail. I don't expect journalists to give up their sources, but if you can get the reporter to tell me – off the record – that it wasn't you, then we can move on to other matters.'

'I can do it now if you let me.'

'Good. Let's take a break.'

Half an hour later, Brewer had talked the reluctant journalist into confirming that he was not the source of her information. Tom had done a verbal dance with the reporter, but managed to avoid committing himself to any future exclusives.

Brewer managed a small smile as he took his phone back. He had the look that Tom had seen so often after a confession – the weight off the shoulders, the relief that it was out of his hands. He seemed eager to give Tom a blow-by-blow account of his fall from grace, but Tom wasn't interested.

'I told you that if you were innocent of any involvement in what happened to Griffin and Hooper then I would let it all go. I keep my promises and I don't want to know any more about it. DC Hayes and I are going to write up a full statement based on what you've said … but there's one more thing before I consign this folder to the shredder,' said Tom, patting the innocuous looking documents, 'and I want your unequivocal undertaking not to discuss it outside this room. Am I clear?'

'Yes. What now?' sighed Brewer.

'Do you remember the budget strategy meeting at the Victoria Hotel?'

Brewer frowned. 'Yes. Wasn't that… ? Of course. It was the night that Griffin and those two boys were killed and Hooper was shot.'

Perhaps there was hope for Brewer. Of all the police staff Tom had dealt with, Brewer was one of the few who included Dermot Lynch and Robert King in the list of victims. Tom had seen the effect of their deaths on their families and he had not forgotten them.

'That's right. I want you to describe, in as much detail as you can, what happened from the moment the chief constable brought things to a close. If it helps you remember, that was at 19:54 – six minutes to eight.'

Brewer rubbed his face for a few seconds. 'I was shattered. Completely knackered – I remember that much. Most of the others had been running on adrenalin because they had so much more invested in the decisions. I was just there to see the process and to comment on the likely media reaction to the various options they put forward. But you don't want to know that, do you?'

'No.'

'I'm telling you I was knackered because it means I can't recall very much. It was like the end of school – as soon as the bell rang, I wanted to be out of there. I remember feeling a little guilty that Evelyn had to help the finance director to pack up, but not very guilty. I left them to it and scuttled away. In fact, I'm pretty sure that I was first out of the door.'

'You didn't stop to switch on your phone, like the others did?'

'No. I'm not the prime minister's press secretary. I don't scour the media 24/7 for items relating to MCPS. There was no emergency, and so my work was done. I just left.'

'Describe exactly what you did and saw.'

'I can't remember. I just went into reception and out to the car park and into my car. Then home.'

'Did you look round? Did you see who was behind you?'

'I think it might have been the ACC. Not Khan – the other one.'

'Thank you. As I said, we'll write this up. Could you be available to read and sign your statement at four o'clock this afternoon?'

Brewer nodded and they all left the interview room.

Back in their office, Hayes said, 'Are you going to pass that on to MCPS Professional Standards? If Brewer has admitted to selling information, he's going to face charges of Misconduct in Public Office at the very least.'

Tom picked up the incriminating folder. 'I gave him a promise and I'm going to keep it. I'll shred this folder on the way out tonight.'

Hayes looked very unhappy at that, and her resolve to be more of a team player was being stretched to the limit. Tom put the file back on the desk and said, 'Thought experiment.'

'What?'

'We used to do them at law school. You create a situation with agreed parameters and then discuss what would happen. Like a scientific experiment.' Hayes nodded her understanding. 'Very simply, what would you have done?'

'In what way?'

'If you were sitting in my seat, if you had the folder with illegal information, how would you have used it to prise open Brewer's shell?'

She exhaled and picked up her pen, tapping it on her desk. 'I think it depends on whether I could live with myself.'

'Go on.'

'Do you remember what you said about the Jigsaw? About this being Operation Jigsaw, and putting all the pieces together?'

'I think about it every time I look at the case.'

'It depends on what's more important – finding the next piece of the jigsaw or giving MCPS a clean bill of health.' She stopped tapping the pen and looked him in the eye. Then she let her gaze travel down to his left shoulder. 'The thing is … Tom, I'm not really sitting in your chair because I wasn't blown up.'

'Are you saying that I've lost my sense of perspective? You wouldn't be the first.'

'No. It's just harder to have absolute standards, that's all. Excuse me for saying this, but if you had been killed in that bomb – if Leonie Spence had been sitting in your chair – what would she have done?'

That was a very good question. He held up his hands in surrender. 'You've got me there. It's hard to do a thought experiment when you can't agree on the starting point.'

Hayes gave him a full-wattage smile, all her white teeth shining. 'We called them dilemmas, not thought experiments. We used to do things like this in my Bible Study group, and I was quite good at it. Probably because I wasn't sure whether or not I believed in God.'

'I think that's a conversation for another day, but I'll tell you this: I made a promise to Brewer to destroy the file, and I will. I never told him that Juliet Porterhouse has a full copy. If she decides that there's a story in it, then that's up to her.'

'That's nasty. Really nasty. I like it.'

'Good. Now, let's get that statement written.'

Clarke had to fill his Zippo before leaving Ribblegate Cottage, and when he opened the cupboard to find the tin of lighter fuel he came across the box containing his Air Force Cross, awarded for his gallantry in Helmand. Why didn't he flaunt it?

He reckoned he deserved a medal for what he had done in Iraq six years ago – flying his Chinook into insurgent fire and getting all the Marines out of the ambush in record time. But he had fallen out with his CO at the time, and he didn't even get a mention in dispatches, so perhaps he and the RAF were even. He still thought they'd only given him the AFC because he had also been invalided out of the service.

The medal was a lie – so why did he feel guilty about showing it off? He lied to people all the time, often for fun, and always for advantage. Perhaps Mina could explain it one day. She was good at that sort of thing. He pushed it further back in the cupboard and took out the lighter fuel.

Hours later, he was getting fed up of light industrial units. It seemed that all the criminal activity in Britain took place in little workshops and warehouses dotted around industrial estates. What was wrong with abandoned factories? Or old quarries? That's what they did on the telly. The showdown was always in an old factory, which echoed with menacing footsteps.

Today's rendezvous with danger was taking place at the Golden East Spice Company in Greater Heathrow, the enormous range of warehouses and units that surround Britain's largest airport. Clarke found it and reversed up to the doors. He saw them rise in his mirror and he continued backwards until the nose of his van was right under the line of the shutters.

His preparation for today had involved lots of elements. One of them was buying an extra-thick coat: another was stealing old Joseph's tweed cap and getting himself a crutch. He could hear shouts from behind the van, but he ignored them and pulled the cap down on his head. Then he grabbed the crutch, opened his door, levered himself very slowly out of the van and put his weight on the crutch. Still ignoring the shouts from behind him, he slammed the door and walked forward.

Ranged around the loading area were four men of Pakistani origin, but very much second-generation. You could tell that from the jeans, the sparkling white trainers and the bling. Lots of bling.

'Are you deaf as well as blind? I said *Move your van back*. I can't get the doors down.'

He was clearly their leader. Taller, slightly older and with a beard. He wore boots instead of trainers, but there was just as much bling.

'Are you Mohamed?' asked Clarke.

'Yeah, I'm Mohamed,' replied the other.

'I'll move the van if we need it,' said Clarke. 'It was painful enough getting out, and I don't want to get back in unless I have to.' He leaned on the crutch for effect and rubbed his left leg.

'Of course we need it,' said one of the others. 'And it's bloody freezing with that door open.'

That was one of the reasons Clarke had bought the coat. None of the other men were dressed for outdoor work.

'We haven't done any business yet,' said Clarke. 'We'll shake on the deal, then I'll get the van in.'

'Whatever,' said Mohamed. 'How much have you got?'

'Half a million US. I reckon that should be worth £240,000 at current rates.'

'Things change. We've got inflation at our end, and the bribes have gone up. Today's rate is £200,000. Take it or leave it.'

Clarke adjusted his crutch. He took off Joseph's cap and wiped his head with his sleeve. The man nearest to the warehouse doors started to shiver a little in the cold. 'That's forty thousand less than I was expecting. I can't go back with that. They'll make me pay the difference, and I can't afford it.'

'That's your problem, not mine.'

'Well, in that case … I'm very sorry gentlemen, but I'll have to leave it and go elsewhere.'

'Not so fast, old man. We've gone to a lot of trouble today. There's an arrangement fee of twenty thousand US dollars. You're not leaving unless you pay it.'

Clarke stared at him. The two men on the outside of the group took a step towards him, and Mohamed's sidekick, the one who had complained about the cold, folded his arms. Clarke held his right hand up to show it was empty and very slowly moved it towards his pocket. The sidekick pulled a gun from his waistband and levelled it at Clarke. 'Freeze. Right there.'

'I'm not armed,' said Clarke. 'See? Finger and thumb.' He put his first two digits in his pocket and pulled out a small remote control.

'What the fuck?' said Mohamed. 'Is that a fucking bomb you've got there?'

'Don't be stupid. I'm not a suicide bomber. I'm just an old man with a bad leg. Have a look at the top of the van.'

Some vans have little vents on the top to circulate fresh air to perishable cargo or livestock. Clarke's van had had no such thing when he bought it, but yesterday, Joe had welded one on top – with a couple of additions, including a little red light, which was now blinking.

'There's something here,' said the one who'd gone to look at the roof. 'There's a red light and some electrics.'

'Live remote feed,' said Clarke. 'My boss said you might not be trustworthy, but I said you should be given a chance. That's why I blocked the door – so the signal could get out, and they can get in if you try anything.'

Mohamed took a step towards the van with shock on his face. His plan had worked. If he had gone in as an ex-forces hard nut, they wouldn't have believed him, but the contrast between the stooped old man with the crutch and the hi-tech surveillance had caught them completely off guard.

'Come on, Mohamed,' said Clarke. 'There's too much at stake for us to get into a pissing contest. Just do the deal at £240,000, and I'll be on my way. No harm, no foul.'

Mohamed looked around his men. This was the crunch point. If he had authority, they would accept him backing down. If Mohamed was short on respect, then things could go wrong very quickly.

Clarke had one last throw of the dice left. 'It was a good try, Mohamed. I'd have done the same in your position, but I'm not in it for death or glory, just the money. I'll open the van, and we'll get started.'

The man with the gun looked up at Mohamed. The leader of the group laughed. 'Okay, mate, deal on.' The gun disappeared and the other men stood back.

'I'm not going to move the van,' said Clarke. 'If I were you, I'd go and get something warm to put on.'

Mohamed jerked his head, and the three others disappeared into the background. Clarke opened the van doors wide and revealed Joe's other piece of welding. Instead of a plastic panel in the door, there was an aluminium cover. It looked shoddy, but this was a van not a limousine. Clarke pretended to fiddle with the cargo until the three other men came back with their coats. This time, they instinctively stood together around their leader rather than spreading out in an arc. Clarke had them exactly where he wanted them.

He unzipped his coat and it flapped open to hide his movements. He removed the aluminium panel and took out his souvenir from Essex – an AK47. He swung it round and dropped his crutch. Soldiers would have dived out of the way as soon as they saw it, but these men weren't soldiers. Or Taliban. They just froze to the spot.

Clarke didn't want to humiliate them, but he wanted to teach them a lesson. 'You. With the gun. Take it out very slowly and put it on the ground, then slide it over. Anyone else makes a move, and you're dead. All of you.'

The man took out his pistol and slid it across the floor. Clarke let it lie. 'Now, the rest of you. Coats off again and turn around. No one's going to get hurt. It's just business. Start with you on the end.'

Mohamed tried to assert some authority by saying *Do it* so that it seemed like the order was coming from him and not Clarke. Either way, the men complied, and in a few seconds Clarke had two more guns. Mohamed, it seemed, was not armed. That was good. Clarke wanted Mohamed to stay in charge of this operation.

'On your knees, all of you. Just until I've picked up these guns. Then we'll get to work.'

'Down,' said Mohamed, and they all dropped.

Clarke put all three guns in his coat pockets and then stepped aside. He pointed his Kalashnikov at the three junior men. 'You three can sit down. Cross-legged. Don't move.' When they had complied, he beckoned Mohamed across and took out a folded piece of paper, which he tossed over. On it was written a set of instructions:

Get the suitcase out of my van and put it on the floor. Empty it. Then get your cash and put it in the case. Add an extra fifteen hundred pounds for me. I don't want that on the tape.

It was cheeky, but if you don't ask you don't get. 'Where's your money?' said Clarke. 'I don't want you wandering off looking for a gun of your own.'

'It's down the back, with the counting machines.'

'We're not going to do any counting today. Which aisle is it down?'

Mohamed pointed down the building. 'Off you go,' said Clarke, and he took up a position where he could cover both Mohamed and the three seated men, who were now shivering violently.

It was all over in ninety seconds. Clarke had their money and his crutch in the van, and they had the US dollars. He even had a bonus to cover his expenses. Job done. He ordered them to lie face down and he put their guns at the side of the room, well out of reach. His last instruction was for them to cross the road and wait. Mohamed looked as if he were about to mutiny, but Clarke said, 'I'm going to get in the van and drive off. I'll be vulnerable when I do that. If you're across the road, I'll have enough time to get away safely. We've come this far, Mohamed. Let's seal the deal.'

They did as he asked, and he climbed into the van, putting his gun on the passenger seat and hiding it with the coat. Carefully, he drove away. On the top of his van, the little red light kept blinking, which it would do all day because it was a child's toy, not a video camera, and there was no backup around the corner.

He had come away with the money and a bonus. It wasn't a stunt he could pull twice: next time, he might need some extra help.

He was about to turn right on to the roundabout when he saw a figure watching him from the corner. He involuntarily slammed on the brakes and his Kalashnikov slipped off the passenger seat into the footwell, and a loud air horn from the truck behind him told him how close he had come to being rear-ended. When he looked again, the man in the cloak had gone. Clarke took a deep breath and slung his coat over the gun. Then he set off for Putney.

Tom and Kris spent Wednesday going through Niall Brewer's statement and preparing for the following day's interview. Tom had taken out the second of the files from DS Griffin and was looking for inspiration. It eventually came when a memory surfaced, and he told his DC that they were going to pay a sympathy call on the Lynch family. He asked Hayes to make the call, and when she had finished, she stared at the receiver with a puzzled expression.

'What's up?' asked Tom. 'Are we *personae non gratae*?'

'If that means she told me to sod off, then no. Mrs Lynch said she'd been planning to get in touch. Strange.'

The temperature was already below zero when they pulled up outside the Lynch house at six o'clock. The car had barely warmed up on the short journey, and they were still muffled up to their noses when Helen Lynch answered the door. She gave Tom in particular a very hard stare, but invited them into the living room, then disappeared into the kitchen.

'I really am very sorry about Patrick,' said Tom.

'And me,' added Hayes.

Fran looked composed, but obviously wounded. The signs of her real age were visible in the wrinkles around her face, and the grey was starting to show in her hair. From her lack of make-up, he guessed that she was so prone to crying that she'd stopped bothering.

The same could not be said about her clothes or the house. Both were still impeccable, and there was no sign of skimping on the housework. Mrs Lynch nodded at their sympathies and offered them a seat; Helen reappeared with the tea tray.

It was Fran who began the conversation. 'Tell me, Chief Inspector, what do you think happened to Pat? I know what the local cops think and I know what the Coroner thinks, but what about you?'

Tom looked at Helen. Her hair was pulled back in its customary ponytail and she was still wearing the corporate uniform. He said to her, 'Could I trouble you to show me something in the kitchen?'

She frowned, but got up and led him through. When Tom closed the door behind him, she folded her arms. 'What do you want?'

'A simple question, but one I didn't want to ask your mother. Could you show me where she found your father's pills and mobile phone?'

Helen pointed to a corner of the worktop at the end nearest the door to the hall. 'Just there.'

'I know you haven't lived here for a while, but was that his normal place? When I get home, I always put my keys, phone and warrant card in a dish. Is that what your dad did?'

Helen nodded.

'Car keys, too?'

'Not always. He sometimes had to take them to open the front door.'

'But on an average day, he'd come in and go out through the back, and leave his keys next to his pills?'

'Yes.'

'Thank you.'

Tom went back to the living room, where Hayes informed him that there could be no funeral just yet because the cemetery ground was frozen.

'Just what you don't need,' said Tom.

'Tell me about it,' said Fran.

Tom drank some of his tea. 'You know that I'm very much not involved with the MCPS, don't you?' Fran nodded, and he continued, 'So can I ask what they said about his keys being probably next to his phone and pills? Why he would have taken the keys but not the other things?'

'They said that it was "just one of those things". They said that not everything has an explanation. They even started to compare his death to a suicide with no note. "Happens more than you think", they said. My Pat would never have done anything that smacked of suicide.'

'I understand. Pat was a man who knew his mortal sins.'

Helen was about to object, but Fran gave him a smile and said, 'Some of them. He was very good about honouring his mother and keeping the Sabbath. He was less hot on "Thou Shalt Not Commit Adultery".'

'As a detective, I reckon the most likely explanation is that Patrick did take his phone and his pills with him, and that the person who stole his car brought them back here afterwards. Which was a terrible risk. The two questions that follow on are: if he did have his pills with him, why didn't he take one when he had an attack, and why was it so important to bring the pills back here? So, the best way of answering those questions is to find out who your husband was meeting. If you had any idea, I'm guessing that you would have told MCPS.'

Fran picked at something on the sleeve of her jacket. 'Yes. Of course I would.'

'I don't think it was someone he knew well. Someone local – like Kelly, for example.'

She shook her head. 'No. That man would sell his grandmother if he could, but he would have done everything in his power to help Pat if he had an attack. He'd have called 999 himself.'

'Which leaves someone from outside. Someone very keen to cover their tracks. I had someone like that in the back of my car recently. He left a bomb behind and ran off. The day before Pat died.'

Fran coloured red, the blood showing a few tiny broken veins as it circulated. 'I'm sorry. I should have asked how you are. It must have been terrible.'

'It was, but I'll feel a lot better when I catch whoever did it. Tell me, did Patrick ever mention having dealings with someone from Northern Ireland – not Benedict Adaire, but someone from the other side? A Loyalist?'

Fran looked into the past, but shook her head. 'I know he did meet someone a couple of times, but he only talked to Dermot about it. From the look on Pat's face, they can't have been easy meetings. Sorry, I don't know any more.'

'Well, if you think of anything – anything that might help, here's my card.'

Tom put his card on the tea tray and adjusted his position. 'How's Elizabeth?'

Fran shrugged. 'Terrible. Being strong for her is all I've got left now. I've even started to look at her when she's getting changed for bed to see if she's self-harming.'

Tom stole a glance at Helen. The line about *being strong for Lizzie is all I've got left* hadn't gone down too well with her other daughter. He said to Fran, 'I've got a question that I'd be very grateful if you kept to yourself. I know what a small world it can be around here.'

'Go on.'

'St Modwenna's is a very small school. I wondered if Elizabeth had much to do with a girl called Pandora Nechells?'

Fran and Helen exchanged a glance. It was Helen who responded. 'Not if we have anything to do with it. She's bad news, that girl. What are you asking about her for?'

'It's her father,' explained Fran to Helen. 'He's the deputy chief constable.'

'That's right. I've been looking through some of DS Griffin's old cases, and it seems he was called out to a shop in Earlsbury one Saturday morning in the summer. The owner had caught Pandora shoplifting. Do you remember hearing anything about that?'

'No, thank the Lord. Was it in July?'

'Yes. Why?'

'Because Lizzie went through a phase of trying to impress Pandora. Even invited the girl to her birthday party. It didn't last because Lizzie and her real friends just aren't cool enough for the likes of Pandora.' She sighed and waved her hand towards the outside world. 'Do what you like. If it'll help bring us closer to knowing what happened to Pat, I don't care. Besides, Hope lost her father, too.'

'Thank you. We won't take up any more of your time.'

Back in the car, Hayes asked if he really thought the bomber had been with Patrick when he died.

'Him or a friend of his, but I don't think we'll find out from Francesca or Helen Lynch. Let's get you home.'

It was a plain van that brought Clarke's first shipment of new money. He received a call, and the next morning he waited at the lock-up in his Land Rover to keep warm. Right on time, the shipment arrived, and one crate was unloaded from the hydraulic ramp at the back. He used his sack barrow to wheel it into a corner. He recognised the driver – it was one of the men who had extracted him from Four Ashes Farm after the shootout with Croxton. The man didn't say a single word and didn't ask him to sign for anything.

Clarke swapped his thermal gloves for latex ones and levered the top off the crate. There was some straw, and then a collection of Afghan village goods. The craftsmanship on some of the metalwork was exquisite, and he put it aside to take to his father at Christmas. Although the old man had sold up the antique shop some time ago, he still liked to keep his hand in.

Underneath the final layer of straw was the cash. Another half million – but this time in Euros. Damn. He was going to have to go to bloody France in this weather, and he didn't fancy trying to smuggle his AK47 through the Tunnel.

He repacked the crate and locked up. Driving back down the yard, he saw the Kirkham men heading into the farmhouse, just as a florist's van appeared. He pulled up and went over.

'It's for a Mrs Kelly Kirkham,' said the delivery driver, holding out a small but intricate Christmas wreath.

Joseph said, 'Some mistake, lad. We've not ordered that.'

'I did,' said Clarke.

'What?'

'Sign for it, and I'll explain inside.'

Joe took the wreath and they headed inside. While they were taking their boots off, Clarke whispered to him, 'Look, I'm not being funny, but I wanted to make up for the pheasants. You give it to her.'

'No. It's you that needs the Brownie points,' said Joe, and he thrust the wreath into Clarke's hands.

Clarke took it over to the table. Kelly seemed genuinely touched. 'It should last outside until the New Year with all this cold and wet weather.'

Joseph nodded his head. 'We haven't had a wreath on the door since Joe's mother left. Thank you, Conrad.'

Kelly flashed him a smile. 'You're not trying to make David jealous, are you?'

'No, never,' said Clarke. 'For the record, I'm seeing someone, but they're away on business. I hope she'll be back next summer.'

'What's she like? Is it serious?'

'I'd like it to be serious, but she's had a lot going on in her life. And she's a bit younger than me.'

'How young?'

'A bit younger than you, I think. She's twenty-seven.'

Kelly looked at him open-mouthed. He might as well have expressed an interest in her daughter, so aghast was her look. Then she remembered her manners. But not for long. 'If you don't mind me asking, Conrad, how old are you?'

'Thirty-seven.'

She sat down with a bump. 'Oh my God. How long since you've seen her?'

Clarke shifted from one foot to the other. Joseph was giving him an evil grin and said, 'See what we have to put up with? She's like this all the time with her mates. Sit down, lad, before you faint.'

'I saw her in the summer, before I went to Afghanistan, and that was only for five minutes. The last time I really saw her was in the spring.'

'You can't see her like this,' said Kelly, gesturing at him from his shaved head to his socks. 'She'll find someone younger if she comes home to you looking like that.'

'Here,' said Joe, 'leave the poor bloke alone. He got blown up this year.'

Kelly was shaking her head. 'You need a makeover, Conrad.'

He looked at her smooth skin and at her husband's cheerful youthfulness. They had been at school together and were of an age. She was right: Mina already had a new jaw and would soon have new teeth. Behind the curtain of hair, she was a young woman who had once enjoyed a vibrant social life. If she made a full recovery, wouldn't she want to do so again?

'Would the baby's car seat fit in the Land Rover?'

'Yeah. Are you taking me up on the offer?'

'If your husband doesn't mind.'

Joe made an expansive gesture with his hand and that made it somehow worse. Clearly the man thought he was no threat to his marriage whatsoever. It was Joseph who spoke up, 'If you're going out, Kell, can you get that new Christmas tree you've been on about? I've some money for it.'

Kelly nodded.

Clarke said, 'Shall we go to Preston?'

Kelly shook her head. 'No. This is serious business. We're going to the Trafford Centre; anything else would be too little too late.'

Clarke drank his tea and suffered the indulgent gazes of the Kirkham family. Even the baby seemed to pity him.

David Nechells walked into the interview room and looked carefully around him before sitting down. He and Tom studied each other for a second. The one chink Tom could see in Nechells' armour was that this was a man who would have preferred to be in a suit. Apparently, the wearing of uniform on all occasions had been brought in by the new Chief; archive pictures of Nechells showed that he had rarely worn it before. Consequently, the buttons glinted rather than gleamed, the creases didn't go all the way to the top of his trousers, and his belt was doing a little too much work to hold in his paunch.

He was still a deputy chief constable though.

'Thank you for your time, sir. We'll try not to keep you too long,' was Tom's opening remark. He cringed inwardly, but couldn't help himself. As if to reinforce his natural superiority, Nechells waved away his apology like Louis XIV accepting the grovelling of some courtier.

Tom gritted his teeth and went through the formal notices, and then he took a deep breath. 'This investigation requires us to take witness statements from all officers and staff present at the budget strategy day at the Victoria Hotel. Can you recall that day?'

'If I have to. It wasn't my favourite day of the year so far. Just as we're starting to make headway with some of the gangs in Birmingham, and we're getting crucial intelligence on Islamist activities, they tell us that we've got to cut our budgets. Not just cut them but slash them. Makes me wonder whether it's worth applying for chief constable jobs in a climate like this.'

Another way of putting him down. Tom pressed on. 'I understand that the meeting went on rather late and finished at six minutes to eight. Can you talk me through what happened next?'

'I turned on my phone, put on my coat and left the building.'

'Did you get any messages?'

Nechells eyes narrowed and his tone shortened. Ever so slightly. 'Yes, I did. From my wife, wanting to know why she was at our daughter's parents' evening on her own. It didn't go down very well.'

'Did you reply to the message?'

'Why on earth do you want to know that? It can't possibly have any bearing on your investigation.'

'I should have made myself clearer. I don't need to know the contents, just whether you actually spent time composing a text message.'

'Yes, but it was a three-word message – *Sorry. Just finished.*'

'And then what?'

'At that time of night, it takes forty minutes to get to Stourbridge if you put your foot down. I reckoned I'd make it in time to see the last few teachers and go back to the others if there was a particular problem.'

'So you left fairly quickly?'

'Yes. I sent the text, grabbed my coat and put it on as I was heading down the corridor.'

'Did you see anyone else?'

'No – or if I did, I don't remember. I just got out and got into the car. What's this about?'

'I'm sure you don't need me to remind you that DS Griffin, DC Hooper, Dermot Lynch and Robert King were all shot that night, and that I'm conducting an investigation into corruption centred on DS Griffin.'

Nechells became tight-lipped. 'I have nothing to add to what I've said already. The meeting finished, I left, I went straight to St Modwenna's. I spoke to no one on the journey and sent only one message. I have no idea what any of the other officers or staff were doing. Oh … the Chief seemed in no rush. I noticed that.'

'Thank you. That's very clear.' *Of course Nechells would notice what the Chief was doing,* thought Tom. *I'll bet he spent the whole day trying to second guess his boss's views and then pretend they were his own.* Tom moved some papers on the desk and prepared himself for the next question. Nechells didn't show any sign yet that he was ready to go.

'How did the parents' evening go?'

'Fine.'

'It's just that I understand that Pandora can be a bit of a handful.'

'Just come out with it,' said Nechells. 'I know what you're going to say.'

'Then I'll say it. Your daughter was caught shoplifting earlier this year, and the store manager called the police. DS Griffin attended.'

'Yes, he did. And before you say anything, I didn't know what was going on until afterwards. I was down in London visiting my mother that day. She'd just come out of hospital. DS Griffin was on duty when the call came in, and he recognised my daughter's name.' Nechells put his hands on the desk. 'I can only imagine that Griffin thought he was doing me a favour. I didn't ask him to – and to be honest, I would have preferred it if he had sent someone who had no clue who Pandora was.'

'Are you saying that DS Griffin was instrumental in convincing the manager not to press charges?'

'I know that for a fact because my wife told me. Griffin didn't have my mobile number, of course, so he rang home and spoke to my wife. It would have happened with any child of a similar age. She hotfooted it down to the station, and Griffin told the manager that – to save them both the trouble of sorting out the paperwork – he would read the riot act to my daughter.'

It was feasible. The police looked after their own, even when it meant bending the law. Griffin would much rather curry favour with the deputy chief than have to administer a formal caution that would go on Pandora's record. 'And did he read her the riot act?'

'Yes. With my wife present. He scared Pandora witless. She's not as tough as she likes to think she is.' Nechells smiled to himself. 'I rubbed salt into the wound by dragging her back to the shop to apologise. It was a very difficult summer holiday this year, I can tell you.'

'Thank you for being so frank, sir. There's just one more question, for the record. Have you had any other contact with DS Griffin?'

'Yes. There was a major incident a couple of years ago, which I led. Griffin was on the team, and I watched him interview a suspect. He was rather good. I spoke to him afterwards. Other than that, I've nodded to him a few times and we've often been at the same events or in the same presentations.'

'And nothing else.'

'No. I've told you that.'

'You have. That's all, sir. DC Hayes and I will be writing up a statement. As Pandora wasn't charged with any crime, there won't be any need to bring her into it.'

'As you wish, but don't leave her out on my account. I would have preferred it if she *had* been charged.'

The deputy chief picked up his hat and left them to it. Hayes was giving him daggers as he walked out of the room, and Tom was desperate for the man not to look back. As soon as the door had closed, she said, 'Bloody typical. Rich white girl gets away with it. Poor black girl gets a record. It makes me sick.'

'Me, too, but I don't think race had anything to do with it. If Nechells had been black – like Khan, for example – I'm sure Griffin would have done the same.'

'Khan's not black, sir. He's Asian.'

Tom held up his hands in surrender, but Hayes wasn't finished. 'And did you see the way he stared at me? If I hadn't been wearing a jumper, I would have had to move. He kept trying to look at my tits.'

There was no answer to that. After the first few minutes of the interview, Nechells had shifted slightly in his seat so that he was facing Hayes, but Tom thought that he was trying to see what she was writing, not to give her the once-over.

'So ... you don't like him. Do you think he's telling the truth?'

She flicked through her notes for a second. 'Yes, I think he is. At least, I don't think he's telling outright lies. I just get the feeling we weren't asking the right questions. But even if we had, I've no idea whether he had anything to do with it.'

Tom had to agree with her.

After all she had been through at the hands of various maxilo-facial surgeons, Mina didn't think it was possible to have odontophobia, but she did: the thought of walking into the dentist's surgery was almost more than she could bear.

The market square in Cairndale was quite sweet, in sort of grim Northern way. Most of the buildings were old, and she was no architect, but she thought that the grey stone looked quite nice. Except that it was the same colour as the grey sky and the grey cobbles which disappeared under the stalls of the Saturday market.

A small section had been cordoned off in the middle, and a notice from Cairndale Town Council said that the Christmas Tree would be erected there from Monday, and that the lights would be switched on at a ceremony next Thursday featuring the Salvation Army Band. Quite a big event, evidently. She felt an awfully long way from Chiswick as the crowds milled past her. Everyone gave her a wide berth, and at first she thought it was because she was the only non-white person anywhere. Then she realised that they were like that all the time. People up here really were more polite.

Six of them from the prison had been dropped off at the edge of the market, and five of the women had gone to Saturday jobs in various shops. They were all close to the end of their sentences and were being allowed a chance to get a reference from a real employer. 'You'll be rich,' Mina had said in the minibus. 'Even at minimum wage, you'll be on three times your prison rates.'

'Aye, but we don't get it, do we?' responded one of them. 'It's all kept back until we leave. I'm due a few hundred now.'

The prison was very open compared to her last place. There were hardly any searches unless you had gone into the community, apparently, and many of the women had mobile phones. Mina wondered if she should get one. The clock struck ten, and she couldn't wait any longer. The dentist's window had a smile in it. A six foot wide smile made of stained glass. It sent shivers down her spine, and she had been standing with her back to it to avoid looking at the nightmare vision. She turned round, covered her eyes and pushed open the door.

A buzzer sounded in the back, which was good, because there was no one on duty. She could tell that it was a private practice because the curved reception desk was made of polished wood and the carpet was thick enough to soak up most of the sounds. Almost immediately, a young and rather attractive dentist came through to meet her.

'Hello there. I'm Luke Morrison: you must be Mina.'

He held out his hand for a firm handshake, and his smile was a wonderful advert for his own work. Except that, surely, he couldn't do his own dentistry, could he?

'Yes. Mina Finch. From the, erm…'

'HMP Cowan Valley. Yes. That doesn't matter here – I'm only interested in your teeth. Go through to the surgery, and I'll be with you in a minute. It's at the top of the stairs.'

He pointed to the back, and Mina walked up the staircase. She had swapped some cigarettes yesterday for the loan of some skinny jeans, which made her feel quite good about herself, and she opened the door to the surgery with a flourish. A few steps into the room, she sensed someone behind her.

'Hello, Mina.'

'Conrad!'

She whirled round and, without thinking, she threw herself in his arms. He lifted her off her feet, and she buried her face into his neck. He had a new smell. A clean, almost industrial smell with a hint of something metallic; it was the first time he hadn't stunk of cigarettes. He held her off the ground for a long time and then lowered her gently to the floor.

She stood back and brushed her hair away. It wasn't just a new smell. He was wearing a new leather jacket over a chunky-knit sweater and a grey knitted cap. Her eyes travelled down to a smart pair of jeans and new brown brogues. On the way down, her eyes had paused where he was showing just how pleased he was to see her. She felt a response inside her and nearly ripped his new jeans off in the surgery.

The thought of the dentist was like the cold wind at the prison. It ran down her back and she swallowed with fear. 'What are you doing here, Conrad? If anyone finds out, you'll go straight to jail.'

'Aren't you pleased to see me?' As he said it, the little smile twitched up the side of his mouth, and she hit him on the chest.

'Of course I'm pleased to see you. I just don't want you to get in trouble. Where's Luke? Why did he let you in here on your own?'

'Luke, the handsome dentist? He's waiting downstairs until I've finished speaking to my client. As far as he's concerned, I work for Dominic McEwan. Someone had to pay your bills.'

She had to sit down, and the only place was on the dentist's chair. She perched on the edge. 'I thought you were going to be in Kabul for a year. What happened?'

'Finished early. I'm working just down the road near Preston. On a racecourse, would you believe?'

'I'd believe anything of you.'

'I can't be too long, but if I play my cards right, I should be able to see you again. Luke thinks there could be quite a few visits.'

She pulled a face. 'That's like aversion therapy. I don't want to be reminded of the dentist every time I think of you. I'd rather think of other things.'

'Me, too. Look, I've brought something for you. Mr Joshi gave me a call.'

He went over to a cardboard box, and she noticed his limp. It was getting worse, not better, since the last time she had seen him. He put the box next to her on the chair and gestured for her to open it.

On the top was a long-sleeved thick woollen pullover in black: it was so soft it could be cashmere. She held it to her face and then threw it over her head. It came down to mid-thigh and the sleeves were too long, but it would be perfect when the wind blew up the valley. Underneath were two pairs of leggings, some walking shoes and, at the bottom, a package wrapped in tissue.

'What's this?'

'Open it and see.'

She unwrapped the tissue paper to find a deep green kameez tunic with red edging and matching red churidar trousers.

'Are they too much? Will the other girls get jealous?'

'Yes, they will, but only if I wear it. This is going at the back of my wardrobe until I'm released. Thank you. I don't know what to say.'

He leaned down and kissed her on the mouth. He did it very gently, as if her jaw were still in pieces, but she kissed him back hard and put her hands behind his head to lock their mouths together. Under the new pullover, she broke out into a sweat. They separated when she heard footsteps coming up the stairs. Luke was back.

'One more thing,' said Conrad. He lifted a little package from his pocket. 'I had the devil's own job getting these.'

She opened the package and found a thin gold chain. On it were two tiny charms. She had to squint to make them out. One was of Ganesha; the other was of a helicopter. She slipped them into her pocket. They would be going around her neck later.

Conrad kissed the top of her head and opened the door. Luke was waiting outside. Conrad thanked the dentist, shook hands and disappeared downstairs. Mina packed away the clothes, and Luke pulled over a stool.

'I'm just going to take a look today,' he said. 'I've seen the X-Rays and the photographs from your surgeon, but there's nothing like seeing the real thing. When I've done that, I'll give you some options as to how we proceed. Okay?'

She lay back, and he prodded and poked around. A lot. On both sides.

'You haven't been near a dentist in years, have you?'

'There wasn't a lot of point.'

'Well, I think I'll start on the left-hand side. There's quite a bit of work to do there, before we get to the main course. Are you busy on Wednesday?'

'I'll have to check my diary. I'm sure I can fit you in.'

'You went speed dating.'

'Go on. Laugh. You know you want to.'

Kate felt guilty all of a sudden, and for no apparent reason. Just because she had been in Dublin enjoying herself, it didn't mean that her cousin couldn't go speed dating if he wanted – or scuba diving in the Thames, or anything else for that matter. Diana Morton was rolling on the couch laughing, then sat up when she realised that Kate hadn't joined in.

'Kate? What are you not telling us? Who have you been seeing over there while we've been snowed into London?'

'I know. It's terrible – I can't remember seeing so much snow over here. It's more like Yorkshire than the South East.'

'Answer the question. You've been in Dublin a fortnight and you've already scored. What are you like?'

Tom had retreated to the kitchen, as he usually did when the talk turned to their love lives. If only he could actually get a woman back to his flat, he'd be well away. Every woman likes a man who can cook. Well, almost every woman. Kate couldn't care less.

'It was nothing. He's just some guy who's on a break from a relationship, that's all,' she said to Di.

Tom came back and joined them. 'How's the job going? Can you talk about it?'

'This time, I can,' said Kate. 'It's a well-known video games company. They're working on the next instalment of their mega-franchise, and they'd got to first build stage.' The others looked at her blankly. 'That means the combat and movement and stuff are all working. They add other elements after that, piece by piece. Except that someone put the first build on a Dark Web store for sale. It could cost them millions.'

'It doesn't work properly, does it?'

'No, but that's not the point. They are very particular about what information they release ahead of the launch. They want every fanatical gamer to pay full price on release, to maximise their profits. Now they'll have to go back and rewrite the story, so that the final version is different. They've hired me to find out who sold them down the river.'

'I thought you didn't do hard-core hacking,' said Tom.

'I don't. I've been using my detective skills. As well as a bit of judicious electronic eavesdropping. It's all in their contracts – the only place I can't listen in is the toilets. I use spies for that.'

'Are you getting close?'

She gave them an enigmatic smile. 'Wait and see. Anyway, Tom, how are you getting on in Earlsbury?'

He told them all about his case, and at certain points in his story, his hand went unconsciously to his shoulder where the skin graft had been made. He sounded determined and resolute, but for Kate, who had heard the full story in York, he didn't sound at all confident.

She swirled her wine around in the glass. 'Even if you find this confederate of Griffin's, do you think it will lead to your bomber?'

He shrugged. 'Who can tell? All I know is that this is the only line of enquiry I'm allowed to pursue. I can't go looking for the bomber directly: that's the responsibility of Lancashire & Westmorland. They're getting nowhere, by the way. They'll scale down the enquiry when it gets closer to Christmas. The only loose end that's not in Blackpool is Patrick Lynch's death. Do you remember him – the money launderer from Earlsbury?

She nodded, but Diana looked a little vague. 'I remember you telling me about him,' said Kate. 'Do you really think the bomber killed him?'

'There's no evidence for that, but I definitely think he was there when Pat died.'

Kate sat back and considered things. Tom brought out an A4 notepad and a pen.

'What's that for?' said Diana. 'Are we going to play word games or something?'

'Sort of,' said Tom. 'We're going to work on my profile.'

Kate and Di exchanged glances.

'Speed dating was a bust,' said Tom, 'so I'm going to try online dating instead. I need to tap into your vast experience as women to produce the perfect profile.'

'Easy,' said Di. 'Don't tell them you're a copper.'

'And definitely don't tell them you used to be a lawyer,' added Kate.

After the meal and the taxi back to the City, Tom gave Kate a nightcap, and added a few more details about the case that he didn't want to share with his sister. When he went to the toilet, Kate looked in his briefcase and stole the Patrick Lynch file. She'd put it back tomorrow, but she needed to take some notes first. She'd had an idea.

Chapter 11

Earlsbury – Dublin – Cairndale – London
Calais – Hampshire – Southport – Boulogne
Monday – Sunday
6-12 December

The snow at the back of Earlsbury nick had been piled up into little banks, and was already going dirty. The last time Tom had come here, Hayes had intervened to pull the local DCI off him when they got into a fight. For his own dignity, if nothing else, he was going to face them on his own.

He identified himself at the door, and was buzzed into the custody suite. The sergeant recognised him straight away. 'Morning, Inspector. Shall I get DCI Storey down? Then we can sell tickets.'

'It's "Good morning *Chief* Inspector" now. If you're going to sell tickets, I want a bigger share of the purse this time.'

The sergeant grinned. 'How can I help, *Chief Inspector*? I wasn't expecting to see you again after Paddy Lynch cashed in his chips.'

'You know me, Sergeant – always sticking my nose into unwelcome places and upsetting people. It's a good job I love my work.' Tom grinned back.

The grin faded on the other man's face. He moved uncomfortably behind the counter. Tom waited until he was about to speak and said, 'Actually, I really would like you to call in DCI Storey. I need a witness when I talk to you.'

'Me?'

Tom said nothing. Thoroughly unnerved, the sergeant started making the phone call. Tom noticed that the two custody officers had paused in their cleaning jobs to watch the encounter.

'He's on his way,' said the sergeant.

'Good. How many males have you got locked up today?'

'None. They've all been released or transferred to the magistrates' court.'

'Then let's wait for DCI Storey in one of the cells. It's more private.' Tom hooked a plastic chair from the lobby under his arm and walked down to the end cell. Dragging his feet, the sergeant joined him a moment later, and Storey was not far behind.

Tom sat on the chair, and the other two had no option but to sit on the plastic mattress. All of them knew that a whole variety of bodily fluids were spilt on the mattresses every week. *If they've done their cleaning properly*, thought Tom, *it shouldn't be a problem, should it?* He took out a folder.

'Thank you for coming. I'm looking into an arrest that was made last year. In the autumn. What recording system does this suite use for CCTV?'

'We changed over to a hard disk system in January of this year,' said the sergeant. 'It was VCR before then.'

'And would the tapes be available?'

'Unless there is an active case, all tapes are destroyed after one year.'

'I thought as much. Do you remember this arrest, Sergeant?'

He passed over the folder, and the man began to study the contents. Storey peered over his shoulder and appeared to grasp the significance of the documents before the sergeant did.

'No. Nothing. Can't remember it, I'm afraid.'

'Are you sure? Do you get incidents like that often?'

'It wasn't an incident. If the prisoner is restrained or chokes on his vomit or overdoses, then that's an incident. This man was released without charge.'

'And you can't remember if anyone other than the people named on that arrest record were present in the custody suite.'

'I can't even remember what I had for breakfast unless I write it down in my notebook.'

'I see. But you are confident that all the details in that record are accurate.'

The sergeant passed the folder back to Tom. 'I signed it, didn't I? They're accurate. I don't make things up. Unlike some people.'

Tom assumed the latter remark was aimed at him, but he didn't care. 'I may need you to make a witness statement to that effect, but I'll serve the proper notice on you if that becomes necessary. Thank you for your time.'

Tom left the suite, and DCI Storey followed him into the car park. For a fraction of a second, Tom felt the hairs on his neck prickle in case Storey was after another few rounds with him, but the man was more worried than angry. At the end of the first phase of the Griffin enquiry, Tom had insisted that Storey take two weeks' leave. The break seemed to have done him good; the man was no longer on the edge of a breakdown.

'Have you got a second?'

'Of course,' said Tom. 'But if you want more than a second, we'll have to go back inside. It's too cold out here.'

'I take it from that file you showed me in there that the clean bill of health you gave my team is no longer valid in the case of one particular officer.'

'I said that none of your team was involved with Griffin, and I stand by that. As for the man you're thinking of, don't jump to conclusions. People often accuse us of throwing mud around to see if any of it sticks, but we don't actually do that. Don't fall into the same trap yourself.'

Storey nodded and considered what Tom had said. 'You're right. He's a good officer, and I'm still short-staffed. I'll try and forget about it.'

'I really hate to say this, but from what I hear, that staffing level might become permanent. Look, could you do me a favour?'

'What?'

'We don't have Griffin's notebooks for that night – it was too long ago. Could you dig them out, and see if he was working with anyone else on the night of the arrest?'

Storey nodded, and they went their separate ways.

Down in the Dublin basement, not a million miles from where the Easter Rising had met its end, Kate had already discovered two affairs, an illegal betting syndicate, and a man who really, really should come out of the closet. She had also discovered that the guy she slept with last Thursday wasn't on a break from his relationship at all. His wife was away on business, and he was trying to order flowers for her return.

She could see how it might be addictive – peering into the intimate, unsuspecting lives of other people. Perhaps that explained why the Stasi became so powerful: the thrill of eavesdropping was definitely compulsive. So compulsive that she would have to find the source of the leak soon or give up before she became hooked. She had narrowed it down to a small group, and was about to cross another one off the list when she paused to think about what Tom had said. *The answer is in the people, not the paperwork.* She put a question mark next to one of the names instead of crossing it out and took a break upstairs.

Out of the basement, her phone pinged with messages once she was back in range of the mast. One was from her father: *When you next in UK? W'd like to meet. Dad.*

She felt worried. Very worried. Her father was the most stoical man she had ever met: he thought displays of emotion were something you encountered in films, not in real people, and it had taken her years to accept that he was just as cut up about his wife's death as Kate had been about losing her mother. In fact, it was only when she accepted that her mother had been married to the man, had loved him and been loved in return, that she realised what her father had lost.

What if he were ill? What if his silences and absences were trips to the hospital for chemotherapy?

She grabbed a coffee and went back down to the basement.

Assistant Chief Constable Malik Khan sat rigidly in the chair, his gaze fixed on a point above Tom's shoulder.

'Before you begin this witness interview, I would like to register my objection to the presence of DC Hayes. It is my belief that her prejudice against me will jeopardise the investigation, and I would like her removed.'

Hayes sat back as if she'd been slapped. Tom could sense her looking at him in appeal, but he kept his eyes focused on Khan. She had to trust him to deal with Khan. No protest came from Hayes, and if she had protested, he would have gotten rid of her immediately. He waited to see if Khan's gaze would drop down, but it didn't. This was clearly a man with huge self-control.

'You assigned DC Hayes to this investigation, sir. If she was good enough then, she's good enough now. Has she ever made a formal complaint against you?'

'You know she hasn't.'

'Has she ever been subject to formal or informal disciplinary procedures because of her attitude towards you?'

'You know that, too.'

'No, I don't. I know that she was never sanctioned, but that doesn't mean she hasn't been subjected to unofficial guidance. Has that ever happened?'

'No.'

'Then we'll continue.'

'If you insist. I would like you to make a note of my objection.'

'Are you sure? Very well: consider it noted. It will appear at the top of your statement for everyone to read.'

Khan realised he'd made a mistake. He was being petty, probably misogynistic and possibly racist. It wouldn't look good if things went further. The man finally looked down from the wall and made eye contact with Tom. He drew a deep breath and said, 'Perhaps I was getting on my high horse. As this is a witness statement, perhaps we'll let it lie.'

Tom wasn't going to have that, and Hayes deserved a lot better. 'The implication being that if you are arrested, you might object at that point. Sorry sir. I'll be proceeding with DC Hayes wherever it might lead us, objection or no objection.'

'Then get on with it.'

Tom opened the file he had taken to Earlsbury division yesterday. 'As part of our investigation into DS Griffin's affairs, we have been checking all his cases, including those which never came to court.' He held up the file so that Khan could read the name on the front. The ACC had to squint, but was too vain to get out his reading glasses. After a second, he realised what he was looking at.

'In October last year,' said Tom, 'DS Griffin stopped a vehicle being driven erratically, and administered a roadside breathalyser test which proved positive. He arrested the driver and took him to Earlsbury police station, where the reading was entered into the custody system. It was over twice the legal limit.'

Khan clearly knew every detail of what Tom was telling him, but his self-restraint was back in place. The man wasn't going to say anything until Tom posed a question.

'However, when DS Griffin administered the test on the calibrated machine at the station, it blew negative, showing that only a small amount was in the driver's system. He was released without charge. That driver was your younger brother, a local businessman. How do you account for that?'

'I don't need to account for it because it's nothing to do with me. If you asked me to speculate, I would say that because Griffin was a detective not a traffic officer, he wasn't used to the new roadside breathalysers we brought in, and that he administered it incorrectly.'

'It's the obvious implication,' said Tom. 'However, there's something unusual about this case because I actually met Griffin before he was shot. I reckon that Griffin was too lazy to stop a vehicle unless it really was being driven erratically, especially that late at night. We now know that Griffin was bent, to use the common phrase, and it's equally likely that when he tested your brother back at the station, Griffin blew into the machine himself.'

'Even if he did, that's still not my business.'

'Not your brother's keeper, eh?'

'I won't dignify that remark with a response. Nor will I answer any questions about my relative who also works in Earlsbury CID, unless you notify me in advance. He still has a career.'

'Then I'll cut to the chase, shall I? Did DS Griffin contact you at any point on the night that he stopped your brother?'

'No.'

'Did you attend Earlsbury police station on that night?'

'Certainly not. As it happens, I was at home with my wife. I know this because my father called me in a state to say that my brother had been arrested. Before I could contact anyone, my brother himself turned up to explain things.'

'Did DS Griffin contact you about the arrest at any time after your brother had been released?'

'No. And I never contacted him.'

'Never? Your brother is arrested, you are the ACC responsible for Griffin's station and the subject is never mentioned?'

'No. The next time I saw Griffin, I may have nodded to him to show I knew, but otherwise it would have been unprofessional of me.'

'What did your brother say when he turned up? It must have been very late.'

'It was. My wife had gone to bed, and I was up late reading reports when my father rang. My brother came round to see me because the reading at the station wasn't zero. That means he had been drinking – something he promised our father that he would stop doing. Completely.'

Tom closed the file and looked at Hayes. She had been writing furiously and making asterisks next to some of her notes. Her ballpoint pen had bitten into the paper so much that she had been forced to skip some pages, so deep was the impression. Satisfied that she had all the details, she nodded for Tom to continue.

He brought up the budget strategy day, and Khan was much quicker to remember it than any of their other witnesses. Had he been tipped off? Was it a sign of guilt?

'I left about fourth or fifth,' said Khan. 'Niall Brewer was out of the door before I'd stood up, and I think David was shortly after him. The chairman of the police authority and his secretary were next. I left with the other ACC. We were still arguing about whose area should bear the brunt of the cuts.'

'Are you sure? About who you left with, and the order.'

'About the order, no. About who I left with, definitely. We stood arguing in the car park until I saw Evelyn and the FD come out of reception. I didn't want them to spot us, so we got in our cars.'

That was interesting. Very interesting.

'One last question. How many people did you see actually driving away?'

'I saw the Chief's chauffeur-driven car at the front. I saw the HR manager leave. I saw the head of anti-terrorism leave. None of the others. They were either before me or after me.'

Tom wrapped up the interview, and ACC Khan left. Although he had answered all Tom's questions, he had behaved as if the wall were three feet further to his right, and that Hayes was on the other side of it: he never looked at her once.

'Could he have done it?' asked Hayes.

'Yes. All he had to do was sit in his car for a minute, pretending to be on the phone. It was dark, starting to rain, and it was late. No one would have noticed him. He could have just got back out and gone in through the fire door.'

'So we're no further forward.'

'I think we are. We've established that both Khan and Nechells could have done it.'

Hayes coughed and played with the pages of her notebook. She flicked a glance at Tom and said, 'Are you going to include his objection to me in his statement?'

'Yes and no. I'll offer him two versions, and he can choose.'

'Thanks, Tom. That meant a lot to me. No one's stood up for me in a long time.'

'If your boss won't stand up for you in public, he – or she – doesn't deserve following. I reckon Khan will remember that soon, and he won't sign up to that objection. Leonie's coming up on Thursday to see how we're doing.'

'Are you worried that she won't back you up?'

'I don't know. That's the problem.'

The trouble with meeting in the library was that he had to take his hat off. Clarke had worried and fretted in the mirror for some time before deciding that his hair had grown out enough to be presentable. The short fuzz had been become something resembling a crew cut, and consequently his bald patch was becoming more visible.

He wandered among the shelves until he found a table with some space. He unpacked his ledgers and started to get to grips with them again. At half past nine, Mina walked up to the table and asked if the other seat was taken.

Wearing the long pullover he had bought her, she looked even younger than twenty-seven. He wondered again how she could want to be with him now that she was no longer married to a man she didn't love, and no longer a pariah because of her disfigurement. He tried to cling on to Kelly Kirkham's words when they had finished their shopping trip last week: *I can stop you looking middle-aged, Conrad, but I can't make you a teenager again. In the end, she either wants you or she doesn't.* He looked into her eyes, and she mouthed a kiss at him. So far, so good.

'Are you alone?' he said. She nodded. 'Good. The librarians here make so much noise talking to pensioners and children that they can't object to polite conversation. How are you?'

'Okay, considering that I've got a three hour appointment with the dentist. What are you up to?'

'Trying to figure out how to lose £240,000 at the bookmakers.'

'Really?'

'Sort-of. That's my new job. Money laundering via the racecourse.'

She rolled her eyes at him. 'Conrad, I thought you were going straight after last time. I don't want to come out of prison just to attend your trial for passing counterfeit currency.'

He shook his head vigorously. 'No counterfeiting this time. Just basic bookkeeping. Except that's one of the things they didn't cover in pilot school.'

She had put her hand on the table as she leaned forward to talk to him. He stretched out and covered it with his. He massaged her fingers and felt her foot make contact with his leg. His good one, fortunately. She slipped her foot up, but the table was too wide for her to get past his knee. With a cough, she withdrew her hand and sat back. 'Don't,' she said. 'You don't want to get me excited before seeing Luke, the hot dentist. I might not be able to keep my hands off him.'

'I've got a solution for that.'

'What are you suggesting?'

'Have a look at my books. That'll calm you down.'

She snorted with laughter and had to put her hand in her mouth. When she came up for air, she brushed her hair aside and smiled at him. He knew at that moment he would never see anyone more beautiful in his life. Ever.

'Leave them with me,' she said. 'There's a one hour gap in my treatment, and they're not picking me up until two o'clock. You can collect them from the dentist's reception. Now go, before one of the off-duty prison officers comes in and sees me.'

He stood up and slid the books across to her. Bending down to pick up his bag, he kissed the top of her head and said, 'I love you.'

She grabbed his hand and squeezed it. 'Me, too.'

He left the library on cloud nine and went for a coffee, taking an outside seat so he could enjoy a cigarette.

With his cravings for nicotine and caffeine satisfied, he went into the bank. 'Could I speak to someone about opening a business account, please? I'm sorry, but I don't have an appointment.'

'No problem, sir. We're quiet today. I'll give Miss Sheriden a buzz, and she'll be with you shortly.'

He took a seat and nearly fell off it when Miss Sheriden emerged. He had never met her before, but he knew her picture and he could tell from the scars on her face that it was the same person. She introduced herself as Tanya, and that sealed it.

'We can fill in some of the paperwork today,' she said, as she led him through to a private room at the back, 'but we might not be able to open the account if you haven't got the right ID on you. It's the money laundering regulations.'

Clarke coughed. 'Do you get a lot of problems with that? Really?'

'You'd be surprised. It doesn't happen much, but I had a bad run-in with it a while ago.'

She could say that again. Tanya Sheriden had been the girl who pulled the thread that started to unravel Sir Stephen's whole operation. She had brought Morton and Lonsdale down on their backs, and her innocent report had started a chain reaction, leading to seven deaths already. And she'd been beaten up by Croxton. Clarke decided that whatever rate of interest he was offered, Praed's bank would not be the best place to start his new business. And then he realised: if Tanya hadn't spotted the irregularity, he would never have met Mina.

It was clearly an omen of some sort, but he couldn't decide whether it was good or bad … the bank could have his money after all.

'Hello, Tom. I'm Leonie. What's your idea of a good night out?'

He stared at her aghast. She had repeated the first line from his speed dating encounter with Elspeth as soon as she walked into the office. And she had done so in front of Hayes.

Leonie looked at his DC. 'Hasn't he told you yet, Kris? Your boss had a close encounter a couple of weekends ago.'

At least Hayes had the decency to look appalled rather than laugh, though he wasn't sure what she was appalled about — Leonie's indiscretion or the idea of her boss going to a speed dating event.

Tom hated to be po-faced. His mother had accused him of it a lot when he was a teenager, and he'd developed his sense of humour partly as a defence against that, but he couldn't help himself today. 'I had rather hoped that would have remained a private matter,' he said to Leonie.

'Too late for that, Tom. Didn't you notice Number Eight looking at you in a funny way? She's a junior at Bridcutt Chambers, and she knows me of old. She recognised your picture from the paper, and she told me over a drink. Even as we speak, the news is making its way up the M40. I'm surprised that Kris hasn't heard already.'

Tom gave Hayes a hard stare, and she started rummaging in her bag. He suspected she was trying not to laugh.

'Okay, down to business,' said Leonie. 'I've come up here to get a full report and see where we're going with this. Let's have it.'

Tom laid it out for her. Their discoveries about Griffin's involvement with three of the suspects, their interviews, the possible timeline for the phone call and his conclusions about where further evidence might be found. The only things he omitted were the dirt on Niall Brewer and Khan's attitude to Hayes's presence in the interview room.

Leonie had been making notes using a mind map, and at the end of Tom's report she underlined a few things, then looked at him.

'This is good work, Tom. And you, Kris. You've discovered a lot and made no waves. I haven't had a single complaint about you from the Chief. In our game, that counts for a lot. When Ogden gave you this job, I wasn't convinced, but I am now. I completely agree with you that someone from the MCPS senior team made that call to Griffin.'

She doodled again. 'I'm eighty per cent in agreement with you about it being either Nechells or Khan, but that's not enough. The only way you'll get definitive proof is to do a full-on assault of those two: phone records, financial records, family interviews, surveillance – the lot. Trouble is

... it will completely destabilise the Command Team here. And there's still a twenty per cent chance that it's someone else entirely. That's not good enough. I can't support deeper enquiries on the basis of this evidence.'

'Are you closing us down?'

'No, Tom, you're misunderstanding me. I said I couldn't support deeper enquiries, not further enquiries. I won't authorise you to interview either of these men again. You can have a bit longer to dig around the issue. See what you can come up with.'

'And if we can't find anything?'

She sighed. 'This is the bit I really hate. Nechells and Khan are both good coppers in their own way. We know that one of them is probably corrupt, but we can't do anything about it. Our only option is to make sure that we whisper in a few ears if they try for promotion. Otherwise, we have no option but to let them carry on doing their jobs. Don't tell me it stinks: I know that already.'

It was Tom's turn to doodle. She was right in many ways. If Kris had suggested a one-woman crusade against Khan, he would have vetoed it, too.

'How long?' he said eventually.

'End of next week. It'll be nearly Christmas by then. You've had no leave since being nearly blown up. Finish off this case and go home to Yorkshire until the New Year.'

'What about you? Where are you going to be if something breaks and I need authority to act?'

She pulled a face. 'I only got out of Sussex on the back of a farmer's tractor last week, and they're sending me to finish the job. There are still hundreds of homes without power, apparently. I'll be staying in a proper hotel this time.'

She put on a smile. 'I'm off back down the motorway. I'll leave you to tell Kris all about the speed dating.'

When Leonie had breezed out of their office, he turned to Hayes and said, 'Don't. Just don't say a word. Not until later.'

'Me? I wasn't going to say anything. Much.'

Kate sat back and listened to the editorial meeting taking place six floors above her.

'… and I'm telling you that there's no way I'll let Shakira get killed off at the end of the second act.'

'Face facts. She's a liability. There's no romantic interest, and the voice acting is terrible. Partly because the lines are awful. This isn't the nineties, you know. Even if women aren't our target audience, they still expect female characters to sound like women, not adolescent fantasies.'

'Adolescent fantasies are what we are selling.'

'I agree, but adolescents are a lot more sophisticated now…'

The argument rumbled on. The designer who had it in for Shakira was top of Kate's list for being the leaker. Any second now, and he'd dig himself a hole.

'Look. You've read the comments from the first build, and every single one that mentions Shakira is negative. She's got to go.'

Gotcha. Kate rang the Chief Exec and told him the name of the person who had leaked their precious game.

'What? Surely to God, no. He's been with this game since the beginning. He lives and breathes this world.'

'And that's why he leaked it. He was so furious about the storyline that he wanted it out in the open, to force you into making changes.'

'Thank you. Thank you very much.'

'Actually, he's got a point. I've played it a few times, and I agree with him completely.'

'I wouldn't say you're typical of our customers, but thanks. I need to think about this and get back to you. I might need you to help me with the interview.'

'Fine.'

Kate shut down her surveillance system, and was about to start writing her final report when something stopped her. Before she left, there was one piece of hacking she needed to do.

She fired up the special programs that the CIS in-house expert had given her and searched the internet until she found Earlsbury Jaguar Ltd. Surely Patrick Lynch would have bought his car here – it was legitimate, after all. Slowly and carefully, she examined the garage's servers until she found the customer database. The actual contact details were well encrypted, but the vehicle details were almost wide open.

In seconds, she had found the record of Patrick's purchase. Clearly, the number plates would have been changed within hours of his death, but you can't change the VIN. She made a note of the number and logged out.

The chief exec rang back. 'You get him to confess and scare the crap out of him, then I'll let him grovel to keep his job. He can give back some of his share options.'

'Are you sure? If it's known that he got away with it, others might be tempted next time.'

'I know. The trouble is that if we sack him, he'll take half a dozen of my best people with him and start a rival house of his own.'

'You're the boss.'

The west of Britain was due to get a respite over the weekend with some milder Atlantic air, and everyone was looking forward to it. Especially the retailers who had seen their pre-Christmas trade fall through the floor with the bad weather. So were the hospitals, which had seen their business rocket upwards.

Tom and Kris were sitting in A&E because his skin graft was hurting so much, and he was worried that it might be infected. Kris was there partly because she might need to drive the car afterwards, and partly because they could talk there as well as anywhere else.

Tom hated doing it, but he had flashed his warrant card and said he couldn't be in the waiting room. The receptionist agreed to call him when his turn came, so they sat in the multi-faith room. It was the only quiet place.

'It doesn't bother you being here?' asked Tom.

'No. It's only a room. God is with us everywhere we go.'

'Fair enough. What do you reckon? Is there somewhere we can go with our enquiry, or should I just pack it in now?'

'Could you just leave it and walk away?'

Tom considered her question. His eyes wandered round the various sacred objects in the room: all dedicated to an absolute truth about the world, and all mutually contradictory. What they had in common, however, was faith.

'Yes. Because I've done it before. When we found two dead bodies in Essex, and I put the first pieces of the jigsaw together, I knew they'd be back, and they were. I've put another piece together here. You could call it the grass if you want – it's green after all the Irish connections. If I walk away now, they'll drop another piece of the jigsaw into my lap sooner or later. I don't want to waste your time if there's nowhere to go right now … so, yes: I would walk away.'

Hayes was looking at the cross on the table at the end. She turned to face him. 'What puzzles me is this: both our prime suspects are very senior officers, right? So what's in it for them? Griffin was ordered to go to that Goods Yard. He was in the pub enjoying himself, so whoever made that call was the senior one in the relationship. How do they gain from all this? There can't have been that much money sloshing around.'

'That's a very good question. I suppose they might have other DS Griffins dotted about the MCPS area, and other crooks like Patrick Lynch. But then again, when they switched the counterfeiting racket to Earlsbury, they chose Lynch to do it. He must have been their top man.'

'They've been very, very careful. I know that much.'

'They have,' said Tom.

They had been very careful indeed. So careful that he couldn't find a single thing that would implicate Khan over Nechells or Nechells over Khan. His phone went off. He was wanted in triage.

When the doctor made him look in the mirror, he winced. That was the first time he had been forced to confront the reality of his injuries. There was scarring in several places on his back, and the skin graft at the top of his arm was inflamed. The doctor pointed to where his skin was a bright red and said, 'The plastic surgeon worked hard to get that join right. If you don't look after it, it will be a terrible waste.'

That was one way of looking at it, he supposed. From his perspective, unless he looked after the graft, he'd have a huge scar and a tight arm.

'We've caught it in time,' said the medic. 'It should respond to antibiotics, but only if it gets some TLC. Have you got any dressings?'

'Yes. Too many, because I haven't changed them enough.'

'Get these from the pharmacy and take the full course.'

The doctor wrote out a script and passed it to him. He stuffed it in his pocket and thanked them for their time. Outside, he signalled to Hayes that he needed to make some calls. When he'd finished, he threw her the keys to his car, and they climbed in. Hayes enjoyed the feel of the driver's seat and then got them going.

'If you promise not to crash it, you can hang on to it for the weekend.'

'Can I take it to the match tomorrow? We're playing away on an all-weather pitch.'

'If you want to. I'm sure it will impress your teammates.'

'Maybe. It'll certainly hold a lot of them. And the kit. Will you want a lift to the station?'

'Yes, please: but I'm not going to London. I'm going to impose myself on my other sister near Liverpool so she can look after me. She can fill this prescription as well.'

'Nice to have relatives in the trade. Are we back to business on Monday?'

'We are. I had an idea in the chapel…'

'You mean the multi-faith room.'

'… I do. It's about Niall Brewer. He was dropped into it from a great height by someone. Why?'

'To make him a suspect.'

'But it did the opposite. Yes, he's guilty of Misconduct in Public Office, but he's not part of the Jigsaw gang. He wouldn't be grubbing for money like that if he was part of a big criminal network, would he?'

Hayes thought for a moment. 'I suppose not.'

'Then why did we get that anonymous email? Who wanted Brewer out of the picture? Assume for the moment that Khan is guilty.'

'Easily done.'

'Then why would he want Brewer cleared of suspicion? It would make more sense if all three of them were suspects. Less chance of us finding the real villain.'

'I like that. It's good. So how do we find out who's got it in for Brewer?'

'When Juliet Porterhouse emailed me that information, she didn't send all of it, I'm sure. She's going to be up north this weekend, so I'm seeing her on Sunday evening for a drink.'

Hayes turned her eyes off the road for a second. 'Is she your type?'

'Knock it off, Constable. Not every encounter with members of the opposite sex is about, well, sex.'

'It's funny you should say that, sir … because I've usually found exactly the reverse.'

Clarke pulled up outside a house in west London and knocked on the door. It was large by London standards, but not so large that the owners had been forced to convert it into flats. He understood that the occupants were on a massive flat-sharing arrangement. It took quite a bit of hammering on the door before a bleary-eyed young woman answered in her dressing gown.

He did a double-take and supposed that, for most people, it was early. For most young people, it was very early on Saturday morning, especially if they'd had a good Friday night. *I've gone native*, he thought, *I'm keeping farmer's hours and going to bed early*. Still, it meant that the roads had been empty. His new van was actually faster on the motorway than the Land Rover.

The young woman raised an eyebrow through the crack in the door. 'Can I 'elp you?'

'*Je cherche Alain*,' said Clarke in what he knew was a terrible French accent. The woman tutted and opened the door wide.

'Upstairs on the right,' she said, and disappeared back into her room.

Clarke took the stairs slowly after the long drive and tried to ease the pain in his leg. Instead of waking any more of the residents, he knocked lightly on the door (helpfully labelled Alain Dupont) and went in.

Alain was alone. If he had a girlfriend, she hadn't stopped the night. The man himself was sitting on the edge of the bed. 'Oh! I thought I heard the door. You must be Georges.'

'George, yes. George Baxter. Do you want me to wait outside while you get dressed?'

'If you go downstairs, there is a lounge and kitchen on the left. Put on the kettle.'

Clarke limped back down and found a communal sitting room filled with bottles, pizza boxes, and two ashtrays.

That was good. He put the kettle on and started to make coffee.

'*Non*! Not that one. Amélie will kill me if her coffee is gone. You must use that one,' said Alain from the doorway.

Clarke did as he was bid and served them two disgusting cups of coffee (*Amélie must have taste*, he thought). He offered Alain a cigarette, and the young Frenchman accepted.

'I was not expecting you until later.'

'Sorry to wake you up, but I had a good journey and thought I'd see you first. If it works out, I can go away and pick you up later. When you've packed and had a shower.'

'Okay. When you offered me the job, you said that I had to pass a final test.'

Clarke nodded and started looking in his pockets for the test paper.

At the end of his meeting with Tanya Sheriden at Praed's bank, she had given him an idea. One of her final questions had been about whether he needed foreign currency facilities for his business, and Clarke, thinking of his impending foreign exchange mission, had said that access to a French translator would be good.

'Try social media.'

Clarke was allergic to social media. Anything which required him to put his name online was anathema to a man like him, but Tanya had shown him, in seconds, how to contact some of the huge French expat community in London.

He gave it some thought and, from an internet café, he had created a profile for George Baxter, and had found four students willing to do a weekend's work for a healthy cash reward. Clarke wanted a native French speaker, but he had to be sure that his new resource could speak idiomatic English. Hence the final test.

'Translate these for me,' said Clarke.

Alain looked at the phrases. 'Where are we going? Most of these words are what you call obscene.'

'Are they? Sorry. I didn't mean to upset you. Do you know what they all mean? Because I have no idea. Someone must be playing a trick on me.'

'I know them all, but I've never used them in English. Well, only once, at a football match.'

'Good man. You've got the job.'

Clarke stood up and took out some of the Euros he'd been delivered. They would count as expenses. 'As promised, here is half the fee in advance. I'll cover your hotel bills as well, of course. Right. I'll see you at twelve o'clock.'

The student looked at the money. When it was in his hand, a small shadow of doubt crossed Alain's unlined face. Clarke stuck out his hand, and the shadow disappeared. Alain would be learning several lessons on this trip. One of them was that online profiles are very easy to fabricate. If only it were as easy to produce a passport in the name of George Baxter as it had been to create the man's profile. Clarke went back to the van and started searching for brunch.

On the way down to the Channel Tunnel, he tried to make as much conversation as possible. He quite enjoyed creating Baxter as he went along. The more Alain believed he was talking to a genuine (if shady) character, the more likely he would be to do as he asked. The only questions he wouldn't answer related to the job Alain believed he was doing. At one point, Clarke even told the truth.

'Did you never learn French at school?' asked Alain. 'Most English people can speak it a little, even if they are too embarrassed to do it in public.'

'I did German. I thought it would be more useful for my career.'

'And was it?'

'Yes. Up to a point.'

When he was a teenager, Clarke's mother had told him that most British servicemen spent long periods stationed in Germany, waiting for the Russians to invade. Either that or in Northern Ireland. By the time Clarke's GCSEs were approaching, the Berlin Wall came tumbling down. He had still spent a lot of time in Germany, though. Until Iraq, of course.

'So why are we going to France if your career is in Germany?'

'I was made redundant in the credit crunch. I've got to take work where I can get it.'

'Okay.'

When they got through Kent, Clarke said, 'It would be better for you if you travelled alone. I'll drop you in Ashford and pick you up at Fréthun station in Calais.'

Alain was surprised, but his question was encouraging. 'Better for me?'

'Yes. For you. Here's the fare, and here's a mobile phone. I'll call you as soon as I'm near.'

Alain said nothing after that but simply got out and disappeared at the station. There was a small chance that he might alert the authorities, but that was a much bigger risk than Clarke approaching the French dealers on his own. Not that Alain would be going anywhere near them. Clarke had promised Ganesha that M Dupont's life would never be at risk.

There were no police at Fréthun to intercept him, and Alain climbed into the van as if nothing had happened. 'It's good to smoke again,' was his only comment.

Clarke drove to Boulogne and dropped his passenger at a motel. He gave him another hundred euros and said, 'I'll see you at three o'clock tomorrow afternoon by the Stade de la Libération. On the cemetery side; you'll find it easily. Enjoy yourself.'

Another reason for choosing Alain was that he was from the south of France. He might take in a movie or go to a bar, but he wouldn't be visiting any friends tonight.

Clarke had researched the area and, if Google Earth was to be believed, he knew where he might find the right spot. He drove past tomorrow's meeting place and parked half a mile beyond. It was getting dark and very damp underfoot as he climbed over a fence into a small wood. Once inside, he pushed through to the far end. Perfect. He watched the target for a while and then retraced his steps.

Kate was almost the only passenger on the Sunday morning flight from Dublin. Her head was throbbing by the time they landed, as she sobered up from last night's celebrations, and she vowed to steer clear of whiskey chasers the next time she drank Guinness. The cold air of England blasted away the Celtic cobwebs, and she turned the heater up on the drive to Hampshire.

Her father gave her a bigger hug than normal, and barely gave her time to put her bag away before he hustled her down the road to his local pub for Sunday lunch. He had even reserved a table. She examined him closely when they met and decided that he looked healthier than she had seen him in years. If he was having chemotherapy, there was no sign of it. Nor were there any shakes, spasms or uncertainty in his movement. She had to lengthen her stride to keep up with him, as she'd been doing all her life.

'It's very Christmas-y in here,' she said. 'Much more festive than Dublin.'

'It's the landlord. Two years ago he bought a load of stock when the other pub in the village closed down. He's the sort of man who never lets anything go to waste. Mind you, there's a good reason why the other place went bust and this one is still thriving. He knows his market, and he gives us what we want. Shall I get us a bottle of wine?'

'Go on.'

While they waited for their food to arrive, her father asked a lot of questions about her work for Anthony Skinner. She left a few names out, but told him most of what had happened.

'You're asking a lot of questions for a change,' she said.

'Didn't need to before: I know the CO of Military Intelligence very well. He always told me what you were up to.'

That figured. Her father was a lecturer at Sandhurst and still very much part of the military establishment.

He rearranged the cutlery on his place setting and asked her if she thought she would make a go of what she was doing.

'I think it's too early to tell. I enjoyed the work in Dublin, but there may not be an indefinite supply of that. You know me, Dad. I enjoy a challenge, but I like the security of a place to fall back on.'

'Me, too. If I hadn't got this job at the Royal Military College, I don't know what I would have done. That's the best and worst thing about the Army.'

'Don't worry about me. I'll be alright.'

'I know you will.'

The food arrived, and her father waited until they were nearly finished before coming back to the subject. 'There was another reason for me asking how you were getting on, you know. A selfish one.'

She put her knife and fork down. Her father was staring at his roast beef. She put her hand out and said, 'Dad, is everything alright? You're not ill or anything?'

He laughed. 'God, no. Just the opposite, in a way.' He put his cutlery down too, but still couldn't meet her eye. 'The thing is, Kate ... I wanted to be certain you'd made the transition away from the regular Army before I said anything to you, and now I know you'll find your way, I want to tell you about some changes in my life.'

He finally looked up and said, 'They're going to be big ones. I'm retiring from the RMC, I'm leaving Hampshire, and I've met someone.'

If she had been holding her cutlery she would have dropped it. Instead, she sat with her mouth open.

'Come on, girl. Spit it out,' said her father.

'Dad! I don't know what to say. Well, I'm thrilled for a start. Really thrilled. But I'm shocked too. Here, give me a kiss.'

To her father's utter mortification, she stood up and leaned over the remains of their food to give him a big kiss on the head.

'First things first. What's she like? How did you meet? How long have you been at it, and where are you going to live?'

Her father chose to finish his meal rather than answer her questions. Like the landlord of the pub, he never let anything go to waste. Whoever he was seeing, she must have the patience of a saint. Kate pushed her plate aside and waited.

He dabbed his mouth with the napkin and leaned towards her. 'If you look at the bar, you'll see two women talking to an idiot with a moustache. Janet is the one with the brown hair. If you're happy to meet her, she can join us for dessert, and you can ask her those questions yourself.'

Kate topped up her glass and drained half of it in one go. Janet had her back to where they were sitting (deliberately, she guessed), and all she could tell was that her father's new woman was neither too old for him nor too young, neither too fat nor too thin.

'I'd love that. Are you sure she won't mind getting the third degree in public?'

'She's been pressing me to introduce you almost since our first date. She's divorced with two children of her own. She can look after herself.'

'Then bring her on. I'd love to meet her. But can I ask you something else first?'

It was his turn to frown with concern. 'What is it?'

'It's Tom.'

The frown disappeared to be replaced with her father's default expression of … well, nothing. It was how he navigated any situation with emotional implications. He admitted that he had abandoned her to the Mortons when she was a child, but he wasn't sure whether they had been an entirely good influence on her. 'Go on,' he said. 'That bomb was a serious business. Raised a fair few eyebrows in the mess.'

'He's made a good recovery, but he's out of the loop on the investigation. Did you read the piece in the *Sunday Examiner*?' He nodded. 'It's true about the Irish connection. I want to do some digging, and I wondered if you could point me in the direction of someone with a background in Northern Ireland. Someone who's not connected to Anthony Skinner's outfit.'

'Are you sure? These can be very dangerous waters.'

'I'm sure. Tom needs my help. He's been there for me and I can't let him down.'

'In that case, there's only one person to speak to: Colonel Shepherd. He hates Skinner, but he spent a long time in Belfast.'

Kate nodded to herself. Colonel Shepherd was one of her own. Ex-Military Intelligence and one-term Member of Parliament. 'Does he still live in his old constituency, do you know?'

'He does. A village outside Cairndale, I believe.'

'Thanks, Dad. That means a lot. Right. Go and tell Janet it's safe to come over. And get another bottle of wine as well.'

Alain seemed fairly relaxed when Clarke picked him up on Sunday afternoon. He said he'd been to a live music venue the night before and had had a good long sleep afterwards.

Clarke drove the van along the back way and arrived at the spot where he'd cut the fence at the end of last night's reconnaissance. He'd been shopping this morning and gave a carrier bag to Alain. 'We might be a while outside, and it's going to get cold. Put these on.'

Alain looked dubiously into the bag and pulled out a thick coat, hat and scarf. There were some woollen socks and gloves, too. All were in black, but that was what Alain was wearing anyway. He shrugged and did a quick change.

Clarke picked up a rucksack and said, 'Follow me.'

There were no complaints as they went through the woods; Alain must have got himself thoroughly mellowed-out to be doing this without asking questions. They approached the vantage point, and Clarke signalled for Alain to slow down and be quiet. They crept forwards until they had a good view of the factory below, where Clarke was due to meet the dealers. He pointed out the spot and then retreated back.

When they were out of sight, he took off the rucksack and moved closer to Alain. The student backed off a pace.

'Here are your instructions. Are you listening?'

'Of course. What are we doing in the woods? I can't talk to the trees, you know.'

Clarke clapped him on the shoulder. 'Good man. That's the spirit. Now listen. You will wait over there for one hour at least. I will call you on the phone when I am ready. You must have it on silent. The line must stay open. Understand?'

Alain nodded.

'Then I'll drive up and we'll wait again. If you see anybody in the woods or hiding behind the buildings, you must tell me straight away. Understand?'

Another nod. By now the fear was visible in his eyes and spreading across his face.

'Another van or cars will come along. When the men get out, you must translate everything they say to me and everything they say to each other. If I whisper, instead of speaking loudly, that means I want you to translate for me. Do it slowly, okay? Now, this is the most important part.'

Clarke opened his rucksack. 'Take these.' He handed over a torch, a pair of binoculars and something he'd picked up in London after brunch yesterday when he'd made a trip to a specialist electrical retailer. It wasn't the sort of gear you could get on the Fylde peninsula. 'If I raise my right hand and point, you must use this on the same man I'm pointing to.'

Alain was shaking his head. 'I am not using a gun. No.'

'It's not a gun. See?' He demonstrated on a nearby tree.

'*Non.* No. I did not agree to do this.'

'Think of the money, Alain. Think of how much you'll get when this is over.'

'No. I'm going home. I don't care about the money. You can have it back.'

Alain started to fumble in his pockets, but Clarke put his hand on Alain's shoulder again. 'Stop. Listen.' Then he repeated the phrase he'd been practising all night, '*Je sais où tu habites. Je sais où habite ta mère. Je sais où habite ta soeur. Et mes amis le savent aussi.*'

Clarke had no idea where Alain's mother or his sister lived, and he had no friends to back him up. But, from social media, he had learned that Alain was devoted to his mother and his sister, and that his father was dead; it's easy to give your life away when you sign up to Facebook.

Alain had gone white. Clarke lit two cigarettes and gave one to the terrified Frenchman. Alain smoked it and then called Clarke something awful in French that he didn't understand. When Alain had got it out of his system, Clarke said, '*Fini*. Enough.' And he raised his finger to Alain's face. The other was silent.

'Good. No more smoking now. Don't use the torch until I tell you. Go on: get in position.'

Alain stubbed out his cigarette and went back to the vantage point. Clarke knocked the end off his smoke and put the butt in his pocket. No sense in leaving DNA around.

He drove away from the woods and waited for the clock to tick round. The sun had gone down, and street lights were flickering into action when he called Alain.

'Is everything clear? No one arrived before me?'

'*Non*.'

'Good. How are you feeling?'

'What do you care, you bastard?'

'I care a lot, Alain, because I might die if you screw this up. Believe it or not, I'm trusting you.'

There was no reply. Clarke drove away from the country lane where he'd parked and on to the access road for the factory. The woods where Alain were waiting rose steeply ahead of him, and the meeting place was in the factory's car park at the back. If you didn't know it was there, you'd never find it.

Clarke reversed his van up to one of the three lights that provided illumination. With the steep slope behind him, it was effectively night-time already. He got out of the van and made his final preparations. Instead of the child's toy in his fake air vent, there was now a wide area microphone and another one up his left sleeve, Secret Service style. He fitted the earpiece under his hat and pulled an eyepatch over his left eye.

His right arm wasn't in the sleeve of his coat. On a sling over his shoulder, the Kalashnikov was dangling. *It's a very big gun, not easy to conceal or deploy from a covert position*, he thought, *I'll have to get myself a pistol*. On the other hand, it is very impressive. The final adjustment was to his Kevlar vest.

He made another check that the communications were working and lit a cigarette.

'Why can't I have one?' said Alain.

'I want you to have both hands free.'

Halfway through his smoke, Alain said, 'I can see lights coming this way.'

Two vehicles came round the corner. In front was a black pickup and behind it a hot hatch. From the smaller car came aggressive music that pounded its way through the gloom. They swept on to the tarmac and parked facing him, leaving their headlights on main beam on to blind him. The car was beyond his van to the left and the pickup to his right. At least the music stopped.

Clarke whispered into his sleeve. 'I can't see properly. What's happening?'

'Three guys just got out of the car. They're standing with their hands inside their coats.'

The pickup turned its lights off. A heavily-set middle-aged man wearing a coach's jacket emblazoned with PSG got out of the truck and walked towards him, stopping about ten feet away. Clarke nodded to him. '*Vous êtes Pierre?*'

'Yes,' said PSG-man. 'Give me the keys, and we won't shoot you.'

Clarke used his left hand to take the keys out of his pocket. He held them up and jingled them with a *Come and get me* gesture.

Pierre jerked his chin upwards and said, 'Throw them here.'

Clarke jingled the keys again then put them back in his pocket. He slowly opened the right hand side of his coat to reveal the AK-47, and lifted his arm to point at the Paris Saint-Germain logo. He held his breath until Alain did his job, and a red laser dot appeared on the man's chest.

Would Pierre call his bluff? It was a genuine laser targeting device, but Alain didn't have a sniper's rifle up there.

The dealer opened his mouth to shout something, and to Clarke's utter amazement, a second red dot appeared, much lower on his body. Pierre didn't notice that one.

The first dot, the one presumably controlled by Alain, started to waver alarmingly, and the Frenchman took his chance. '*A droite!*' he screamed to the others and he started to dodge to his left.

And then three things happened at once.

First, Alain shouted, 'They're coming to your left with guns!' Then Clarke shrugged the coat off his right shoulder and raised the Kalashnikov, and at the same moment, the French leader collapsed in a heap, clutching his right knee.

Clarke had to take his first two shots standing up because the van would have blocked him. Looking straight at the headlights of the car, he shot them out in turn. From beyond the van, pistols were fired – and one shot slammed into his chest, knocking him over as the Kevlar absorbed the impact.

In the sudden darkness after the lights went out, the shots stopped. Clarke rolled to his left, ripping off the patch and closing his right eye. For a second, he had the advantage of night vision and used it to peer under the van.

If the three shooters had carried on round the vehicle, he would have been at their mercy. Instead, he had a chance to aim at their legs, and used it to fire three single shots. One hit home and blew apart the man's ankle. His colleagues scattered.

'Where are they?' he shouted to Alain.

'One coming to your left.'

He rolled on to his back and got a clear shot as the man rounded the van, hitting him in the stomach before he could raise his gun.

'Behind you.'

Clarke was flat on his back. He couldn't move in time, so he pointed the rifle over his head and fired on automatic. As he did so, a pistol shot ricocheted off the tarmac six inches from his head.

None of his bullets hit the third gunman, but they did their job. There was no more pistol fire. Instead, Clarke heard the car door open and slam shut. He rolled to a crouch and prepared to duck away, but the other man had had enough. The engine roared and tyres squealed as he fled the scene.

Clarke ignored the man he'd shot in the stomach: if he wasn't dead already, he would be very soon. The other two would be in agony – but in combat, adrenalin will allow you to do things that seem impossible afterwards. Either of them could be picking up a gun right now.

And that was exactly what Pierre was trying to do. He couldn't roll on to his right side because of the damage to his knee, and that allowed Clarke to slip the AK-47 off his shoulder and use it as a club to knock the other man's gun out of his hand.

Shouldering his weapon, he moved round the van in a crouch to find the third man trying to stem the bleeding from his ankle. He had dropped his pistol when he fell, and Clarke picked it up as a souvenir.

He stood up and then crouched back down again, because his own adrenalin levels had obscured the pain from where he'd been hit on the vest. He took a deep breath and straightened up slowly. In his left ear, he heard a shout, followed by Alain saying something in French.

'What's the matter? Are you okay?'

There was silence then Alain said, 'Georges, there is a man here with a big gun. He says he is a friend of yours.'

'Can you see his face?'

'*Non*. He is wearing a mask.'

He offered a silent prayer of thanks to Ganesha. Alain couldn't be a witness and might be spared. 'Give him the phone and don't do anything stupid.'

'Hello, *Georges*,' said Will Offlea.

'I don't know whether to thank you for saving me or damn you for setting me up. Twice.'

'Twice?'

'Mohamed at Heathrow.'

'Bad luck. Nothing to do with me, though.'

'What's going on here, you prick?'

'Is Pierre alive?'

'Yes. Good shot on his knee, by the way.'

'Thanks. Give him your phone.'

Clarke took a moment to sort himself out. He placed the rifle on the top of the van and put his coat on properly. He dug out the pistol he'd confiscated and grunted in satisfaction. It was a French police model SIG and would do very nicely. He checked the clip and then pointed it at Pierre. Finally, he dug his phone out of his pocket and handed it over.

He heard both sides of the ensuing conversation through his earpiece. He heard it, but he didn't understand a word. Offlea was in France for a good reason: he spoke the language like a native. Even so, Clarke could tell an argument when he heard one.

While waiting for them to finish, he slipped on some latex gloves and picked up the other two pistols. He ejected the clips, cleared the chambers and chucked the guns into the night. The man he had shot in the abdomen was dead. The one with no ankle left had made a tourniquet, but it wasn't working. Clarke found a stick and showed the man how to twist it inside the bandage to halt the blood flow.

Eventually, the stream of French stopped, and Pierre shouted, 'Come.'

He collected his phone from the Frenchman and Offlea said, 'Pierre's going to play nicely. We'll rendezvous at the hospital. Just take the road into town and follow the big red H signs. I'll bring Alain.'

'You better had. How are the Frenchmen going to get there?'

'Reinforcements are on the way. You'd better get out before they arrive and start shooting.'

The last time he had met Juliet Porterhouse, Tom was so preoccupied about getting back to work that he hadn't really noticed her as a person. Would he recognise her in the pub if she were dressed up for a night out? In fact, wasn't she wearing a hat when she sat in his mother's hall? Yes, she was.

He needn't have worried. From the other side of the Lounge Bar, she waved at him and came over to give him a metropolitan air kiss. At least she seemed genuinely concerned about his injuries and was quick to offer him a drink.

'I've had a bit of relapse with my skin graft,' he said, 'and I'm on antibiotics. Luckily, my sister's a GP and she said the ones they gave me are quite safe with alcohol. I'll have a pint of Lancaster Bomber, please.'

'Is that a joke?'

'No. It's a very nice pint of bitter, considering it comes from the wrong side of the Pennines.'

She went up to the bar, and he settled down in the corner. Without her hat, she looked a little older than he thought. Fifty plus? Something like that. She would be about the same age as Francesca Lynch, he supposed, but didn't spend as much on her appearance — neither at the hairdresser's nor the plastic surgeon's. On the other hand, Juliet hadn't just come through a double family tragedy. Not that he knew of.

Juliet was casually dressed in jeans and a cardigan, but she moved with a confidence that came from succeeding in a man's world. He had chosen a fairly quiet pub on the outskirts of Southport where no one was likely to recognise him as Fiona's brother. Everyone else was engrossed in their own business and didn't give them a second glance. He relaxed a bit, and relaxed a bit more after he'd taken a sip from his pint.

'I'm not dragging you away from your family, am I?' she asked.

'They deserved a break from me. I've left them watching *I'm A Celebrity – Get Me Out of Here*. Good luck to them. What about you? Why are you up here?'

She pulled a face. 'My paper is very anxious to let the government know that they have to make deep cuts in public spending. They've sent me up here to look at local council budgets and how they're responding to the proposed grant settlement. You're losing interest already, aren't you?'

'Does it show?'

'Yes. Not that I blame you. It's going to have a good headline though – *Ripe for the Plucking. How Councils are STILL wasting YOUR money.*'

'Bit of a change from the Blackpool bombing and IRA connections.'

'I was lucky with that story. The *Sunday Examiner* is reinventing itself as a seven-day internet-led news organisation. I happened to be on call when the story broke.' She shrugged. 'I don't often get a quiet drink with a chief inspector, even if I did have to come all the way out here for the privilege. What's up?'

Juliet had finished her second glass of wine, and judging from the size of the glass, it had as many units of alcohol as his pint. He hoped she wasn't driving. 'Would you like another before I get started?'

'Go on.'

He fetched her drink and considered his words carefully. 'It's about that email you sent me.'

'I thought it might be.'

'All the financial information was in a spreadsheet, but it came from two different banks. I looked a bit more closely: it was you who created and completed the spreadsheet. I think the information was genuine – don't get me wrong – but I don't think it was delivered to you like that.'

'You're not a detective for nothing, are you?'

He rolled his eyes. 'Please, no. My brother-in-law has said that five times already this weekend.'

'I won't say *it's a fair cop*, then.'

'No. Don't. Just tell me whether you received the information in a different format.'

'Of course I did. Now we get to the interesting part. Why do you want it? If it was just confirmation you needed, I'm sure you could get a warrant in no time.'

'I could. It's a bit more complicated than that.'

She played with a drip mat, flipping it over a couple of times. 'None of the other papers are anywhere near this story. I can afford to wait a bit before I do anything with it. Especially if there's more to come.'

'I hope there is. You know I can't give you an exclusive. Anything I do concerning an arrest will be public knowledge, and I can't offer you access to any dawn raids because there won't be any.'

'If you gave me an off-the-record background interview it would make a huge difference to me. I'd get priority on the story, probably get it in the daily edition, and get a cut of the syndication rights.'

He thought back to his discussion with Kris in the multi-faith room at the hospital. All religions require faith and trust. He was going to put his trust in Juliet.

'I can tell you that Niall Brewer is no longer a person of interest in connection with my main investigation. I can also tell you that I'll either be making an arrest this week or going back to London to lick my wounds.'

She pulled a face.

'Sorry. That sounds a bit literal, doesn't it?' he said.

'Yes. Not a nice image for a Sunday evening.' She leaned in towards him. 'But you're telling me that there's something in those accounts that could ruin Niall Brewer? Something to do with maintenance payments, I think.'

'You're getting warm. Very warm.' It was his turn to lean in. 'Now tell me, what format did the bank records come in? If I use a warrant to get bank records, the printouts have the name of the force across the top.'

Juliet took a sip of wine and kept him waiting for a few seconds. 'That's what puzzled me. The records for Brewer's ex-wife were on MCPS headed paper, but the name of the requesting officer, the reference number, and all the account details had been blanked out. The ones for Brewer's account were screenshots of his own online banking pages.'

Tom sat back. That was what he wanted to know, all right. It pointed the finger very firmly in one direction. 'Thank you. That's very interesting.'

'Do you want me to send you the originals?'

'No. Then I'd have to enter them as evidence then.'

Juliet sat back too and finished her wine. She gave him a playful smile, and that's exactly what she had done. Played him. When she saw him in York, she must have made a very quick character judgement and decided that he wasn't the sort of copper who would be heavy handed with her. By releasing the details slowly, she had hooked him and reeled him in like a fish. He finished his pint and said, 'Where are you staying?'

'A new hotel by the docks in Liverpool. It's nice down there; I didn't realise how much it's changed.'

'Do you fancy another drink? Then I'll order you a taxi.'

She opened her mouth to protest and realised he was serious. 'You're going to make me leave my car out here, aren't you?'

'Yes. There are regular trains from Lime Street in the morning, so you can come back for it. There's something else you should know as well.' He leaned forward and whispered to her. 'Some of my best friends are tax inspectors.'

She snorted with laughter. 'It's a fair cop. I'll take a taxi and fill in my tax return on time. Same again?'

When she returned with the drinks, he asked about her life. She told him that she had just finished divorcing her second husband. She was getting more work at the paper now that her youngest child had gone to university. 'God help her, though. There's not going to be any decent jobs when she graduates.'

'Can you tell me something? Has your paper ever run any features about online dating?'

After he saw her into the taxi, he stood in the cold, waiting to see if she had told the driver to go round the block and return for her car. While he was waiting, he sent a text to Hayes: *We have a new suspect. See you tomorrow. Tom.*

After five minutes, satisfied that the roads were safe from Juliet's driving, he took a taxi himself back to Fiona's house.

There were more cars coming out of the hospital than going in. Clarke drove round for a while until a black Jaguar with GB plates came in and chose a spot under one of the lamp standards. Instead of the usual soaring clusters of lights, they were short and stubby. Must be a helipad nearby.

Clarke pulled his hat down and hunched into his coat when he got out. Offlea stood tall and proud next to his own vehicle.

'Won't you be rather obvious on the CCTV?' asked Clarke.

'Welcome to France. They have hardly any of it over here. Civil liberties and privacy are a much higher priority in this country. They wouldn't want Big Brother clocking them every time they went to see their mistresses.'

'Good for them. What happened tonight, Offlea? Why did the French come mob-handed, and why were you lurking in the bushes?'

'I thought Pierre might try something stupid when he heard I was out of the picture. Mohamed did, didn't he? If I'd broken my cover and contacted Pierre first, he would have tried to kill me, and that would have been messy. This way, he's learned his lesson, and we can finish the business.'

Clarke shook his head and sighed. He didn't want to take the Kevlar vest off yet, just in case there was more trouble, but every time he took a deep breath a pain stabbed through his left ribs.

'You nearly spoilt everything with your man and his wee observation post, you know,' said Offlea. 'He'd taken the best position, and I had to go around. I nearly didn't arrive in time.'

'If I hadn't recruited Alain, what were you going to do when they arrived?'

'Give Pierre a call. Tell him he was in my cross-hairs.'

'You stupid idiot. You were going to leave me standing around four armed men, *and you were going to call him on the phone?* What if he didn't answer?'

'I'd have fired a warning shot, Conrad, sure I would. Look out: here they come.' Offlea pointed to the entrance, and Pierre's pickup truck drove towards them. He started to get into the Jaguar.

'Did you talk figures with Pierre?' asked Clarke.

'Yes: £340,000 for half a million Euros.' Offlea shut himself in the car, and Clarke stood with the van between himself and the approaching pickup. He took out the SIG and held it down.

The truck stopped with its bed towards the back of his van. In the front, he could see Pierre and the man with the tourniquet in the passenger seats.

The driver got out and lowered the tailgate. There was a cardboard box on the bed, which he picked up and dumped on the floor. The expression on his face was one of combined fury and hatred. Clarke opened the back of his van and pointed to the suitcase containing the euros. He couldn't lift it and hold on to his gun; the pain in his ribs wouldn't let him. Reluctantly, the driver swapped the box for the suitcase and closed the van doors. Before he got in the pickup, he spat on the floor.

'Another Waterloo, eh?' said Clarke loudly. He just couldn't resist it. The pickup drove away, heading for the entrance to casualty.

Offlea got out again, and Clarke pointed to the car. 'Where's your Range Rover? This isn't your style.'

'Amelia Jennings has it until she can collect me. Much as I love the French, and I love them dearly, my work with CIS can't wait. I need to get back in circulation before I'm old news. Probably after Christmas.'

While he was talking, Clarke had been admiring the car. He wondered if he was too young to be seen driving one. Would Mina think him completely middle-aged if he collected her from prison in a Jaguar? He paused at the nearside rear wheel. 'Did you know you've got a flat tyre?'

Offlea came around and looked. There was damage to the wing and the tyre was partially deflated.

'Damn. I wondered what that warning light was all about. I'll have to get it fixed before I try and get rid of it.' He kicked the tyre in disgust at the poor quality of French roads, and swore – in French.

'Where did you learn to speak French so fluently?' asked Clarke.

'I started at school and got the hang of it. After the ceasefire in Ulster, I got bored: I joined *la Légion étrangère*. With them, you either learn fast or you're out. Or dead.'

Another good reason not to argue with the man, thought Clarke.

Offlea jingled his keys, and said, 'Do you want Alain back or shall I get rid of him?'

'Hand him over.'

Offlea opened the rear doors and helped Alain to get out. He had tied the young student's wrists and blindfolded him, but thankfully he hadn't locked Alain in the boot. Offlea took out a knife and cut the bonds.

'Are you okay?' said Clarke to Alain.

'I guess.'

'Good. Let's go.'

He opened the passenger door, and Alain felt his way into the vehicle, still blindfolded. They drove out of the hospital, and Clarke headed for the main road to Calais, pulling up just short of the *On* ramp.

'You can take the blindfold off now.' For the first time since the shootout, he lit a cigarette. He passed it to Alain and lit one for himself.

Caressing the image of Ganesha on his lighter he said, 'I'm sorry.'

'What for? For lying? For kidnapping me? For letting your crazy friend loose? What's it all about, eh? What is this all about?'

'Money, of course.'

'Are you selling drugs or buying them or what?'

'No drugs, Alain: just money. Pure and simple cash. I sold some Euros and bought some sterling. Happens all the time.'

'Not like that it doesn't.'

No, it doesn't, thought Clarke. Nor could the money really be described as pure or simple. It was neither of those things. Nor was it dirty. It was just paper with pictures of the Queen on it: the rest was down to the people who used it.

'You saved my life, Alain. Without your intelligence during the engagement, I would be dead.'

'I was frightened.'

'I don't blame you.'

'No. You don't understand. I was frightened that if they killed you, they would come after me. My case was in the back of your van.'

So it was. So it was. But if Clarke hadn't left it there, would Alain have bolted? Best not to think about that. 'You enjoyed it, though,' he said.

Instead of protesting, Alain snorted. 'You're right. I did enjoy it at the time. I didn't think that things like this really happened.'

'They don't happen very often, but they're more common than you think. The dead man will never be found, and the gunshot wounds will be written up as accidents.'

Clarke dug into his pockets. 'When they count the money, it's going to be a bit short.' He took out a bundle of Euros from the suitcase and counted them out into Alain's hand. 'This is the rest of the fee we agreed: this is for your train fare back to London. You'll be there before bedtime. And this is for lying to you.'

Alain nodded and folded away the money. 'What are you going to do?'

'Drive straight to Calais and drop you at Fréthun. Then I'll rest up overnight, fill the van with fags and booze, and drive to Cherbourg. You'll never see me again.'

'Good.'

Clarke pulled on to the A16 and headed north. They would be in Calais in less than half an hour, and he had one last question for Alain. 'When the other man came up to you and took the phone, did you hear what he said to Pierre?'

'No. He tied me up and put the coat over my head. I couldn't hear anything.'

That was deliberate. Offlea was saying something to Pierre that he didn't want Clarke to find out about. It was a good job that the advanced Bluetooth control unit he'd installed in the van included a digital recorder.

They were about five minutes from the station when Clarke said, 'I know you're not going to go to the police, but it's possible that they may come to you. Don't worry. Tell them everything that happened except for one thing. Don't ever *ever* mention the man in the ski mask.'

'What man?'

'Excellent. That's the right attitude.' He pulled up outside the Eurostar station and turned to Alain. 'Good luck.'

After a second's hesitation, Alain held out his hand and said, '*Adieu, Georges.*'

Clarke shook hands with him, and then Alain was gone. Clarke did check that he'd left the money behind when he took his bag from the back, but he wasn't worried about him talking to the cops. Not for a few years, anyway.

He had been telling some of the truth when Alain had asked about his plans. He was definitely going to rest, definitely going to stock up with fags and booze, but he wasn't going to Cherbourg. He was planning to see an old friend in Germany before he crossed back through Holland. He might even drop into the Christmas market.

Chapter 12

Earlsbury – Fylde Peninsula – Cairndale

Monday – Wednesday

13-15 December

Fiona dressed his wound and pronounced herself satisfied with its progress, then she gave him a lift to the station. It had been good to see her again properly: since she had married fourteen years ago, he couldn't remember ever seeing her away from family gatherings. Their relationship just wasn't like that. She had also crossed over into Lancashire, which certain members of his family had yet to come to terms with.

There was no ice to scrape off her car, either. 'It really is warmer and wetter on the west coast,' she said. 'Much more pleasant, though I'm sure Granddad would say that it's not so character-building.'

'True.'

She pulled up near Southport station and looked over to him. 'Are you going to be careful, Tom? If they tried to kill you once, it could easily happen again.'

'If you knew there was a cure – something that could stop one of your patients dying – would you just give up on them if the NHS said they couldn't have it?'

'Of course not, but NHS trusts don't usually plant bombs in people's cars.'

'I'll think of a better analogy on the train and let you know.'

She leant over to kiss him, and he made his way to the platform. When he arrived at Earlsbury, Hayes was waiting for him, and he had to walk around his car to check for damage. When he had discovered no dents he said, 'You can drive us to BCSS if you want.'

'Shut up and get in.'

They set off, and Tom asked her how the match had gone on Saturday. Her expression said it all.

'Only our third win of the season, and the first away from home. I even scored.'

'Well done.'

'Thanks. Now who's this suspect?'

'Someone who stands to gain from Niall Brewer being taken down. The only person on earth who could benefit is Nicole Rodgers, his deputy.'

'I did wonder. But for her to get hold of that information – she's only in media relations. She doesn't have that sort of access.'

'That's what I wanted to see Juliet Porterhouse for. She told me that the information on Brewer's bank account came from screen shots of his online banking.'

Hayes flicked a glance over at him. It didn't make sense to her.

'Think about it this way, Kris. It could only have been someone who had access to his details. It won't be his new girlfriend; I doubt it's his PA – but his deputy? She has access to his office, his notebooks, his computer. If he wasn't careful about his passwords, she could easily hack his account.'

They arrived at the station and headed for the canteen. 'Sounds good,' said Hayes. 'If he gets suspended and / or arrested, she will be acting MR manager. The court case could take months. By the time he's sacked, she would be in pole position for the job. I like it.'

Tom tucked into his second bacon sandwich of the day, and Hayes remembered something. 'I had a call from DCI Storey on Friday afternoon. He said you wanted to know the name of the officer with Griffin on the night that Khan's brother was arrested.'

'Mm. Did he find out?'

'Yes. It was DC Angela Lindow. She's on maternity leave, apparently.'

'She is. I saw her bump when I first came up here. The baby must be a couple of months old now. Are you ready, Kris?'

'What for?'

'Bending the rules. We haven't got time to go through the proper channels. It's this week or never. I want you to stalk her – find out her routine and intercept her in a public place. Ask her for ten minutes of her time and find out what went on that night. Are you up for it?'

He watched her carefully. Her eyes flicked about the canteen as if checking for eavesdroppers. He could sense the conflict which ended when she blew out a breath. 'In for a penny, sir. I'll get on to it this afternoon. What are you going to do?'

'Talk to Evelyn Andrews and get her friend in HR to courier Nicole Rodgers' records over here. Then we can start digging.'

Patrick Lynch had not been a hoarder. So much of his life was lived by word of mouth that he had left very few physical relics for Fran to sort out. Helen had offered to help, but this was one job she was going to manage on her own.

In the gap between his arrest and whatever had happened down by the canal, Pat had started to wind up his businesses and cancel his contracts. Fran had already shipped a load of paperwork to their solicitor for probate, and to defend the Proceeds of Crime order which the police insisted did not perish with her husband.

That didn't leave a lot. Fran was the custodian of family memories: all the photographs, children's certificates and holiday souvenirs were her department. In fact, when it came down to it, the only thing that needed sorting was

Patrick's golfing cupboard in the garage. She could get at it so easily because there was an empty space where his Jaguar should be.

The funeral home had been on the phone. The thaw over the weekend had allowed the cemetery to start catching up with the backlog. They could fit her in before Christmas if she wanted. She did.

It had begun properly now. The church was booked, Earlsbury Park Golf Club had fallen over themselves to offer their premises for the reception, and the funeral home was handling a lot of the other details. Fran had laid down the law. Her children could read a lesson at the funeral, but the eulogy was being given by the priest. That's what he was for. All she was doing today was trying to find something of Pat's life that was uniquely his. All she had turned up so far was golf.

She sorted it into three piles. The trophies and certificates she would return to the club: they might have a use for them. All the actual equipment (which she knew was worth a lot of money) would be sold on eBay eventually. And there was a third pile. Of rubbish.

Fran was feeling grubby and dirty after working her way through three-quarters of the stuff. She decided she would take a quick look at the rest, then clean herself up, before collecting Elizabeth from the train. She reached into the back of the cupboard and found another bundle of old scorecards which she put straight into the black bag and then, right at the very back, she felt a golf ball in a bag. That was odd. Pat was very careful with his balls and didn't leave them lying around.

She fished it out and found an ordinary-looking ball in a ziplock freezer bag. There had been nothing like that anywhere else. She flicked it round and discovered a label – *Red Hand Insurance*.

She was about to empty the bag and put the ball with the others she'd collected when she made the connection.

The Red Hand of Ulster. The man from Blackpool. The bomber who had blown Benedict Adaire to Hell, and who had tried to send Morton the same way.

The only conceivable reason for keeping this at the back of the cupboard was that it had the man's fingerprints or DNA on it. She went back into the house and found Chief Inspector Morton's business card, and then gave him a call.

Tom put the phone down and told Hayes that they were going home via Patrick Lynch's house. He didn't say why. She had just returned from her visit to Angela Lindow and she was itching to tell him something, so he didn't deny her the pleasure.

'Angela was nice. I walked up to her in the supermarket and admired the baby, then I showed her my warrant card. I just asked her straight out if we could chat. She said *yes*, and we went to the in-store café. It's all down to you, sir.'

'What is?'

'She went to see Ian Hooper a couple of weeks ago, and he said that you'd been straight with him. Once she realised I was working for you, she was happy to talk off the record and would be happy to make a statement if we want.'

That was nice to hear. Tom reckoned the ratio of comments was still about ten to one against him – ten *Gestapo* for every *Good Bloke*. It was still good to hear. 'You don't work for me: you work with me,' he said to Hayes. 'What did she have to say?'

'I reckon that Angela was on to Griffin. She knew the case as soon as I mentioned it, and she'd obviously thought something was dodgy at the time.'

Tom sat up and took notice. 'In what way?'

'According to her, there was never any real surveillance going on at all. Griffin was very vague about his source, and the observation didn't start until eleven o'clock at night. It finished as soon as Khan's brother appeared, weaving down the road in his car. Angela reckons that Griffin was waiting for him and just wanted her there as a witness.'

'Was there anything wrong with the initial arrest?'

'No. She says that the bloke was obviously drunk, and Griffin used the breathalyser exactly in accordance with instructions. He was bang to rights, sir. The funny business started when they got to the station.'

'What happened?'

Hayes put down her notebook. 'That's the thing. She has no idea, because Griffin sent her home before they went inside the custody suite. That's why her name isn't on the arrest record.'

'Did she ever ask him what happened?'

'Yes. He said that the machine at the station was malfunctioning, and it took them so long to get it fixed that Khan had sobered up enough to pass the test. She says that she feels guilty now for not checking it out, but why would she? We've all known police equipment to malfunction. Besides, she trusted the custody sergeant.'

'Okay. Conclusions?'

'Griffin was either trying to curry favour, like he did when he let Nechells' daughter go, or he did actually blackmail Khan.'

Tom wasn't convinced. Like he'd said to Khan, Griffin was lazy. He wouldn't be out at night on a mission like that unless he thought he would get something from it. 'He could have been ordered to do it.'

'What do you mean?'

'If he were working for Khan, he could have been ordered to give the brother a scare. We don't know enough about the Khan family dynamics to see how big a deal the brother's drinking might be. If ACC Khan were being held responsible for his brother, if their father really did treat him as his brother's keeper, it would be a good move. The brother is arrested, he sees how close he is to disaster and then he's let off. It's a lesson and a warning – next time it might not be Griffin who arrests you.'

Hayes nodded her understanding. It was a powerful motive and it fitted the new information from DC Lindow. Tom made a note in his file, and Hayes asked him what he'd discovered about Nicole Rodgers.

'She's twenty-nine, single and worked in London before getting the job here four years ago. Her annual appraisals have always been outstanding, but there have been two complaints about her by women: both said that she made a pass at them during staff functions.'

Kris's nose twitched and she was on her feet. She came round to his desk to look at the complaints as if he'd just told her that Rodgers was suspected of war crimes. She stopped halfway and realised that she'd shown too much interest in his news. Instead of approaching his desk, she went to the coat stand and took a tissue out of her pocket before returning to her seat.

There is a public perception that more women police officers are gay than in the general population. The same goes for women's football teams. Tom had no idea whether either of these beliefs were true, but if Kris Hayes was being close-lipped about her sexual preferences, he couldn't blame her. As a black woman, she would suffer enough problems without coming out as a lesbian. On the other hand, if she really was gay, she might be able to follow lines of enquiry that were closed to him.

He lifted the file and said, 'In both complaints, HR decided that there was no case to answer because it was at a social function, and Rodgers wasn't using a position of authority to pressure the women.'

'Good,' said Hayes. 'If Rodgers had been a man, no one would have complained, would they?'

'Perhaps not.'

When Rodgers had been in their office, she had completely blanked Hayes. Kris had said it was because

Rodgers had been unhelpful during her ordeal as a whistleblower. Could there be more to it than that?

He picked up a different file and said, 'She lives in a converted factory between Earlsbury and Birmingham. It's a rather exclusive development, I think, and she has one of the better flats judging by the online brochure. I've checked with the Land Registry and there's a mortgage on it for £170,000.'

Hayes' eyebrows shot up. At her age, she would no doubt have a good idea of the mortgage market and how difficult it was to get one since the credit crunch.

'You're right,' said Tom. 'That's over *five times* her salary. I wish I could get a mortgage like that, but I doubt that the Consolidated Mortgage Bank of St Jude has much presence on the High Street.'

'St Jude? Where on earth is that?'

'The Republic of St Jude is a tiny enclave on the coast of South America. It used to be part of British Guyana, but it broke away and ditched the Queen. As they say in the geography books, its principal economic activities are trade and finance. Or, as we used to say in the Fraud Squad, they're all smugglers and money launderers. We've got more chance of finding out what's going on in Beijing than we have of penetrating their financial regulations. And don't forget, there was a St Jude connection to the golf club.'

Hayes mulled over this and did a couple of calculations in her notebook. 'The repayments must be a huge percentage of her salary.'

'They should be. At normal values, she should have less than a thousand a month to live on.'

'You don't buy many designer outfits for that, and she's got a lot. I should know, I've seen enough of them.'

'That's what I thought. I haven't told you about her car, yet. I got Pete Fulton to do a credit check on her. She's making regular payments on a finance agreement for her trendy Mini. Are Minis trendy?'

'For white girls, yeah.'

'So, there we are. Miss Rodgers is living a very luxurious lifestyle without the salary to justify it. I've met women – and men – like her before, but they've all had family money to get them started. I could understand it if granddad had left her the money for the flat, but she's got a huge mortgage.'

Kris was giving him a grin that he could only describe as feral. She would rather be getting her teeth into ACC Khan, but if he was off limits for now, she'd quite enjoy taking a chunk out of Nicole. Before she started salivating, he closed down his computer. 'Come on: it's getting late, and I need to see Fran Lynch.'

After thinking about it overnight, Tom decided that the best place for Francesca Lynch's golf ball was in the incident room at Blackpool. He wrote DCS Hulme a note saying that there might be forensic evidence giving a clue to the identity of the bomber, and asked to be kept informed if a Mr John Lake got in touch. He packaged it and marked it for urgent delivery and turned his attention to Nicole Rodgers.

'Our first job,' he told Hayes, 'is to reconstruct the original email that was sent to Juliet Porterhouse. If we're going to avoid getting bogged down with Niall Brewer, we need to recreate what was done ourselves.'

'How do we do that?'

'I've been thinking about Brewer again. He's going to be in deep trouble, regardless of what we do, but we need one last favour from him. He's coming over here this morning. I want you to go on another charm offensive, this time with his ex-wife.'

'It doesn't sound like they had a very amicable divorce. Why should she help us out?'

'That's where you'll have to trust your instincts. All we need to know is her bank details. You can track back from that to discover who submitted the request for her records. The former Mrs Brewer works at a commercial radio station now. Go and see her, and mention her husband's name. Give the impression that he might be in trouble. If she says, "Good," then you can imply that her help will make it worse for him. If she shows concern, imply that her help might dig him out of the hole.'

Hayes weighed up his suggestion. 'If he goes down, her maintenance payments are going to stop pretty quickly.'

'Look, Kris, I thought you were starting to work it out for yourself. One of the big differences between being a detective and being in uniform is that when we catch a villain, there's often collateral damage afterwards. The only way to come to terms with it is to think of innocent victims as already victims – it's the crime that hurts them, not us. We're just a delayed consequence of the wrongdoing.'

She started to put her things together. 'You should be a pastor, you know. You can argue your way out of all sorts of tight corners.'

'It's better than fighting my way out.'

'Not always.'

She left, and Tom went back to Brewer's personnel file. Tucked in the admin section were his bank details. He went to the online banking screen and left it ready. When Brewer himself appeared shortly afterwards, he looked a lot less chipper than when he left last week's interview. He was very reluctant to enter Tom's office, and even more so to sit down.

'Let me guess,' said Tom. 'You've confessed to your new partner.'

'She lost no time in telling me what a stupid idiot I've been.'

'You have. In fact, you've been an utter moron.'

'No need to sugar-coat it. Just give it to me straight.'

'You need to resign today.'

Brewer looked stunned. He thought that confessing to Tom in return for immunity would be the end of things: to have it shoved back in his face was clearly not what he was expecting.

'I can't,' said Brewer. 'I'm in debt up to my eyeballs, and in this economic climate, there's no chance of finding an equivalent job.'

'I'm sorry, Niall. You've been stupid – criminally stupid – and if I had the resources, I'd prosecute you.' This made things even worse. Brewer looked as if he were about to get up and walk out. 'However, it's not up to me. I reckon you've got a choice. You can either tough it out until MCPS' own Professional Standards people find out what's going on or you can resign and hope that they'll ignore you. I can't give you any better advice than that.'

'I'll have to talk it over. This isn't a decision I can make on my own.'

'Yes, it is. If she's the right person for you, she'll stand by you and help you rebuild your life. If she's not, the sooner and quicker she buggers off, the better. You're going down, Niall, but I can give you one last victory. You can help me take down the person who shafted you.'

'What do you mean?'

'We didn't get all this information ourselves. Someone dropped you in it from a great height, and you get one shot at revenge. If you agree to resign today, I'll tell you who it is, and you can give me some evidence to nail them.'

Tom let him stew. He'd said his piece, and it was down to Brewer whether he went down with the sinking ship of his own career or dived overboard into the future without a lifebelt.

'I'll do it,' said Brewer with a shrug, then he slapped his hands on his knees. 'Who was it? What do you want from me?'

'Call Evelyn Andrews first and make an appointment with the Chief Constable. Tell her what it's about, then there's no going back.'

'Now? In here?'

Tom nodded, and as Brewer started to dial, a tremor crept into his hand, but he kept his nerve and five minutes later it was done. He would be seeing the Chief this afternoon and clearing his desk at five o'clock.

Tom turned the monitor round so that Brewer could see the online banking screen. 'It's Nicole Rodgers,' said Tom. 'She's after your job and wanted you out of the way as quickly as possible.'

Brewer let out a stream of four-letter words that was audible in the corridor. Tom let the volcano subside and said, 'I want you to log on to your banking, check the request logs and bring up your calendar.'

When Brewer had done what he asked, Tom had all the information he needed. He released the soon-to-be-ex media relations manager to his future.

'Good luck, Niall.'

'Thanks. I'll need it.'

'And you don't need me to tell you that you must not go anywhere near Nicole Rodgers. Send someone else to clear your desk if you have to, and tell no one about this until I say so.'

'I understand.'

They shook hands and he left. Tom sent Kris a text message instructing her to meet him at the canalside building where Nicole had bought that expensive flat.

Tom arrived there first and Hayes was third. The second person was the developer who had been and gone before Kris arrived. The first thing Tom asked her was how she had got on with the former Mrs Brewer.

'She was busy. When I started to tell her what I wanted, she just handed over her debit card and told me to copy it down. I was in and out in less than two minutes.' Hayes looked up at the name etched into a stone course running through the red brick. 'I'm not sure I'd want to live in a place called Grinding House.'

'Apparently the council insisted,' said Tom. 'Something to do with the listed building status preserving the name of the original owner.' He pointed to the locked door. 'The developer wouldn't even let me inside without a warrant, but I don't think there's any need. He said that there are twenty-four flats. Sorry, there are twenty-four *apartments*. Twelve have been sold, including Miss Rodgers' spacious residence. Come on: we can see it from the other side.'

They took a path to the side, which led round to a recycling section and then a locked gate on to a canalside communal area. There was even some sunshine on this side of the building. They peered through the railings and agreed that *Yes, it must be very nice in the summer.* As far as they could tell from the brochures provided by the developer, Nicole Rodgers lived one step down from the penthouse, but still had a balcony with views out towards the Malvern Hills.

'Where does that leave us?' asked Hayes.

'Thanks to you and thanks to Niall Brewer, we've got everything we need except for Leonie's permission. It's getting cold; I'll ring her from the car.'

They got in their cars and headed back to BCSS. Leonie Spence answered on the third ring.

'Not disturbing you, am I?' said Tom.

'No. I'm going through CCTV from a custody suite, so anything's better than that.'

'We've had a breakthrough. I want either your presence or your permission to arrest Nicole Rodgers, the deputy media relations manager. I should tell you that her boss resigned today.'

'Do you need me to come up?'

'No. Kris and I can handle it.'

'Good. Go for it, Tom.'

Olivia greeted him with an amused expression when he turned up at the stables. 'Are you sure you're up to it? This horse had a long career over the jumps before he came to us. He knows his own mind.'

'What's the worst that can happen? I'm already a laughing stock to your family.'

'No, you're not. Dad says you're good at your job and Mum's taken a shine to you, I can tell. I don't want Herdwick Boy to get the better of you. You could get injured.'

By way of an answer, Clarke lifted his jumper and shirt to reveal a massive bruise on his chest. 'I got that changing some money,' he said. 'A few more won't hurt.'

'What is it with you and showing off your injuries? Are you trying to prove something? I saw you lift up your trouser leg when you were talking to Gerard the other night.'

'Sorry. It's my way of showing that I suffer for my art. Let's get saddled up. Where are we going?'

'Have you ridden over the gallops at a racing stables before?'

'Only once.'

'Well, take it easy. I'll lead and I don't want you to try and overtake me. This isn't a race.'

Clarke tried to adopt a humble expression and got to know his mount for the day. Herdwick Boy (or Herdie) was rather old, but he was in good condition. Olivia told him that the horses at her centre were used by the university for a variety of experiments, often in conjunction with pharmaceutical companies.

He wasn't embarrassed to use a mounting block, and when in the saddle, he waited for Olivia to show him the way. 'We'll go up the ridge,' she said.

Following behind her, he decided that he had been right: she did look much better in jodhpurs than a cocktail dress.

They walked out of the yard and along a track before she turned on to a course that led up a slight hill, and then they started to trot.

The cold air burned his throat and within seconds his chest was screaming at him from the bruised area. His leg joined in, too. Clarke rode with the pain and fought hard to stop Herdie from opening his stride into a gallop. By the time they reached the top, he was sweating from just about every pore in his body. Olivia was barely out of breath.

'Beautiful up here, isn't it?' she said.

When he had stopped hyperventilating, he had to agree with her. It wasn't a ridge so much as a gentle hill, but it commanded views of the estuary and beyond. To his left, the impossibly green track of the racecourse looked like enamelwork with the Sporting Hotel as a gem on top. He looked to the right and across the flat peninsula: Blackpool and its Tower looked like a sleepy little village. Sunlight broke through distant clouds and he could see sand stretching towards the beginning of some hills.

'Is that the Lake District?'

'Yes. In front of it is Morecambe Bay. We took the horses across last year with Cedric.'

'Should I know him?'

'He's a legend. The Queen's Guide to the Sands. He's the man who knows every gully, channel and sandbank. It's one of the most dangerous places in Britain without him.'

Clarke looked behind to the stables and farmhouse where Olivia lived. She was right. On a day like this, it was difficult to imagine anywhere more beautiful. With every beat of his heart, his ribs and his leg reminded him of the sacrifices he had made to get there. He would love to bring Mina up here and show it to her. He looked from the view to Olivia and something clicked in his head, as if he'd been turned round 180 degrees and saw the world from a different direction. The beautiful English countryside was still there, as was the English rose mounted on her horse, but he could see them differently now.

He made himself a promise: Conrad Clarke was now a man with a plan. A big plan.

'Are you ready?' said Olivia.

'After you.'

When they got back, there were two Range Rovers in the stable yard. Not unusual in itself, but next to one of them was Amelia Jennings.

She was standing with her arms folded and an expression of thunder on her face. Olivia didn't notice her sister, and Clarke didn't draw her attention to it. They dismounted, and Olivia said that one of the lads would see to the horses this time. 'Next time, you'll have to sort him out yourself. How do you feel?'

'Like I've just ridden the Grand National. And won. Thank you, Olivia: that was the most fun I've had in ages.'

'Good. You really can do it as often as you want. I won't need to supervise next time. Cup of coffee?'

'Yes, please, but I'd better see what your sister wants first.'

'Amelia? Did she call you or something?'

'No. She's standing out there giving me daggers. At least I think it's me.'

'Good luck. I'll see the survivors in the farmhouse.'

He stretched his limbs and tried not to limp as he walked over to Amelia.

'What did you say to him?' was her opening remark.

'Say what? To who?'

'Gerard. I saw you talking to him at Livi's party. What did you say to him?'

'Nothing. Why?'

She had been leaning against the bonnet and lifted herself off to go for an all-out attack. 'Because when I went to the Legends gig at the O2 on Saturday, I was humiliated. Humiliated, Conrad.'

'What happened?'

'I went up to the VIP line, and they told me that my name wasn't on the list. And it got worse. Not only did the paparazzi see me being turned away, I had to watch Gerard arriving with his wife. On Friday, he was telling me that going to this gig was important to him because they were one of his biggest bands. On Saturday I'm dumped. Dumped in public.'

'I'm very sorry.'

She jabbed him in the chest with her finger, and he winced. She didn't notice. 'That's not the worst of it. On Monday, he's interviewed by some whore on this gossip website. He tells her that the reason he's back with his wife is *All down to Nostromo*. It won't mean anything to anyone else except you and me. So tell me, Conrad – named after your mother's favourite writer and author of *Nostromo* – what did you say to Gerard?'

Clarke tried to look guilty, which was quite difficult, because he really wanted to do a lap of honour around the stable yard. 'We just got chatting, and he said that you were wonderful, but he missed his kids. I just said that he should go for what he really wanted in life. I thought he would choose you because, well ... who wouldn't? I'm really sorry, Amelia.'

'How are you going to make it up to me?'

He went forward and put his hands on her shoulders, then he brushed the hair away from her face. 'You're still the most alluring, captivating and maddening woman I've ever met. And the best shag so far.'

She smiled. 'Okay. You're forgiven.'

For what? He hadn't done anything wrong. He hadn't even lied – just paraphrased. He had to give her credit for living in the moment, however. The sunny outlook had returned to her face, and whatever Gerard had meant to her was now history. She offered him her arm, and they marched towards the farmhouse. Clarke took the opportunity to dip his hand in her pocket and he took out the keys to the Range Rover. Will Offlea's Range Rover.

He didn't linger over coffee and outstay his welcome; he wanted to make sure he had some quality time outside. He went to his own vehicle and retrieved the tracker he had picked up from his friend in Germany. When Offlea announced that Amelia had custody of his car, Clarke thought he was bound to get access to it sooner or later; he just hadn't expected it to be this soon. He opened the boot and fitted the GPS tracker and broadcaster at the back of the spare wheel. He didn't care where Amelia went, but as soon as he sent a signal, it would wake up and start broadcasting Offlea's movements.

Job done, he dropped her keys in the mud, then took them back to the farmhouse. He briefly told Amelia that he'd found them on his way out. She was in the middle of telling her sister how brutal Gerard had been, and barely had time to thank him.

On the way back to his Defender, an unknown number came up on his phone.

'Hello, Conrad. It seems I owe you a hundred pounds,' said Anthony Skinner.

'Hah! Kate delivered the goods, then. I knew she would.'

'Big bonus for her, bigger bonus for CIS. That bet was a good investment.'

'Give the cash to Jennings next time you see him. I'll be expecting it.'

'I'm sure you will. There's something else you can expect, too. The woman wants to see you.'

'I thought she would. What do you want me to say?'

'Whatever you want. Lying has never been much of a challenge to you, has it?'

'Give her my number and tell her I'd be happy to see her any time she's up north. You could give her the hundred quid if you like; she'll probably be up here before Jennings.'

The magistrate had signed the search warrant for Rodgers' flat without hesitation, but she hung on to the paper before handing it over.

'Misconduct in Public Office is a serious matter, especially when the person concerned works for the police.'

'Yes, ma'am,' said Tom.

'I don't know whether to hope you're wrong or hope you're right about this. Either way, this woman's life is never going to be the same again. Here you are.'

It was Hayes who spoke first. 'She didn't need to say that. We know what we're doing, and we know the consequences. At least, I do now.'

'You've changed your tune. I hope you're not becoming a bitter and twisted cynic.'

'No. We only need one of those on this team, and you do the job so well.'

'I shall rise above that.'

'Sorry, sir. I didn't mean it. You're not bitter or cynical.'

'You left out "twisted".'

'Did I? Freudian slip.'

They got into his car, and she adopted a more serious tone. 'I think I get where you're coming from now. All of these things we're investigating — they're all terrible. They're all a breach of trust. It's like going into a situation and expecting someone to have your back. And they don't. The more I look, the less I like it.'

'That's one approach. A good one, too. Let's get after Miss Rodgers. According to my sources, she's in BCSS, but we'll take her to Earlsbury for interview. It's quieter there, and I'm back on speaking terms with DCI Storey.'

When they tracked her down to a remote office at the station, she was humming a tune and looking very pleased with herself as she shuffled files into a transportable crate.

She gave them a smile when they knocked on her door. 'You've just caught me,' she said. 'I'm done here, and I'm off to HQ to take over the reins now that Niall has resigned.' She paused for a second and took in their expressions. 'That wasn't anything to do with you two, was it? I hope not.'

Nicole Rodgers was triumphant. She had put up her hair with an elaborate series of clips and she was wearing a cream and black geometric dress which could have been tailored to fit her. She stood poised by her desk, one suede boot crossed over the other. Tom wondered what was off about her appearance. Later, Hayes told him that she was wearing bronze eye shadow, which didn't go with her pink lipstick.

'DC Hayes, could you do the honours?'

'Nicole Rodgers, I am arresting you on suspicion of Misconduct in Public Office. You do not have to say anything, but it may harm your defence if you do not mention when questioned something which you later rely on in court. Anything you do say may be given in evidence.'

While Hayes administered the caution, he watched her go from shock to anger to hatred in the space of twelve seconds. She uncoiled her legs and stood in the brace position, as if they were going to attack her. Tom took a step back and said, 'We are taking you to Earlsbury police station where we will conduct an interview. You may exercise your right to legal counsel when we arrive. I hope we don't have to handcuff you, Miss Rodgers: that's not our style. However, I must ask you to surrender your bag to DC Hayes, and we will conduct a search of this office before we leave.'

Rodgers pursed her pink lips, but stood aside. Tom and Kris rapidly searched the drawers and cupboard in the office, but found nothing until Hayes looked in the crate. At the bottom of the files was a cheap mobile phone. She showed it to Tom and Rodgers, and then dropped it in Rodgers' handbag.

'Let's go,' said Tom.

When the custody sergeant at Earlsbury had finished processing her, Tom showed her the search warrant for her flat. 'There's an officer on duty to make sure no one goes in before we can get down there to search it. We'll take your keys — saves breaking the lock.'

Rodgers said nothing. The only words she had uttered since her arrest were in response to questions at the custody desk. Tom showed her into an interview room to wait for her solicitor. 'I've heard some people say that having their house searched by the police is worse than being burgled,' he said. Rodgers stiffened and glared at him. 'I'll get DC Hayes to tidy up. I'm sure you'd prefer a woman's touch.'

'That remark was totally out of order. I could report you for that.'

'Really? What for?'

'You shouldn't be talking to me without a solicitor present.'

'I can talk to you all I want: I just can't use anything you say in evidence. We'll be back.'

Tom and Hayes went to get their papers together. Kris said to him, 'Are you going to push that in the interview, sir? I mean ... the gay angle.'

'Absolutely not, Kris. I was just getting under her skin a little. Time will do the rest.'

An hour later, Tom had a discussion with Rodgers' solicitor in the corridor, while Hayes set up the video and audio tapes in the interview room. Sometimes it was good to tell the suspect's brief what was going on; today Tom said nothing other than that his client could expect to answer questions in relation to contact with the media.

'But that's her job,' said the solicitor.

'It's my job to have contact with villains,' said Tom. 'That doesn't give me the right to take bribes.'

The solicitor gave an exasperated sigh, and they settled down in the interview room. Hayes repeated the caution.

'Please describe your relationship with the late Detective Sergeant Griffin,' was his opening gambit.

Rodgers looked at her brief, but he just shrugged. If a client chooses to answer questions, the solicitor's role is quite limited in a well-conducted interview. She turned back to Tom and said, 'I knew him, of course but so did half the force. He was quite a larger-than-life figure, and I sometimes prepped him for statements to camera.'

'I see. And did he ever pass you any information?'

'He told me things. How else could I work with him? Even you've told me things, Inspector.'

'Specifically, did he ever pass you any financial information?'

Bingo. Her eyes gave it away immediately, and he knew he'd made the right decision. Now all he had to do was prove it.

'No,' she said. 'I've no idea what you're talking about.'

'I'm talking about a request for the financial records of Mrs Brewer. The former Mrs Brewer. DS Griffin requested one a few months before his death, and a copy of that document was recently passed to a journalist. In other words, after Griffin was murdered.'

She shifted uncomfortably, but said nothing.

'Do you have a question?' said the lawyer.

'Along with those records, some information from Niall Brewer's bank was also given to the journalist. That information was obtained directly from online banking, using his office computer at a time when he was in Worcester.' He let that sink in. Rodgers was having difficulty swallowing. 'Did you obtain those records? Did you pass those records to Juliet Porterhouse of the *Sunday Examiner*?'

'No.'

'We will be searching your flat, because I don't think you sent that email from work. I know that the email account was a webmail one, but even so, our warrant has already uncovered the IP address from where it was sent. It ties back to your building. I suspect that we'll find evidence on your laptop. It may take a few days, but we'll get there. Obviously, you'll be released on police bail until then. And suspended from duty. But we'll keep you here for a bit longer first.'

Nicole Rodgers immediately started whispering to her solicitor. Tom knew then that they would find what they wanted at her home. 'My client does not wish to comment at this time until any further evidence is presented,' was the lawyer's conclusion.

'As you wish. Now, I'm going to get hypothetical for a moment: you don't need to comment. If we find evidence that you received that report from DS Griffin, it begs a question. He had no reason to request Mrs Brewer's bank account, did he? So he must have been acting for you. If he did that favour for you, what else did you get him to do? DS Griffin was a thoroughly bent copper, as you know. What really concerns me is how he died and who sent him there.'

He let his speculation hang in the air between them for a couple of seconds, then he pressed on. 'I'm going to read from one of your own statements to the press, Miss Rodgers. It concerns the conviction of a drug dealer from last year. "Midland Counties police will pursue offenders to ensure that they do not profit from their crimes. We will investigate, freeze, and seize all their assets to ensure that they pay the full penalty." So it seems that you are well aware of how the Proceeds of Crime Act can be used to drive someone into the ground. I used to work the money laundering desk in the City: I'm quite good at it. When we connect you to DS Griffin, we can pursue you for a share of the corrupt earnings he was receiving.'

She knew what he was on about all right. She bent in to whisper to her lawyer, and he became quite animated. He shushed her with his hands and asked for a break in the interview. Tom nodded and took Hayes with him out of the interview room.

'Have we got her?' she asked.

'Oh, yes. We had her as soon as I said we'd got a search warrant. The question is, who can we pull down with her?'

Rodgers' lawyer appeared a few minutes later. 'My client would like to volunteer some information that will allow you to make a much bigger arrest, but she needs an assurance that no action will be taken against her for her stupid mistake in contacting the press.'

'How big an arrest?'

'Very big.'

Tom looked at Hayes who said, 'It's a big ask, sir. We could have Rodgers in a cell shortly, and a guaranteed conviction.'

'DC Hayes is right. I can't guarantee anything unless Miss Rodgers is willing to make a full statement, testify in court and offer additional evidence.'

'I'm sure she can do that,' said the lawyer and returned to his client.

'Well done, Kris. That was nicely put: *We could have Rodgers in a cell shortly*. I like that.'

'Pleasure.'

The detectives returned to the interview room and restarted the tapes.

'I believe you have something to offer,' said Tom.

'The person you are looking for is Deputy Chief Constable David Nechells,' said Rodgers.

Tom held his breath.

'Two years ago, we began a relationship. During that relationship I became aware that he was receiving money from certain sources, which could only be illegal ones. Because he manipulated me and coerced me, I began to … carry out certain tasks on his behalf. This included liaising with DS Griffin and gathering information to ensure that Patrick Lynch and others were not investigated.'

'Did you benefit from this relationship with Mr Nechells? I mean, financially?'

'He paid for part of my mortgage, but that stopped when Griffin was murdered. He said that it would be too dangerous to see each other.'

Hayes spoke for the first time. 'But that wouldn't have stopped him making the payments.'

Rodgers face said it all. She had been living the good life, and it had all been snatched away. That's what a sense of entitlement does for you: it clouds your judgement, so that you don't see where the money is coming from, only where it goes.

'Would I be right in thinking,' said Tom, 'that you tried to implicate Niall Brewer because you needed his job to continue your lifestyle?'

'How else was I going to pay for things?'

He didn't answer that. Instead, he said, 'How did you obtain the information about Mrs Brewer?'

'David used to keep things at my apartment. He liked to have information on people and he used Griff to find it. I took my own copy before he went away.'

'How long has Mr Nechells been linked to Griffin?'

'Since before he was appointed as deputy chief. Griffin started in the Met before transferring back here. David was asked to investigate a miscarriage of justice involving Dermot Lynch. He used Griffin to pay off the Lynch family, and that's how it all began.'

She shrugged her shoulders. That was her story. Nechells had seduced her, started an affair and bought a love nest with his share of Patrick Lynch's illegal profits.

'You're willing to testify to all this in court?'

She nodded.

'For the tape, please.'

'Yes.'

'Your statement may be enough for disciplinary proceedings against Mr Nechells, but what other evidence can you offer?'

'I taped our last two conversations. They're in a safe place. In the first one, you can hear him ordering me to steal the key from the evidence room and go to Griffin's house. He told me to remove any evidence of where Griffin played golf. You can hear me saying that I'd already disposed of two mobile phones for him, and that it would be dangerous for me to go to the house. In the second tape, when he came round to clear out his rubbish from my apartment, you can hear him admitting that Lynch's money was paying Pandora's school fees. There's other stuff too.'

Tom looked at Hayes and their eyes said *High five* to each other. Tom asked about the location of the tapes and suspended the interview.

Outside, he told Hayes to track down the recordings and secure them, then begin the search of Rodgers' flat. He said he was going to contact Leonie for further instructions.

'Can I ask her one more question, off the record?'

'So long as it doesn't jeopardise our enquiry.'

Hayes stuck her head back through the door. Tom could see that Nicole had already pushed back her chair and relaxed. Hayes said, 'Miss Rodgers … the tapes are off, but I just wondered why you came on to those two women who complained about you.'

Rodgers looked down her nose at Hayes and said, 'They were pestering David, both of them. I thought it would freak them out if I got up close and personal. I was right.'

That was too much for Tom. He leaned over Kris's shoulder and said, 'You might want your lawyer's help in drafting your resignation. The sooner the better, I reckon.'

On their way out, Hayes said, 'Bitch.'

That just about summed it up as far as Tom was concerned.

With so much local anaesthetic in her face, it was difficult for Mina to talk, let alone kiss him: even her nose was numb. Conrad appeared at the dentist's surgery shortly after Luke Morrison had finished drilling her jaw and inserting holes for screws that would eventually give her more teeth. That was a job for the next session.

'You look like you've been wunning,' she said.

'Wunning?'

She made a real effort to make her tongue work. 'RRRRunning.' It sounded more like a dog barking than a word.

'Riding. Olivia Jennings let me loose on one of their experimental horses. I need the exercise and it gave me a chance to see the world from a new angle.'

What on earth is an experimental horse? She didn't have the energy to ask, so she frowned and uttered a sort of interrogative grunt.

'I'll tell you in a minute,' he said. 'I spoke to Luscious Luke on the way in. He seemed very pleased with today's work.'

'Easy for him to say.'

'You poor love. I wouldn't bother you, but we need to take every chance we can get.'

She took his hand and kneaded his fingers; it was a lot easier than talking. When the anaesthetic had taken effect, Luke had begun drilling. The bottom jaw had a section of allograft in it – a piece of someone else's bone, tested and matched in much the same way as a marrow donor. The drill went through it quite easily, but when it came to the upper jaw, she experienced the drilling as sound. The vibration travelled along her skull and straight into her inner ear. It was like being given an extra sense, but one she never wanted to experience again.

She had realised something while she was being drilled: something that had to be said no matter whether she bit her tongue or not. She returned her focus to the staff break room where they were sitting. Conrad's attention had drifted away, too.

'You said that you loved me last week,' she said.

He snapped back to the present. 'Yes, I did. And I mean it.'

'That's the problem, Conrad. I've seen you in action too many times and I know that you're the best liar I've ever met. I believe you. I really do, but that's only today, and that's only a feeling. If you're going to love me, you have to make me a promise.'

'Anything. Well, almost anything. See? I'm telling the truth again.'

'That's just it. I want you to promise me that you will never, ever lie to me. Even if it hurts me more than a lie, you must tell me the truth.'

He didn't hesitate. He got down on one knee and made his promise. Then he couldn't get back up again and had to roll on his side. She giggled.

'I told you I'd been riding,' he said. 'And I definitely need the exercise.'

'Good. Now tell me what's wrong. I could feel it when you came in the door.'

'I will, but can you answer a boring, mundane question first?'

'If it's quick. That last speech hurt a lot.'

'Did you find anything off beam in those ledgers?'

It was her turn to be put on the spot. She wasn't sure about what she'd found, but if it meant a lot to him then she would have to speak.

'Yes, I did. I think. When that other man started the exchanges, he was getting a much better rate. All of a sudden, it dipped on all the transactions. Not just on one currency, but on all of them.'

He nodded and reached into his leather jacket to pull out a piece of paper. She took it off him and raised her eyebrows at the first line:

Hi Conrad. This is what you wanted. Lovely to see you again and thanks for last night.

'Conrad? Who is this and what did you do with her?'

'Are you sure you want to know? I can't lie to you any more.'

She flushed deeply. If he had been with some old flame while she was locked up in prison, no wonder he was troubled about telling the truth. Her nose started to tingle as the tide of anaesthetic receded, and she knew she was in for some physical pain. Why not get it over with all at once? 'Tell me.'

He gave her a massive grin, and she decided that he needed to get his teeth whitened.

'It's from a woman called Martha. She's German, and we had a thing going when I was stationed over there – ooh, must be six years ago now. I dropped in to see her on Monday night and I did duty as a babysitter for her and her husband. I even paid for their meal.'

'That's very noble of you. Why do I think that you're not telling me everything? No matter. How did she introduce you to her husband and what did you want?'

'Do I have to have wanted something?'

'Yes.'

'I'll come to that. She introduced me as "someone from the old days". Her husband has to accept that sort of thing because she works in national security. He assumed I was a spy.'

He went quiet again. Something was troubling him in a way she hadn't seen since the end of their time together in London, when everything was going pear-shaped and people were starting to get killed. She put her hand on his again. 'What's the matter, Conrad?'

He blew out his cheeks and felt in his pockets, until he remembered that he couldn't smoke in here. 'I went to see Martha because she's fluent in French as well as English. I needed someone to transcribe and translate a tape recording. This came through today.' He drew attention back to the piece of paper.

Mina read it. It was a conversation between a man called Red and another designated as Pierre. It seemed that Red had done something, something terrible to Pierre's leg. Then Red insisted that Pierre go through with a transaction at a rate of 80% and that he would still have to pay 5% to Red later. There was some arguing until Red threatened to shoot him in the balls. Pierre caved in after that.

She finished reading and looked up at Conrad. 'What is this to do with you?'

'I was there. You remember Barbarossa, the guy whose job I took over? He's "Red" in that conversation, and he knows I don't speak French. What he didn't know was that I'd taped everything. It's proof that he's been skimming a lot of money – in cahoots with the dealers.'

'Did he shoot this man Pierre?'

'Blew his knee off from over two hundred metres away. And that's not all. I've been told off once today already for doing this, but you need to see it.'

He lifted his shirt and showed a massive black and yellow bruise over his ribs. She instinctively reached out to touch his pain, but he flinched away. 'Sorry,' he said. 'Still rather painful.'

'You look like you've been hit with a baseball bat.'

'I was shot. It's what happens when you wear body armour that doesn't quite fit properly. You should see the other guy, though.'

He tried to smile, but it was a poor effort. She reached up and touched his face instead of his chest. 'You can't go on like this,' she said.

'I know. That's the decision I came to this morning. I want to get out.'

'Good.'

'There's just one problem.'

'Only the one?'

'If I remember correctly, "I want out" were Vinnie Jensen's last words before Gareth Wade broke his back in two.'

'Then don't say them out loud.'

Chapter 13

Earlsbury – London – Cairndale
Wednesday – Saturday
15-18 December

The milder weather in Earlsbury had been deceptive. That morning, a massive cold front had swept in from the North Sea and covered the south east of England in several inches of snow. It showed no signs of stopping.

He wasn't able to get hold of Leonie until early evening.

'I can't believe it.' she said. 'I'm ruddy snowed in *again*. This time I even managed to crash my car. I'm stuck in bloody Sussex.'

He told her about Nicole Rodgers' confession and the evidence against Nechells. He asked if they should wait until she was mobile.

'God, no. I never intended to steal your thunder, Tom: I was just protecting you. I don't think you realise just quite how much you looked like a crazed loon when I first met you: I just didn't want you to ruin your career by arresting someone unnecessarily – because if you had, I'd have got rid of you straight away.'

'That's good to know.'

'You'll see what I mean tomorrow when you arrest the creep.'

'Good luck with your car.'

'At least it wasn't bombed.'

Tom disconnected and rang the chief constable on his personal number.

'One minute,' said the Chief.

There was a sound of shouting through a muffled hand over the mouthpiece. He seemed to be still in the office and talking to Evelyn. When the Chief came back on the line he said, 'Where do you want to interview him?'

'I don't mind, sir, but I'd prefer it to be Earlsbury.'

'Good. I'll bring him down myself. We've got a breakfast meeting in Coventry, but I'll tell him there's business in the Black Country first.'

A crazed loon? No one had ever called him that before. He wondered if it were a look he should cultivate for the purpose of intimidating suspects.

Kate had two screens connected to the laptop in her studio flat. One of them was showing that transport in the South East was hopelessly disrupted, except for some inter-city trains running out of Euston. That was good because Cairndale (the nearest station to Colonel Shepherd's house) was on the West Coast Main Line. She just hoped that Conrad wasn't in East Anglia or somewhere equally inaccessible.

The other screen was mostly scrolling text as her sniffer program went to work. The hacker who had gone with her to Aberdeen last month had set up a program which was testing, probing, hacking and scanning every automotive database in the UK for the VIN belonging to Patrick Lynch's Jaguar. It would run quite happily on its own, and there were so many layers of cloaking between her and the target that it was fairly slow. She was going to leave it running overnight and tomorrow when she went away.

That left one thing – Conrad. Skinner had given her his number along with an envelope containing one hundred pounds in cash. She dialled it.

'Hello?'

'Hello, Conrad. It's Kate.'

'Aah. Anthony said you might call. He also said you might want to see me.'

'If you don't mind. Where are you?'

'In the North West, not too far from Preston.'

'That's great. I've got to go to Cairndale tomorrow. Do you know it?'

'I was there this morning. Are there any trains running? It looks pretty bad down your way. If you're in London, that is.'

'I am in London, but there are trains running. Where shall we meet?'

'How about you get the train to Cairndale, and I'll meet you at the station? I'll take us for lunch and spend some of that hundred pounds you've got for me. You deserve a share.'

'What for?'

'I'll tell you over lunch. Just text me when you know the time of your train. Oh, and wear something half-way smart.'

Tom had insisted on keeping Nicole Rodgers in custody overnight until the CPS could thrash out the small print of her deal. He had great delight in letting Hayes choose a change of clothes for her after they'd finished searching the flat. As predicted, all the forensic evidence was there to nail her for Misconduct in Public Office. The tapes of her and Nechells having a domestic had also been retrieved from a safe deposit box.

There had been a late-night phone call from Kate who confessed to going into his place to raid his wine store. She sounded like she had already made inroads into one of his better reds.

'I'm finally going to lay Vinnie's ghost,' she had said.

'How? With a séance?'

'Don't be silly. The ghost inside me, Tom. I'm going waaaay up north tomorrow to get some answers.'

It sounded as if there was something else she wanted to tell him, but either she'd had too much to drink or not enough. She finished by telling him that London was a disaster zone as far as transport was concerned.

'If things go according to plan tomorrow,' he said, 'I might stay up here for the weekend. There may be a lot of paperwork.'

'Have fun.'

The weather had turned colder again overnight, and both Tom and Kris were wrapped up warm as they waited for the Chief to arrive with his passenger. It was barely light when the Chief's official Mercedes drove around the back of Earlsbury's police station: the rear of the Victorian building with its utilitarian extension seemed especially shabby when the gleaming black vehicle pulled up. The rear windows were tinted, and Tom couldn't see who was in the back.

The driver got out, his gun clearly visible under his uniform jacket. He opened the offside rear door and, very slowly, DCC Nechells got out. The driver shut the door, slipped back into the car and drove off.

David Nechells was left standing in the middle of the car park. He had no coat to go over his uniform, and the frost glittered under the street lights around him.

Tom moved towards him, and Nechells looked at the exit. Sensing that he might run, Hayes walked quickly off to their left to block his route. Nechells adjusted his peaked cap and turned to face them.

He had let Hayes administer the caution to Rodgers yesterday, but Nechells was his prize. He showed his warrant card and placed the Deputy Chief Constable under arrest.

The first shock to Nechells' system came when he asked for a lawyer.

'I'm afraid that's not possible, sir. That particular solicitor has already been engaged by Miss Nicole Rodgers, and as Miss Rodgers may be giving evidence at a future trial, you need to find alternative representation.'

'Get on to ACPO. I'll use whoever they nominate.'

Tom was in the Police Federation, as was Hayes: Nechells had the benefit of being represented by the Association of Chief Police Officers.

The custody sergeant drew Tom aside and said, 'Do you want me to do the full monty? Belt, shoelaces and tie confiscated, and lock him up in a cell?'

'Yes. It may be a while before the ACPO solicitor gets here.'

'Righty-ho.' The sergeant put his head on one side. 'Could you get a permanent posting here? I've seen more action on your watch than we normally get in a year.'

'Much as I love the Black Country, I'm going to spread the love elsewhere.'

When the custody sergeant asked Nechells whether he wished anyone to be notified of his arrest, he nominated his wife. Tom objected.

'We have reason to believe that there may be evidence at your home which might be compromised. We'll tell her shortly, when we execute the search warrant.'

He left him in the tender care of the sergeant and took Hayes with him to the Nechells' house, along with the deputy chief's keys.

'Blimey,' said Kate. 'I can see why you wanted me to wear something smart.'

She pivoted slowly in the grand entrance to Hartsford Hall which displayed its original seventeenth-century staircase to great effect. There were photographs on the board outside of elegant brides descending to rapturous applause. It was way above anything she'd eaten in before. 'I hope the food's as good as the venue.'

'It's got a Michelin star, so it had better be good.'

Clarke had undergone something of a transformation too. He looked smarter than she'd ever seen him out of uniform, and he had shaved off most of his hair. The receptionist led them straight through to the dining room.

As they passed the fireplace, she could smell pine resin going up the chimney, and that was reinforced by the majestic Christmas tree near the staircase. The dining room was more discreetly festive. Unlike the pub where she had enjoyed Sunday lunch with her father, Hartsford Hall clearly believed that less is more when it came to decorations. She wondered if that were partly because they had no intention of offering a Christmas menu: it was the two-course set lunch or nothing. The price for one person was higher than her Dad had paid for the whole bill.

Conrad insisted that they enjoy the food before getting down to business, and Kate didn't object, because once she'd eaten the amuse-bouche, she made herself a promise to eat in somewhere like this at least once a year.

She let herself enjoy two glasses of wine and was thoroughly relaxed when they took coffee by the log fire in the hall. Conrad nipped out for a smoke.

Clarke took the last drag on his cigarette and stubbed it out in the mock-Georgian planter filled with sand. He had thought long and hard about Kate, and how to win her over. The food and wine were a bonus – and would help him convince her today – but Intelligence officers have notoriously good memories. He needed a story that would still be as credible tomorrow, when she'd sobered up and was back to her microwaved meals in London. He returned to the fire and made himself comfortable.

'What do you want to know, Kate?'

'As much as you can tell me.'

He nodded and looked into the fire before speaking. 'The British Army is not without its faults, but it's an honourable body of men and women.' He looked up at her. 'I rehearsed that last night. Do you think it sounds too pompous?'

'Do you ever take anything seriously?'

He made a move towards his left trouser leg then remembered what Olivia had said. Who was he trying to convince by showing off his wounds all the time? Himself, of course. He pretended to brush some lint away instead. 'It's true, though. You should know that. Would you have put up with private military contractors having the run of Army resources?'

'I might have.'

'Not really. You'd want to know what was going on. You'd want to know whether their missions were kosher: whether you were being implicated in something you couldn't agree to.'

'And you didn't? You were happy to go along with this.'

He shook his head. 'We were a carefully-chosen team. Carefully chosen for our ability to put a support mission together and keep our mouths shut. There were three of us: Vinnie would allocate resources from the supply chain, Wade would load them on to a helicopter and then fly with me when we took the mission out.'

'Where were they? The missions?'

'All in Pakistan. The PMCs were only doing what the regular Army couldn't – that is, make direct strikes on Taliban targets across the border. The Yanks like to play with their new toys – those drones – but they need boots on the ground. As ever.'

There was a grain of truth in what he had said. She must have been aware of the rumours that PMCs were doing dirty work in Pakistan on behalf of NATO governments. And they were. The problem was that Clarke's work for Operation Red Flag had nothing to do with missions: it was the straightforward theft of money intended for reconstruction projects. According to Jennings, some of it did indeed subsidise black ops over the border, but Clarke suspected that most of it went on refurbishing St Andrew's

Hall and subsidising the racecourse. And Amelia – she was very high-maintenance.

Kate had been thinking while she finished her coffee. 'There must have been more than three of you in it. With all due respect, Conrad, you might have been able to smuggle booze on to the Camp, and God knows what else out of it, but even you couldn't have organised something on this scale. I was duty Intelligence officer for years out there. I never got so much as a whiff of what you were doing.'

'Of course we weren't on our own. These missions were facilitated at a very high level, but I'm not giving that away.'

'What about the money? Why were Vinnie and Gareth being paid for their work? And why did Skinner say he'd never paid you a penny?'

'I was their shop steward. I said it was so risky that the PMCs should make a contribution. Those guys deal in millions. As for me, I don't need the money.' He gave her a grin. 'I'm going to let you into a secret: I won the lottery a few years ago. Not enough to retire on, but enough to buy myself a helicopter business. I was just waiting out my twenty years for a decent pension, then I was going to set myself up. I still am when my leg's better, and I can get my pilot's licence back. Next summer, I hope.'

He was getting close to the crunch. The lottery part was also half true; he looked forward to telling Mina the real story one day. 'I didn't do it for money: I did it for favours and contacts.'

She closed her eyes and accepted what he had said. Her boyfriend had been on the take, and she had to acknowledge it. He pressed on. 'It's finally time I told you what happened on the day he died.'

She leaned forward and put her cup down. He had his receptive audience: now it was show time.

'Vinnie wanted out. He'd had enough and he wanted to quit, so he could be with you. He'd borrowed the ring from me the night before, but I had no idea what he was going to do.' He shook his head in a show of unhappy memory. 'We were testing Madox out to see if he could join the team. I don't mind flying on my own, but an extra pilot would have made life easier, especially in the bigger choppers. While Madox was making the pre-flight checks, Vinnie told us that he was quitting. Gareth was furious – we couldn't operate without an insider from Royal Logistics, and Vinnie had no one else to offer in his place. That meant a hiatus in our operation and a hiatus in payments. Gareth hadn't been very wise in his investments.'

'Go on. What happened next?'

He let out a sigh. 'I gave Madox an illegal order – to buzz the mosque in that village. It was to see whether he could be tempted. Unfortunately, Gareth saw it as a chance to take it out on Vinnie. There was a dreadful fight in the back. Wade fired his weapon and missed. There's no armour on the internal partition. The shot went straight through the screen and hit Madox.'

'Why didn't you take over?'

'Madox was doing a great job with a really delicate manoeuvre when he got hit in the arm. He pulled the stick just enough to make us collide. We'd hit the mosque before I knew what was happening. Vinnie and Madox died in the crash.'

She sat back and considered what he had said. It was enough to hang him several times over, but would she go to the Military Police or would she accept it? It was like a delicate game of bridge with no trumps. He had one card left to play. Would it be enough? Kate led with the final question.

'If Gaz Wade was so angry, why did he commit suicide?'

'Two reasons. One was that our superiors, the ones I'm not going to identify, had a word with him and said that he would go to jail unless he put things right. The second reason was those investments of his. They had plummeted in value, but they were linked to his life – if he died, for whatever reason, they paid out in full. I also think that he was so frightened of you and of his wife, and so guilty for what he'd done, that he couldn't live with himself. Camp Bastion can be a very lonely place.'

There. He'd played his card. He sat back and waited for her response.

'It's so sordid. So messy. Poor Madox: he didn't deserve that.'

'He didn't. That's why I'm telling you now. There was an innocent victim on that chopper, but it wasn't Vinnie, I'm afraid.'

She looked at her watch, and he knew he'd won the trick. If Kate had mentioned justice for Madox's family, he would have been in trouble. For whatever reason, she had decided that nothing would bring him back, and that he should rest in peace.

'I've got to go,' said Kate as she stood up. 'Thanks for lunch.'

'Where do you want to be? It's no bother to drop you off.'

'Would you mind terribly giving me a lift to the golf club? It's back through town and near the coast. It's odd, you know, but my cousin has just done an entire case which hinged on evidence from golfing.'

'Den of thieves, in my opinion. You should do something more wholesome, like going racing.'

'Racing? You?'

'I've taken a sabbatical from all things military. I'm working at a racecourse and our first meeting is on Boxing Day. I'm off to Wolverhampton on Saturday to see how it's done.'

He drove back to Cairndale, over the railway then out to the coast where the clubhouse was to be found. He dropped her off and took a different road, which led up a small incline. At the top was a viewing point. No one was there today, so he jumped out of the Land Rover and lit a cigarette. The whole of Morecambe Bay was stretched out before him in the winter sun, its sands glistening with a billion ripples of reflected light. He saw the squat iron pillars of the Arnside Viaduct taking a train over some river which cut its own special channel through the sand.

Beyond the beach, beyond the serrated markings in the sands, beyond the viaduct and the river, beyond some grassy mounds, lay the granite blocks of Grange over Sands. Beyond Grange, hills rose up until they were overtopped by the giant, capped-white-with-snow fells of the Lake District.

It would be a long time before he would be well enough to walk across the sands. Before then he would have crossed his own personal river: a Rubicon with a Red Flag in it. He'd be out of the Rainbow, and be either free or dead. He'd taken the first step today by convincing Kate to back off. She would be safe now she'd stopped sticking her nose into things.

By the time they resumed their interview with David Nechells, all hell had broken loose across Midland Counties Police Service. Officers from other stations were dropping by to see if it were true that the deputy chief was under arrest, and Tom had been forced to call in an independent Scene of Crime contractor to finish the search of the rather well-appointed family home.

Even though Nechells had tried to cover his tracks, there was plenty of evidence to be had. It was after lunch when Tom took his folders into the interview room: DCI Storey had volunteered to man the recording equipment and keep any rubberneckers at bay. Prosecutors from the CPS had also descended and were sitting next to Storey to keep an eye on things.

'Interview resumed. For the purposes of clarity, I will be asking you questions relating to a variety of offences.'

Tom went through the laws he thought Nechells might have broken and then asked if he wished to comment.

'My client does not wish to comment at this time. He wishes to see what evidence you have gathered,' said the ACPO-nominated solicitor.

Tom started producing documents. To every question, Nechells gave a *No Comment* answer. Instead, his solicitor queried their warrants, their logs, their chain of evidence and their ability to relate the evidence to his client.

That was fine. Tom was very willing to play the long game with Nechells: he was willing to release him on police bail and wait until all results were back. However, he had saved the best bits until last.

'I am showing your client a list of numbers found in an old diary in his desk. I've checked these myself and they relate to accounts in St Jude. Do you know anything about them?'

'Were they in my client's name?'

'No. As you would expect with St Jude, the ownership is opaque.'

'Well, it must be a coincidence.'

'Perhaps.' Tom focused his attention on the policeman and not the lawyer. 'You may not know this, Mr Nechells, but things are changing in the world of offshore finance. It's all Al-Qaida's fault. The Americans have come down heavily on places like St Jude. They now respond positively to requests for information – but only when criminal proceedings are involved. I will be charging you with money laundering, and the bank has agreed to freeze the accounts, with immediate effect.'

A little of the blood drained from Nechells' face. Tom added some insult to the injury. 'I rang the bursar at St Modwenna's school, and she confirmed that one of these accounts was used to pay Pandora's school fees. That should be a telling detail for the jury.'

The lawyer started to object, but realised that Tom hadn't actually said anything wrong. Everyone around the table could see it, though: a working class jury would not take kindly to school fees amounting to tens of thousands of pounds being paid from a dodgy offshore account.

It was time for the last cut. Tom set up the MP3 player and stated the origin of the evidence. When he said *Clandestine recording by Miss Nicole Rodgers*, Nechells almost grabbed his solicitor by the throat to ask for a break.

Ten minutes later the lawyer said, 'My client has instructed me to discuss these matters with the CPS, with a view to a selective guilty plea to some small matters. I don't think we need to hear the tape.'

'Oh, I think we do. These are not "matters", these are crimes. There are some questions I'd like to put to your client based on the tape. DC Hayes, could you run it for me?'

Nechells looked at the ceiling, the walls, the table and the floor ... anywhere but at Tom or the little loudspeaker that was playing out his last two nights at Nicole's flat.

Hayes turned off the MP3 player and Tom said, 'In that tape, you are clearly heard directing Miss Rodgers to interfere with evidence. Can you explain this?'

'No comment.'

'Also, on this tape, you are heard to make the following statement: "I told Griffin to be careful at the Goods Yard. It's not my fault he was drunk." Did you telephone DS Griffin from the Victoria Hotel in Edgbaston and order him to go to the Goods Yard?'

'No comment.'

'I'll be charging you with murder by association at the end of this interview.'

The lawyer looked sceptical. 'The CPS will never pursue that.'

Tom let the silence gather around Nechells like wolves closing in on a wounded animal, but Nechells still didn't get it. He looked inconvenienced rather than guilty.

'Interview suspended,' said Tom, and pressed the button to stop the tapes. 'I will pursue it. Every officer – every decent officer – in MCPS will be rooting for me to convict the man who sent Ian Hooper to get shot.' He slammed his hand on to the table. 'Do you know that? Do you know that you betrayed every honest copper on the force when you made that call?'

The lawyer puffed out his chest. 'Chief Inspector, you are playing to the gallery – and that sort of conduct won't play well with the jury, because it won't be admissible. You turned off the tape.' Tom noticed that while objecting on behalf of his client, the man had moved well away from him. If he could have got round the desk and on to Tom's side, he would have.

'I admit it. I was playing to the gallery a little. The recorder is switched off, but the video link is still on. I hope that what I said gets round the force by tomorrow morning. Oh ... I've got something else for you. It came at lunchtime.'

He took an embossed envelope out of his folder, addressed to Mr Nechells. 'It's from the chief constable. It's a written confirmation of the verbal suspension he issued in the car this morning. I shall have great pleasure in returning your warrant card to him tomorrow.'

Tom stood up. 'DC Hayes, will you escort Mr Nechells to the custody suite? I believe his lawyer has some work to do with the CPS.'

Kate didn't have time to think between being dropped off outside the clubhouse and being greeted by Colonel William Shepherd MC, previously of Military Intelligence. He signed her into the club and took her through to the lounge, where she accepted another glass of wine.

Colonel Shepherd was older than her father, but seemed to lead a healthier lifestyle, judging by his slight tan and upright stance. He did favour his left arm a little. Arthritis? They talked of the weather for a minute then he asked about her service. She told him.

'How can I help you?' he asked. 'I know the sort of things that Skinner and Jennings' mob gets up to, and I can't say I approve of them.'

'Sorry, sir. Who's Jennings?'

'Sir Stephen Jennings. He was a Regular until he left the Army and bought a stake in CIS. He was CEO for many years, and he's still the chairman. Skinner is very much a man in his image.'

'After what I've heard today, I'm not sure I approve of them either. I don't think I'll be working for them again, and I haven't done anything so far that I'm not proud of.'

'Fair enough. I didn't think you would. What's the problem?'

'Did you hear about that bomb in Blackpool?'

'The one that killed Ben Adaire? Of course. You're not the first person to ask me about that. What on earth is your interest?'

'It's my cousin. He was the survivor, and he's the police officer chasing the people behind a big money laundering operation. It got very serious when he turned over some rocks in the Black Country.'

'I see. I couldn't give MI5 any names, so I won't be of much use to you either.'

'Tom – my cousin – believes that there is a leak in one of the police forces connected with this gang. He's held back on one piece of information: the bomber had a red hand and dagger tattooed on his left forearm.'

Shepherd gave nothing away, but he didn't respond immediately. He finished his gin and swirled the ice cubes around. Eventually he spoke. 'You never served over there, did you?'

'No, sir. I was with Signals then, and I spent most of my time in Latin America before the Twin Towers came down, but I've talked to plenty of officers who did.'

'Northern Ireland wasn't the finest chapter in Military Intelligence's history, you know. We let MI5 get their feet under the table and we became just an army of occupation. The counter-terrorism stuff was mostly out of our hands, but you know all that. What you don't know is that certain sections of the Army weren't very happy about it, and decided to start their own initiatives.'

'I've heard the accusations of co-operation with Loyalist paramilitaries.'

Shepherd shook his head. 'Some took it further than that. They recruited some of the hotheads from Loyalist gangs, and they gave them military training. You didn't hear that from me.'

'No, sir.'

'When the peace process started, there was a general amnesty. Benedict Adaire was given a new identity in Britain, as were other IRA men. That's how your cousin identified him, I believe, because he was on the system. Those men from the Loyalist gangs were never arrested. MI5 said that your cousin supplied some fingerprints the other day. No record anywhere. I'm afraid that I can't help you.'

'You've been a big help, sir. Now I know what sort of person I'm looking for, it helps me narrow it down a lot.'

'Good luck, and be careful. Do you want a lift to the station?'

'If you're going that way.'

Kate had thought about it on the train home last night. She thought about it on the way to North London this morning, and she was still thinking about it when she put flowers on Vinnie's grave. Seeing the flowers already on the grave made up her mind. Vinnie didn't need her to mourn him: she would let the dead lie.

If she stirred things up now, what would happen? First, Vinnie's parents would be wrecked when their son was exposed. Then, someone like Tom would be appointed to look into Vinnie and Wade's financial affairs. Did those little children she'd seen in Pembroke deserve to have their lives wrecked again for what their father might have done? Finally, there was Madox's family. They were the only ones who would gain anything – instead of having caused the crash, their son would be exonerated as a victim of Wade's greed. It wasn't enough. It wouldn't bring him back.

That left the question of her own position. She couldn't go up to the authorities and say, *Look what I found.* They either wouldn't believe her or she'd be palmed off with more rubbish. No, to get to the bottom of this mystery would require her to go to the press and stand in the spotlight for a long time while all her income dried up and she was vilified from all sides. On the whole, the world would not be a better place if she spoke out, because once the fuss had died down they'd carry on as if nothing had happened.

She stood for a moment in the snow and thought about what a generous, considerate man Vinnie had been. He had respected her as a woman and as a soldier. It was rare to get both in a man: they either baulked at her position in the military or treated her as a sexless android. She felt something run down her spine and linger on her backside. Was it the icy wind or the memory of his hands? Without looking back, she walked out of the churchyard and left the dead to their rest .

She stocked up on some food from the Metro store and returned to her flat. As she passed her laptop, she glanced at the screen. There was a hit.

One of the databases had returned an entry for Patrick Lynch's Jaguar with a date after his death. It was the central registry of a tyre workshop chain that was registered in Leicester. But where was the branch?

She had to tread carefully going into the system to find the table with the branch details. She cross-referenced the index and thought that at first the table was corrupted. According to the result, the workshop that had recorded Lynch's car was situated in Longuenesse. That couldn't be right. She dug further and realised that YouAuto plc was also the proud owner of VousAuto SA in France, and that Longuenesse was a suburb of Saint-Omer, south east of Calais.

According to the job sheet, the French garage had replaced a run-flat tyre. The vehicle had false plates, but some diligent employee had listed the VIN correctly and recorded that Mr Smith had paid in cash. The most interesting part was the fitter's notes. She had to resort to the internet for a translation, but she finally worked out that the car had also suffered some damage to the bodywork, and the garage had booked it in to Boyard et Fils to have a dent knocked out and the paintwork sprayed. Mr Smith would collect it direct from Boyard et Fils on Saturday.

Tom had left a message for her last night saying that he'd made a big arrest and wouldn't be coming home until next week. She didn't want to bother him with what might be nothing and – let's face it – international co-operation needed a bit more to go on than this. She couldn't expect the Lancashire & Westmorland Constabulary to issue an International Arrest Warrant on the basis of a hacked database. She could be in France by teatime, and Saint-Omer was only half an hour from Calais.

Kate dug out her passport and started packing again. Those Euros she'd brought back from Dublin would come in handy.

'I can't do TV.'

'Yes, you can,' said Hayes. 'You know how much you loved being ambushed last week. Go and get your own back. Besides, it's your fault.'

'How is it my fault?' said Tom.

'You forced the media relations manager to resign, and then arrested his deputy. There's no one left at MCPS to appear on television except the unpaid intern. Besides, it's not their case, is it? You arrested Nechells, so you should go on TV to explain it.'

'You're just trying to wind me up.'

'I know.'

The horrible thing was that Kris might be right. This was definitely a CIPPS case, and not a local police matter. The only problem was that with Leonie snowed into Sussex and the CIPPS press office being in Lambeth, there was no one on the ground in Birmingham to give an interview. Not that he could say anything: the whole thing was *sub judice*.

'Pass me the property file again.'

They were surrounded by paperwork and besieged on all sides by the CPS, ACPO, people from the TV, and anyone else who wanted a piece of the action. They only person leaving them alone to get on with their job was the chief constable.

Tom opened the file containing all property transactions involving the parties concerned. He had searched the Land Registry for all mentions of Nechells, Griffin, Lynch, Rodgers and their families, and any companies they were directors of. It was pretty thick.

'Get some Post-it notes and a pen then help me clear the floor.'

They shoved all the other folders on to the desks, and Tom started laying out the property records on the floor in a way that corresponded to a map of Britain. Hayes provided local knowledge of the Black Country. Every time there was a profit or loss, she wrote the amount on a sticky note and Tom fixed it on the sheet. The breakthrough, when it came, was not in the Midlands but in Twickenham.

Three years ago, Nechells had bought a house from his own mother (who was in a nursing home) but sold it two months later at a loss of one hundred thousand pounds. The buyer had been a property management company registered in St Jude, but they in turn had sold it to DS Griffin within six weeks for the same amount. Griffin had sold it to a member of the public the following year for a profit of £120,000, and used the money as equity for the house they had searched only a few weeks ago. It was enough to convict Nechells of money laundering.

'Well done, Tom,' said Hayes. 'I wouldn't have spotted that.' She offered her hand and helped him up from the floor.

'We'd better get this lot cleared away,' he said. 'The CPS are due any minute.'

'How do you think we'll do?'

It was the question Tom had avoided all last night and all this morning. DCI Storey had done his job, and Nechells' name was forever blackened in the Midlands. No police officer would ever speak to him again, unless they were trying to arrest him for something. Even if Nechells dodged the worst of the charges, just one conviction would be enough to vindicate Tom's determination.

While Hayes filed things away, Tom decided that the most alarming reaction had come from Nechells' wife.

Mrs Nechells had returned from her job at Earlsbury Sixth Form College to find the police had already turned their house over. Tom had apologised for not informing her and quickly brought her up to date. Within seconds of meeting the woman, he had decided she wasn't part of his criminal activities.

'Will it all come out in court?' It was a standard response from a fraudster's spouse.

'I think that depends on whether he contests any of the charges. If he pleads guilty, there will be a statement of his crimes, naturally, but no cross-examination of witnesses or drawn-out accumulation of detail. I should point out that the press are very likely to be here soon. If you and your daughter want to avoid them, I suggest you pack a bag and get out before they arrive.'

'I meant the affair. Will that come out in court?'

He paused before replying. Mrs Nechells was of an age or slightly older than her husband, and she made a startling contrast to Nicole Rodgers. Her hair was not dyed and she was bordering on overweight. Although she was an assistant principal and teacher of Religious Studies, her appearance was like something out of a film about Oxford colleges: Mrs Nechells appeared to have grabbed whatever was clean this morning and put it on.

'The affair wasn't a crime: it was what he did to other people that will send him to prison. He may be directly involved in getting an innocent officer shot.'

Mrs Nechells waved this away as a minor concern. 'Will it come out that he spent all that money on one of his bimbos? That's what I can't stand. My husband has been ploughing his own furrow for some years, Inspector. That's between him and God. What I don't want people to know is that he stole money to do so.'

Tom couldn't answer that. On the way back to Earlsbury Park, Hayes had answered it for him. 'I think God is more likely to forgive David Nechells than his wife ever will.' That just about summed it up.

Tom jerked to his feet when the chief prosecutor for the West Midlands arrived. This was always the most depressing part of the job: going through the evidence and having to stand by while someone else decided whether it was in the public interest to prosecute, and whether there was a realistic chance of conviction.

There had already been one meeting last night, and Tom brought the man up to speed on what they'd discovered this morning. After that, he had to ask Hayes to leave them alone.

'Tell me,' said the prosecutor. 'Why did you charge him with murder by association? He wasn't there on the night. We'll never prosecute that.'

'I know. It's just my way of letting MCPS know what he did, one copper to another. If Nechells had been a civilian, I wouldn't have bothered.'

This was clearly a foreign concept to the CPS. 'We'll move on, shall we?'

Over the next hour, they fought back and forth over the charges, until there was a list of things that the prosecutor could put to the ACPO solicitor. A telephone call was made, and Tom insisted that Hayes was present when the final score was read out: Nechells was going to plead guilty to conspiracy to pervert the course of justice, but at the moment would be pleading not guilty to money laundering.

'That was your boss's idea,' said the prosecutor to Hayes. 'He reckons that enough evidence will eventually emerge for the money laundering to stick. We'll definitely get him sent to prison for conspiracy, though. The rest can lie on file until he stands up in court and admits it all.'

'I'm glad we've sorted that out,' said Tom. 'It's a big weight off my mind.' He gave the man a smile. 'Now that you've taken over the case, you can do the media.'

When he had gone, Tom looked around at the files. 'A good result, Kris. Well done and thanks. This must be the biggest case you've worked on so far.'

'You're not joking, sir. I never expected to be doing something like this so soon after coming out of uniform.'

'Well, savour the moment. Today is the best day. From now on, it's just paperwork, and pressure to move on to the next case. I'll be raising a glass tonight and enjoying every drop.'

Hayes looked uncomfortable, but didn't comment.

'In the meantime, I've ordered a cake. A proper sticky chocolate gateau will be delivered here at four o'clock, and you will join me in a big slice.'

'Can we take it home afterwards? My mom loves chocolate cake, and I don't want you mixing cake and booze on your own in the hotel.' She had spoken with a smile, but he could tell there was something else underneath.

'If you like. I could definitely manage two slices before sinking into an alcoholic stupor.'

'No, that's not what I mean. It's my mom. It would mean the world to her if you told her what's been going on. I just can't seem to find the words.'

'That would be a pleasure. I can also break it to her that we'll be working all weekend, otherwise I won't be able to go home for Christmas. Do you want to go to church on Sunday or play football on Saturday?'

'Football. But don't tell my mom.'

'On your own head be it, but I may come and watch if I've got nothing better to do.' He picked up a bag and put it on her desk. 'You can carry on going through the contents of his laptop until the cake arrives.'

Hayes put her hand on the bag and considered him. 'I can't work out whether you're being serious or not. About coming to watch me play.'

'That's all part of my plan. You'll be looking over your shoulder all the way from the dressing room to the touchline.'

She gave him a grin. 'If you do come, the kick-off is at two o'clock. We don't have floodlights.'

The body shop of Boyard et Fils was in a good location for surveillance. Kate drove past it in her hire car during the evening and saw the perfect place to keep watch. Across the road was a patch of rough ground used as a public car park:

her hire car would fit in perfectly. Satisfied, she returned to the motel and crashed out.

It was so cold the next morning that she had to chip ice off the car for ages until it warmed up. She didn't arrive at the observation point until well after eight o'clock, the time she expected the garage to open. It would be horrible if the Jaguar were already gone.

She took up position and watched as the first employees of Boyard et Fils arrived for work, all of them leaving their cars near her. Ten minutes later, she breathed a sigh of relief as the Jaguar was moved out of the workshop and left at the front, ready for collection.

At about nine o'clock she realised that it was too cold to sit in the car without the engine running. She had to have it going in short bursts when there were no pedestrians nearby.

At ten o'clock she needed to pee. Soldiers got used to that, and she filled an old water bottle. A few men had arrived and left, and a badly-dented Saab had been delivered. At half past ten, a man was dropped off by taxi. That looked promising. Two minutes later, he emerged from the office and pointed to the Jaguar; the indicators flashed as he unlocked the doors.

She had worked out that if the car turned left, he would pass her location: if it turned right, she would have to try and intercept it. The man got into the car and started the engine. He adjusted the seat then moved off. He turned right.

Kate pulled out into the traffic. There was a junction ahead of her. If she didn't see the Jag, she would have to make a right turn and hope for the best. The lights turned red, and she saw the target vehicle cross in front of her, heading away to her left.

She caught up with him and left plenty of vehicles between them. The Jaguar and its GB number plates stuck out in the traffic, so she took her time. They headed through the outskirts of Saint-Omer, and then out to the north east, over the canal. If they carried on along this road they would be in Belgium before long.

The traffic thinned, and Kate had to drop back even further. The next time they came to a roundabout, she only just caught sight of the Jag turning left on to a smaller road. She had to give way for a few seconds, and when she had got round, she could just see its rear disappearing up a side road. That was too dangerous. Kate slowed down and pulled into a lay-by just before the turning. The Jaguar's destination must be up the lane somewhere. She would give it a minute and then follow.

She was in France, so it was a left-hand drive car and she was pulled in to the right-hand side of the road. She stretched out her arms as best she could and shuffled in her seat. A white van came down the road, then – as it got near – it swerved over and pulled up right in front of her, blocking her exit.

She and the other driver jumped out of their vehicles at the same time, and she found herself eight feet from a man with a gun. He was holding it down, out of sight from any passing cars, but it wouldn't take long for him to raise it up. He was wearing a knitted cap and was muffled against the cold, but something about his face looked British. Maybe it was the pale skin.

'Let's not hang about here,' he said. 'Let's go for a wee chat.'

It was a Northern Irish accent. Shit. How had they tracked her? What had she done wrong?

Kate relaxed her stance and worked out the distances. It didn't look good.

'I don't think so,' she said. 'The last time one of my family got in a car with you, things didn't go well.'

'That was a mistake,' he said. 'We're past that now. I just want a word, that's all.'

'Let's talk here. We're both wrapped up warm.'

'Stop messing, woman, and get in the back of the van.'

Kate was the best analyst she knew. She could look at the evidence and read the situation. This man had killed at least two people, and had tried to kill Tom. He wanted her in the back of his van. She had told no one where she was. No one would come looking for her. The most likely scenario involved him torturing and killing her. He had let her see his face.

'That's a big gun. What is it? A Glock 22?'

'It's a 32. Now get in the van.'

He was eight feet away. If she ran at him, he might try to fight or he might try to shoot her. If he fought, she would take her chances. If he shot, he might miss.

If he hit her anywhere except an arm, the bullet would rip her apart. She didn't want to get shot, but she wanted to be tortured even less.

Kate dipped her knees and lowered her head to charge. As she did so, she saw him starting to lift his gun.

Chapter 14

Wolverhampton – Earlsbury – Fleetwood – Cairndale – Oxford

Saturday – Sunday

18-19 December

'I suppose it counts as flat racing, seeing as there aren't any jumps.'

'No. It has a category all of its own – All Weather racing. You're right, though – there aren't any jumps.'

Clarke was standing between Julian Bentley and Amelia Jennings near the track at Wolverhampton Racecourse. It was one of the few meetings going ahead since the weather had taken an icy grip on the countryside.

'Not many here,' said Amelia. 'Are you two going to stay outside for the race?'

The forecast was for things to get even worse. A cold front was due to bring strong winds and snow down from the Arctic and to hit the west coast. All three of them were wrapped in several layers, and Amelia was bouncing on her toes to keep warm.

'Conrad needs to see how the bookies react as the riders come out,' said Bentley. 'He needs to see what happens to the odds. A lot can change in the last few minutes of a small meeting like this.'

Clarke had wondered where they were going when they drove under the railway viaduct and past the small workshops to the racecourse. He would rather be here than doing any Christmas shopping, but it was a close call. Bentley had compared Wolverhampton's operation to one just north of their own. 'Cartmel only has seven meetings a year. A year. Wolverhampton has well over a hundred. It's all down to the bookmakers – they need a guaranteed racecard at all sorts of odd times. You can't go racing at Fylde on a winter's night.'

'I'm going to leave you boys to it,' said Amelia. 'I'm off to our box to get warm.'

She retreated up the steps, and Clarke watched several punters make their way down to the track as the riders warmed up their mounts beyond the rail. As large wads of notes were brought out and wagered on the impending race, the bookmakers made frantic signals to their assistants and demanded to know what was happening online. Two or three of the prices changed quite substantially in the last minute before the starter brought the horses under orders.

Clarke had watched the runners quite carefully as they came out, and he reckoned that one of them looked just a little bit happier in the cold – just a little bit sharper as he moved – and the jockey had a smile on his face. Clarke put his fifty pounds on that one.

The race was over before the small crowd could really get excited about it. That didn't stop the horses doing their best, and Clarke's horse in particular seemed to enjoy himself. Clarke wasn't the only one who had had that idea, and his winnings were pretty meagre. He only discovered he'd backed the firm favourite after placing his bet.

'I need a drink,' said Bentley.

'Me, too. I'll buy you a shandy with my profits.'

'I don't think Amelia knows what a shandy is.'

'What's she doing here? Bit off the beaten track for her, isn't it?'

'She told Olivia she's finding it hard in London at the moment. I believe your name was mentioned.'

'What, mine?'

Bentley laughed, and they worked their way through the bar to their box. 'She does have a job with us, you know.

She's in charge of VIP hospitality and she's come up early for the Boxing Day meeting.'

'Not going back to Daddy's for Christmas?'

Bentley gave him a sidelong look. Clearly, he'd overstepped the mark. Sir Stephen's was not a name to be taken in vain.

'We all go down to St Andrew's Hall on Christmas Eve. We have an early Christmas lunch then we go back up to Fylde in the afternoon to oversee the preparations for Boxing Day. That's if it goes ahead.'

Bentley pushed open the door to their box, and Amelia was pouring three glasses of Champagne. There was a great view of the track, and on the far side, Clarke caught a glimpse of his hallucination. The man in the cloak and floppy hat seemed to be staring across the track and right into their box. He took a step towards the panoramic window, but Amelia's voice made him turn his head.

'Champagne, everyone. I've had some good news.'

'Oh?'

'William's coming back. He's just sent me a text to say he's decided that he'd rather be in Fylde. I'm picking him up from Preston tonight.'

Clarke felt very uneasy. Will Offlea never did anything without a reason. No matter how desirable Amelia might be, he doubted that her charms alone would have brought him back from France.

They drank the champagne and talked about the Boxing Day meeting, until Clarke made an excuse that he needed a smoke. He left the box and headed outside. As soon as he'd lit his cigarette, he called Alain in London.

'What do you want? You promised I'd never hear from you again.'

'I know. I just need you to do a small favour. You can do it without even standing up.'

'Why can't you do it yourself?'

'I still can't speak French, even after our little adventure. Look, can you go on to a few French news websites? Has anything happened in the last day or so that I might be interested in? Start in the Pas-de-Calais and work down. That's all.'

'I'll call you back.'

As the riders were lining up for the first race at Wolverhampton, down the road in Earlsbury the teams were coming out for Castle Women vs Tettenhall Tigresses, and Tom was wondering what he was doing standing at the edge of a muddy field when there was still ice on some of the puddles. Just before they split up for lunch, he had said, 'If there's any reason why you'd prefer me not to be there, just say. I really am only doing it to stop myself going mad in the hotel.'

'No, you can come. Just don't embarrass me.'

So there he was. He took up a position at the end of the thin line of spectators. He could spot boyfriends, husbands, a couple of the players' children and a few parents. There was a sprinkling of young women, who could be anything from cousins to girlfriends to unused squad players. If the team had a squad that big, of course. When they changed ends after the toss, Tom was mortified to realise that Kris's position at right back would put her immediately in front of him. He tried to hide behind a man with a pushchair.

Castle had a male coach who let his opinion be known from the moment the whistle blew. The home supporters took their lead from him, and there was a constant stream of advice, imprecations and abuse hurled from the touchline. The Tigresses' female coach was just as loud, but she saved most of her invective for her own players. It wasn't a winning strategy, and after fifteen minutes, Hayes dispossessed their winger and put in a very impressive cross-field ball which the Castle forward took down and took forward until she put it in the back of the Tigresses' net. During the celebrations, Tom heard his phone ringing.

He had to take off his gloves and dig it out of his pocket. What was his mother doing ringing him now?

'Where on earth are you, Tom? Sounds like a wrestling match.'

'Long story, Mum. How's things?'

There was a long pause, and Tom checked the screen to see if the call were still live.

'There's no easy way to say this, dear,' she said. 'I've just had a call from Kate's father. The police came to see him not long ago and told him that Kate's dead.'

'Dead? What do you mean?'

'I'm sorry, Tom. She was killed this morning. In France.'

'There must be a mistake. She's in London.'

'Her father says not. She's been identified from her passport. She went over yesterday and…' His mother took a deep breath. 'She was shot. The French police think it might have been a carjacking that went wrong.'

Tom had wandered away from the pitch, and behind him, the shouts of the fans sounded like devils screaming for the gates of Hell to be opened.

'Have you got his mobile number … her dad's?'

'I'll text it to you. I'm so sorry, dear. I know how much she meant to you, I've always known you two had a special bond. She was so special, so full of life.'

She was that. She was all that and so much more. And what on earth was she doing in France?

'Thanks, Mum. I'd better get going. I'll be in touch.'

'Are you alright? To have this happen so soon after the bombing … it's going to put a terrible strain on you. Are you sure you shouldn't take some time off?'

'I'll see. Don't worry, Mum. I'm not going to go off the deep end. Bye.'

He went back to the touchline and found one of the Castle substitutes, a tall, heavily-set woman who looked like she might have been better off playing netball – but what did he know? What did he know about anything?

'Excuse me … I'm really sorry to bother you.'

'Yeah? Are you alright duck?'

'No, I'm not. Look, could you do me a favour? Could you tell Kris Hayes that I've had to go? I've just had some bad news.'

''Course I will.' He was conscious of the woman giving him a top-to-toe evaluation now that she knew what he wanted. 'Who shall I say left the message?'

'Tom.'

'Righty-ho. I'll tell her. Whatever's happened, I'm sorry.'

'Me, too. Thanks.'

He trudged back to his car and flopped into the driver's seat. He couldn't stay at the match, but he had no idea what to do next. He started the car and headed for Earlsbury Park. He was going to pack his bag and head for London to pick up his passport.

'*Allô Georges*. It's me, Alain.'

'Good man. Have you found anything?'

Clarke was watching the bookmakers shout the odds for the third race. He retreated up the steps away from their noise.

'The only news that might interest you is the death of a British woman outside Saint-Omer.'

That sounded bad, but there were lots of English women in France and, sadly, they died on a regular basis. Just like they did in Britain. 'Have you got the details?'

'Yes. A thirty-six year-old woman was found next to a car on a road north east of Saint-Omer. She had been shot once. She travelled from Britain yesterday, and it was a hire car. Police are appealing for witnesses and they are withholding her name until her family have been informed. That's it.'

'Thanks. That's very good to know.'

'Should I be worried?'

Clarke checked his watch. If Offlea was meeting Amelia at seven o'clock tonight, there was no time for him to go on a murder spree in London.

'No. Not at all. Go and spend some of those Euros, and enjoy yourself.'

He disconnected from Alain and immediately dialled Sir Stephen Jennings. He could hear music in the background.

'Sorry to bother you, sir, but can you talk?'

'I'm in Oxford helping Susan do the Christmas shopping. Hang on a sec.'

There was a muffled sound, and Jennings came back on the line.

'What's up, Clarke?'

'I've got a bad feeling, sir. I'm with Amelia at Wolverhampton races, and she let slip that Offlea's broken cover. He's coming back to England this afternoon.'

'Damn. He swore he'd give it until the New Year.'

'That's not all. A British woman was killed this morning near where Offlea was staying in France.'

'How do you know where he was? Never mind. Why do you think there's a connection?'

'They're not releasing the dead woman's name, but she was on her own and she was shot. She was the right age to be Captain Lonsdale.'

'Damn and blast. That bloody family will be the death of me. Did you see what happened in Birmingham on Thursday? Her bloody cousin went and busted one of our Principal Investors. That puts him one step away from Operation Red Flag. I hope Nechells keeps his mouth shut.'

'Martin Nechells? I remember him. Wasn't he on the embassy staff in Basra and Kabul?'

'He was, but this is brother David. That's what I mean – they're getting close. Martin was a key player in Red Flag, and he brought his brother in later. Look, I'm going to have to make some calls, but the numbers I need are back at the

Hall. I'll leave Susan to her shopping and get a taxi. I'll call you as soon as I know something. Are you sure that Offlea's meeting Amelia tonight? Not Olivia?'

'They had something of a fling, I believe.'

'Good God. I thought he was having an affair with Olivia. I'll call you back.'

Clarke turned round just in time to watch his horse, Colour Me Hopeful, kick out the sand and put in a tremendous finish. He didn't know whether that was the universe giving him a positive sign or being tremendously ironic.

Tom didn't go straight to the hotel. He stopped at BCSS to write Hayes a list of instructions for her to complete in his absence the next day, and to leave a voicemail with Leonie telling her what had happened. Shortly afterwards, he was clearing out his bathroom at Earlsbury Park when Leonie called him back.

'Hello. Are you back in London?' he said.

'Yes, but my car isn't. I got your message, Tom, and I'm really sorry about your cousin. Really, really sorry.'

Something in her voice made him sit on the edge of the bed. 'Thanks. She was like a third sister to me.'

'I know. It's really shitty when something like this happens, and I hope the French police get their act together. But they don't need you.'

'I need to find out what's going on. Kate sometimes flew under the radar at work.'

'And no one will talk to her cousin about that. I'm not being Queen Bitch here, Tom, but you've just made one of the most high-profile arrests in the history of CIPPS. You need to get that case nailed down, and you can't do it in France. I trusted you to crack it on your own, and you've repaid that trust. Don't let me – or yourself – down.'

There was no mistaking her tone. This wasn't a conversation that could go anywhere else other than to get him in serious trouble. She was right about the French police, though. Not only could he not speak the language very well, he had no jurisdiction, and if a French relative turned up to one his own investigations, he would shut them out completely.

'You're right. I suppose I just wanted to know what's going on.'

'Of course you do, and I'm sure you'll call in every favour you can to get the inside track. I know I would, but you can do that in Earlsbury. If there really is a good reason for you to be elsewhere, let me know.'

'Thanks.'

There was a knock on the door, and he opened it to find Hayes, kitbag in hand, standing outside. He waved her in and pointed to the armchair.

'It's my cousin, Kate Lonsdale. She was killed in France this morning.'

Hayes shot out of the chair and opened her arms. He stood up and embraced her. She had taken out the cornrows in her hair, and a mass of damp curls was emerging from her head. He buried his face in it and started to cry. Kris held on to him as the sobs came out until he realised what he was doing, and the wrongness of having his arms around a junior officer outweighed the rightness of her comfort. He pulled back.

'Sit down,' she said, pushing him gently on to the bed. 'I'm going to put the kettle on, and you're going to tell me all about it.'

The last race had been and gone, and Clarke was now carrying a wallet stuffed with twenty pound notes. He had tried to lose it all on an outsider but, on the track, he could do no wrong. He wondered if that, too, were an omen. Amelia had caught the train up from London that morning, and they were giving her a lift back to Fylde. Jennings sent him a text at half past four, and Clarke asked, politely but firmly, that they stop at the next services.

He walked into the trees and called Sir Stephen's number.

'It's bad news, I'm afraid,' said Jennings, as soon as he answered. 'It was Lonsdale who got shot, and she was on Offlea's trail. Damn fool.'

Clarke stared through the trees at the filling station forecourt where Bentley was messing with the car, and Amelia was buying them cups of coffee from the vending machine. It was over. It had to be over now. There was no way that Offlea could escape from this. Lonsdale was a recently retired Military Intelligence officer. Far too many questions would be asked, and her cousin would be asking them the loudest.

'Kate was very good at her job,' he said to Jennings. 'How did he cotton on to her?'

'He was tipped off. Do you remember our source in the City Police? He put a tap on to her broadband connection. Everything that appeared on her screen was downloaded to his servers. He noticed a huge amount of activity and discovered that Lonsdale was chasing a vehicle in France. Word was put out on our network, and Offlea must have intercepted her.'

Clarke closed his eyes and remembered Kate sitting across from him at Hartsford Hall, her jacket straining across her broad shoulders, and her trousers just a little bit too short. She was special: too special to be killed on a French road by someone like Offlea.

'He's gone too far,' said Clarke. 'Should we tip off the police?'

'Good God, man. Are you mad? I agree he's gone too far, but he needs to leave the country for good, not go to jail.' Jennings drew a breath and almost shouted down the phone. 'Especially when he's near one of my daughters. You'll be able to get hold of him tomorrow. Read him the riot act and tell him to get lost, or he'll be for the high jump.'

'Yes, sir. I'll keep you posted.'

So that was it. Offlea shoots a woman like Kate Lonsdale in cold blood, and Jennings treats it as a disciplinary matter in the barracks. The others were standing by Bentley's car, waiting for him to rejoin them.

He dropped the phone in his pocket, and half an idea came to into his head. When Amelia handed over his cappuccino, he took out his wallet and peeled off half a dozen twenty pound notes.

'Here. Get yourself a bottle of champagne and a takeaway for tonight. I'd rather someone else had some fun with it.'

'Aah. Poor Conrad. You can join us if you like.'

The grin on her face was a dare. It said *I'm up for a threesome. Are you?*

'I don't think William would like that, somehow. It doesn't pay to get on his bad side, you know.'

Bentley gave him a quizzical look, but said nothing. They got in the car and headed north.

Juliet Porterhouse loved this time of the week. Even after twenty-five years in the business, there was nothing to beat the rush of putting together a Sunday paper. Although the hot metal presses were ancient history, the bustle and chaos of Saturday evening gave her a bigger buzz than she could get from anywhere else. The icing on the cake was that *Ripe for the Plucking* had been given a prominent position, and her name was first in the byline.

She folded her arms behind her head and shouted over to the news editor to ask if they'd heard any more from their source in Scotland Yard about the dead woman in France. He was busy shouting *No* when her phone rang.

'I've got a man for you,' said the switchboard. Juliet doubted that very much, and even if they did, she didn't want one tonight. Not in that way.

'Put him through.'

'Is that Juliet Porterhouse?'

'Yes. Who's calling?'

'I'd rather not say at the moment.'

Anonymous calls are fairly common for journalists: that's how some of the biggest stories start. On the other hand, some of the biggest nutters refuse to give their names. This one had a fairly posh voice and sounded almost apologetic. No alarm bells yet.

'Fine. How can I help?'

'You could do us both a big favour if you gave me DCI Tom Morton's mobile number.'

Juliet took her feet off the desk and paid attention. 'That would be a breach of all kinds of trust, and probably the Data Protection Act.'

'But you didn't say *No*, did you? I might have some very important information for him. I promise that I won't bother him unless I need to. I won't tell him you gave me the number, and I promise to let you know if I've got something.'

'Is this related to the case in Birmingham or the bombing in Blackpool?'

'Nice alliteration. They're both related to each other, as I'm sure you know.'

She didn't know that at all. When the story broke about the deputy chief constable, she had pestered Morton's press office, but they strongly denied a link. She hadn't contacted the man himself because she had a feeling he wouldn't say anything.

'You're not going to stalk him, are you?'

'If I wanted to stalk him, I'd go and sit outside his office or break into his flat. This is rather more urgent than that.'

'And you promise you won't mention my name.'

'If you don't mention mine.'

'Ha ha. Have you got a pen?'

She gave her caller the number and wondered whether she should tell Tom about it. She was still debating with herself when the magazine editor shouted out that it was time for the pub. She decided not to disturb Tom's Saturday night. After all, the presses were rolling and it was too late to stop them.

The cottage where Amelia Jennings was going to entertain her William was closer to the motorway than Ribblegate Farm, so she had been dropped off first. That meant that Clarke couldn't get at Offlea's Range Rover to activate the tracking device.

Not to worry. Amelia was planning a gourmet supper, and even a strange creature like Will Offlea wouldn't be able to resist having Amelia for dessert if she were on offer. That would take a while, and at midnight, the tracking device would wake up and call home. Clarke set up the command that would bring it fully awake and start broadcasting its location over the internet to his laptop. He put a bag of things together and took a shower. Then he dressed in his rough gear and set the alarm for 0500. Finally, he climbed under the duvet and went to sleep.

He turned off the alarm and swung out of bed. While the kettle boiled, he checked his laptop. He had to squint and check again: according to the tracker, Offlea's Range Rover was a quarter of a mile away. In the farmyard.

Clarke shoved on his boots, coat and hat, then grabbed his bag and climbed into the Land Rover, throwing the bag into the passenger footwell. The direct route was up the lane, but there was a shortcut across the pasture that would bring him round the back and let him get close to the farm without being seen. He shoved the Defender in gear and drove into the field.

He kept to the side of the hill and worked his way around to the north of the farm. When he turned to follow the quad bike tracks, he turned off his lights and slowed down. Coming up out of the dip, the first thing in sight was the two stone buildings where he kept his van and where all the money laundering gear was stored. And the money.

The roller shutter door was wide open and the interior was on fire, and rapidly turning into a huge blaze. He sped up and came to the track down to the farmyard. The Kirkhams didn't have their yard lights on at night, but he could see a shadow in front of the farmhouse. The shadow would be about the size of a Range Rover.

The entrance to the yard was too narrow for him to risk passing through without lights, so he turned them on, and immediately saw the man himself bending down by the farmhouse door. In the new light, he could see discarded petrol cans. Offlea lit a rag that was hanging from the letterbox at the same moment that Clarke slammed on his brakes and jumped out of the cab.

'What are you doing?' he shouted, half hoping that his voice would start to rouse the Kirkhams. He saw Offlea go for his gun, and Clarke dodged back behind his vehicle. His own weapon was in his bag.

'I'm eliminating the variables. This shower are the only ones who know my face and aren't part of the Rainbow.'

Clarke opened the back door of his Land Rover and was about to crawl inside, when Offlea shouted from the yard. 'I'm out of here, Clarke.'

The Range Rover's engine roared and shot away towards the main road. Clarke blew the horn several times before going up to the farmhouse. Through the curtainless windows, he could see flames running all through the kitchen.

'Joe, Kelly, Joseph!' he screamed at the top of his voice. A window opened upstairs, and Joe stuck his head out.

'We're on fire. We can't get out.'

Screams from Kelly came through the gap, and little Natasha started to wail. Clarke remembered the workshop where the pheasants had been hung. There was a set of ladders.

'Get everyone into your room. I'm coming.'

He ran across the yard and skidded on the ice. His left leg gave way, and only a quick roll in the air stopped his hip from crashing into the concrete. He got up and scuttled into the shed. Across the yard, the screams were joined by coughs, and he could hear the roaring of flames. From the cowshed, the beasts joined in with a chorus of distress.

He found the light and, as the fluorescent tube flickered on, he grabbed the ladders and fell over again. They were long enough to reach to the top of the barn and needed two men to lift them.

The pain in his back from the fall outside was making his eyes water. He scoured his fist across them and dragged one end of the ladder towards the farmhouse.

Kelly screamed at him. 'It's the baby. I can't carry the baby.'

He glanced into the downstairs rooms, and all he could see was orange. Thank God for the new double glazing: if the windows had blown out, they would all be dead by now. He lifted the end of the ladders and got underneath. He pushed up and walked backwards until the front end was at the right height.

'Stand back,' he yelled, and dragged the ladders forward until the top end crashed into the window of Joe's room. They were too unstable to be used without someone footing the bottom rung. He ran forward and said, 'Drop the baby. I'll catch him.'

There was an argument from inside the room, and Joe appeared with a small screaming bundle. Clarke stood directly below the window, braced himself … and Joe let go.

The blanket flapped in the breeze for a second, and then the bundle landed in his arms like a dolly catch to mid-off. He sank to one knee in relief and took a deep breath. He placed the baby away from the blazing building and placed his foot firmly on the ladder. Kelly came out first and squatted on the ladder as if she were about to go down a slide at the park.

'Turn round,' shouted her husband, but she froze, unable to move.

Clarke reached up a hand and encouraged her forwards. She started to slide down the ladder and was halfway towards him when she overbalanced and pitched on to the floor. A painful crack came from her left wrist as she tried to break her fall.

Joe was waiting at the top, and Clarke was relieved to see that little Natasha was clinging to her stepfather's back like a monkey. Joe wasted no time in getting down, and Joseph followed. Smoke was billowing from the window by now, and both men were coughing violently. Old Joseph was holding his chest in agony.

Clarke left them to it and went to Kelly, who was gripping her left wrist and moaning. He almost dragged her to her feet using her right elbow and pushed her away from the fire. There was first a crack, and then a blast of glass showered him as the windows blew out. Joe had been facing the house and clutched his face in pain.

Kelly had fallen to her knees again, but came to her senses when she saw the little bundle in front of her. She picked him up with one hand and checked his little body for injuries before clamping him to her shoulder and wrapping her injured arm around him for protection.

Clarke looked around him. They were all alive and they would all recover. Even Joseph was coughing rather than collapsing, but they were in their nightclothes, and the temperature was below freezing.

Something was glinting silver in the headlights. Paranoid that Offlea might have put down a landmine, he walked over and examined it. It was the tracking device from Offlea's car. Shit.

'Come on, all of you. Into my Land Rover. You'll get hypothermia in minutes out here. Especially Natasha.'

He led them to his vehicle and opened the rear. Joe helped his wife and children into the back, and Joseph followed. Clarke drove on, giving the house a wide berth, and heading for Ribblegate Cottage.

'It wasn't me, you know,' he said.

'I know,' said Joseph through his coughing. 'I'd just got up for milking when I heard a shout and looked out. I could see that bloody Irishman getting in to his car. By then I could already smell the smoke. Thank God you were here.'

Clarke arrived at the cottage and led them inside. They were all shivering, and he put on the fan heater in the sitting room, then dragged quilts from the bedroom to wrap round them. When they were all safe, he took Joe aside: there was blood running down his cheek from flying glass, but he scarcely seemed to notice it. 'You can call 999 now. Tell them that I was on my way out when I saw the fire in the shed.'

'The shed?'

'Yes. He set that one first then came for you. Make sure they take you to hospital first. The police won't bother you until later. I'll have it sorted by then.'

'What are you going to do?' There was anger burning in Joe's eyes, and Clarke could see the echo of the flames that were consuming his house.

'Don't ask.'

He turned away and grabbed his Kevlar vest from the cupboard. Joe saw it and gave him a small nod. 'I'll put the kettle on then make that call,' he said. 'You can get away.'

'Thanks. Help yourself to my clothes. I've a feeling that you're going to have to wear them to milk those cows.'

Joseph put his hand on Natasha's head. 'Aye. You know what they say.'

Together, Joe and Clarke replied, 'They won't milk themselves.'

Clarke looked at Natasha's little head, and something the child had said came back to him. *Smelly fish.* He had an idea.

'Where's a good obvious landmark in Blackpool … somewhere in the open?' he asked the Kirkhams.

'The Cenotaph. Just by the North Pier,' Joseph responded.

Tom wanted his phone to ring if there was a call, but stay silent when he got an email. It took a few goes to work out the settings but, satisfied, he set the alarm and dropped on to the bed. The voice of Kate's father boomed around his memory. *The French police are beginning to see sense … Starting to realise this wasn't a robbery … She looked so peaceful.*

Mr Lonsdale had been calling from Saint-Omer, and he had been pulling every string he could to make the French police upgrade the enquiry from a robbery to a major incident. It was his tone that had bothered Tom. He couldn't work out whether it was resentful or sympathetic. Mrs Hayes had put it like this: *He's lost his daughter, and he's jealous of you for being closer to her than he was. There's no right or wrong to grief.*

Kris had dragged him back to her mother's house. He had been fed and watered, and not a single drop of alcohol had passed his lips. It was a very strange feeling – he was shattered, but still compos mentis. Thinking about the Hayes family Christmas tree, he slipped into a deep sleep.

Is that a siren? Fire? God, no, it's my phone.

He banged his knuckles on the bedside light trying to pick it up.

'Hello?'

'Morton? I want to talk to you. I'm going to ring you back in five minutes when you've woken up.'

The call was disconnected, and Tom tried to work out if he was dreaming. He heaved himself up in bed and put the light on. It was a quarter to six in the morning.

He went to the bathroom and made some tea. Bang on five minutes, his phone rang again.

'We need to talk.'

'Who is this? How did you get my number?'

'I'm the man who can tell you who killed your cousin and who put a bomb in your car. He's done plenty of other things, too, but we'll focus on those.'

'Go on. I'm all ears.'

'I might be able to offer you more. I might be able to tell you where he is, and I might be able to open up the whole can of worms, but I need immunity.'

'That's not mine to give, and even if it were, I'd need to know what I was giving you immunity from. You might be worse than him, whoever he is. You might be him.'

Tom knew it wasn't the bomber. This man's voice had a deep rasp that was nothing like the bomber's smoother tones, nor was there any trace at all of the Belfast accent. It was just a question of reeling him in, because this man was afraid of something: he was either afraid of the Jigsaw men, or he was afraid of being caught.

'I'm not like him,' said the voice. 'I haven't murdered anyone. Simple as that. This is a one-time offer, Morton. I want your personal guarantee that you won't arrest me or cause me to be arrested, and that you'll fight any attempt to prosecute me. If you don't accept, I'll deal with the man myself, and the whole operation will carry on as if nothing had happened. Except, of course, that – if you get too close – you might find that Kate Lonsdale was only the first member of your family to be silenced.'

Something had changed in the caller's voice. There was an element of fear, yes, but there was a lot more than that.

It sounded personal in some way. It wasn't a hoax, because the caller knew that Kate was dead when her name hadn't been released yet. Even so, Tom wanted to draw him in a little further.

'This man — the man who bombed my car. Do you know him personally?'

'I do.'

'Does he have any distinguishing marks?'

There was a pause. 'You mean the red hand tattoo on his wrist?'

'That's him. What do you mean by saying that you can offer him to me?'

'I said I might be able to offer him. He's gone to ground, and I'm going to look for him now. Look, I've got to go. If you decide to go ahead, head up the M6 straight away, and I'll text you a meeting point.'

Tom's hand started to shake. It was exactly what had happened last time. *Head up the M6 and I'll give you further instructions.* 'No way. The last time I did that I ended up with third-degree burns. Give me a meeting place now.'

'Equally, no way. I don't want to miss this chance because you've arranged a reception committee. The meeting place will be in the open. I'll get there first and you can decide yourself whether it's too risky.'

'If I come, it won't be alone. I'll have one other person with me.'

'Fair enough. Remember, this is all dependent on me finding him. Don't hang about, Morton. Get going.'

The call ended, and Tom was alone with his cup of tea. That was just about the story of his life.

If he alerted Lancashire & Westmorland now, there was nothing they could do. He could try to get a triangulation on the phone call, but that would take hours at this time on a Sunday morning, and would probably come back to a service station. They usually did. Nor could he call Leonie. She would simply say *It's not worth it.*

Almost as soon as the caller had linked the bombing with Kate's murder, he had known he was going to accept the deal. He had been faced with a lot of decisions in this case: decisions where going forwards meant risking everything, but going backwards would be a form of suicide – because he couldn't live with himself afterwards. He was going forwards.

But what about Hayes? Could he risk putting her in harm's way? If he were in her position, how would he feel? Well, he'd want the choice. It was as simple as that.

He rang her mobile, and gave her the choice of going to church or heading up the M6 and into the unknown.

It had taken him longer to talk to Morton than he expected, and Clarke was conscious that it could all go pear-shaped very quickly if he didn't get moving. He turned round and headed for Offlea's cottage. He wasn't expecting to find him there, but Amelia might have something to offer.

As he drove up the lane, he thought about what Offlea must have done at Ribblegate Farm. After Clarke's last two visits to the money launderers, there was half a million in used sterling in that shed. Offlea would have taken it with him.

Was the whole thing a plan? Jennings said that Offlea had been allowed to clear out the counterfeit Euros from Garlic & Sons before skipping off to the continent. With all the skimming that Mina had identified – and the rest – that could give him upwards of two million in cash. Could he have planned this? Could he have planned to cause mayhem and get out with the money, knowing that Jennings would give him a safe conduct pass?

Probably. And his relationship with Amelia probably fitted nicely into the plan, too.

Clarke had wanted out before, but when Offlea killed Kate and set fire to the farmhouse, he had done something which Clarke could not allow to go unpunished. He had rung Juliet Porterhouse to get Morton's number so that he could shop Offlea anonymously, but the fire at Ribblegate had made it personal. He was going to inflict the punishment himself.

He braked sharply when he saw that the lights were on in Offlea's cottage. Was she on the phone, looking for someone to comfort her after being abandoned again?

He took the SIG pistol out of his bag and stuffed it inside his coat, just in case. When he went up to the house, he found the door ajar.

This was very wrong. Could Offlea have murdered Amelia, too? Surely not. He had said the Kirkhams had to die because they weren't part of the Rainbow. Amelia was most definitely part of it, and any harm to her would bring the wrath of Sir Stephen down on Offlea's head.

He pushed the door open and shouted Amelia's name. There was no reply. Nor was there any time to mess about, so he strode in and looked around. She was gone. The remains of their supper were scattered throughout the room, and a fire was burning out in the grate. Offlea had taken her with him.

That left him one chance. One chance to stop Offlea getting away scott-free. He jumped into the Land Rover. Well, he jumped into it as much as a man with a gammy leg, bruised ribs, a sore back and near-frostbite can be said to jump. He felt sixty, not thirty-seven. That didn't stop the vehicle performing, and he set course for the north western end of the Fylde peninsula.

Laundering money and meeting Mina were both dangerous, but not all that time-consuming. Clarke had done what any good officer would have done and explored his environment when not actually at work. Offlea had made a habit of returning to Ribblegate Farm from some of his missions with a load of rotting fish in his van. Why would he do that and where would he be operating from? There was only one place on the whole of the west coast that would fit the description, and it was just up the road: Fleetwood.

He had noticed the wind picking up when he left his own place, and it was definitely gusting as he came out of Offlea's cottage. By the time he arrived at the outskirts of Fleetwood, he could feel it gently rocking his vehicle. If Offlea was going to escape by boat, he was a brave man. But Clarke already knew that: he was less sure that Amelia would fancy the trip.

It was still pitch black and wouldn't start to get light until well after seven o'clock, later if the cloud cover was anything to go by. He was also very conscious of being one of the only vehicles around at this time on a winter's Sunday morning. If Offlea were on the lookout, he would spot Clarke's Land Rover immediately. On the last roundabout before approaching the docks, he reluctantly turned around and headed back into Thornton-Cleveleys. He was about to give up when he saw a taxi dropping off some very drunken revellers at a private house. The taxi remained idling at the kerb, and Clarke pulled in behind him.

He went up to the driver's window and said, 'I need you for an odd job.'

The driver was Asian and gave him a wary look. 'You drunk, mate?'

'No. Haven't touched a drop.' He still had his winnings in his pocket from yesterday's racing, so, to get the driver's attention, he peeled off two twenty pound notes and said, 'That's the tip. I'll pay whatever else is on the meter afterwards.'

The money sealed the deal, but the cabbie had some limits. 'I finish at eight o'clock. I'm not going to Manchester or nothing like that.'

'Just Fleetwood. Promise.'

When the driver didn't object, Clarke opened the door and made himself comfortable. 'I think my wife is having an affair,' he said. 'I think she's with a man in a Range Rover in Fleetwood. I want you to drive around, especially near the docks, so I can look for them.'

'What's she doing out here at this time of the morning?'

'We live on a farm,' said Clarke. That seemed to do the trick, and the driver pulled away. With many townies, simply stating that your occupation was *farmer* seemed to explain almost anything. He could have said his wife was at a cannibal barbecue, and the man would only have commented that Fleetwood was a smokeless zone.

There was nothing by the docks, but Clarke did notice that a couple of the fishing boats already had lights on them. They circled around a little until there was twenty pounds on the meter. Clarke handed over another note and told the driver to go round to the beach.

'You mean the Explanade?'

'If you say so.'

There was no sign of him on the main road, but off to the right, almost down to the sea itself, Clarke saw a parking area with several vehicles in it. 'Put your light on. Pretend you're for hire and go down there,' he said.

The driver obeyed, and Clarke lay across the back seats. They drove into the car park, and several vehicles revealed themselves. One of them was a Range Rover, with the courtesy light on. It was them.

'Great. Take me back.'

'Bad news, was it?'

'Oh, no. It means I can divorce her now. I get custody of the sheep.'

'Right.'

With Offlea safely down by the water, Clarke had an obvious question to ask at the dock. He told the driver to stop for a second as he lowered the window and shouted to a man heading for the quay.

'Excuse me. D'you know what time the fishing boats sail?'

The man looked so stunned to be spoken to at this time in the morning that he simply answered the question. 'High tide's at half past nine. We'll be sailing some time after nine. If everyone turns up.'

'Thanks.'

On the way to his car, he sent Morton a text message:

I'll be standing at the Blackpool cenotaph from 0815. Gone at 0820.

He didn't get a reply.

Tom had given custody of his phone to Kris. When the mystery man's text came in, they were just north of Manchester. 'Do you know it?' he asked her when she'd read the message to him.

'Dunno. I've only been to Blackpool once. We used to go to Rhyl when I was little, or Aberystwyth. We got a ferry to France once. I'm talking too much, aren't I?'

'No. It all helps keep my mind off this. Are you sure you want to come with me?'

'For the umpteenth time, sir … yes I am. Look what happened last time I walked off the job.'

'We'll stop at Charnock Richard for a comfort break. There's time.'

The wind at the service station blew his coat around, and there was just enough light to see that it was very overcast. The radio had promised snow at some point. Relieved and refreshed, they made good time on the empty roads and arrived at the top end of Blackpool prom at just before eight o'clock.

Strictly speaking the cenotaph wasn't on the road, but on a tarmac apron just off it, sandwiched between the Metropole Hotel and the North Pier. There was no one about.

'Are you sure you don't want to call for backup?' asked Hayes, about as often as he'd asked her whether she wanted to bail out.

'No. He will either offer me something I can use properly or it will be a dead end. If it's a dead end, no harm done. If we can use his information, I'm going nowhere without backup.'

'What now then?'

'We park in full view of the cenotaph and wait.'

Tom did just that. The monument, a tall needle of white stone, emerged from a garden, and was backed by memorial boards (also in white stone). He and Kris both flicked their eyes constantly between the cenotaph and the digital clock on his dashboard. When it showed 08:14, they spotted a man crossing over from where an all-night burger van was located. He walked slowly to the cenotaph and seemed to be limping on his left leg. When he arrived, he took off his glove and put his head inside his coat to light a cigarette. He had brought a polystyrene cup with him, which he raised in salute at their car. Tom nodded to Hayes, and they got out together. As they crossed the tarmac, they both slipped on hats and gloves against the wind.

The man was equally protected. He wore thick outdoor trousers over walking boots, and what looked like a skiing jacket. Whatever it was, it seemed too big for him. Most of his head was covered with a hat on top and a scarf below. As they got closer, he took a last drag on his cigarette, but instead of flicking it away or grinding it under his foot, he knocked off the glowing end and put the butt into his pocket. Was he being careful about DNA, or respectful of the memorial?

'Is it a deal?' said the man.

'Have you got something for me?'

Tom had to repeat himself because the wind was whistling around the buildings.

'Yes. I can tell you exactly where he is and what he's doing. You get that in return for keeping me out of it.'

They were almost shouting now. Tom had thought long and hard about this, but he hadn't discussed it with Hayes.

If the shit hit the fan afterwards, she had to be innocent of any complicity.

'I'll do my best to keep you out of anything up to murder or torture. I'm not going to let any killers walk away.'

'You won't be. Shall we talk in your car or mine? It's a bit breezy out here.'

'Mine.'

The man stuck out a hand. 'I'm Conrad Clarke. I've heard a lot about you.'

Tom was already shaking his hand when it all clicked into place. Of course. He was the man who was flying the helicopter when Kate's not-quite-fiancé was killed. He pointed to Kris. 'This is my partner, DC Hayes.'

Clarke shook hands with her, too, and they walked in silence to Tom's BMW. Tom pointed firmly for the other man to get in the front. He didn't want anyone sitting behind him again. Except for Hayes. He trusted her to have his back.

'Is our deal still on? Immunity for me, in return for the killer and the organisation?'

'Yes. Come on. You said this was urgent.'

Clarke turned to him and said, very simply, 'The man who killed your cousin and who bombed your car is called William Offlea. He is about to board a fishing vessel at Fleetwood and leave the country. He has a woman with him who is entirely innocent, but who may be a hostage if you're not careful. He also has at least half a million pounds in cash.'

Tom could hear Hayes writing furiously in the back. 'Is he armed?' asked Tom.

'Of course. He has a big Glock pistol. Real cannon it is. He's also very handy with a sniper's rifle.'

'And the rest of the organisation?'

'One step at a time, Morton. I've kept my side so far.'

Tom's hand hesitated over the ignition key. 'You could have led Kate to him. You could have stitched her up ... maybe you didn't pull the trigger, but you could be as guilty as William Offlea.'

'No. I risked my neck to save her arse in Hong Kong. Why do you think I'm here, Morton? She was one of the best, and I want Offlea to answer for what he did to her. That and other things.'

'What other things?'

'Later. Just drive and get on the phone. The boat could sail at any time after nine o'clock.'

Tom started the engine and dialled 999.

Clarke drummed his fingers on the armrest as they drove past the Fleetwood retail park and towards the quay, where the fishing boats were bobbing on the full tide. It was fully daylight now, not that it gave them much help.

'There,' said Clarke. 'That's his car.'

They passed the Range Rover, and they could see that it was empty. 'How many boats are getting ready?' asked Morton.

'I can see at least two,' said DC Hayes in the back.

'I can see three,' said Clarke.

Morton turned round at the traffic island, and his phone rang. He pressed the console button and identified himself.

'This is Superintendent Stocks. I can't get hold of DCS Hulme yet, so I'm taking operational command. There is one ARV leaving Blackpool on its way to you. We are scrambling another, but it will be at least half an hour. Two patrol units are on standby at Blackpool & Fylde College. That's just down the road, but I'm holding them back. Blackpool are getting together another team in the Area Support Van.'

'One ARV?' said Morton. 'Is that all?'

'It's Sunday morning. What's the situation?'

'We're at Fleetwood Quay now. The target vehicle has been located, but the targets have left it. We believe that they are on one of three boats which are getting ready to sail.'

'Damn,' said Stocks. 'Too many variables.' There was a noise in the background. 'The ARV is in position at the College. Are you sure that there is only one person armed?'

Clarke shrugged. Morton had told him not to speak when he was on the line to the police. It was possible that the entire boat was full of armed men or that Offlea was acting alone. He really had no idea.

'We can't confirm that.'

'Then I can't authorise intervention. Maintain observation and let me know if you see anything.'

Clarke leant over and whispered *chopper* in Morton's ear.

'Has aerial support been activated, sir?'

'I've been on to Inskip, and they're warming it up, but the crew say the weather's too bad for observational flying. "Like swimming through a sewer at midnight," were his exact words.'

Bunch of wimps. Morton pulled up opposite the quay now that the road was getting busier and so they wouldn't stand out. Clarke took out his binoculars and scanned the three boats. There. It would have to be Amelia who gave the game away – she was standing in the prow of one of the boats like Kate Winslet in *Titanic*. He tapped Morton urgently on the shoulder and pointed.

'Sir? We've been able to identify the boat,' he told Control. 'It's called *Cuchulain's Pride*. Should we intervene?'

'No. Repeat No. I'll put the wheels in motion to track the boat. We'll get him now.'

All three of them watched from the car as the ropes were cast off, and the boat started to slip out into the estuary. Morton reported it to Control with a mixture of pain, anger and sorrow in his voice. For his trouble, Stocks ordered him to go to Blackpool police station at once, and disconnected the call.

There was a moment of shared frustration in Morton's car. The chief inspector drummed his fingers on the wheel; the young black detective shuffled around in the back and gave a big sigh; Clarke thought of just how close they'd been to nailing the slippery bastard, if only the chopper had been scrambled. And then it came back to him – only one person had ever used that phrase – *swimming through a sewer at midnight*. Clarke hadn't expected to hear it again, but it gave them a chance.

'Sod that,' he said. 'Are you going to give up now?'

'What can we do?'

'Drive to Inskip.'

'Inskip? I don't know who he is.'

'It's not a person, it's the place where your helicopter lives. It's only ten minutes from here if you put your foot down. It's your last chance because, believe me, that boat will have no passengers very soon, and you'll never see Offlea again. Unless he's pointing a gun at you, of course.'

'What are we going to do when we get there?'

'Wait and see.'

'Go on, sir,' said Hayes from the back. 'It won't hurt to postpone the awkward questions for a bit.'

Morton put the car in gear and shot off down the road. When they passed the College a few seconds later, they all turned to look at the three police cars lined up outside.

It took longer than ten minutes to get to Inskip because throwing a BMW saloon around icy corners was not one of Tom's strong points. He drove on to the small airfield and found that the police helicopter was in a separate compound. A private security firm at the gate waved him through when he showed his warrant card.

'Almost as lax as the Army,' said Clarke. 'You wouldn't get into an RAF base that easily. Pull up over there.'

Tom knew nothing about helicopters, but there was unquestionably one on the ground in front of him. When Clarke opened the car door, Tom could hear the engine. Was the man going to try to talk the crew into letting him borrow it? He must be desperate if he thought that was a likely proposition.

'Come on,' he said to Hayes. 'Be ready to arrest him if things get heated.'

Even with his limp, Clarke's longer stride took him into the building before them. They arrived just as a man in a flying suit came into the lobby. Clarke and the pilot looked at each other, and Clarke nodded. 'Captain Bob. It's been a long time.'

'Clarke? What the hell are you doing here?'

'Let's step outside, shall we?'

Without waiting for an answer, Clarke put his arm around the pilot's shoulder and propelled him towards the door. The man resisted, but Clarke shoved harder, and the pilot stumbled forwards. Clarke jerked his head at Morton to follow them, and they walked out into the wind and thickly falling snow.

Clarke went to put his arm around the pilot again, but the man lashed out and deflected him.

'Lay off, Clarke. You've got no authority here.'

Tom stepped forward to separate the men. The pilot was white with rage, and his top lip was quivering, but he made no further move to strike out.

'Show him your warrant card, Morton,' said Clarke.

Tom identified himself and held up his ID, but the pilot didn't look down from his staring match with the other man.

'This is Flight Lieutenant Roberts, or it was before he was kicked out of the RAF,' said Clarke with an edge of contempt.

'I resigned my commission, Clarke. If you say anything else, I'll sue you.'

Clarke pointed at Tom. 'This officer survived a bomb blast last month. Yesterday, his cousin was murdered. The killer is on that boat. If you don't get after him, I'll tell your co-pilot what happened in Basra.'

'Nothing happened in Basra.'

'Oh, yes it did. Besides, I do have authority here. I'm on a mission for Skinner.'

Roberts went from white to puce in half a second. 'Damn Skinner, and damn you, Clarke. I'm not taking that chopper out in this weather.'

Clarke unzipped his bulky jacket and showed something inside it to Roberts. When Tom tried to see what it was, Clarke pulled it closed again and said, 'One last chance. Give me your co-pilot and tell Control that you've changed your mind. I'll fly the bloody thing.'

'You're mad. You always were.'

'But I'm a better pilot than you'll ever be. That boat is getting away, and I'm going to count to five ... One ... Two ...'

'Sod it. Kill yourself if you want, but Sammy hasn't done anything to deserve this.'

'I need a co-pilot whose voice won't upset Control. It's you or him.'

Fear and rage battled over Roberts's face. It was the fear that won out. 'I'll tell him it's a security operation and that he's sworn to secrecy.'

'Don't forget Tom here. He's coming with us.'

From behind them came a female voice. 'What about me?' said Hayes.

'Beat it,' said Clarke to Roberts. 'Now.' The pilot went back into the building, and Clarke turned to Hayes. 'It's Kris, isn't it? I need one of you to be in the helicopter, but the other one needs to be in the car and following the coastline. I don't mind which.'

Tom remembered the conversation on the way north. 'Have you ever been in a plane?'

Hayes looked down. 'My Dad was scared of flying. I think I inherited it.'

Roberts emerged from the building with a much younger man, who was also wearing a flying suit. They were accompanied by two others in overalls, who started to work on the helicopter. Snow had already settled on the ground, but it seemed to be running off the rotor blades as water. Tom dug the car keys out of his pocket and pressed them into her palm. 'Head back to Fleetwood, and I'll call you when we're in the air. Or text if it's too noisy.'

She walked off, and Tom stood next to Clarke as he lit a cigarette.

'Is this a suicide mission?' asked Tom quietly.

'Suicide? No. It's very dangerous, though.' He pointed to the chopper. 'These things have an autopilot just like fixed-wing aircraft. They can fly through anything except very gusty wind conditions. Have you ever been on a plane when it seems to drop in mid-air?'

'Once. My ex-wife screamed her head off.'

'You probably dropped about twenty metres. A helicopter will drop up to forty metres or more, which is fine, unless your altitude is only thirty metres. In that case it's not fine at all.'

'Oh.'

'Cigarette?'

'Even the thought of imminent death doesn't make me want to smoke, thank you.'

'Well, let's get going then.'

They walked up to the two police pilots. Roberts pointed to the other man and simply said, 'This is Sammy.' And then he walked away.

'Squadron Leader Clarke. Call me Conrad.'

They shook hands, and Clarke introduced Tom. 'Can you get him fixed up in the back? I'll make myself comfortable.'

Sammy opened the massive door and pointed to the handrail. Snowflakes blew in around Tom as he climbed aboard, and a big flurry of them rushed past his shoulder when Clarke opened the other door. Sammy efficiently pointed out the seat harness mechanism, and Tom was strapped in.

There were already lights on the instrument panel, and Sammy started to push buttons and turn knobs. Tom closed his eyes and thought all the way back to the day that Tanya Sheriden had approached him. Since then, as he had carefully put each piece of the Jigsaw together, there had been a trail of death: Brookes Burton, Miles Finch, Joe Croxton, DS Griffin, Dermot Lynch, Rob King, Benedict Adaire and his sidekick, Patrick Lynch, and now Kate. Plus the injuries to Ian Hooper, Tanya and himself. He would be very surprised if there weren't others that he didn't know of. Would it end today, or would the Jigsaw claim more victims?

Tom didn't believe in any God who would answer his prayers, so he didn't offer one, but if Kris – or Clarke – were going to pray, he wished them the best of luck. He smiled to himself. Conrad Clarke didn't strike him as the praying type. He opened his eyes and saw Clarke stick his hand in his pocket and pull out his lighter. Tom was about to object, but he saw Clarke rub his fingers over an enamel design that looked like the Hindu god Ganesha. Well, well.

Conrad slipped the lighter back into his pocket and said in a loud voice, 'Ready.'

Sammy craned his head and gazed around. 'Clear left. Clear right.' It looked anything but clear to Tom: he could barely see the building at the edge of the helipad.

The pilots put on their helmets, and at the last moment Clarke pointed to the intercom set next to Tom. While he was fiddling with the wires, the engines roared and the blades began to spin.

The downdraught blew away the snow, and Sammy informed Control that they were about to take off. Clarke's hand hesitated over a couple of switches, and Sammy said, 'Look, mate, have you flown a Eurocopter before?'

Clarke flicked a switch and moved something. They lifted off the ground, and it was too late.

Once they had risen into the snow, Tom started to panic. He couldn't see a thing except white flakes against a grey background. He clutched his knees and closed his eyes until they banked to the right, and he opened them again. He still couldn't see anything.

'We're heading east and then north to avoid Blackpool Airport,' said Clarke. His voice sounded reassuringly calm.

'Then where are we going?' asked Sammy. 'The thermal imaging camera loses range in snow. That boat's got a forty-five minute head start on us. Looking for things at sea is a bugger.'

'I know. I used to fly air-sea rescue before it became fashionable and Prince William jumped on the bandwagon.'

'Did you ever meet him?'

'Once or twice. Nice bloke.'

They banked again, and Sammy said something that made no sense at all to Tom, but he said it calmly. That would have to do for now. Tom lifted his headphones and was nearly deafened by the roar of the engines. He took out his phone and sent a text to Kris:

Airborne. Heading over sea. May lose contact. If we crash, can I have a humanist funeral?

'Have you got the Irish Sea chart there?' said Conrad.

Sammy unfolded a map from the bucket above the console.

'Where would you go if you were fishing illegally for scallops?' said Clarke.

'How should I know?' said Sammy.

'The Isle of Man,' said Tom. 'My fishmonger's based on Morecambe Bay, and he says that the Isle of Man has the biggest and best scallop beds around.'

'Perfect,' said Clarke. 'And that would be a good place to take large amounts of cash too, I wouldn't wonder. Right, Sammy, plot me a course from Fleetwood to the Isle of Man.'

There was a crackle over the radio, and Sammy adjusted a dial.

'This is Police Control.' Tom recognised Stocks's voice. 'We have been informed that Pilot Roberts is not on this flight. Please advise. Over.'

'One moment,' said Sammy. He pressed another switch. 'We're on intercom and they can't hear us. What am I going to say? If they think this is a terrorist situation, we'll have a brace of Typhoons after us.'

'Leave it to me,' said Tom. Sammy flicked the switch back over. 'This is DCI Morton. For the status of this mission, please refer to Mr John Lake at Security Liaison. Over.'

'Confirmed. Please advise who is in command of the helicopter. Over.'

'Squadron Leader Conrad Clarke on attachment to Consolidated International Security,' said Clarke. 'Do not – repeat – do not broadcast this. Over.'

'Confirmed. We'll check it out.'

'We're over the sea,' said Sammy, more for Tom's benefit than anyone else's.

It seemed impossible, but the snow was worse than before. It was starting to gather at the bottom of the windows. Tom felt in his stomach that they had gone down, closer to the water. Sammy seemed oblivious and was setting up the camera.

They flew for a few minutes, and then they plunged. The cockpit lurched to the left, and bile rose in his throat. He grabbed the seats in front of him and squeezed his eyes closed. Then they lurched up again, and the engine noise changed to a whine. In seconds, blazing light flooded through his eyelids, and he thought they'd crashed. He opened them and he could see the sea.

'Sweet Jesus,' said Sammy. 'Don't do that again.'

'I'll try not to,' said Clarke. Then he turned to look at Tom, who wanted to scream *Watch where you're going*. 'We've hit the edge of the clouds. Should be easier now.' Then he turned back and banked again.

There was a discarded, half-full bottle of water in the back. Tom unscrewed the top and tried to swallow back the bile. Only then did he realise how much his heart was pounding.

They might have been out of the cloud, but the winds were still blowing. The helicopter rose and fell with alarming frequency, but the pilots seemed to ignore it. They began a sweep search, and Tom started to look out, too. The waters below were flecked with white, and instead of waves, the whole sea seemed to rise and fall in hills and mounds.

'They won't have got this far with swell like that,' said Sammy. Tom looked to his left and was shocked to see that the Isle of Man was almost upon them. He didn't know they'd been going that fast.

Clarke banked to the right and flew away from the island. He held a steady course for a few seconds then said, 'They'll be flying below the radar. Metaphorically speaking.'

'What do you mean?'

'If they switch on all their navigation gear, they'll give away their position. They'll be doing it the old-fashioned way, in which case they may have over-corrected for the swell and the wind.'

He banked left and rose a little. Tom could see more clouds rolling down from the north.

'Got something,' said Sammy. 'Over to the east.'

Clarke changed course and reduced altitude. They were rather too close to the water now. 'That's them. Has to be.'

He rose and started to circle. Tom peered down and saw the boat. When he'd drunk the water, he'd also found a pair of binoculars and he put them to his eyes. It was hard to focus on the boat when both of them were moving.

'What are you going to do?' asked Sammy.

'Fly in front of their bows. Just once. They won't know it's me up here: they'll think it's the police.'

The helicopter rolled and descended, and passed so close to the boat that Tom could see the expressions on the faces of two men in the wheelhouse. Clarke lifted them up and started to hover above the boat. It was hard to tell, but judging from the lack of wake behind it, the boat seemed to have stopped. Clarke confirmed it. 'They won't stay still for long in this swell. They'll have to get moving again before they get rolled over.'

Tom had a chance to focus his binoculars, and what happened next unfolded like a weird silent movie. Two figures appeared from below: one man and one woman. Neither were dressed like the fishermen. 'Is that Offlea? With the woman?' he said.

'Probably,' said Clarke.

Tom looked again, and the man raised a long-barrelled rifle towards them. Before Tom could shout a warning, the woman knocked it out of Offlea's hand, and it skittered across the deck and slid into the water. Offlea didn't slap the woman across the face: he punched her. Hard. She fell backwards, and only a thin strut stopped her from going over the side. Offlea disappeared, and Tom shouted out what had happened.

'Please, Ganesha. No.' said Clarke.

One of the fishermen jumped down on to the deck and staggered as the swell lifted the boat. He clipped himself on to the safety line and dived on top of the woman as the boat rolled towards the water and her legs disappeared. He struggled and pulled and got her back on the deck. She lifted her hand and started to crawl towards the hatch.

'She's okay. He's got her.'

'They're on the move,' said Sammy. 'They're turning about.'

Clarke lifted the helicopter, and they watched as the boat gathered speed. 'They're heading due east. Where will that take them?'

Sammy consulted his chart. 'Cowan Sands. Near Cairndale. Mind you, the tide's going out now, so they'll hit land before that.'

'Tom? Send Kris a text. Tell her to point your satnav towards Cairndale Links Golf Club.'

'Will we get a signal up here?'

'We're just passing Barrow-in-Furness. Those masts reach a long way up into the air, you know.'

He checked his phone, and Hayes had replied to his last message:

Yes. Humanist funeral OK, but no cremations or burials at sea allowed. Please be careful. X.

There wasn't much he could do about being careful, but he resolved to update his will after this was over. He sent the text that Clarke had asked for and added: *We're over the worst*. He hesitated with his finger over the 'X' button, but decided against sending his constable a kiss.

It was slow progress across Morecambe Bay, and occasionally Clarke lifted them up to avoid an air current. When they gained height, Tom could see the sand beginning to be exposed at the edges of the waves. Whatever plan Offlea was making, further sailing couldn't be part of it.

'Fuel warning, sir,' said Sammy. A new formality had entered his voice as if this was a message that Clarke could not avoid.

'Roger that. I'll take her to land in five minutes.'

All three of them watched the fishing boat head towards a small river estuary, then veer to the left a little. The clouds were gathering again, and Tom could feel waves of frustration coming off Clarke. With two minutes left before he had promised to land, the fishing boat simply stopped. It had hit a sandbank, and for a second it paused and then tilted to the right. Starboard?

'I'm going to put her down on the beach,' said Clarke. 'Sammy, you move the chopper away as soon as I get out. You can land on the golf course: it's just over the sand dunes. Morton, tell Hayes to commandeer a 4x4 or better still, a Land Rover. There'll be some in the car park.'

'I'm coming with you,' said Tom.

Clarke didn't respond. He moved the helicopter away from the stranded boat and dropped it on the sands. He turned to Tom and opened his jacket. Underneath the padded coat, he was wearing a bulletproof vest and had a gun. 'No, Tom,' he said. 'This is mine to finish.'

The rotors started to slow down, and both pilots were shrugging off their harnesses. Sammy showed exemplary gymnastic skills, and flipped himself over the console into the pilot's seat. Clarke was already out of the door while Tom was still trying to work out how to get the straps off.

'No, wait,' he shouted.

'Sorry,' said Sammy. 'We're starting to sink. I need to lift off.'

As more snow came towards them, Sammy lifted the chopper with a wobble and hopped over the sand dunes to plonk them down on the ninth green. 'That's it,' he said. 'No fuel left. There's going to be hell on, when they have to bring the tanker out here to refuel it. I'd better tell Control what we've been up to.'

Tom ran, scrambled and staggered his way up the sand dune. When he got to the top, he could see nothing but sand and snow. He slipped down the dune towards the beach and called Hayes.

When Clarke dropped out of the helicopter and ducked under the rotor blades, he was half hoping that Morton would follow him, but Sammy was too quick and the chopper disappeared over the dune.

He'd looked up Morecambe Bay on the internet and found out all about the Sands and Cedric, the Queen's Guide. The message had been very clear: to wander about with no expert help was very dangerous. To do so in a snowstorm was tantamount to suicide.

He had a mental picture of where the boat had grounded and where the helicopter had landed. He could only guess that Offlea would avoid the Cowan estuary and head north rather than south. Clarke struck out north west, away from the golden beach and into compressed grey sands. The snow wasn't as thick as before, but it reduced his visibility drastically. He was scanning ahead of him when he pitched forwards into a gully.

Where did that come from? Was it all like this? He scrambled up and knocked the sand off his coat. More carefully this time, he pressed forwards. A little grassy area appeared, which might give him some height. He was about to climb on to it when he saw the sand move in front of him. Quicksand? Too risky. He skirted right and found a drier patch. Dropping to a crouch, he moved on to the grass.

The wind blew a flurry of snow, and then it cleared. Offlea was ahead of him to the right, dodging the gullies as best he could, with a huge rucksack on his back.

Clarke smiled inside. Money could weigh you down on life's journey if you weren't careful. He scuttled off his mound and found a gully that would take him towards Offlea's track. He risked another glance: the man was too focused on his feet to look up. Clarke ran forwards until he had Offlea between him and the sea. He shrugged off his coat and immediately started to shiver. Taking off his gloves, he stood up and raised his pistol.

'Game's over.' he shouted.

Offlea took two more steps towards him, and he had to repeat himself. The man looked up and laughed.

'You sneaky bastard. How the fuck did you get here?'

'On your knees, Offlea. Hands in the air.'

The other man whirled around and presented the rucksack to Clarke, effectively a bulletproof shield. Clarke swore to himself, but held his fire. When Offlea turned back, he was armed with his Glock. He dropped to his knees and raised his weapon.

There were no more words. They both had body armour, so it was a question of who could hold their nerve and take the best shot. Clarke breathed in, took aim and fired. As the recoil travelled through his arm, a hammer struck his left shoulder, and he fell back into the trench.

Hell fire and damnation. He rolled on to his side and sneaked a look over the gully top. Offlea was flat on his back.

Clarke moved his shoulder gently, and the pain sent lights in front of his eyes, but he couldn't feel any shattered bones grinding. He let his left arm dangle and raised his gun. Step by step he walked towards Offlea, and nothing moved. He saw the gun still in Offlea's right hand and he stopped. He moved in half steps until he saw Offlea's head. Clarke had hit him in the face with a Parabellum bullet. He wasn't going anywhere.

Clarke lowered his weapon. Was that still Offlea in front of him, or was the essence of Offlea on its way to somewhere else? Down to Hell, possibly, or floating away over the sands to be reincarnated as a viper? Clarke would find out himself one day. He was content to wait.

Over to his left, he could see the boat in the distance and two figures making their way towards it. They hadn't looked his way yet. *Priorities. Got to get your priorities right for survival*, he thought. *Enemy eliminated, step one. Secure your environment, step two.* He put his gun away and went back to retrieve his coat and gloves before he became hypothermic. *Step three, plan your escape.*

He took Offlea's Glock and looked at the rucksack. With his shoulder, there was no way he could carry that. He opened the top and saw that it was stuffed full of money. He took half a dozen bundles and shoved them inside his coat before turning to the shore. He took a direct route to the beach, and ahead of him, he could see a Land Rover parked on the sand. Morton and Hayes were approaching the boat, and it looked like Amelia had jumped down to join them.

He hated running (another reason he'd never made it as a modern pentathlete), but he started to jog towards the Land Rover. His leg ached, his shoulder was so sore he had to run one-armed. That was odd enough, but his back was throbbing, too. He kept going until he his breath was ragged and he was about to slow to a walk when he saw the group of three figures turn towards the shore. He sucked deep and put on one last burst.

He slapped the bonnet of the Defender as if it were the finish line of a race and jerked open the door. Hayes had left the keys in the ignition. Brilliant. Before the others knew what had happened, he had reversed the Land Rover down the beach and up the slipway to the Golf Club.

He drove steadily back into Cairndale and was relieved not to see any police cars yet. He crossed the railway bridge and turned into Midland Square. All of the short-stay spaces outside the station were free, so he just abandoned the vehicle and walked down towards the river and across into the old town. There was one rather primitive CCTV camera pointed at the Market Cross, which was easy to avoid, and he ducked into the coffee shop. Why not? He deserved it. He bought a takeaway triple-strength black coffee, and left the shop to find a quiet corner where he could get out his fags and his phone. He chose the entrance to an alleyway by the library.

First of all, he called Joe. 'It's over,' he said. 'Any chance of a lift from Cairndale library to Blackpool?'

'Yeah. I'll be there in half an hour.'

Then he called Morton. 'Sorry about that, but I've got unfinished business.'

The policeman sounded pretty hacked off. Clarke couldn't blame him. 'You've no idea how much unfinished business there is. I'm so deep in shit here I may never see the sun again.'

'I won't let you down. Listen, I haven't got long. If you want to get the ringleaders, there's something you need to do.'

'There's something you need to do. Get your arse back here.'

'Not going to happen, old son. You need to get young Hayes out of there now. You need to send her home in your car, and you need to have her on standby tonight. I doubt very much that your colleagues up here will let you wander off.'

'What's Kris got to do with it?'

'I assume you trust her: you need someone you trust in the Midlands tonight. Text me her number. Oh, and there's a dead body about a quarter of a mile away from you. You need to find it before the tide turns.'

'Oh, shit.'

'Sorry. He wouldn't give himself up. That woman you've rescued... What has she said?'

'She's refusing to say anything. She's in shock and she needs medical attention on her eye.'

'Tell her Conrad says not to say a word until tomorrow, then get her to hospital. No one must know where she is for a while. Everything could be in danger if she's discovered.'

'I'll do what I can.'

'Thanks. Text me that number now because I'm about to sling this phone in the bin.'

Business concluded, he started to sway and he couldn't stand up any more. He had to slide down the wall and put his head between his knees for a while. With his backside freezing on the cobbles, he drank his coffee and smoked two cigarettes. Neither of these measures stopped his hand from shaking. When Joe arrived, he couldn't get up off the floor and had to crawl to the bollard and heave himself up.

'You look like shit, mate.'

Joe had come, but he wasn't happy. A surgical dressing covered most of his cheek, and the impact of losing his home was just sinking in.

Clarke leaned on the roof of the pickup. 'I'm sorry you got tangled up in this. I really am.'

'It weren't your fault. You're not his boss. Kelly said that the money he was paying us to look the other way was too good to be true. I guess she was right. Are you getting in or what?'

He got in and closed his eyes. Joe didn't ask any questions, and by the time they got to the motorway, he was asleep.

'Where do you want to be?' said Joe, as they passed the football ground on the way into Blackpool.'

'Long-stay car park by the North Pier. I'll direct you.' The taste in his mouth was awful. Truly awful. When they arrived at their destination he turned to Joe. 'Are you fully insured?'

'Yes. Thanks to you. If you hadn't paid the rent on the cottage in advance, Dad wouldn't have had the money for the premiums. We'll do all right. Eventually.'

'How's Kelly's wrist?'

'In a cast. They said she didn't tear any ligaments, so it should heal properly. Are you going to tell me what's going on? The police only let me leave the farm because I said I needed vital agricultural supplies.'

'That man who tried to kill you … his name was William Offlea. He's dead. End of story. You must use the cottage to live in while they start rebuilding the farmhouse. And you must take this.'

He took the bundles of cash from Offlea's rucksack out of his coat and handed them over. Joe raised his eyebrows and flicked through the bundles. 'There must be thirty grand here,' he said.

'Couldn't carry any more. Book yourselves into a hotel for Christmas.'

'Thanks, Conrad. For this, and for saving our lives.'

Clarke patted him on the shoulder and started to climb out of the truck. 'Kelly was right. I know it's hard being a dairy farmer right now, and I know you needed the money, but it *was* too good to be true. There's a slippery slope in all this. I should know.'

He waved and closed the door. Joe drove off back to his family, and Clarke picked up his vehicle. His first stop was going to be that outlet village in Fleetwood. He needed a new coat.

Tom watched Hayes drive out of the golf club just as the first police cars arrived, sirens blaring as they sped round the corner. The ambulance was just behind them. He turned to the woman from the boat who was wrapped in a big coat provided by the man who had loaned them his Land Rover. That was going to be a difficult conversation, but not yet. The woman was shivering so badly it took him a few moments to get her attention.

'We're sending you to hospital. You need help.'

'Where's William? Is he okay? Has he got away?'

'He's safe.' It was only a lie if you looked at it in a certain light. If you looked at it in another way, it was true – nothing bad could happen to William Offlea now.

'I've got a message for you. From Conrad. Do you know him?'

'Good Old Conrad. Nostromo. Is he okay too?'

'Yes, he's fine. He says you have to keep quiet until tomorrow. Just say nothing at the hospital, okay?'

'I've got it. Yes, I've got it. Mum's the word.'

He doubted that she would be in a fit state to say anything to anyone for some time. The first of the uniformed officers approached, and he held out his warrant card. 'Take this woman into protective custody. Complete isolation and guard at the hospital.'

To his utter surprise, the policeman nodded, and directed his partner to take the shivering woman into the ambulance. In the second vehicle were three officers. A male sergeant and woman constable got out of the front, and from the back came a senior officer, whose uniform would have given the chief constable of MCPS a run for its money.

'Commander Ross, Cairndale Division,' he said.

'DCI Morton. I've just dispatched a witness into protective custody, sir.'

'Is this a live situation? Is anyone in danger?'

'Not here.'

'Then let's go inside. I can't hear myself think in this wind.'

Ross's voice had a Scottish accent, but one that had been honed on the parade ground. He turned towards the clubhouse and marched through the front doors. Tom followed and saw Ross's back disappearing into a side room.

'What's the situation, Morton? All they told me was that you'd been party to hijacking a police helicopter. Either that, or I've got the security services running amok on my patch. Which is it?'

That was the question: had Tom sacrificed his career to get Offlea? When Clarke had rung him at a quarter to six this morning, he had known that he would have to go through with whatever happened, but it was still happening.

Just because Offlea was dead, that didn't mean the nightmare was over.

'I'm not sure, sir. I was acting on information supplied to me to pursue a very dangerous suspect. I can't say exactly where the authorisation came from.'

When Kate had described Conrad, she had called him the best liar she knew. Perhaps it was rubbing off on him. His phone rang, showing the control room number.

'Excuse me, sir.'

He took the call, and Stocks said, 'I've finally heard back from Security Liaison. It seems that Mr Lake was on holiday, and not in charge of your operation. I told them the details, and they've said that they'll authorise it retrospectively. They very much want an urgent word with Mr Clarke. Apparently he left the RAF some time ago.'

'I'd like a word with him too. He's gone AWOL but he said he'd be in touch. I've got Commander Ross here. Could you have a word with him?'

Tom passed over his phone and looked around for a chair to collapse into. Ross spoke for a few minutes and passed it back. 'Right, laddie. Where do we start?'

'Take your pick, sir. We've got a helicopter on the golf course with no fuel, a dead body on the sands with the tide coming in, and a beached fishing boat.'

Ross gave him a broad smile that seemed right out of place in the situation. He squared his shoulders and said, 'What's your game, son? Do you play golf?'

'If I never see another golf course, sir, it will be too soon.'

'Good. Because after today, you'll be barred from every course in the country. They don't like having their game interrupted, and they like helicopters on their greens even less. We'll start with the body, I think. Lead on.'

Tom climbed to his feet and zipped up his coat. What he really, really wanted was a cup of tea, but he didn't think that was an option at the moment.

Clarke arrived at St Andrew's Hall at half past seven in the evening. He parked down the lane and sent a text message to Kris Hayes.

Time for action. Head South on the M40 and wait for instructions at the Cherwell Valley Services. Clarke.

He had dropped into Ribblegate Cottage – briefly – on his way south to take a few things and to pick up some of the strong painkillers he'd been hoarding since the operations on his leg. They were just about allowing him to function. Hayes responded that she was on her way. Good. He had to give her time to get down the motorway, so with the engine running and the radio playing, he drank his coffee and smoked a couple of cigarettes. Not a single car came down the lane past him. At eight o'clock, he put the Land Rover in gear and drove over the crisp snow lying on the gravel in front of St Andrew's Hall.

He went round the back and rang the bell. Lady Jennings answered the door, and he could tell that she was very worried.

'Thank God it's you, Conrad. Stephen's going frantic, and he won't tell me what it's about.' She held open the door and waved him in. On the way through the kitchen she said, 'It's something to do with Amelia, and I can't get hold of her. Olivia says she spent the night with Offlea, and now he's disappeared. Do you know what's going on?'

'Yes. I've come here to sort it out.'

'He's in the study. Through here.'

There was a small panelled door at the back of the grand hallway that led to Jennings' den, a little space with not much room for more than a desk, a chair and some cupboards. He was on the phone when Clarke opened the door, but slammed down the receiver when he saw his visitor.

'Come in, man, and shut the bloody door. What in Heaven's name is going on?'

'I'm going to have to sit down,' said Clarke. Jennings pointed to a hard-backed chair in the corner, and Clarke pulled it forwards. He put the small satchel he was carrying next to his chair. The satchel was a refurbished Victorian officer's case, and had been a present from his proud father when he got his Wings. He asked Jennings what he had heard so far.

'I've heard that you've been very bloody stupid, that's what I've heard. I've heard that you used Skinner's name in some awful misadventure, and as a result Offlea is dead and Amelia is missing. *What have you done, man?*'

Clarke took a very deep breath. 'It's Amelia I've come about. Olivia, too, but mostly Amelia. She's alright, I think, but the police are holding her in protective custody. It's just a question of whether she goes down for what Offlea did or whether she's treated as a witness.'

'She's innocent. She had nothing to do with that man.'

Clarke leaned forward. Jennings leaned back. 'Did Offlea ever tell you where he kept the money?' Jennings shook his head. 'Thought not. He kept it on a farm and he didn't tell the owners what he was up to. Amelia spent last night with Offlea. Her DNA is all over his cottage. At five o'clock this morning, Offlea took all of the money and burned down the shed.' He paused, and Jennings didn't seem to think this was unexpected. 'Then he set fire to the farmhouse to eliminate the witnesses. There were three adults and two children in that building. They only got out alive because I was there to help them. Their home is utterly destroyed.'

He looked deliberately around the room to make his point. Jennings caught up with his train of thought and became very angry.

'That doesn't make you an avenging angel, Clarke. Just tell me where Amelia is, and I'll get her out.'

'Too late. It's just a question of whether or not I swear on oath that I saw her with Offlea when he set fire to the house. I can implicate her in lots of other things, as well. I'm quite a good liar, as you know. I can take down Bentley and Olivia, too.'

'How much do you want?'

'It's over, Jennings. I want the whole story, and I want you to fall on your sword. To save your family.'

Sir Stephen was taken aback. 'No. You can't threaten me like that.'

'Yes I can. I can walk out of here and be in police custody in minutes. You can't stop me, and things have gone too far for your friends to bail you out now. You may have bought some important people, Jennings, but you haven't bought the whole of Lancashire & Westmorland Constabulary and you haven't bought Tom Morton. Rather the opposite, I'd say, after what your lieutenant did to his cousin.'

'I could make you a very good offer.'

Clarke slapped his hand on the desk. 'No! The only way I'll ever be safe from you is to know that the whole thing has stopped, and it has to stop now. Choose, Jennings. Choose your bloody Rainbow or choose your family.'

Jennings sighed and looked around the room, just as Clarke had done. There were a couple of regimental souvenirs on the wall, and several family photographs in gleaming frames on the window ledge. One side of his life was going to be destroyed. There was never really any question of which one, though. Family always came first.

'What do you need to know?'

'Have you got a drink in here?'

'No. Too dangerous.' Jennings got up and went as far as the door. He shouted for Susan to bring the decanter and two glasses, and when she appeared with them he said, 'Don't worry. Conrad's going to work something out.' Over his shoulder, Susan smiled at Clarke.

Jennings poured them both a drink and started his story. 'Do you remember the TV Programme *Death on the Rock*?'

'How old do you think I am? I don't remember it, but I do know about it.'

'That was the last time we sent the SAS to do government dirty work. Everything they've done since then has been something that the prime minister can defend in the House of Commons if he has to.'

'But the dirty work didn't stop.'

'No. It never does. There was a bit of argy-bargy for a few years, and then a project called Operation White Light was set up. That's the one thing you can't tell the police.' Clarke nodded his assent, and Jennings continued. 'Money was channelled from the secret vote when necessary, and various private military contractors were paid to do our dirty work.

'The problem was that these companies wanted the money legitimately, not in used fivers. That's where the Rainbow came in. Have you ever read Keats?'

'No.'

'There's a line somewhere about *Unweaving the Rainbow*. It's in *Lamia*, I think. That's what you get if you put white light through a prism – a rainbow. Operation Rainbow is the money laundering arm of White Light.'

This was all fascinating, thought Clarke, but he hadn't got all night. 'You can't have been involved from the beginning.'

'What? No. It was all set up when I came on board – and it will continue, under another name, when I resign. What you want to know about is the various elements – Red Flag, Blue Sky and so on.'

'In a nutshell. And I need proof.'

Jennings got up and moved a regimental crest from the wall. He slipped back one of the panels and revealed a safe, set into the rough brick. Clarke reached for his gun in case Jennings tried something, but all that appeared from the safe were some notebooks and several mobile phones, each one in a plastic bag.

'These are all labelled,' said Sir Stephen. 'There are full details in the notebooks as well.'

'Names?'

'Red flag started with Martin Nechells. He was a diplomat in Basra, and realised that a lot of cash was being wasted on corruption in the Iraqi government. We got talking, and we decided that it could be a source of cash for White Light operations. Much better use of government funds. Later, we brought in his brother and a friend of theirs called Ray Fleming. It was Fleming's brother-in-law who provided all the intelligence.'

Even now he was denying it. Jennings, Offlea, both the Nechells brothers – and, presumably, Anthony Skinner – were all kidding themselves that they were undercover heroes. Why couldn't they just admit they were crooks? Clarke was proud to be a crook, and to have come from a long line of crooks. His father was an antiques dealer, and his grandfather had been a solicitor. Biggest crooks around, both of them.

Clarke put the notebooks and phones into his satchel. He also turned off the voice recorder that had captured Jennings' confession. He didn't want the next act to be preserved for posterity. He took a swig from his drink and asked about Skinner.

'Complete plausible deniability,' said Jennings. 'He knows about it, but he's only a beneficiary.'

'I thought as much.'

He finished his drink and Jennings did the same. 'Time's up,' said Clarke, and poured Jennings another measure. 'You might need that.'

'Have I got time to flee the country before you get to the police?' said Jennings with half a smile.

'I thought you would have understood the classical reference. When I said that I wanted you to fall on your sword, I meant it literally.'

Clarke reached into his satchel again, and pulled out an object wrapped in cloth. He put it on the desk and unwrapped it. William Offlea's Glock 32 lay inside. He took out his SIG to discourage Jennings from trying anything foolish and said, 'The time for talking's over. I'm going to wait outside the house until I hear the shot. I'll give you twenty minutes to write a note. If you're not dead by then, I'll do to your house what Offlea did to the Kirkhams.'

He stood up and backed towards the door. From the moment he had unwrapped the gun, Jennings' eyes hadn't left it.

There really was nothing more to say. He left Sir Stephen Jennings to contemplate his fate and slipped out of the study. Susan was waiting in the hall, and Clarke closed the door behind him.

'It's going to be okay,' he said. 'Stephen's just making some calls. He should have some good news for you in much less than twenty minutes.'

'Thank goodness. That's such a relief, Conrad. Thank you so much for sorting this out. Can I get you another drink?'

'Don't mention it. Sorry, but I've got things to sort out too. I'll see myself out.'

Lady Jennings was too much the hostess not to escort him to the back door, but she didn't ask any more questions. The door closed behind him and he got into his Land Rover. He had no intention of burning down St Andrew's Hall. That wouldn't change anything: it would just make him guilty of murder and arson. It wouldn't ruin Sir Stephen's family, or change anything else in the world because it was very hard to change the world. Gandhi had done it, Hitler had done it, Sir Isaac Newton and Nelson Mandela had both done it – but he wasn't like any of them.

Sir Stephen's family had lived in St Andrew's Hall for a long time. Some of them were good people and some were bad, and most were a mixture of the two. Perhaps the next master of St Andrew's would be a better man than his father. In a few years, Clarke planned to pay a visit and find out.

Conrad had arrived as a tradesman and left as a tradesman: he was quite content with that. He drove out of the grounds and along the lane at a dangerously fast speed towards the motorway.

Sir Stephen Jennings stared at the gun until Clarke closed the door. He checked his watch and saw that his deadline was nine o'clock.

He rubbed his hands on his trousers and looked out of the small window. Would Clarke be waiting outside, petrol can in hand? He doubted it very much. Unlike the gun in front of him, he suspected that the threat of arson was more metaphorical. For one thing, he had noticed the recorder in Clarke's bag.

It wasn't much of a choice. He could sit tight and deny everything and spend years fighting the law before they punished him, or he could finish it tonight. Like the choice between his family and the Rainbow, it was no choice at all.

His note was very short:

Susan, I'm sorry. Please forgive me. I love you.

He took two wills from the safe. They were both dated the same day, and his solicitor had kicked up a fuss about creating two different documents. The stupid little man had only agreed after Jennings invited him and his wife for dinner. Susan had no idea why she was entertaining them, but she did her best.

Both the wills gave St Andrew's Hall to his son, with full, immediate possession. Susan's name had never been on the deeds, and the will made it clear that his daughter-in-law had no interest in the property, either. That was for his son to decide. He felt sure that he would do the right thing. The main difference between the documents was Amelia. In one of them, she was cut off with as little as the solicitor would let him get away with, which was just enough to prevent her challenging the will in court. The other document was much more generous, and included some of his shares in the racecourse.

There was a tiny fireplace in the room and a box of matches next to it. All he ever burned in it were documents. He took the two wills and considered. Amelia needed his help now more than ever. He lit a match and burned the one which left her nothing. If Amelia had a share of the business, it would give her some focus, and make Olivia more inclined to look out for her sister.

He took another drink. The hardest part was losing control, of not seeing how things turned out after he'd gone. He checked his watch. Five to nine.

He finished his drink and picked up the gun. With a few practised movements, he checked that it was all in order. He closed his eyes, said the Lord's Prayer under his breath, and pulled the trigger.

Chapter 15

Earlsbury – Cairndale – Throckton
Tuesday to Sunday, Christmas Week
24-26 December

After recovering Offlea's body from the sands, Tom had been whisked off to HQ in Preston and kept more or less incommunicado while enquiries were made and wheels were put in motion: all that changed when Hayes called him in the evening. She gabbled out a story about being handed Top Secret material in a service station and that she was now standing over a dead body in some mansion.

The ringleader – the carpenter who had cut out all the pieces of Tom's Jigsaw – was dead by his own hand.

After that, things happened very quickly. Someone from Special Branch was put in charge of the operation, and Tom heard that Nechells' brother had been arrested, along with various other people in Jennings' files. At least they were keeping him in the loop.

He knew it had all been worth it the next morning. Pete Fulton got in touch to say that the City of London Police had raided Horsefair Court. They found that Kate's broadband connection had been intercepted and that they had traced the feed back to Doug Rickman, the Systems Administrator for the City Police. Rickman had got his sister and brother-in-law to rent their flats to Tom and Kate precisely so they could keep tabs on the first enquiry. Kate's laptop had been found in Offlea's rucksack. She had tracked the killer through Lynch's Jaguar. It was brilliant – and thoroughly illegal – but she had paid the price with her life.

On Monday afternoon, he asked if he could go to Patrick's funeral the next day. 'No,' was the short answer. He called Leonie.

'Tom, could you not have waited until after Christmas to go all James Bond on me? I've got more paperwork on my desk because of you than I've had in years. Seriously ... well done, though. You've single-handedly guaranteed our future, I reckon.'

'That's good to know. Can you do me a favour?'

'At the moment, I'd give you almost anything. Make the most of it.'

'This case is so political that they don't really need me, do they?'

'I wouldn't put it like that. You need to hang in there.'

'Not really. It's you that should be fighting for CIPPS, not me. You do it so much better than I ever could.'

'Naked flattery. I like it.'

'Take over from me at the top level. Let me go back to Earlsbury and finish the case against David Nechells. I don't want him to slip through the net.'

'Are you anxious to get back to your little DC?'

'No. You should know me better than that. However, I do want to go to Patrick Lynch's funeral tomorrow.'

'Oh. I see. Leave it with me, Tom.'

Half an hour later, DCS Hulme came in and told him that he was being reassigned. He picked up his bag and scrounged a lift to the station. Hayes picked him up from Wolverhampton an hour after that.

'Wow, sir. I can't believe we're both still alive.'

'Tell me what happened in Oxfordshire. You weren't making much sense on Sunday night.'

Somehow, Hayes was still driving his car. He didn't mind. She left the station and started the slow drive through the Black Country.

'It started with another of those *Meet me in the middle of nowhere* messages that they all seem so fond of. I reckoned that if I didn't follow it up, Clarke might just disappear.'

'You're probably right, but it was very brave of you.'

'And that was very patronising, sir.'

'Sorry. I'm still learning.'

'You're forgiven. I wasn't nearly as brave as you getting in that helicopter, though. What was it like?'

'I'll tell you later. Back to the rendezvous.'

'I drove to this service station and waited. After ten minutes, Conrad Clarke drives up and winds his window down. He passes me all these phones and notebooks, and tells me to write down this address. It was St Andrew's Hall. I asked him what's there, and he says, "I hope that there's a dead body. Nothing to do with me, this time".'

'Did he threaten you?'

'No. Not at all. It got quite silly when he handed over this armoured vest. He said that I had to be careful not to dislodge the bullet because it was proof that Offlea shot him first.'

'Hah! We'll probably never know the truth about what happened out on the sands.'

Kris paused. 'Then it got scary. He passes over this gun, butt first. I'd never touched a gun before, Tom. I never want to again. I asked if it was loaded, and he gave me that smile of his, and he said, "Not much use, otherwise, is it? I'd hang on to it, but I used it to shoot Offlea, and you'll be after me if I use it again".'

She paused again; Tom said nothing.

'After that, it just went mental,' she said. 'I rang 999 on the way to the Hall, and Control said that no one from the house had reported anything. I had to go round the back to get in, and I found the widow going through his safe, stepping over her husband's body and walking around his brains. It was a hell of a mess. Not only that, she was really rude. She told me it was none of my business, and that I should eff off. I can't get my head round that. I was about to arrest her when the local uniforms showed up. D'you know, one of them actually doffed his cap when he came into the study?'

She shook her head and asked him how the woman from the boat was doing.

'Not very well. That was Jennings's daughter. Apparently she was running away with Offlea when we interrupted them. Not only is her boyfriend dead, but her father is too.'

There were more details to exchange, and soon they were at Kris's house: he was leaving her there and taking his car to Earlsbury Park. She hesitated before getting out.

'Tom, can you give me an honest answer?'

He remembered the X at the end of her text message. Was she going to say something personal? He hoped not.

'Go on. I've never lied to you before: I'm hardly likely to start now.'

'How much of this is going to come out? How much is going to get buried by the secret services and Special Branch?'

'Enough. I don't know what Clarke said or did with Jennings, but the evidence he gave you means that we've got all the Jigsaw gang right where we want them. Everyone who we've arrested so far will go to prison – but only for Misconduct in Public Office, or money laundering, or both. All the murder charges are going to be pinned on Jennings. And Offlea, of course. I heard rumours about death squads and all sorts, but that's going nowhere. We did it, Kris. We got the lot of them.'

Her frown turned into a smile. 'We did, didn't we? Are you sure you won't come in for tea?'

'No thanks. I'm scared that your mother might try and get the truth out of me.'

'See you tomorrow.'

She left his car and walked carefully up the icy path. Tom summoned the energy to get into the driver's seat and took himself to the hotel. He ate the biggest portions on the menu and drank a half-bottle of wine. He was asleep before the ten o'clock news.

No one really noticed the weather at the funeral: it was sort-of cold and damp, but not properly winter. The church was packed, and heavy with the smell of incense and pine needles from the Christmas trees.

Tom and Kris were early and sat in an empty row of seats. People he'd vaguely seen during the investigation nodded to him in a friendly way, but they sat elsewhere. By the time the service started, they had been joined on their row by Ian Hooper and Erin King. When the family appeared behind the priest, they all stood. Francesca had Elizabeth next to her, and her older daughters behind. As part of the same group, Tom was surprised to see Theresa and Hope King. James King slipped into their pew and embraced Ian Hooper warmly. Another interesting development.

The service passed, as did the interment, and Kris seemed a little reluctant to return for the reception.

'Are you sure we'll be welcome?'

'Yes. Francesca wants to know what happened. Besides, it's at Earlsbury Park. I've started having my mail delivered there, you know. It feels more like home than Horsefair Court.'

They made small talk over the sausage rolls until Francesca came across to them. When the conventions had been observed, Kris asked, 'How's Pat's mother?'

'She's had a stroke. She's in hospital. Tell me something good, Inspector. I need it.'

'I don't think there's anything good about what's happened, Mrs Lynch.'

She gave him the bearing-up-under-the-circumstances smile that widows use. 'You're alive, aren't you?'

'It's good of you to pretend that my welfare counts as good news.'

'You can have the benefit of the doubt today. It's nearly Christmas, after all. Go on: tell me what's been happening'

Tom put down his plate. 'We'll never know exactly what happened to Patrick, but I'm pretty sure that his death counts as murder.'

Francesca didn't blink. 'How do you know?'

'Can I start at the beginning?' She nodded, and he continued. 'During the Troubles in Northern Ireland, that man Benedict Adaire was an armourer for the Republicans.'

'I'm not my husband,' she said. 'I'd call him a terrorist, even if Patrick wouldn't have.'

'So would I. Adaire specialised in bombs, and one day he planted a device that blew up the spectators at a parade. It killed all but one member of a family called Offlea: mother, father, young boy and a five-year-old girl. The only one who escaped was actually in the parade. He was their oldest son, William Offlea.'

'He's the one who got shot in Cairndale?'

'Yes. After his family was blown up, he was taken into care. While he was there, a soldier called Jennings recruited him for undercover work. They paid for him to go to boarding school in Wales, and he was given specialist training by the Army. All completely unofficial. When he went back to Belfast, he started taking his revenge, one Republican at a time.'

'My God.' She shook her head in bewilderment. 'Did that really happen? Did you really turn young boys into killing machines like that?'

'Me?'

'The British.'

It was very strange to hear a woman with a Black Country accent refer to him as being British, as if that meant he was from a foreign country. 'Both sides did it. The Republicans went to the USA or Libya: the Loyalists came over here. When the ceasefire was declared, Adaire became a serious player in the drugs world, and Offlea carried on working for Jennings, after a spell overseas in the French Foreign Legion. Jennings had a number of Principal Investors: David Nechells was one of those. He arranged things, and his fixer was DS Griffin. When Griffin was killed, they sent in Offlea to sort things out.'

'Was Offlea definitely the one who killed Adaire and who tried to kill you?'

'Yes. The day after, he came down here, driving a van. It was the one Patrick was found in. Whether he did something to your husband, or whether Pat had a heart attack, we can't tell. However, there's no doubt that Offlea did nothing to help him. He probably stopped Patrick taking his pills and he made no effort to call 999 or give CPR. That makes him a murderer in my book. Afterwards, he came to your house and planted the tablets and the phone.'

Francesca looked out of the picture windows at the golf course, the one where Patrick had apparently done most of his business. Including at least one meeting with William Offlea.

'That's not all,' said Tom. 'He stole Pat's Jaguar, and my cousin traced it to France. Offlea found out and he killed her. In cold blood.'

She put her hand out and touched his arm. 'Dear God, no. When was that?'

'On Saturday. It was the beginning of the end: after that, things unravelled very quickly, and one of the gang turned on the others. Jennings shot himself on Sunday night to avoid a scandal.'

There was a moment's silence while they digested Tom's story. Francesca had personal charge of one of the waiters and waved him over. She handed a glass of champagne to

Tom and offered one to Hayes who politely declined it. 'Don't argue,' said Francesca. 'You need take only one sip. You won't be over the limit. This is a toast to my husband's memory.'

'I can't. I really can't,' said Hayes. 'I'll toast him with this.'

'Then here's to Patrick.'

They raised their glasses and drank. Francesca offered her hand to Hayes and then to Tom.

When she had gone, Kris muttered, 'Would she have done that to a Moslem? I don't think so.'

'Careful. You don't want to get a crucifixion complex.'

The scalp showing through her hair went red, then pale brown, then red again. 'Some things just aren't funny, sir.'

'Yes, they are. Anyway, I can't think of a better place to make an off-colour religious joke than at a funeral, can you?'

'I suppose it's better than the other thing that happens at a funeral.'

'What's that?'

'They say everyone gets horny. That's not going to be a problem for me with you around.'

'Hayes, that hurt. Just when I thought you were getting to like me.'

'I thought I fancied you for about five minutes but, in the end, all white guys look the same to me.'

'Careful. If you carry on like that, I'll leave you alone with Leonie the next time she's here.'

Hayes was stumped. 'She's not gay. She's a real man-eater.'

'Possibly, but she prefers women. It came to me after seeing Nicole Rodgers.'

'That tart.'

'Yes. Rodgers flirts with men because she's a tease: Leonie does it because that's her way of intimidating the opposite sex. It's protective colouring: nature's way of warning people off her.'

'There's hope for you yet.'

'Talking of hope, have you decided what to do after we've finished with Nechells?'

'I was going to tell you later,' said Hayes. 'I've decided that even if I have to work twice as hard as you to get the same recognition, I'd rather be a copper than anything else. I spoke to DCI Storey yesterday, and he said I could join his team at Earlsbury.'

'That's brilliant. Well done, Kris. Does he have a vacancy?'

By way of an answer, Hayes put her drink down and went over to the bar. She came back with Ian Hooper and James King. Hooper looked very nervous and hung back, but King shook Tom's hand and expressed his condolences for Kate's death.

'Go on,' said King to Hooper. 'Tell him.'

'I'm sorry, sir,' said Hooper. 'I've decided to leave the force. You were right. It's not for me.'

'I'm sorry too,' said Tom, 'but that's not what I said. I told you to work it out, that's all.'

'Well he did,' said King. 'I went to see him when Patrick died, and we got talking. You know what, Mr Morton? Queen Victoria's album has advance sales that are going to put us in the big time. Next year we're going to crack America.'

'I'm pleased to hear that,' said Tom, 'but what's it got to do with Ian?'

'Vicci needs people she can trust. She doesn't ever want to lose sight of who she is. If we go to the States, there's going to be a lot of issues with security. Ian's going to start on our next UK tour, and then be head of security over there.'

'Wow,' said Tom. 'Congratulations. What about Ceri? And Erin? Or shouldn't I ask.'

Hooper cast a glance over to the corner where Theresa King was sitting with Hope, Elizabeth and Erin. 'Erin's just a friend. Always has been. Ceri's going to take a year out from teaching and come with us to America. Vicci says that she can be the founder member of her entourage. Erin's been headhunted, believe it or not. She's going to Manchester to handle the choreography for a chain of clubs. It'll do us all good to get away.'

Tom raised his glass to them. 'To new beginnings,' he said.

Christmas in an open prison, especially a women's prison, is a little like Christmas in hospital. As many of the inmates as possible were being released on licence, and the ones left behind were having to make the most of it.

Rules and regulations put a limit on the decorations, but the women did their best, and the association area looked almost festive. Mina was having a break from dental treatment and had volunteered to work in the numeracy classes. She thought she might have something to offer and, besides, she would do anything to avoid being sent out to the gardens. Not that anyone was doing much outdoor work with six inches of snow on the ground.

Just before class on the Wednesday, she was handed a short-notice therapeutic visiting order.

'Your therapist's coming to see you this afternoon. You've got dispensation to use the Family Room.'

'But I haven't got a therapist.'

'Yes you have. It says so here.'

The officer pointed to the relevant box on the form. *No. It couldn't be, could it?* According to the form, she was being treated by Dr Conrad Clarke PhD. She stuffed the order into her tunic and went into class: during a group session, one of the students pointed out to her that she had written 4+8=2.

She was so distracted she almost forgot to enjoy her lunch. Although she had holes in both jaws now, it was another two weeks before the teeth went in. But that didn't stop her enjoying every meal. She passed on dessert (or rather she passed her dessert on to someone else) and had been waiting twenty minutes by the gate before she was called through.

The officer accompanied her to the corridor where the Family Room was located: and coming along from the other end was an old man in a suit, with one arm in a sling and the other carrying a heavy case. He lifted his head, and she bit her lip so hard that blood came into her mouth and her eyes watered. The old man was Conrad.

She walked the rest of the way with her eyes fixed on the floor, and stood outside the room like a naughty girl outside the headmistress's study in a children's book. Conrad and the officer exchanged paperwork, and his voice sent shivers down her arms. She had dreamed of his voice only last night, echoing in the temple, and now he was next to her. *But he looked so old.* She thought of all the nights that Miles had come home from work, when she had prepared food for him that she couldn't eat without putting it through the blender. It was a lukewarm, puréed life: a life with no texture, no taste and very little spice. She would only be twenty-eight when she left prison. She couldn't go back to a lukewarm life. Not now.

The officer opened the door, and she was left standing outside. She heard him explaining the facilities and panic buttons to Conrad.

'In you go, Mina,' said the officer. She walked into the room with her eyes still on the carpet. The door was closed behind her.

'My landlord said I looked like shit,' said Conrad, 'but he was being polite. I actually look like I've gone ten rounds with Death and only won on points.'

She lifted her eyes and met his gaze. The blue in his eyes was different, somehow. Last week it had been a pale blue, like his RAF uniform. Today it was greyer, flintier, harder … but it wasn't a day older than when he first took her by the hand.

She brought her hand up to her mouth and wiped it with her sleeve. A mixture of blood and saliva streaked across the fabric. She couldn't speak.

'I'll leave if you want,' he said. 'I know I'm too old for you, and I can understand that you've got a new life ahead of you. I don't want your pity, Mina. I want all of you. Completely.'

He wasn't begging. He didn't drop his eyes or look away. Across the room, she felt it. She felt the life in him like a fire. Miles had never burned like this. Conrad wasn't going to drain her as living with Miles had done: he was going to make her burn like him, and she wanted that very much.

'Yes,' she said. 'I've got a new life, and I want to spend it with you.'

'So come here.'

He held out his right arm. The left one was pinned to the opposite shoulder with a strap, and he was obviously in pain. Instead of running across the room, she walked like she was in the temple. He wrapped his good arm around her, and she put her fingers on his chest.

After a long time, he kissed the top of her head, and she pulled away. She had so many questions that all she could do was open her arms and say, 'Why?'

'Put the kettle on, and I'll tell you.'

She started to make the tea, and he settled into a chair. Not the couch where she could sit next to him, but a high-backed chair. When he was down, he threw his head back and sucked in air through his teeth. She said nothing until the tea was made and she put his mug on the low table.

'It's over,' he said. 'I'm free of it all.'

She bowed her head and gave thanks to Ganesha. 'What was the price?'

'As well as the ongoing leg situation, I now have a hairline fracture to the clavicle and two cracked ribs in different places. It will all heal.'

'Have you been arrested?'

'No. Just the opposite. I've been given a starring role for the prosecution next year. I'm going to be "Squadron Leader J", and give my evidence from behind a screen. That's if there's a trial. I doubt it, somehow.'

'Tell me.'

'Before I do, you should know that this conversation is probably being recorded. And not by me.'

Over two mugs of tea, he told her. At some points he flicked his eyes up to the ceiling, and she knew that he couldn't tell her the whole truth yet. At one point, towards the end, he looked down. She made a mental note to come back to that, and she also asked him to pass on a message at one point. He agreed.

She was sitting on the couch with her legs underneath her, enjoying the comfort, enjoying his story and just enjoying his company. There were so many questions she wanted to ask that she didn't know where to start. The serious questions could wait: he was here, and that was enough for both of them. She picked on something light and asked him what he was playing at with the fake doctorate.

'It's not fake. I'm a fully qualified Doctor of Occult Studies from Miskatonic University in Arkham.'

'Isn't that in…?'

'H P Lovecraft. It cost me fifteen dollars for the certificate. Part of the deal I did with MI5 was that I could see you once for a proper visit. They put me down as your therapist, so I thought I'd better get a qualification.'

He was grinning, but the troubled look had come back into his eyes. She uncurled her legs from the sofa and leaned across the table to take his good hand. 'I know there are things you're holding back, and I know the reason why. That's fine. But you have to tell me what happened after you saw DC Hayes. What happened on the way to London?'

He looked away. 'I will tell you, I promise. But not in here. Not until you're free.'

She owed him one secret. He could keep it for now.

'I've got something for you,' he said. 'After I gave you those clothes the other week, it struck me that I bought you that sari-thingy and I didn't buy you any shoes.'

He was right. She didn't have the heart to tell him on the day, but churidar trousers were no use without a proper pair of sandals. 'Where are they?'

'With the warden. Wrapped up for Christmas. I've got something else for now.'

He stood up and reached into his expensive-looking leather case. From inside, he carefully withdrew something in bubble-wrap and unfolded it.

He pulled out a healthy sprig of mistletoe covered in white berries. 'Merry Christmas, Mrs Finch.'

'Merry Christmas, Doctor Clarke.'

Boxing Day was crisp, cold and perfect for a walk up the hills towards Rievaulx Abbey. Last year had been wet, but they had laughed all the way there and back. Today they were quiet. It was the first time that Tom's grandfather hadn't led the expedition, because his chest was still too bad to be out in the cold. It was also the first time that they hadn't spoken to Kate.

Tom, his father, his uncle and his sisters all paused on the top of the hill. They never actually went to Rievaulx – they just stopped to look before turning back. There was a dry stone wall that marked the edge of Rooksnest Farm and up here the wind could be felt much more keenly. His uncle was the first to turn around, saying that he had to look after the sheep. Fiona was next, muttering about her husband and the children. Diana (as usual) didn't have the right clothes and was shivering. She patted his arm and left him with his father. The two men carried on looking into the distance.

'Do you want me to go?' said his dad.

'No. You're all right.'

On their left, the sun was just about to kiss the top of the hills.

'If we stay here any longer, we'll need a torch,' said his father.

'Was that a philosophical statement or Yorkshire common sense?'

Judge Thomas Morton, soon to be Sir Thomas, hooted with laughter. 'You'll do, Son. You're a chip off the old block, and no mistake.'

'Aye, 'appen I am that.'

Tom broke away from his memories and turned back towards the farm.

'Are you going back to that Mr Bleaney box?' said his father.

'Once. To clear it out. Then I'm going to buy somewhere before the market recovers too much, and I'm priced out.'

'Good. That's the best thing I've heard all Christmas.'

They finished their walk in silence, and the farmhouse kitchen was as warm as it always was, no more no less. The fact that it was now technically the seat of the second Baron Throckton hadn't changed its homely nature. He hoped that Granddad lived long enough to boast about his title in the pub. His mother handed him a mug of tea and a note when he'd finished taking off his boots.

'Someone called. Said it's personal. Could you ring this number.'

He studied the note and didn't recognise either the number or the dialling code. He ate a mince pie and called the number. An older sounding woman answered the phone.

'Hello. This is Tom Morton. I was asked to call this number.'

'Hang on a sec,' she said. He heard the receiver being placed down and footsteps receding. Then the woman's voice shouted, 'Conrad. Telephone.'

That man had a nerve. What was Clarke doing ringing him on Boxing Day and pretending it was personal? And how did he get the farmhouse's number?

'Is that you, Tom?'

'This is DCI Morton, yes. What do you want?'

Clarke ignored his tone and wished him a Merry Christmas. Tom had no option but to do the same, and then he asked, 'Where are you?'

'Same as you: I'm at home with my parents. It's not like Rooksnest Farm, but it's home all the same.'

'How did you…? Oh. Kate must have told you about it.'

'She did. She told me how happy she was up there. That's why I've rung: my girlfriend asked me to pass on her condolences about Kate. She's very sorry for your loss, Tom.'

'Have I met her? You're not seeing Amelia Jennings, are you?' The mere thought of Conrad making a move on Amelia after killing Offlea and forcing her father to commit suicide was just incredible. Surely the man wasn't that twisted? Anyway, Amelia had never known Kate.

'You have met her, and she did meet Captain Lonsdale, but she can't get to the phone at the moment. She's in prison.'

Of course. Mina Finch. That was the final piece of the Jigsaw. No wonder Clarke wanted to smash it to bits just as much as Tom had wanted to piece it together.

'You shot Joe Croxton,' said Tom.

'You arrested Mina for that, and she admitted it.' Tom could hear the amusement in his voice.

'She killed him, but you shot him first. The way you twist things, Conrad, you should be a lawyer, not a pilot.'

'I've got a new job since we last met: I'll enjoy telling you about it one day.' His voice changed again. 'I'm not winding you up, by the way. Mina really did ask me to pass on her condolences. Kate was a good woman. One of the best. Merry Christmas, Tom.'

'And you, Conrad.'

He poured himself more tea, slipped his feet into some wellingtons, and went back outside as the last of the sun was disappearing. He raised his mug towards the light.

'To New Beginnings, Kate. To New Beginnings.'

His words were soaked up by the snow, the trees, the stones and the fields. He took a long swallow from the mug and went back inside to join the rest of his family.

THE END

The new Tom Morton book, 'A Serpent in Paradise', is available on Amazon for Kindle and will be available in print by Summer 2015.

Keep reading for a sample.

Conrad & Mina's story will be continued in 'The Thirteenth Witch: The Casebooks of Dr Clarke, Vol I' also by Paw press, due to be published in 2015.

Author's Note

Thank you for reading this book; I hope you enjoyed it, and I hope that you enjoyed the first two as well.

The two survivors of the Operation Jigsaw case (and Mina) will be taking very different paths into the future. Tom will be continuing his career with CIPPS, and his next case will take him to Cheshire: to the world of WAGS and bags in *A Serpent in Paradise*; there's a sample here.

Conrad will be heading into the unknown. I've always wanted to write a paranormal thriller, and with Dr Conrad Clarke, I get the chance. Was the figure in the cloak a memory, or was he something else? What wasn't Conrad telling Mina about the journey from St Andrew's Hall to London? All will be revealed in *The Thirteenth Witch: Casebooks of Dr Clarke, Vol I*. I'm going to write the next Tom Morton book first, so the *Casebook* will be out in 2015.

For all the news on current and future books about Tom and Conrad, please sign up for my mailing list: visit the Paw Press Website.

In this book, all the characters are fictional and so are most of the places: the whole town of Earlsbury exists only in my imagination - and yours, of course. At the end of this book, I briefly introduce the town of Cairndale. That is where several of my future books will be set. We'll be back there before too long.

Hong Kong, London and Dublin are real enough, but as they're only bit-part players in this book, they don't count.

Both CIPPS and the MCPS are fictional, as is the newly introduced Lancashire & Westmorland Constabulary.

About the Author

Mark Hayden is the writing name of Adrian Attwood. He lives in Westmorland with his more famous wife, Anne.

Adrian has had a varied career working for a brewery, teaching English and being the Town Clerk in Carnforth. He is now a part-time writer and part-time househusband.

The first of his books, the *Operation Jigsaw* trilogy have now been published on Amazon and he hopes to release two more in 2015.

Continue reading for an extract from the next Tom Morton book — *A Serpent in Paradise*.

A Serpent in Paradise

by Mark Hayden

A Tom Morton Book — No 4

Copyright © Paw Press 2015

Available now from Amazon for Kindle.
Print Version available Summer 2015.

Chapter 1

Thursday 26 December
Boxing Day

The police were waiting for them as they turned off the bypass.

Blue lights emerged from the hidden farm track, and Lucy grabbed her brother's arm before he could put his foot down to race them.

'Gianni, no. Enough. You're not even speeding.'

She saw him glance ahead. It was half a mile to the 7Bridge Estate entrance, and the Maserati would easily outrun the police over that distance.

'No,' said Lucy. 'It's too important to risk an arrest. Just pull in.'

Gianni slammed on the brakes and cut into the side of the road. Behind them, the police car went into a skid and came to rest half over the white line. If someone had been coming out of the Village...

'Don't get out,' she pleaded, but Gianni wasn't going to miss the fun. He threw off his seat belt and leapt out, just in time to watch the police car reverse from its dangerous position in the middle of the road, and tuck itself behind Gianni's vehicle. There were two officers inside. That could make things awkward, because the driver had been embarrassed in front of his colleague. Or her colleague. Lucy slipped out of the car as well, and tried to be inconspicuous.

They were both men, and they both approached the Maserati in silence. Lucy noticed that the non-driving policeman had three little silver stripes on the shoulder of his hi-viz jacket. When they got closer to the car, Gianni squared up to them, an insolent grin on his face.

'Is this your vehicle, sir?' asked the younger policeman.

'*Non sono inglese*,' said Gianni, offering them his driving licence.

The officer looked at it and passed it to the sergeant, who tapped it against his hand. 'This is a full UK licence, sir. You must have learnt English to pass the test.'

'*Non capisco.*'

The constable turned and whispered to his colleague, but Lucy could still hear him. 'Sarge, even if we don't arrest him, this will still get back to their security people.'

The sergeant's face set in a grim expression. 'You should have thought of that before you started to chase him.'

Lucy decided to intervene. 'Excuse me, officers, but if you want to question my brother any more, you'll have to arrest him and get a translator. He's done nothing wrong today, so just breathalyse him and let us go. It is Christmas, after all.'

'Who—?' The younger officer started to speak, but the sergeant held up his hand.

'Thank you, Ms Berardi.'

'My name's Lucy White. Gianni's my half-brother. I live in the Village, not on the Estate.'

The sergeant tapped the licence against his hands for a few seconds more. A gust of wind blew Lucy's coat open, and she shivered. Finally, the sergeant made up his mind. 'It's gonna snow soon,' he said. 'There'll be crashes up and down the M6. There always are on Boxing Day. C'mon, take his reading.'

The constable reluctantly pulled out an intoximeter and gave Gianni the instructions. In English. He complied without going through the farce of waiting for a translation from Lucy. Two minutes later, they were on their way.

'*Cornuto*,' snarled Gianni.

Lucy. 'You'll say that to their faces one of
)t of people know what it means now.'
it he is: his dick is small and his wife sleeps
han.'
oing to tell Max Nolan about being stopped?'

Gianni drove carefully towards the Village, then turned into the Estate access road. 'Of course I will tell him. This is more harassment from the police. What else do we pay security for, if not to sort out our problems?'

There was no sign on the turning, nothing to announce the road as the entrance to Cheshire's largest and most exclusive gated community. It had been over a year since Lucy entered the 7Bridge Estate via the residents' entrance. Although her family still lived there, and she had spent Christmas Day with them, she always walked through the Village and signed in at the security gate in the service area.

The drive to the residents' entrance was long, too long to walk, and was lined with trees on both sides. Among the trees were the CCTV cameras. They picked up the Maserati's number plate and the security system recognised it as belonging to an official Resident of the Estate. By the time they arrived at the bridge, the way was clear, and they crossed into 7Bridge, waving to the patrol officer on duty.

Any vehicle not on the system would be greeted by a ram-proof barrier and a patrol officer. Attempting to skirt the barrier would land the driver in the river. The patrol officer would direct the vehicle back through the Village to the service area. There were no exceptions: only full residents could nominate vehicles to pass through here. Given that the footballers, boy-band stars, hedge fund managers and entrepreneurs who lived in 7Bridge often drove up in new vehicles, they were quite often stopped at the barrier. It was one of the many things that Lucy's father had to sort out for them, though he usually delegated the cars to his assistant — Lucy's friend, Grace. There was other business with cars, which Lucy handled, but she was getting fed up with that.

Gianni drove slowly through the Estate. He may have escaped the police, but he wouldn't risk the wrath of the Estate patrol: a formal warning from the head of security, Max Nolan, was much worse than three points on your licence. Lucy checked her phone. The Japanese guests were due to arrive in fifteen minutes, which gave her just enough time to calm her brother down. They crossed over the mound, and Gianni stopped the car next to the visitors' reception.

There were two entrances to the Estate: Gianni had driven the Maserati through the residents' entrance — but all guests, no matter how important, had to arrive at Visitor Reception, next to the service buildings, and be signed in at the security desk.

Paul Warren, her father's attorney, was waiting on the other side of the security fence, stamping his feet against the cold.

When they had passed through security, Paul gave her a hug and wished her a Merry Christmas. He was Dad's oldest friend, but he was also Lucy's godfather, and had been there for her on many occasions. The bristles from his moustache tickled, like they always did, and Lucy was glad that he was going to the match with Gianni and one of the visitors. He might keep her brother in check.

The service area was even more exposed than the lay-by where the police had stopped them. Lucy pulled her woollen scarf higher. A stray gust brought the odour of cooking oil from the Hartley Catering building. 'Why am I doing this?' she asked. 'It's Boxing Day.'

Gianni grinned at her. 'What would you rather do, *cara mia*? Spend the afternoon with our stepmother, or take Mrs Ikeda to the 7Bridge Spa? When was the last time you went for a full afternoon of *la dolce vita*, eh?'

'Before I moved out, that's when — and you know it. I can barely afford the Village Café these days. That's why I was hoping to be invited to watch the Trafford Rangers game with you and Dad. I haven't missed a Christmas game in years.'

'Signor Ikeda could be a big sponsor. That is why Papa is paying you to take Signora Ikeda to the Spa, and why Holly is paying you to babysit tonight.'

'I'd rather go to the Nugent Ball than look after the Nugent children.'

'No, you wouldn't. You cannot say you are poor and go to the ball. You are not Cinderella.'

'Now then, you two,' said Paul. 'I think I can see lights. What is it we do again, Lucy?'

'We bow first, then you say *Konnichiwa, Ikeda-san,* because Gianni can't pronounce it.'

Paul practised the phrase as a stretch limo glided towards them.

Thu 26 evening

Football fixtures are governed by many factors, but the biggest of all is television. On Boxing Day this year, Trafford Rangers had played at lunchtime, and Chelsea were playing later. The rest of the Premier League and all the divisions below them kicked off at the traditional time of three o'clock. Salton Town FC, newly promoted to the Championship, had made the relatively short journey from Cheshire to Burnley. They were now about to leave.

The seats at the back of the team bus were known as Cripple's Corner: they were reserved for the walking wounded after the game. Dean Rooksby was there because he'd bashed his shoulder into the goalpost. His left arm was strapped across his chest, and the painkillers were threatening to send him to sleep. His head jerked up as the rest of the squad piled on to the coach. Leading the charge was his best mate, Travis, with a bottle of beer in one hand

and a teddy bear in the other — a teddy bear swaddled in a Salton Town FC scarf. Just behind him was Dean's central defensive partner, Ricardo 'Rich' Menghini.

'You all right, Deano?' said his friend.

'No, I'm not all right. I'm going to miss the cup match, not to mention the derby.'

'Eh? Is not good,' said Rich.

'Did you hear?' said Travis, pointing to the Italian. 'He got another yellow card after you were taken off.'

Dean tried a smile. 'Careful, Rich. They can't do without both of us.'

Menghini made a violent gesture towards the window, '*Arbitro cornuto!*' he said.

'Yeah, we know,' said Travis. 'All the refs pick on you because you're so attractive and they're jealous.'

'Is true. This referee... he is so ugly, no woman goes near him.' With that assertion, Ricardo went back to his seat.

'This is yours,' said Travis, placing the teddy bear on the empty seat next to Dean. 'That fat blond bird who's always waiting outside said she hopes you get well soon.'

'Leave off, Travis. Her name's Emily, and she's the supporters' club secretary. She interviewed me last season for the newsletter. She's really nice.'

Travis thought for a second. 'Yeah... she was really sweet, actually. She still ate all the pies, though. C'n I get you anything, man? Beer?'

'Naah. I can't drink with these pills, but can you get my phone out? It's in the locker.'

Their manager, Gus Burkett, was very strict about rules on the bus. On the way to games, all electronic devices had to be locked away. Travis fished in the locker and handed Dean his phone.

At the front of the coach, Gus's well-padded figure mounted the steps. 'Seats, lads,' he said. That was another rule: sit down when arriving and departing.

Dean had been Man of the Match again today — not bad for a teenage centre half. His heroics with the goalpost had cleared a shot off the line and earned them a hard-fought draw with Burnley, one of the promotion favourites. He'd been stretchered off after making the clearance.

'Cheer up, mate,' said his friend. 'You'll be playing in the Champions League with Trafford Rangers next year.'

'Maybe,' said Dean.

Travis waved to him and swayed back to the table where they normally sat together. The lights dimmed, and the coach pulled out of Turf Moor.

With some effort, Dean unlocked his phone and saw a message from Madison: *Hope you're OK. Call me when you can.* He dialled, and she picked up on the first ring.

'Dean, love, what's happened?'

'Did you see it?'

'Yes, I bloody well did. Three times. Twice in slow motion. No one knew if you'd broken it or not.'

'The physio doesn't think it's broken, but I'll need a scan tomorrow to check it out.' He sighed. 'I'm gonna be out for a couple of weeks at least. You can practise being a housewife. For when we're married.'

'Lay off, Dean. It's not funny seeing you on a stretcher like that. Do you want me to stay in tonight and look after you?'

In the pause after her question, Dean could hear the sound of a hairdryer and a girly laugh: Maddi was already round at Holly's, getting herself glammed up.

'You go and have fun. Not too much fun though. I'll be asleep when you get back.'

'Thanks, love. Text me when you get home.'

'Yeah. Love you, fiancée.'

'Love you too.'

Concentrating on his phone had made his shoulder ache. Dean had no idea whether he could even undress himself, never mind get something to eat. He called Gary

White, his agent. Injury clearly brought privileges, because Gary himself took the call and asked how badly he was hurt.

Dean filled in the details and then, with a little hesitation, said, 'Gary, you know Madison's going to this do in Chester?'

'So are we. Robyn's just getting ready.'

'It's just that Mum and Dad have gone abroad for Christmas, and I don't think I can look after myself tonight.'

'Don't worry, Dean. That's what living in 7Bridge is all about. I'll put in a call to Natasha. Personally. There'll be a nurse waiting for you in Salton. It'll have to be a bloke, though: you might need lifting. He can drive you home and look after you. Besides, I don't want Madison coming home to find a hot Filipino in your bedroom.'

'Cheers, Gary. It's a good job I'm not gay, then.'

'Don't even *think* those thoughts. Gotta go.'

Dean relaxed properly for the first time since the goalpost had brought his afternoon to a premature end. He swiped his way through to the *Salton Advertiser* match report on his phone. They had given him 8 out of 10 for his performance — making him the top of the paper's player rankings, much to the skipper's annoyance. Dean grinned. His finger hesitated over another website. Should he read it? No. He'd find out soon enough what the Mother Superior was saying about his fiancée on that website of hers.

Mother Superior. Maddi had said it was irony or something. Dean didn't see what was ironic about a super-heated gossip queen calling herself after a nun. Sometimes he didn't get the references on the *SeenIn7Bridge* website, and Maddi had to explain them. No, it could definitely wait until he got home. He looked at the lights of Manchester, and remembered the diamond sparkles in the engagement ring. He fell asleep with a smile on his face, and the phone slipped from his hand.

Down the coach, Travis heard the clatter when the phone hit the floor, and peered over his shoulder to see if Gus was watching. With the coast clear, Travis sneaked back and did what any good friend would do: he picked up Dean's phone, placed the teddy bear on Dean's lap, and then took a picture. Using Dean's own Twitter account, he posted the picture with this message:

Feeling better now I'm curled up with Teddy from @EmilySaltonTown. Love you Blondie!

Travis had done his good deed for the day, and felt much better when he sat down.

Thu 26 evening

At the back of 7Bridge, lights were shining in most of the service buildings, including the Estate Office. The Estate manager, Saul Blackstone, had the top floor to himself. Half of it was office, and half of it was a small flat where he had spent too many nights. Including this one.

He was in the tiny kitchen making coffee when he heard his name called.

'I'm in the flat, Max,' he shouted back.

When Max Nolan (the security ops manager) came through, Saul asked what he always asked: 'Status?'

'Calm on the Estate,' said Max, and handed over three days' worth of reports covering the meagre break that Saul had allowed himself this year. He did not want to be back at work on Boxing Day, but he didn't have any choice.

'I should hope it's quiet: it is Christmas.' Saul pointed to one of the coffees, took the other one, then flicked through the reports on the way to his office.

'There's been another incident with the police,' said Max.

Saul glanced at the police incident: *A 7Bridge Collective car, travelling below the speed limit, was pursued and stopped for no reason. The driver was breathalysed. Negative. He reports that the attitude of the police was confrontational and that they only backed off when they realised there was a non-resident witness.*

'Who was driving the car? And who was the witness?'

'Giovanni Berardi was driving. His sister was the passenger.'

Saul grunted and tossed the reports into his out tray. This was getting out hand. A lot of the talent liked fast cars, but didn't like getting points on their licence. Their agent's attorney had come up with a scheme, which Saul would have vetoed if it weren't for the fact that Gary White, super sports agent, was a resident of the Estate and owned 20% of the holding company. White's attorney had set up a company called the 7Bridge Collective, which was the legal keeper of all the fast cars. Every time one of the cars tripped a speed camera, Paul Warren would ask for pictures. The driver was usually unrecognisable. He would declare that the company was unable to say who was at the wheel, he would be summonsed to court and he would stand impassively in front of a furious magistrate and be fined £1,000. A corporate body does not have a driving licence, so no one got any points.

Shortly afterwards, the real guilty party would make an anonymous cash payment to the Collective, routed via the books of White-Berardi Sports Management. A £1,000 fine would discourage normal people, but these are not normal people: for most of them it was less than 1% of their weekly wage. The police knew exactly what was going on. They had started lying in wait and stopping every fast car in north Cheshire.

Last week it had come home to roost when a squad car chased a Maserati down the access road and nearly crashed into the barrier. Max's patrol officers had stood their ground, and the policeman had a screaming fit, threatening to arrest them, until he realised that he was on HD CCTV.

Saul would have to do something, but not until after the holidays. There was a more pressing problem to attend to.

'Is Hoskins here yet?' he asked.

'I left him in your lobby, to keep him out of the way.'

'Let's get the show on the road.' Saul picked up his iPad and went out to the lobby, where their newly engaged cyber-detective was waiting.

They had emailed and spoken, but not met before. Hoskins might sound like a geek, and talk like one, but he looked like a teddy bear, right down to the fluffy sweater that must have been a Christmas present from his mother. Saul looked again: the man had a wedding ring. Good for him. Saul still reckoned that his mother had bought the jumper, though.

Max made the formal introduction. Saul said, 'Thanks for coming on Boxing Day. I know we're paying you handsomely, but it's still a big sacrifice for you.'

'My youngest is only one,' said Hoskins. 'Too young to know what's going on, but old enough to get completely hyper. I'm glad of the break.'

Saul would have liked to have a one-year-old again, but that was unlikely at the moment. Perhaps next year the lawyers would stop holding him and Miriam to ransom, and let them divorce each other in a civilised way.

The preliminary contact with Hoskins had been all about his credentials. Saul was not willing to discuss specifics until he had a signature on the confidentiality agreement. That had arrived in the last post on Christmas Eve. 'I'll put this in very simple terms, Neil,' said Saul. 'Princess Karida, who represents the Estate's majority shareholders, and who lives in Sevenbridge Hall, has ordered me to stop the Mother Superior.'

'Who's the Mother Superior?'

'Let me show you.' Saul opened his iPad and flicked through to the *SeenIn7Bridge* website. Hoskins showed no sign of recognition. 'This website is written by someone in or from the Estate. She calls herself the Mother Superior. It's been unpleasant for some of the residents and staff for some time, but things are getting worse. This is the straw that broke the camel's back.'

He clicked through to a posting from five days ago, and they all crowded round the screen to read this message:

*Happy Winter Solstice! Today is the shortest day of the year, and it's also a pagan festival. A little bird told me that 7Bridge has its very own pagans.

A series of grainy pictures accompanied the post, showing the Christmas tree on the green and the surrounding grass covered in snow. Across the images a group of women, naked apart from their running shoes, were seen to race each other round the tree. All but one of the women had their faces digitally covered with black squares. The one woman whose face was visible raised her arms in triumph in the last picture. Clearly she had won the race.

'Who…?' said Hoskins.

'Doesn't matter who the woman is,' said Saul. 'You can look it up later. What matters is that these images were taken just across the green, from inside a holly bush.'

'As soon as this was posted online, I went to see where it was taken from,' said Max. 'The ground was frozen, and I found a deep indentation. Whatever these ladies were getting up to, someone knew about it in advance and planted a camera there.'

'Nasty,' said Hoskins. 'Can't you just go after the website?'

'We tried that last year,' said Saul. 'Unfortunately, they've done nothing that's actually criminal. We got a court order to force the web hosts to take it down, but couldn't get one to force them to reveal the site owners. All that happened was that a really scurrilous web magazine took over: *Hot & Viral*. We can't touch them.'

Hoskins stroked his beard. 'I see.'

'You probably don't see, yet. I need a name. If it's an employee, I can sack them and sue them. If it's a resident, they'll get thrown off the estate. The residency agreement allows me to revoke their residency status for this sort of thing.'

'There are privacy issues with residents,' said Neil.

'Not on this Estate,' said Max. 'So long as we use a reputable third party – that's you by the way – we can sniff around the Estate's Internet links.'

Hoskins smiled. 'The fact that you've brought me down from Cairndale says that this is a priority.'

'Princess Karida is paying,' said Saul. 'You have the wealth of the Ghar'aan royal family to draw on.'

'I'll start in the morning,' said Hoskins.

Thu 26 evening

Lucy White strode along the footpaths through the 7Bridge Estate, whistling along to the music in her earphones, secure in the knowledge that no treacherous ice lay in wait around the corners. This wasn't because the Estate was immune to nature, though it sometimes felt like that. It was because the residents paid so much in management fees that there would be an uproar if unauthorised ice were discovered on the footways. Not only that: if one of the talent hurt himself, the court case would cost tens of millions. It was the blessing and the curse of 7Bridge: complete service with no hint of spontaneity. On the whole, she was glad she had moved out.

The earmuffs kept out the cold, but trapped the music inside, making her head echo with the beat. She broke stride to dance a little, then did a shuffle, snapping her fingers and coming to rest under the streetlight when the music stopped. She looked up at the CCTV camera and pointed into the lens. 'Yeah! That's right!' she said to the camera, just as the red light winked into action. Damn. Someone really was watching her now — perhaps even Sergeant Nolan himself. She flinched, but held her ground for another second to show she meant it, then turned slowly towards the Visitors Gate. Instead of passing through, she waited in the shelter of the building.

Despite the cold, Lucy felt good: a whole-body massage, a steam room and an essential oils head massage will do that to you. She had enjoyed the company, too — Mitsumi Ikeda was a lot like Lucy (if six years older). Mitsumi had been an unmarried elementary school teacher in Miyagi — until one day a former pupil had come to endow them with a new building, and he had fallen in love with his hostess.

Kaito Ikeda was a *lot* older than Mitsumi, but she said that was okay because he was a big kid, and she just treated him like one of her students. They were on their honeymoon. Mitsumi had insisted that they spend Christmas at a country house hotel in the Lake District. She had been to England as a student, and wanted to go back to a happy place. That's what she'd said: a happy place. She said the hotel had made her very happy.

Kaito was happy too. He had spent the afternoon at Barton Bridge stadium enjoying the hospitality of the White-Berardi executive box, wearing his gift: a blood-red Trafford Rangers shirt with *Ikeda* and the number 7 on the back. Trafford Rangers had beaten Arsenal 2-1.

Tonight was the highlight of Kaito and Mitsumi's visit, and Lucy was waiting with the special pass to get them into the Estate. Right on time, the car pulled in. Her father had arranged for the luxury limousine which had brought them from the Lakes this morning: he had replaced it with a monstrous stretch version, big enough for eight. Lucy leaned in to the security office and handed over the pass, then walked up to the limo.

This car came with a footman (it was the only word she could think of to describe a man whose job it was to leap out and open doors). He was already in place before she got there.

'Evening miss.'

'Hi. I'm not going to the Ball, you know.'

'I guessed. Enjoy the ride, even if it is only round the bend.'

She climbed in and joined the Ikedas at the back. Kaito half rose from his seat to bow, and Lucy managed the same before collapsing into a padded chair.

'I had to stop him bringing the shirt,' said Mitsumi. 'He wants John Nugent to sign it, but I told him that was rude.'

Gianni would have arranged a good deal more than a signed shirt, so Lucy just smiled. Kaito looked smart in his tuxedo, except for the wild hair. Mitsumi looked … well, put it this way: Mitsumi didn't scrub up quite as well as her husband. When they had arrived this morning, Mitsumi had been shrouded in the most beautiful Hermès scarf, a Christmas present from Kaito. Lucky her. In her winter coat and boots, she looked chic and well-polished. She hadn't made the transition to evening wear so comfortably. Lucy and Mitsumi were the same height (five foot four), and Mitsumi had gone for something that only a much taller woman should have attempted. *Never mind*, thought Lucy. *No one will say anything except to ask who designed it.* The answer, of course, was Dior.

The limo had started moving without Lucy noticing — and then it swung to the right and they were there, pulling into John and Holly Nugent's residence. The footman was at the door before they'd stopped moving. How did he do that?

'Please,' said Lucy. 'After you.'

Mitsumi nudged her husband and he moved first. '*Arigato*,' he said, giving another bow.

Gianni was waiting outside, and her brother led the Ikedas towards the front door. Lucy gave them half a minute, then slipped out of the limo. The footman hadn't moved.

The others had disappeared, so Lucy walked into *Casa Nugent*. That's what she called it, because what else would you call a Spanish-style mansion stuck in the middle of a

Cheshire snowdrift? The main doors were thrown open to the night. When you don't pay your own heating bills, it's easier to leave them open.

Inside the hall, she levered off her boots, slinging them to one side to land under the second-largest Christmas tree in 7Bridge (the largest was on the green). The hall was like something out of an opera. In fact, the stage at La Scala seemed shallower than *Casa Nugent*. A marble staircase descended from a colonnaded gallery to meet the black and white tiled floor. Short passages led back to the catering kitchen and the family kitchen, and to either side of the hall were double doors: stage left to the family quarters, stage right to the party room.

'Auntie Lucy!' Peeking round the door to the family room was Holly's oldest child, Ellie. She beckoned furiously for Lucy to come over.

'Wow, kid,' said Lucy. 'Love the outfit.' She wasn't Ellie Nugent's real auntie, of course, but she had known the Nugents since both families had moved into 7Bridge when Lucy was eleven, which is why Lucy was babysitting tonight. Holly had an au pair, of course, but she also practised what she preached: family values. The au pair was in Poland and not due back until Sunday, so Lucy was the most trusted stand-in.

Ellie was wearing a blue dress that came to just below the knee. Anything shorter would have emphasised just how thin her legs were. At twelve years old, Ellie was going through a growth spurt that, with the black heels, made her almost as tall as Lucy. Her waist-length hair was kept in check with a matching Alice band; in fact, the only thing missing for the full *Through the Looking Glass* effect was an apron. Her feet were in first position. Ellie still hoped to be a ballerina; Lucy hoped she'd grow out of it soon.

Ellie disappeared into the squashy, comfy, childproof family room. Lucy followed. When they were out of earshot, Ellie said, 'Tell me who those people are. The...' she searched for a politically correct description.

'You mean our Japanese guests?'

'Stop teasing me. Yes, I do. Why are they here. And why are they going to the Ball? Mum's never taken anyone except Sheena, and this year she's taking Madison and these people.'

'*These people* are Kaito and Mitsumi Ikeda. I think they've come over to sort out something with your dad. Anyway, Kaito's a big fan of Trafford Rangers, and Mitsumi thinks your mum walks on water. Much prefers her to Victoria Beckham.'

Ellie's face fell. She sat on the only upright chair in the room, sweeping the skirt of her dress out of the way without thinking. When Lucy sat down like that, she always thought about moving her skirt afterwards, not before. Away from the cold, she dumped her coat on a beanbag.

'I thought they might be someone different, you know?' said Ellie. 'Someone from outside 7Bridge and football.'

'They'll be gone soon, and then we can enjoy ourselves.'

'That's right! Now they're here, I can get changed.'

Ellie jumped up again and clattered into the hall. On the way upstairs, she passed her mother coming down.

Holly Nugent still had her ash-blonde hair in giant rollers, and wasn't wearing her shoes yet, but otherwise she was ready for the ball — the fourth Nugent Boxing Day Benefit Ball.

'You look great,' said Lucy. 'The empire line always works for you.'

Holly made a slight grimace. 'You mean I've got big tits, big hips and I've eaten too much turkey.' She waved her hand. 'Thanks so much for tonight. I'm surprised that Robyn allowed you over here to babysit when she's going herself.'

It was Lucy's turn to grimace. 'One of the perks of living in the Village instead of on the Estate is that my stepmother is no longer my keeper. She asked me to babysit, but I said that you'd got in first, and that you paid better.'

'You can't put a price on peace of mind,' said Holly, and Lucy felt as if her life was on elastic. One minute she was being treated by Ellie as if she were a responsible adult, an Auntie, and the next minute she was being paid to babysit as if she were still a teenager. *I'm twenty-six*, she thought. *I have my own business*. When her bad angel started to remind her that the business was hanging on by a thread, and was underwritten by her father's money, she screwed up her eyes and tried to forget.

'Have you done story-time yet?' she asked Holly.

'Going to do it now.' Holly checked the time on her Rolex Pearlmaster, and had to hold her arm away from her body to get the hands of the watch in focus. 'We've got to leave in half an hour, so I'd better get a shift on. You go ahead and make yourself comfortable – and listen – I think I've got another client for you. One of the African players has his family over for Christmas.' With that, she headed back upstairs, a lot less elegantly than her daughter.

There was a blast of noise from across the hall and the doors to the party room opened. The sound resolved itself into the commentary from Stamford Bridge, and John Nugent was standing in the doorway.

'Hello, Lucy,' he said. 'Are they anywhere near ready, yet, do you know? I'm struggling with small talk in here.'

John Nugent, captain of Trafford Rangers and England, was already in his evening dress. It was bespoke, to fit across his shoulders, and it barely creased when he lifted his arm to drink from the bottle of San Miguel. John Nugent was the first man that Lucy had formed a crush on (with millions of other girls), and he was even more handsome now that his stubble was flecked with grey. He took a step towards her and reflections glittered from his watch, his earring and even his shoes. Lucy felt a shiver that was only partly from the breeze from the wide open doors. Another man appeared behind him — John's teammate, Murray Cavendish. He was thinner and shorter than John and had a high-pitched Edinburgh accent and red hair. He had only been with Trafford Rangers a few years, and because he wasn't one of her father's clients, Lucy didn't know him very well. His tuxedo was expensive but off the peg, and his shoes weren't shoes at all — they were black leather trainers.

'Good result this afternoon,' she said to the men.

John waved his hand dismissively. 'Should have been easier. Two years ago we'd have cruised through a game like that. Have you seen Holly?'

'She's reading the boys a story. She said they'd be down in less than half an hour.'

He took another step forward and looked over his shoulder. 'I'm used to fans, but not in my own house. I'm not sure who's worse — Mr or Mrs.'

'You mean the Ikedas?'

'Yeah. Whatever. When Gianni introduced them, I thought Mr Ikeda was gonna topple over, he bowed so low. He kept saying my name, too. Then he says things in Japanese and she translates them. That's when she's not staring at the door waiting for Holly to appear, like the second coming.'

Murray took another swig of beer, and appeared to be enjoying every moment. 'Ikeda said that my cross for the second goal was driven by a divine wind. I like that.'

'Shut up, you. You're not helping,' said John. He turned back to Lucy. 'Neither is your brother. He keeps saying how good I'll look on posters in Tokyo.'

'Mmm. You will,' said Lucy. 'Especially stripped to the waist. You might have to dye your chest hair, though. Or finally get it shaved.'

John went back into the party room, and grabbed Murray's hair on the way. 'At least it's not ginger,' he said.

Murray winced with pain, and sloshed beer on his trainers. He cursed, and saw a discarded Santa sack under the tree. Without thinking, he polished his shoes and threw the sack into a corner. A roar from the crowd drew his attention back to the game. Lucy shivered on top, but could feel the underfloor heating toasting her feet.

'I don't like him,' said a voice from the stairs. 'That was Jack's Santa sack from Granddad Nugent. He uses the same sack every year, and now it's got beer on it.' Ellie had changed from Disney princess back to little girl. Her hair was loose, and she was sporting pink pyjamas under a towelling dressing gown. Her face was barely visible over the double duvet she was carrying.

'Careful, love,' said Lucy. 'Don't trip on the stairs.' She dashed up to take the duvet from Ellie before there was an accident. 'Who's this?' she asked, spotting the five hunky faces on the duvet cover. It looked like a boy band, but not one that Lucy had seen before.

'Five Dimensions,' said Ellie over her shoulder. 'They're going to be *massive* this year. They were in the grand final of *Sing for Glory*. I thought you'd know all about that.'

Lucy tossed the duvet on to the couch. 'Why would I? Some of us are allowed out on Saturday nights. Right, what's it going to be?'

Ellie flung open the cupboard under the massive TV and pulled out a stack of DVDs big enough to equip a small shop. They were rooting around and arguing about which film to watch when Lucy heard voices from the hall.

'Let's go and check them out,' said Ellie.

'Why not? C'mon.'

They went up to the double doors, and Lucy peered round. Ellie peered from underneath her arm.

The hall was big enough for John, Murray, Gianni and Kaito and Mitsumi Ikeda to form a reception line at the bottom of the staircase with the Christmas tree as a backdrop. The two footballers were waiting with their hands folded in front of them, as if they were defending a free kick. Gianni was next, and then the Ikedas. Mitsumi's hands were clasped to her mouth, her eyes riveted above. Her husband was still looking at John. That was weird. Heels began descending the staircase, and Kaito finally looked up.

Holly was in white — a sweeping gown that emphasised her cleavage. Sheena Cavendish had gone for red (which clashed horribly with her husband's hair), and she had neglected the legs *or* cleavage rule. The third woman was Madison Greenwood, fiancée to 7Bridge's newest resident, Dean Rooksby. She was younger than Holly and Sheena, younger even than Lucy. The green floor-length gown suited her perfectly.

'Have you heard what happened to Dean?' whispered Ellie. 'She shouldn't be going out when he's injured. She should have gone to Burnley.'

Lucy didn't care whether or not Madison neglected her boyfriend, but she did care that the red carpet for the Nugent Benefit Ball would be papped all over the Internet. *No one will notice the handbag*, she thought, and tried to forget the sight of Madison leaving the house with a Paola Berardi clutch.

John and Murray took their wives' arms, and Gianni did the same to Madison. Lucy liked Maddi. In fact, Maddi was putting together a refurbishment plan for the House of Lucia, her shop. Not that Lucy could afford it, but Maddi was an intern with the Estate's interior designer, Anthea Godfrey: the House of Lucia project was a practice assignment. Gianni had arranged the internship, and brought Maddi round to the shop. Lucy hoped that he wasn't going to get too close.

At the last moment, Holly turned and gave a little wave to her daughter. Ellie beamed back.

'What's that about Dean?' asked Lucy.

'He damaged his shoulder this afternoon. Madison should have been with him.'

With Dean being one of her dad's up-and-coming young clients, Lucy was surprised she hadn't heard. And what was with Ellie's attitude? 'Did you work that out for yourself — that Madison shouldn't have gone out tonight?' she asked.

'Sort of. It's what the Mother Superior said.'

'Aah.' That would be the anonymous author of the *SeenIn7Bridge* blog. She called herself the Mother Superior, and every female who set foot on the Estate was a target: resident wives, visiting girlfriends, the senior support staff — all were fair game, and there was a lot of detail that only an insider could know about. Everyone said that the Mother Superior was a complete bitch, but they all read the blog and spent hours discussing who the author might be. Apparently.

Lucy tried to ignore it, mostly. Now that she lived in the Village, the blog rarely mentioned her. While Ellie made a final choice between three DVDs, Lucy looked up *SeenIn7Bridge* on her phone, and read the latest entry:

*Let's hear it for early kick-off times! WAGs with men at Trafford Rangers can get home in plenty of time to put their slap on before the red carpet bash in Chester. Who has a ball on Boxing Day? HOLLY NUGENT, of course. She's persuaded the B-listers from our favourite soap MERSEYGATE to grace her charity bash, which means that Holly may not be the oldest person there! I hope you laid off the Christmas Pudding, Holly — a moment on the lips, and all that.

*BTW, a little bird tells me that MADISON GREENWOOD will be there too. Why isn't she going to support Dean at Turf Moor — especially now they're engaged? Well, who'd want to be seen in BURNLEY when there's a red carpet and paparazzi in Chester? Just because you can, Maddi, it doesn't mean you should. Try being more supportive next time.

Ellie really shouldn't be reading this, but Lucy wasn't going to suggest that Holly took her daughter's phone away. Or her iPad, or her MacBook.

Lucy was still worried about potential pictures of Madison, though. The handbag that Maddi was carrying tonight was one of Mama's designs. Gianni and Lucy's mother lived in Italy, and she supplied a lot of Lucy's designer stock. Gianni had bought one of the bags, and said that he was going to give it to Dean for him to pass on as a gift. Lucy would have loved the publicity, but if Gianni had actually given the bag himself, someone would say something on Dean's Twitter feed, and then there would be trouble.

On the table in front of the couch was a variety of snacks and treats, most still in their supermarket packages. 'Didn't you get Sonia to do the feast?' she asked Ellie.

'I wanted this to be special. We have Sonia's food all the time, but I wanted the things I really like.' She held up a DVD box. 'We'll watch this one.'

Lucy accepted the box from Ellie, checked the age rating, and put the disk into the machine. Ellie worked the remote, and Lucy slipped off her pullover and socks, then spread the duvet over the couch. As the menu came up on the screen, Lucy and Ellie snuggled up under the quilt.

'Will you put my hair into a braid?' asked Ellie. 'Now that Christmas is over, it's such a pain having it loose all the time.'

'I'll do it before you go to bed. Now pass the gummy bears,' said Lucy. 'You're nearest.'

Printed in Great Britain
by Amazon